Wheel Of D

John Roberts

WHEEL OF DECEPTION

Blake Langford returns to his family home in London after the death of his mother. As he sorts through her possessions, he discovers an old photo of her with a man he does not recognise from many years ago.

As he begins to dig deeper into his family's past, conflicting stories lead to a young couple who went missing over 70 years ago.

When a dog walker discovers a body of a young woman half way out of a grave, Blake has many unanswered questions for an undertaker who is not willing to cooperate and a corpse that may link back to his own family in ways he never expected.

When the body count continues to climb, Blake needs to find closure in a world of death and violence but who can he trust?

Trigger Warning: Contains scenes of torture and violence.

John Roberts

John Roberts was born in a small market town called Banbury in the UK. In 1999, he moved to Southampton where he now lives with his wife and son. He has been a freelance writer since 2008 with varied success, a long suffering Newcastle United FC supporter, Formula 1 fanatic and works the night shift at a local supermarket.

Wheel Of Deception is the fourth book in John's new adult fiction series, featuring his protagonist, Blake Langford. A man with a troubled past who has to fight his own demons to look after those that he loves but nothing is as straightforward as it seems. This novel is split across two eras of the Langford family as decisions made in the past cause ripples in the present day.

John Roberts is also the author of the children's series; Bennie Barrier's Big City Adventures and co-author of the children's adventure series, "The New Adventures Of Cornelius Cone And Friends" with his friend, Steve Boyce. All of these adventures can be found on Amazon Kindle and in most well known book shops worldwide.

For Gloria And Steve
We May Only Be Passing Through But Memories Live
Forever

Wheel Of Deception

Blake Langford's Family Tree

Steven Langford - Brother

Jenny Langford - Sister

John Langford - Father

Emily Langford (Handanowicz) - Mother

Frederick Langford - John's Brother

Evelyn Handanowicz - Emily's Twin-Sister

Mary Langford - John's Sister

James Handanowicz - Emily's Brother

Edith Wise - Emily's Sister

Victor Wise - Emily's Brother

Mavis Langford (Lee) - Blake's Grandmother

Dana Handanowicz (Wise) - Blake's Grandmother

Edward Langford - Blake's Grandfather

William Handanowicz - Blake's Grandfather

Alfred Langford - Blake's Great-Grandfather

Gerald Wise - Dana's 1st Husband (Edith's Father)

Chapter One

A Mother's Love

Thursday 2nd October 2008

Blake Langford breathlessly crossed the finish line and glugged a mouthful of water down as his team completed the assault course at RAF Upper Heyford. The cool liquid provided welcome relief as the former air force base provided the ideal facilities for Special Branch to push their agents through endurance tests that would serve them well as they travelled around the world.

"You improved your time from last year," Alison Pearce smiled as she showed him the times for their team.

Samir and Joe eventually caught up a few moments later. The training facility was just what Blake needed after taking some long overdue leave from Special Branch. His last case, investigating the trafficking of students in and out of London, had taken its toll on him. Having the break allowed him to come back refreshed and ready to take on a new challenge.

"I see you can move your ass when you want to," Joe laughed.

"Kicking a football around a field with my son keeps me young. Anyway, you're not doing too bad yourself for being three months out of hospital."

"It'll take more than an exploding shed to keep me down."

"Speaking of which, have you found any leads from Zodiac or Reaper?"

"We're still looking into it but nothing so far," Samir replied.

"What about The Crystal?" Blake asked.

"All major operations have been shut down but that doesn't mean that there won't be any streams going in from the dark web," Joe replied.

"Keep me posted if you find anything," Blake said before picking up his towel and heading towards the changing rooms.

Joe and Samir watched him as he left.

"Do you think he's ready to come back?" Samir asked.

"Grief can change a lot of people but I've known Blake for a long time. He's like a dog with a bone. As soon as he grabs hold, he won't let go. Come on, two more circuits then we'll go for a beer," Joe replied before running back to the start line.

Samir watched Blake and Alison leave before following Joe to the start line. He felt uneasy about their alliance but knew he had to keep them close if he was to find out how much they knew about his involvement in The Crystal.

Alison met Blake outside after he had changed his clothes and returned to the car park. They walked from the main entrance together. "I didn't want to mention it in front of the other two but I think Joe is pushing himself too hard," she said as they arrived at Blake's car.

"In what way?"

"Trying to prove himself again. Samir led him into a dangerous situation that almost cost him his life."

"You don't trust Samir?"

Alison sighed. "It's not that, it's just..."

"We all have skeletons in our past that we'd rather hide away from. Samir admitted his mistakes. It takes a lot to admit to bribes in front of Eric and not be concerned for your future in Special Branch."

"Joe told me that Samir and Zodiac were friends. He was willing to cut Zodiac a deal in exchange for information. That deal led them to the house where Joe was almost killed."

"Do you think it was deliberate or did Zodiac lead them into a trap?" Blake asked.

"I don't know. Maybe I'm reading too much into this but something is off. I'm not sure what it is but I just have this feeling."

"Personally or professionally?"

"What do you mean?"

"Samir and you were close for a while."

"That was a long time ago, Blake. He's changed."

"In what way?"

"The job makes us all a lot harder. It takes a lot longer to let people in."

"Does having Samir in the team make you feel uneasy?"

"I loved him once. Now he's more like a brother. He's good at his job and can be a valuable asset. I just don't know if I'd trust him to have my back if I was in trouble. He led Joe into that garden and the explosion left him severely burnt. We split when I realised that he'd rather save his own skin than mine."

Blake thought about that for a moment. "What are you doing this afternoon?"

"I have to visit my mother in Basingstoke. It's her birthday tomorrow and I promised I'd go and see her."

Blake thought of his own mother who had died from a stroke only six months ago.

Alison noticed his demeanour change. "I'm sorry Blake, I didn't..."

"It's okay, it just doesn't seem real sometimes."

"A mother's love is never forgotten."

Blake pulled out a photo from his jacket pocket and showed it to Alison. There were two men and two women in the photo which looked like it had been taken on Lepe Beach many years ago. There were also three children playing in the sand in front of them, two boys and a girl. "Soon after Mum's death, I received a key to a safe deposit box in London. This photo was inside the box."

"I didn't realise anyone still used safe deposit boxes anymore," Alison replied as she looked at the photo. "Is this your grandparents with their children?"

"The two boys are my father John and his brother Fred. The girl is Edith Wise, my mum's older sister who died in 1956. My father's parents are there and so is my grandmother on Mum's side but nobody seems to be able to identify the man with his arm around my grandmother," Blake explained.

"Could've been a family friend?"

"Family friends didn't hold each other like that in 1948."

"How do you know when it was taken?"

Blake turned the photo over and showed the date on the back.

"Do you think there's more to it than that?" Alison asked.

"The family solicitor has asked to see Jenny, Steven and myself tomorrow for the reading of Mum's will. Apparently, there was a delay due to the contents of the will and the need to find out everyone who is due to inherit from it."

"Surely it should just be you three as Emily's children."

"Apparently not but none of us ever knew the contents of my parents' wills when they wrote them around the time of their marriage in 1977. Anyway, Steven can't make it so it'll just be Jenny and me going."

"I'm sure it's just a formality. You know how these solicitors like to drag things out for maximum fees."

Blake nodded. "If you're concerned about Samir, I could ask Eric Gordon to consider moving him off of the team."

"If he can keep the partnership professional then so can I."

"Trusting your team can be the difference between life and death."

"Then I hope I can trust all three of you when it counts," Alison smiled.

Blake replaced the photo in his pocket. "I guess you're right. I'll see you soon."

Alison headed over towards her car as Blake climbed inside his. He knew what Alison was saying was logical but something was still eating away at him. He just wasn't sure what.

***

The following day, Blake and his sister Jenny, arrived at Cartwright And Sons Solicitors on Bond Street, London. After a short wait, they were ushered inside one of the offices and sat opposite a large mahogany desk.

"Here we have the last will and testament of Emily Avis Jane Langford along with a scroll that was given to Cartwright Solicitors when the will was made," Julia Cartwright explained as she handed Blake the scroll.

Blake unrolled the scroll to reveal a letter dated August 12th 1977. A crumpled piece of yellow paper fell out of it and landed next to Jenny's foot. She carefully picked it up and noticed that it seemed to form part of a map.

"This was written the day before our parents were married," Jenny said as she read the scroll.

"Yes, your father, John Langford, was also present at the time. Your mother thought it important that the exact details of her will were kept quiet until she had passed away. Obviously, other interested parties will have been contacted after her death," Julia confirmed.

"What other parties? Us two and our brother Steven are her only living relatives!" Blake replied.

"That's not strictly true Mr Langford. You see, the will includes a benefaction that came from her late father. She was entitled to just over sixteen and a half percent of this benefaction if it was ever claimed."

"I don't understand. When our grandfather, William Handanowicz, died, the estate was split between the family."

"William Handanowicz was not Emily's father. The will contains a HM25 clause in it."

"What's a HM25 clause?"

"Harvey Matchbox twenty-five is a clause where a large benefaction is split through several members of the extended family. The benefaction comes from a sum of money that was written off in 1940. That money, if found, would be split six ways between the surviving relatives of your mother, Emily Handanowicz, now Langford, Evelyn Handanowicz, Victor Wise, Frederick Langford, Mary Langford and Patricia Hughes."

Blake sat back in his chair struggling to piece the information together. "Who put the benefaction in place?"

"Someone by the name of Jack Walter Smith, who died August 21st 1948."

"Does this mean Jack Smith was our grandfather?" Jenny asked.

"That scroll confirms that when Jack Smith died in 1948, the gold that was robbed from a bank in Portsmouth in 1938 and then written off two years later, was left as inheritance to his children. The problem was, the gold was buried and eight pieces of the map were given to relatives to keep safe. You have the first piece of the map. If you find the other seven pieces, it will give you the location of the gold."

Blake laughed. "I'm sorry but I'm not buying this treasure map fairytale. What the hell is going on here and even if this is true, how come nobody else has uncovered this in the past seventy years?"

"You're right to be sceptical Mr Langford but I have been doing some digging myself and it all seems to line up," Julia confirmed.

"How much gold is there?" Jenny asked.

"Nobody knows for sure, but the estimated value of what was taken by my calculations would be in the region of three million pounds."

Blake shook his head. "My family come from a long line of law-abiding people, Miss Cartwright. I worked my way through the police force, so did my father, my grandfather and my great-grandfather. Are you saying that they covered this all up? And if so, why?"

"All I have is what Emily Handanowicz placed on file in August 1977 right before her marriage to your father, John Langford."

"Why was this all contained in our mother's will?" Jenny asked. "Why haven't the other beneficiaries had the same information that we have?"

"Emily was very protective of her family. She took on the burden to protect not just her three children but the entire family. Now that her secret is out, it's only a matter of time before the rest of the beneficiaries will come knocking. Until then, the estate will be held in trust until everybody's whereabouts and connection to this benefaction have been accounted for."

"But my mother, Emily, my uncle Fred and aunt Mary are all dead," Blake explained.

"That may be so but the remaining few are still alive. Mary and Fred had no children. You are Emily's children hence the benefaction was triggered after her death and you stand to inherit her share."

"So what do we do now?" Jenny asked.

"If I were you, I'd speak to as many family members and friends of the family that you can and try to figure out what really happened in 1938 which led to Jack Smith leaving his fortune to your family ten years later," Julia replied.

***

In a rundown two bedroom basement flat in south-east London, Tom Gibson walked out into the back garden as rain fell heavily. He wandered over to a brick shed and unlocked a silver padlock. He opened the door and tossed a carrier bag of food into the dimly lit space. Pleading eyes came from a young woman caged behind steel bars at the back of the shed. She quickly gathered the food out of the bag and began to eat the stale bread he had given her. Her eyes bloodshot from crying and a combination of sedatives gave her a vacant appearance. Tom closed the door and locked the padlock once again before heading back inside the flat.

He began tapping away on a laptop, connecting investors to crypto-currency in a program known as The Crystal as the front door slammed shut.

A blonde haired woman appeared in the doorway of the lounge. "Any news from Andrea?" she asked.

"Nothing," Tom lied. "I'm sure she'll let us know when she's back."

"You have a letter here."

He turned to face her as she handed him the brown envelope with Cartwright And Sons Solicitors printed on it. He opened it and smiled as he read the letter.

"What is it?" she asked.

"Of course," Tom smiled as he quickly searched for obituaries on his laptop. He turned the screen to face her.

"Emily Langford?"

"Don't you see what this means Jade?"

She shook her head.

"Emily Langford was the missing piece. She held the second piece of the map. With her death, the inheritance moves to Blake. It was only a matter of time. When he discovers his whole life was built on a lie, it'll finish him!"

Jade moved towards him. "Don't you think this obsession with the Langfords is going too far?"

Tom glared at her. "I was never good enough in John Langford's eyes for his precious daughter. They stole what was rightfully ours. Our inheritance, our futures! How the hell can you defend them?"

"Jenny Langford was my friend in Uni. She'd never deliberately go out and hurt anybody."

"Yet she failed to tell you that she was your cousin."

"She probably didn't know."

"Probably," Tom huffed. "That family covers up more than a corrupt politician!"

"I don't believe that."

"Money changes people."

"No, it changed you. If it wasn't for Samir letting Zodiac go, he'd have taken you down with him."

"Zodiac knows what to do. If Emily had the declaration in her will then her brother James must have the next piece."

"Aren't you getting too old for all this Indiana Jones stuff? How do you know if there really is treasure to be found?" Jade asked.

"Jack Smith was my grandfather. He robbed a bank in 1938 and got away with it. After the war, he planned to give it all to my mother Patricia but he died before he had the chance to. She had to grow up in foster care because Blake Langford's great-grandfather couldn't keep his nose out of her business. Those bastards have been corrupting the police force for four generations. Playing the self-righteous detectives and sergeants throughout whilst their wives were sleeping around. My grandfather survived the war, he had his fun and then the Langfords killed him to make sure his secret remained hidden. Not anymore."

"Your mother was in foster care from when she was a baby. How the hell do you know if she was even telling the truth?"

Tom reached inside a drawer under his desk and pulled out an old metal cigarette case. He opened it and inside was a lock of light brown hair. "When my mother was given up for adoption, Jack gave her a lock of his hair in this cigarette box. It was proof that she was his daughter. It has since been DNA tested. It is our blood line Jade! He planned to come back for her. Then the bombing started. He went off to fight in the war and my grandmother, Ada, was killed in one of the blasts near Portsmouth. When he returned, injured from battle, he found out that she had been killed. He slept with two of the nurses who cared for him before deserting. When he returned to the south coast, he found out what really happened the night his daughter, Patricia, was given up and it cost him his life. It was the talk of the city for many years after. That's why she came back to London and I vowed to make amends one day."

Jade watched as Tom held a photo of his mother in his hands and traced the outline of her face with his finger. She turned and left him heading towards the bedroom. She had also received a letter in the mail. She had recognised her grandfather's writing immediately. She opened it and read the letter before picking up her phone and scrolling through her contacts until she arrived at Victor (Grandad). Her finger hovered over the call button for a moment before she closed it down again. She knew she needed to get close to Tom to find out how much he knew about the family legacy but visiting her grandad would open up a lot of deep wounds from her past that she wasn't ready to face.

She slipped the letter back into the envelope and hid it in the bottom drawer of the cabinet in the corner of the room. Thousands of questions flooded her mind. If the money really was hidden somewhere, how could they find it and how could she stop Tom from blowing it all on crypto-currency. She opened her laptop and began searching for significant dates from 1938. She needed to go back in time...

Chapter Two

A Time For Letting Go
Saturday 27th August 1938

"For goodness sake Jack, sit down! You're wearing a hole in the floor!" Charlie snapped as they heard the screams of childbirth coming from the bedroom upstairs.

"It's the wrong time, Charlie. We've got the big one on Saturday and Ada having the baby early has thrown a spanner in the works," Jack replied as he continued pacing up and down the lounge area.

"We go ahead as planned whatever happens. We have one chance to make this work and I won't let anything get in the way of our future!"

"And what about Ada?"

"She needs to make a choice. You knew that before you got yourselves into this mess. You take her and live out your lives here or you take a chance and leave a mark on this world."

At that moment, the sound of a newborn baby crying echoed down the hall. Jack looked over at Charlie who walked over towards the back door.

Jack checked his watch. "Seven o'clock tomorrow night, I'll be there to set it up."

Charlie nodded before leaving the house.

Jack took a deep breath before heading upstairs. He stood for a moment outside the bedroom door before gently knocking. A moment later, the door opened and he saw Ada holding a baby in her arms whilst the midwife continued to help her mother, Joan, with the towels and blankets.

Jack knelt down beside the bed and looked at the baby in Ada's arms.

"She has your eyes," she smiled.

"She?" Jack asked.

"Yes, Patricia Ivy Smith."

Jack smiled as he held them both closely to him. He knew they needed to savour this moment as it may well be one of their last together as a family. After a couple of minutes, he excused himself from the room and headed out of the house.

Wandering through the busy streets of Portsmouth, he headed towards The King's Hat pub next to the guildhall. As he entered, the smell of tobacco and stale beer attacked his senses. He saw a man in a black trench coat standing in the corner drinking beer from an overflowing glass. Jack walked over to the bar and exchanged his money for a pint of bitter before joining the man in the corner.

"Everything as agreed?" the man in the trench coat asked.

"Charlie knows what to do," Jack replied as he enjoyed a mouthful of ale.

"Bob takes over from the night guard at four o'clock. We'll have about half an hour to get inside before the rest of them arrive."

"That should give us enough time."

The man in the trench coat looked over Jack's shoulder as two police officers entered the pub. "You ought to be careful about the company you keep," he snapped before slamming his glass onto the bar and walking out of the pub.

One of the police officers walked over towards Jack who calmly finished his pint.

"You think it's acceptable to be here when your wife is giving birth do you?" the officer asked.

Jack turned around to face him. "Your wife and daughter are fine without me."

"Never a truer word said in jest. Get home where you belong Smith or I'll make sure you don't get anywhere near my grandchild."

"Calm down Ern, I was just leaving," Jack smirked as he pushed his way through the crowd and left the pub.

One week later, just before four o'clock on the morning of Saturday 3rd September 1938, a huge explosion echoed around Portsmouth City Centre. Dust filled the air as the walls of the City Bank fell and shattered into small pieces of brick and concrete. Police cars, fire engines and ambulances arrived to remove people who were caught up in the blast and to extinguish the flames from the explosion. Witnesses claimed that a bomb had just exploded inside the bank and two men and a woman had been seen climbing into a truck and speeding away from the city. In three minutes, it was over and gone. As the dust settled, police officers were left to try and piece together what had just happened.

***

When Joan Hughes entered the grocery store later that morning, she was met with stunned silence by the shopkeeper behind the counter.

"Is something wrong Iris?" Joan asked.

"Where have you been? The police have been trying to find you all morning."

"I was at home. Nobody came around. Oh no, has something happened? I need to find Ernest...."

At that moment, Joan heard a baby crying. Iris opened the door that led into the stockroom behind the counter and beckoned her daughter to come into the shop. As she approached, Joan looked at the baby in her arms and gasped.

"No! No! Where's Ada?"

"We were hoping that you could tell us," Iris replied.

"There must be some simple explanation... Some reason. They would not leave Patricia behind."

"It's obvious isn't it."

Joan looked at Iris.

"He's gone back to his old ways. The bank. The explosion. We all heard it on the wireless this morning. You should never have let your Ada hook up with a man like him. You know what they say..."

Joan moved towards Iris' daughter and took Patricia into her arms. "No, what do they say?"

"Once a thief, always a thief. Your Ada was silly to think that she could change his ways."

"Jack Smith is a most respectable man and he has always provided for my daughter in their marriage. This is just a misunderstanding. Good day to you..." Joan snapped before storming out of the shop.

"What did I say?" Iris asked after she had left.

"Some people just don't want to hear the truth mama," her daughter replied.

Joan stormed back into the family home and found her husband Ernest standing in the kitchen still wearing his coat as he looked out at the back garden.

"You knew, didn't you!" Joan snapped.

"It's just part of our inquiries for now..."

"You were out all night! Tell me Ern, where are they?"

Ernest turned to face her and saw Patricia in her arms. "Where was she?" he asked.

"Where are they? Why aren't you out there looking for our daughter and Jack?"

"My superior thinks that because I am Ada's father, I should be excluded from the investigation. Where was Patricia?"

"Iris Jones had her in the grocery shop," Joan admitted as she tried to fight back her tears.

Ernest thought back to the previous weekend when he saw Jack Smith in the local bar drinking with someone he didn't recognise. Surely they couldn't have been planning the bank robbery whilst Ada was having the baby, could they? He battled with himself weighing up whether to tell Joan about their short exchange but decided to keep that information to himself.

"What can I do to help?" he finally asked.

Joan looked at him through tear-filled eyes. "Find our daughter," she replied before heading upstairs with the baby in her arms.

Ernest watched her leave before picking up his hat and coat and leaving the house, looking for answers but not expecting many to arrive.

One Year Later...

Joan and Ernest Hughes were sitting at the dining table with their one year old granddaughter Patricia when a message from the Prime Minister, Neville Chamberlain, interrupted the music that was playing on the radio. As he told the nation of Hitler's failure to respond to British demands to leave Poland and that the UK will be at war with Germany, a feeling of dread overwhelmed them.

"Do you know what today is?" Joan asked.

"Sunday," Ernest sighed as he tried to lose himself in the headlines of the newspaper he was reading.

"It's been one year since Ada and Jack went missing."

Ernest's face turned red. The lines of too many red wines traced a roadmap on his cheeks. "I think we have bigger things to worry about than some small-time crook and our selfish excuse of a daughter running away from their responsibilities!"

"How can you be so cold?"

"I'm forty-five years old Joan! I should be enjoying the fruits of my labour. Playing bridge at the Golf Club, going fishing down on the beach and now it looks like we're about to head into another battle that nobody can win. I had enough of that when I was a young man."

"Well I'm sorry that the world didn't ask for your permission before joining a fight for freedom!"

Ernest stood up from his chair. "Any more lip like that and I'll..."

"You'll do what? I've had it with you Ern. Ever since Ada disappeared you've changed."

"What do you expect when your only daughter runs off with some low-life and you're powerless to stop it?"

"And why do you think she ran away with him in the first place?"

Ernest raised his hand and struck Joan across her face, sending her into the dining chair before she regained her balance.

"You have no right to speak to me like that! All I've ever done is work hard to provide for this family and for what?"

"There's more than just you hurting in this family, remember that before you lash out again," Joan replied before picking up Patricia and heading out of the house.

She had been planning this moment for a while. Ernest's outburst had finally given her the courage to follow it through. Joan had already packed a small suitcase full of clothes for herself and Patricia and had taken it to a friend's house the previous day. She walked towards Southsea seafront before heading down Palmerston Road towards the shops. She turned into a sideroad where her friend, Florence and her husband, Ron, lived.

Joan entered the house with Patricia in her arms. As the door closed behind them, Ron led her to the dining table where three sheets of paper were laid out.

"Are you sure about this?" Florence asked.

"I can't keep her in that environment and with the war starting, she has a better chance away from here," Joan sighed as she signed the papers.

Ron collected the signed documents from the table and placed them into an envelope.

"What now?" Joan asked.

"You'll stay here for tonight, there is a train leaving for London at ten minutes past nine in the morning. We need to be on that train.

We will head towards Hammersmith to finalise all of the details. It's a time for letting go, Mrs Hughes," Ron replied.

Florence led them both to a spare bedroom with a double bed that had been made up with soft blankets and a selection of cuddly toys laid out on the bed. For the rest of that evening, Joan played and held her granddaughter close before they both fell asleep together as night fell. The following morning, Florence waved them goodbye at the railway station as Ron, wearing a long trench coat, joined them both on the train to London. From that moment on, Joan knew that their lives would never be the same again.

Chapter Three

One Hand Out Of The Grave
Friday 31st October 2008

If Blake Langford had broken a mirror, he wouldn't have expected the misfortune that had come his way. He drove his silver Ford Mondeo up the slight incline of his driveway towards Southward Cottage, his home that overlooked Lepe Beach, before parking his car behind a blue Nissan Note belonging to his sister, Jenny. He stepped out of his car and headed inside taking note of a spherical dent with accompanying scratches on the rear bumper of his sister's car.

"Good morning, looks like somebody had a disagreement with something outside," Blake said as he entered the dining room where Jenny and Paula were sitting at the table enjoying some coffee.

"Nothing gets past you does it?" Jenny smiled as she hugged Blake.

"Having a fight with the lamp post again?"

"It wasn't there when I reversed it!"

Blake laughed as he poured himself a cup of coffee. "I'm sure it just appeared out of nowhere. Seriously though, do you want me to try and do something for that dent?"

"No, it's okay, Dan will take care of it."

"Oh, who's this Dan then?" Paula asked.

"Just a friend..." Jenny smiled. "Anyway, the police have allowed us to go back into mum's house and recover what we can from the explosion."

Blake's expression changed. "I doubt there's much left to salvage after what happened."

Whilst Blake and Jenny's mother, Emily Langford, was ill in hospital, Tom Gibson, the leader of a student trafficking group in

London had planted a bomb in the Langford family home. Blake, his colleague Alison Pearce, and Jenny had been lucky to escape before the bomb exploded, mostly destroying the entire house. The general feeling was that Gibson had set up the bomb to target Blake. Jenny and Tom had been in a relationship several years earlier which Blake felt, still had an influence on how that assignment ended. Tom Gibson, Ian Bleeker and Zachary Zhal were still out there running free in Europe. Blake hated loose ends and knew that it was only a matter of time before their paths crossed again.

"They're looking to demolish and rebuild it but they've put some scaffolding in place to allow us to search through anything that we can salvage," Jenny explained.

Even though years of training had given Blake the tools he needed to cope with most things, he had struggled to compartmentalise what had happened to him and his family over the past year or so. After the death of his fiance Rachael Evans, he discovered that he was a father and had an eight year old son whom he barely knew before then losing his mother to a severe stroke that caused her to have a brain haemorrhage, he felt like the world was conspiring against him and there was little or no clue as to where he should turn next. "I'm not interested in any of it," he snapped. "Mum and Dad are gone and the house is just an empty shell of what it once was."

Jenny lifted a small dented metal box out of a bag and placed it on the table.

"What's that?" Blake asked.

"Photos from when Mum and Dad were kids. Our photos from years ago. Somehow they survived the blast. Thought maybe you'd want to reminisce..."

"What's the point Jen? What's done is done. We can't bring them back so there's no point in rehashing the past!"

Jenny opened up the box and pulled out a black and white photo of a man in a suit standing next to a pregnant woman at a railway station.

"Blake, look at this," Paula said.

Blake looked down at the photo.

"Isn't that the same man who was in the photo that you found?" Paula asked.

Jenny looked at them both. "What photo?"

"A few months ago after the Gibson case and our trip to France, I received a letter in the mail from Goodman, Parker & Knowles in London," Blake explained.

Jenny gasped. "Mum's safety deposit box!"

"You knew about it?"

"Yeah, she had used it for years to store away valuable jewellery and money when times were tough. What was inside the box?"

Paula stood up from the table and walked over towards a wooden cabinet in the corner of the room. She opened a drawer and pulled out a small plastic bag and an old black and white photo. She brought them over to the table and laid them down alongside the photo that Jenny had selected. The new photo showed two men, two women and three children on Lepe Beach in 1948.

"Mum's engagement ring, dad's old Rolex watch, I think that might be Grandma Handanowicz's ring and I'm not sure of the other one," Jenny explained.

"Where does the Handanowicz name come from?" Paula asked.

"Mum's parents were Dana and William Handanowicz, our grandparents," Blake replied. "They died a long time ago."

"That's not an English name. I never knew your mother had foreign parents," Paula replied.

"No, our grandad was originally from what used to be Yugoslavia but he settled here after the war. Mum, aunt Evelyn and our uncle Jim were all born in Southampton," Jenny explained as she took a closer look at the two photos. "Oh my God!" she gasped.

"What?" Paula asked.

"That's Dad's parents, Edward and Mavis Langford alongside Grandma Dana Handanowicz and that other man," Jenny replied.

Blake nodded. "That's what I noticed. The Langfords and the Handanowicz's at least knew of each other in 1948."

"Wait, Mum wasn't born until 1949 so who are the children in this photo?" Jenny asked.

"Dad, uncle Fred and aunt Mary," Blake confirmed. "Dad was nine years older than Mum. Fred and Mary must have been around six at the time."

"That means your Dad was born in 1940 and Mary and Fred were born in 1942. Wasn't your grandad fighting in the war back then?" Paula asked.

"Our Grandad, Edward Langford was a local police detective and he didn't get drafted until the beginning of 1942. From what I remember of their stories, Aunt Mary and Uncle Fred were twins and they were born whilst Grandad was away," Blake explained.

"Your grandmother must have been through so much during that time. The bombing and being pregnant as well as looking after your Dad."

"She was a nurse and helped look after the war wounded so I guess she had like minded people around her to help at the time."

"So where is Grandad Will?" Jenny asked.

"I've been doing some research online and it looks like our Handanowicz grandparents didn't get married until April 22nd 1949," Blake replied.

"And mum's birthday was August 16th 1949," Jenny gasped.

"Maybe they realised that she was pregnant and then quickly arranged the wedding so they wouldn't be frowned upon for having sex before marriage. Back then, there was a social stigma around unmarried mothers, wasn't there?" Paula asked.

Blake nodded as he looked at both photos and turned them over. On the back of the beach photo it read 14th July 1948 and the photo from the train station was dated 24th March 1948. There was a smudge below the date on the train photo which he looked closely at but couldn't quite make anything out of it.

"So Dana was pregnant in the train photo and not in the beach photo," Paula said as she tried to work out the dates.

"Are there any photos of Grandad Will before Mum was born?" Blake asked.

"Not here but they may have gone up in smoke. Why?" Jenny asked.

"I'm thinking that Grandad Will might not have been our biological grandad," Blake replied.

"How do you get that from a random photograph?" Jenny asked.

"Back in 1948, you wouldn't lay a hand on a woman that you were not married to in public. He has his arms around Grandma in both photos."

"That's pretty flimsy Blake, he may have been a close friend and Grandad Will might have been taking the photo."

Paula picked up the railway station photo and walked over towards the study. She turned the desk lamp on and studied the smudge underneath the date. "I think I've got something!" she called out.

Blake and Jenny joined her in the study.

"It's very faint but I think that is a J, something, something, K and then a space before an S," Paula pointed out.

Blake and Jenny took a closer look.

"It's got to be the name of a person or a place," Jenny said.

"The obvious name for the time would be John or Jack but John or Jack S isn't going to get us far," Blake sighed.

"There might be someone who would know," Jenny replied.

"No, we're not going there!" Blake snapped.

"He's Mum's sole living relative from that generation Blake!" Jenny pleaded.

"I'm not going all the way out to Greece to track down Uncle Jim in his private villa simply for a little bit of fact-finding for a family tree. That man is poisonous. He'd walk over anyone to chase a fiver in a force-ten gale!" Blake fumed.

"Aren't you just a little bit inquisitive?" Paula asked.

"Why should I be? Mum and Dad are both gone. Let them and whatever they got up to in the past rest in peace with them," Blake sighed.

"But why did Mum find that photograph important enough to lock away in a safety deposit box? There has to be more to this Blake! Maybe the map is connected to it in some way," Jenny replied.

"What map?" Paula asked.

Blake took a deep breath. "Just some fairytale story that the solicitor tried to sell us the other day."

"They must have had a reason to bring it up."

"I need some air," he replied before heading out of the back door and walking down the wooden steps at the far end of the garden towards the stony beach below.

Paula and Jenny stood by the door and watched him leave.

"He's too stubborn for his own good, just like Dad," Jenny sighed.

"What did your Uncle Jim do that was so bad?" Paula asked.

"Nobody knows the full story but it almost cost Dad his job at Scotland Yard. There was a huge family row about twenty years ago and then Uncle Jim just sold up and left. Last we heard he had a villa out in Rhodes, one of the Greek Islands."

"Was Jim your Mum's only sibling?"

"No, she had Evelyn, her twin sister and an older sister too, called Edith, but she died when she was only a teenager in 1956."

"I'll talk to him. He'll come around eventually," Paula replied.

"I hope so," Jenny said as she returned to the dining table to finish her coffee. "How are you bearing up?"

"Me? I'm fine. Just trying to get on with things again. After Dad fled the country with our money, there's not much left to say anymore."

"You can't blame yourself Paula. He played on your sympathy and even though what he's done over the years was wrong, he's still your father and deep down you still love and care for him."

"Yeah, and look how that turned out. I know there's a lot going on with your family since Emily passed away but mine seems to be as disjointed as ever too."

"I would have done the same thing in those circumstances. You can't change the past, only learn from it."

"I guess you're right. Sorry, I've just had a lot on my mind lately," Paula sighed.

"Andrew Broughton?"

"His funeral was two weeks ago and I just can't seem to get him off of my mind. Crazy huh? I have everything I want here with Blake and Michael and yet I'm still tied in knots with a guy who physically and mentally abused me ten years ago."

"It's not crazy at all. We can't help who we fall in love with."

"But why do I always go for the high maintenance ones?"

"Is Blake high maintenance?"

Paula shook her head. "I don't know Jen. I'm so confused about everything right now. There's deaths and betrayals every way we turn at the moment and I'm struggling to know whether I'm coming or going."

Jenny didn't reply.

"I know his job takes priority and occasionally Michael and I would become collateral damage, I just didn't think it would be this hard."

"Blake loves you both and will do anything to protect you. You just need to trust that when things get rough, he will make the right decision."

Paula walked over towards the window and looked out at the beach. "I know all of this but why am I still unsure of myself? Why do I have my ex ingrained in my memory and why am I full of distrust for Blake?"

Jenny joined her at the window. "Only you can answer that. When Tom returned after fifteen years, I still had that fantasy in my mind of the dreams we shared when we were together. But that's all they were, dreams. Sometimes you need to love someone enough to let them go. Tom will always have a place in my heart but he'll never hurt me again. You need to decide how to move forward. With the ghost of Andy and what might have been or with Blake. Only you can decide."

Paula thought about what Jenny had said. She knew that Blake was still fighting his own thoughts and emotions about her sister Rachael's death and the guilt he carried for not being able to save her. She felt the same about Andy. If only she had been there, maybe he wouldn't have been poisoned. The flip of a coin. Whichever way she looked at it, there were pros and cons on both sides. Andy's death had hit her harder than she ever wanted to admit. It filled her with thoughts that she had never felt before. Doubts and fears that had been buried for so long. She knew she needed to face up to them sooner or later and whatever the consequences were, she would have to accept them. But right now, she still didn't know which way to turn. So much had gone wrong recently and her confidence was at an all-time-low. She just hoped that somehow, she still had a chance to fight for what she truly wanted when all was said and done.

"Where's Dad gone?" Michael asked as he entered the room.

"He's just gone for a walk, is everything okay?" Jenny asked.

"Yeah, I just thought we could have a rematch on the Playstation."

"Well how about you show me," Jenny replied as she led him away.

Paula watched them leave. She knew that Michael was beginning to feel the tension in the house between her and Blake. He'd been through so much at such a young age after losing his mother and relocating from Miami to The New Forest in the UK but there was still that nagging doubt in her mind and she struggled to figure out who or what could change it.

***

Later that night, a man walking his cocker spaniel through the fields of the New Forest National Park heard a muffled sound like somebody trying to scream. His dog darted towards East Boldre cemetery.

"Spike! Come here!" the man called out as he swung his torch around in all directions trying to find out where his dog had run off to.

He heard his dog barking and whining. He shone his torch up to see a sign displaying the cemetery's name on the gate that had been left open. "You would pick this place on Halloween night!" he grumbled.

Using his torch to light up the muddy pathway, the man followed the whines and barks of his dog into the cemetery.

"Spike! This is not funny! Where are you!" he snapped.

At that moment, he noticed his dog sitting beside a grave, whining.

"There you are, come here boy!" the man called out but the dog wouldn't move.

"Spike! Come on, here boy!" He tried again.

The dog remained seated next to the grave. The man walked towards him. "What's gotten into you?"

As he approached, the dog barked at him. "What's wrong?"

As the man waved his torch around he stood frozen to the spot. Next to where Spike was sitting was an unmarked grave and from the centre of it pointing to the sky was somebody's arm and hand.

Chapter Four

Alfred Langford
Wednesday 6th September 1939

Joan Hughes returned home on Wednesday morning and noticed eight bottles of milk had been left in the porch with a note from the milkman. Thoughts flooded her mind as Ernest would always take the milk in and pay the milkman in advance. She thought about the argument on Sunday, her trip to London to leave Patricia at the adoption agency and the lonely night she had spent at Florence and Ron's house last night.

The bruising on her face had only just started to fade and she knew when she told Ernest that she had given up Patricia, he would likely lash out again. Tears stung her eyes as the reality of her tough decision began to hit her. She knew Patricia would be better off away from here but now she needed to find the courage to face her husband's fury. She slid her key into the lock and opened the front door. The smell of stale tobacco and alcohol caught her attention as she wandered through the kitchen and into the dining room before entering the lounge.

The morning sun shining through the curtains gave the room a green glow. A pile of letters had been left unopened on the arm of the sofa and a glass with a small amount of whiskey inside it had been left on the coffee table. Joan tutted to herself because a coaster hadn't been used and the glass had left a watermark on the table. She placed a coaster underneath the glass and then smiled at herself for the absurdity of her pickiness given the circumstances they found themselves in.

"Ernest?" she called out. "Ern? Are you home?"

The house was deathly silent. Joan felt a cold sweat overwhelm her body as she carefully began climbing the stairs. As she reached the top, she heard someone breathing heavily.

"Ern?"

At that moment, an ironing board flew past in front of her and clattered into the wall at the top of the stairs.

"What on earth..."

"Where the hell have you been?" Ernest slurred.

Joan looked towards the bathroom doorway and saw Ernest leaning against the doorframe. He was wearing a ripped shirt, trousers with a belt hanging loosely from the waist and looked as if he hadn't shaved for a few days.

"What happened?" Joan asked.

"Answer the question!"

"I had to get away for a few days."

"You've been with him haven't you!"

"Who?"

"You know who, that bloody copper who goes to The King's Hat!"

"Alfred Langford? He's married and we've only spoken a couple of times. How dare you..."

Ernest lunged at her but Joan managed to step back before he slumped down in the doorway of their bedroom. "You should... know your place," he grimaced.

"No, you should understand that I'm the only one looking out for us whilst everything else is falling apart!"

"What's that supposed to mean?"

"In case you haven't noticed, there is a war going on and rather than doing anything to help, you're drowning in whiskey hoping that it all goes away. Look at the state of you. Call yourself a Police Officer? You're pathetic."

Ernest stood up and attempted to walk towards her. He lost his balance and hit the door of Patricia's bedroom open. He looked inside the room before turning back to Joan. His eyes were bloodshot and piercing. "Where is she?"

"Safe."

"Where is she? Tell me!"

"Safe! Away from you and away from the coast."

Ernest swung his fist in her direction and made contact with her cheek before falling against the doorframe of their bedroom. Joan staggered back to her feet and began heading towards the stairs. Ernest crawled towards the chest of drawers in the bedroom and removed his gun from the bottom drawer. As she reached the hallway, Joan turned around and saw him standing at the bottom of the stairs aiming the gun at her.

"You won't leave this house alive," Ernest spat as he began to move towards her.

"What happened to you? What happened to the man I married?" Joan replied, trying with all her strength to keep her voice calm.

"We were fine. We were happy until you let Ada go off with that lowlife common criminal. Then to top it all, my wife becomes the city whore and takes turns at my colleagues."

"Jack Smith was a good man. He worked on his father's farm land for years!"

"He's a petty thief! A criminal. A shoplifter. He robbed the City Bank and is now on the run with our only daughter! Now tell me, where is Patricia?"

"At the adoption agency. You'll never see her again!"

Ernest froze for a moment, unsure of how to react. "No, no, why? Why would you do that?"

"Isn't it obvious! You're out of control Ern!"

Ernest fired the gun at the ceiling sending a shower of wood and plaster sprinkling all over the room.

"You had everything a woman could want! A family, a home, a husband, I gave you everything!" he fumed, his face turning red and his eyes piercing as they glared at Joan.

She tried to open the front door but the lock had jammed.

"Don't even think about escaping!" he shouted as he staggered towards her.

Joan quickly looked around and found a glass ashtray on the sideboard. She picked it up and threw it at Ernest. The ashtray hit him on the side of his head with a sickening crack. He fell to the floor with blood seeping from a cut at the side of his forehead.

"Oh my God! No! Ern!" Joan gasped as she rushed towards him. "I'm so sorry, I didn't mean..."

As she crouched down beside him, Ernest grabbed her arms and swung his whole body weight on top of her to pin her to the floor.

"No wife of mine is going to walk out on me alive!" he cussed as he wrestled with Joan on the floor.

Joan saw the gun on the floor next to them. As if reading her mind, Ernest reached for the gun. She brought her knee up and made contact between his legs. He momentarily let go of her, giving Joan the opportunity to get up. Ernest reached for the gun but she kicked it towards the front door. She tried to run towards the door but he grabbed her ankle, sending her crashing to the floor, hitting her head on the sideboard in the hallway. As she regained her senses, Ernest was standing over her. Blood was dripping from the cut on his forehead leaving a large bloodstain on his shirt.

"You just couldn't leave things alone could you? You had to chase your freedom. You are my wife and that means you do what I tell you to! You knew that! You knew that!"

Joan nodded nervously as he aimed the gun at her head.

"Things could have been so different Joan. We could've been happy..."

"We still can be..." she stammered.

"Not now, once I've taken care of you, I'll pay a visit to your little friend and make sure he knows the pain of betrayal."

Joan noticed an umbrella that had been left beside the front door just behind where Ernest was standing. She needed a distraction and that could be it.

"And then what Ern, if the police find out what you've done you'll be spending the rest of your life rotting in jail!"

"Who are they going to believe, a copper wet behind the ears or me?"

At that moment, Joan kicked out causing the umbrella to fall. The noise distracted Ernest long enough for her to grab his arm and knock the gun out of his hand. He wrestled and tried to overpower her but she found strength from somewhere to push him away and tried the door again. The door opened and they saw a police car driving down the road towards the house. Ernest grabbed her hair and dragged her back before slamming the door shut. Joan backed herself against the wall. He lunged at her once more. She dodged him and kicked his kneecap, sending him down to the floor once more. As she tried to get to the door, he grabbed her leg once more and pulled her down on top of him. Joan clawed at his face, drawing blood from his cheek. Ernest smiled menacingly as he brought the gun up between them. She saw it and grabbed the barrel of the gun and pulled with all of her might to aim it away from them.

Another shot fired into the ceiling sending more wood and plaster sprinkling around the room. Ernest managed to cock the gun once more and held her head close to him. With all her strength, Joan caught his hand with her fist sending the gun towards his chin and suddenly, it fired once more.

There was a sudden deathly silence in the house. Joan began gasping for air as she exhaled a breath she hadn't realised that she was holding. She looked down at Ernest's body and the pool of blood that was coming from his head. She vomited on the floor at the sight and the stench coming from his body. A loud knocking at the front door caught her attention.

"Hello! Mr Hughes? Mrs Hughes? It's the police!" Alfred Langford called out.

A feeling of panic ran through Joan's body as she saw her husband's body laying on the ground.

"Mrs Hughes? Joan? Are you all right?" Alfred called out again.

Joan carefully climbed over Ernest's body and opened the door. She was thankful to see a friendly face and quickly ushered Alfred inside. As he entered though, his friendly expression quickly hardened.

"Oh my God. I need to call this in. Joan, what happened?" Alfred asked.

Joan fell to her knees and cried. "It was an accident! I didn't mean to kill him! How did you know?"

"Someone called the station because they heard a gunshot. Tell me everything that happened."

Joan told Alfred Langford everything including her journey to London to give up Patricia to the adoption agency and Ernest's increased violent outbursts since their daughter's disappearance. Alfred listened intently, nodding, taking notes in his notebook and trying not to interrupt until she was finished. When she had finally finished, two more police cars appeared outside.

"They're going to arrest me aren't they? I'm going to spend the rest of my life in jail for protecting my granddaughter," Joan sighed.

Alfred took a deep breath and looked down at the gun on the floor. He picked up a cloth from the kitchen table and walked over towards the gun. Using the cloth, he picked up the gun and placed it in Ernest's right hand before returning the cloth to the kitchen table.

"Why? What..." Joan gasped.

"That's where the gun should have been. Ernest Hughes was an arrogant bastard who should have been put in his place a long time ago. As far as anyone else knows, there was a family argument and he committed suicide. Do you think you can stick to that story?"

Joan looked down at Ernest's body and then back at Alfred. "Why are you doing this for me? He's one of your own. You should be throwing the key away."

"I once had a friend in a similar situation to yours. Nobody was willing to help her and she ended up dead because of it. If you're willing to support this, I will make sure that nothing happens to you. You did what you needed to do to protect your granddaughter. You deserve a chance to see what you did was right."

A knock at the door interrupted their conversation.

"I need an answer Joan..."

She nodded before heading over towards the door. A police detective with two more officers were waiting for them. Joan walked out whilst Alfred Langford told the detective the new version of what had happened. When he finished briefing the detective, he wandered over towards the waiting ambulance. Joan was sitting on the edge of a wall talking to a nurse.

"Do you have anywhere to stay until we have cleaned up your home?" Alfred asked.

"I can stay with friends, thank you Officer Langford," Joan replied.

"Well, I hope things work out for you Mrs Hughes and my condolences for your loss," Alfred replied before heading back towards his car and driving away.

Alfred Langford gave Joan one final glance as he drove away from the house. He had a feeling that this wouldn't be the last he would see of the Hughes family.

Chapter Five

Picking Up The Pieces
Saturday 1st November 2008

Blake Langford inhaled deeply as he parked his car outside the charred remains of his family home at 124 Alfredson Road. He had driven up to London from his home on the south coast to where he shared many family memories with his sister Jenny, who was sat alongside him, and their brother Steven along with their parents and grandparents. Now however, the house looked like a decaying shell that was slowly falling to pieces in front of him. He felt numb. There was no longing, no attachment to the bricks and mortar that had been the home of the Langford family for so many years.

"Are you okay?" Jenny asked.

"Yeah, there's just been too many weird things going on lately. I'm struggling to piece it all together. If mum had some kind of family secret, why didn't she tell us?"

"I guess there are some things we need to keep to ourselves until we're ready to confront them."

"Or until it's taken to the grave."

"She wouldn't want us to mull over what might've been. Out of tragedy, at least you and Steven are talking again."

Blake smiled at the thought of his brother. They had been at each other's throats for years but after Steven had woken up to a house full of murdered students, Blake had been the only one who had stood by him and helped to prove his innocence.

"He's gone off the radar lately. Have you heard from him?" Blake asked.

"He's gone on some kind of silent retreat. Somewhere in Cambodia. A spiritual healer has convinced him to go into a monastery for thirty days to help him find himself again."

Blake looked at his sister shocked. "Are we talking about the same person here? Our brother, the gobshite of the nightclubs who can barely keep his mouth shut for two minutes, has gone away on some woo woo pilgrimage to what…. Find Jesus?"

"Grief takes people on different journeys Blake. Sometimes, you need to face the truth and admit that you need help."

"Why do those who insist on giving advice never seem to take it themselves?"

"Meaning?"

"Tom Gibson?"

"What about him?"

"Knowing that he's still out there somewhere."

"I grieved for Tom a long time ago. The man I knew and loved was not the man I saw at that underground station."

"I just don't want you to rush into another relationship on the rebound…"

"The rebound from what Blake? I discovered that the man I loved from ten years ago is in fact a callous bastard who faked his death, led his team into a death trap and is now trafficking young girls across Europe. As far as I'm concerned, he's dead to me and he has been for a long time. What I have with Dan now is just a close friendship and in time, who knows?"

"I'm just worried about you…"

"Coming from the guy who's recently proposed to the love of his life's sister…"

"You know that's different. Rachael and I were over long ago."

"Yet you're standing at her graveside at every opportunity you get."

"Sometimes the heart takes a while to catch up with the brain. We do stupid things in the name of love and then get burnt because of it."

"So you should understand that the feelings I had for Tom are now over and I'm ready to move on. You share a beautiful son with Rachael and you and Paula will be great parents for him as he grows up. Don't let the chip on your shoulder prevent you from being there for Michael and making the best of what you have. I'm still picking up the pieces of my life but in the end, we all need to find closure and move on."

Blake looked over at their family home. The windows were all boarded up and the white PVC front door had now been replaced with a dark grey metal one. He wondered what their father, John Langford, would have thought of the situation they now found themselves in.

"Did mum ever speak much to you about her family before she married dad?" Blake asked.

"Not much more than what we all knew. Grandma Dana married Grandad William in 1949 and they had mum a few months later before Uncle Jim came along in 1951. Have you thought any more about contacting him? He's the only one who could possibly know why that photo was in the box."

Blake shook his head. "Sometimes we just need to let things be and after what Jim did to Dad, I don't want to bring up any more bad memories. We've had enough aggravation already. The photo was taken three years before he was born anyway. Chances of him knowing anything are very slim."

Jenny nodded noncommittally.

"Grandma Dana was married before she met Grandad William though, wasn't she?" Blake asked.

"She was married to someone called Gerald but he died during the war. He was Edith's father but she died in 1956 of Pneumonia. Do you think Mum was trying to tell us something with that photo or was she just keeping hold of it for sentimental reasons?"

"It's probably nothing and I'm just overthinking it but why did she keep that specific photo in her safe deposit box? Even the guy at the depository seemed to be familiar with mum and gave his condolences for her."

"I know she did visit there regularly because her friend, Sandra, commented on it a while back," Jenny conceded.

"Do you think she may have information about why mum was so meticulous about that box?"

"I guess it wouldn't hurt to ask."

Blake pondered that for a moment. "I'll keep it in mind. I guess we can't put it this off any longer," he sighed as he opened the car door and headed over towards the house with Jenny following close behind.

They collected several boxes of ornaments and whatever they could salvage from the charred remains of the house and placed them in the back of the car. After the bomb had exploded and blown out most of the front of the house, Blake had arranged for scaffolders and builders to attempt to make the remains of the building as secure as possible but the reality was, it would have to be completely demolished and rebuilt.

Blake was usually very good at compartmentalising things but the memories of his childhood and his parents lives in this house over the years panged him anew as he looked at what the remains of the building had become. As they locked the door and returned to the car, Blake noticed a black BMW had pulled up on the opposite side of the road.

"Trouble?" Jenny asked as she nodded in the direction of the car.

"I don't think so," Blake replied as he wandered over towards the car.

As he approached, Joe Knight stepped out from the driver's seat. A roadmap of veins and shrapnel scarring on the left side of his face told the story of a shed exploding during a stake-out with Samir

Khalifa a few months ago. Blake still felt guilty for sending them to the address where they were pursuing a lead on a known criminal called Zodiac but after a lengthy stay in hospital, Joe was back in the field again and Blake was pleased to see him.

"I see they can't keep a good man down. Good to see you Joe," Blake smiled as he shook his hand. "What brings you here?"

"Thanks, Blake. Unfortunately, I wish it was under better circumstances. Gordon needs you to come in. Some weird stuff has been flagged up from Hampshire Constabulary."

"Hampshire?"

"Yeah, last night a man was walking his dog through a graveyard and gave himself a fright."

"What rational man would wander through a graveyard on Halloween night anyway?"

"Your guess is as good as mine but when his dog ran over to an unmarked grave, he discovered a hand sticking out of it," Joe replied.

"Halloween prank taken too far?"

"That's what the police thought until they dug deeper shall we say."

"Meaning?"

"They dug into the grave and discovered a young woman who had recently been buried alive."

"And the hand was her failed attempt to escape?" Blake asked. "That's a rough way to die."

"The plot thickens, early indications show that the young woman could well be Andrea Louise Smith."

That took Blake by surprise. "The same Andrea Smith that was staying at the chateau in Toulouse with Graham Evans?"

"The same."

"But how? Why? I thought she was on the red list. If her, Gibson, Zodiac or Evans returned to the UK they'd have been flagged up."

"That's the thing, there is no record of any of them returning to the UK since they left after the trafficking case went south."

"It doesn't make any sense. Whose grave was she buried in?"

"The grave at East Boldre cemetery was unmarked and there seems to be no paper trail. All we know is that it apparently belongs to someone who died in the 1980's but so far, the authorities have been unable to get permission to exhume the body for identification."

"Why? Surely if the body is a John or Jane Doe then there are no connected relatives to the deceased, therefore no red tape."

"You'd think so but the undertaker, a Mr Paul Crowther, refuses to give up the paperwork that was processed by his father whom he inherited the company from. Without the legal paperwork, the authorities cannot proceed with the dig any further."

"So, have the French police contacted Graham Evans?" Blake asked.

"He claims that Andrea left the chateau around a month ago and was meeting up with some friends in Monte Carlo. He hasn't seen or heard from her since."

"And they bought that?"

"They had no reason to suspect otherwise. The final will of Elliot Francis left the estate to Graham Evans so he is legally, as far as the French authorities are concerned, living at the chateau alone."

"Except he isn't. Gibson and Zodiac are still out there and he probably knows where they are."

"The trail's gone cold Blake. Derek Copsewood isn't giving anything up despite facing ten years behind bars. The only chance we had to get them was on that freight train and they slipped through our fingers."

Blake swore under his breath. He had been tracking a student trafficking ring across London led my Derek Copsewood, Tom Gibson and Zachary Zhal, better known as Zodiac but despite him and his team rescuing the missing students and Derek Copsewood giving himself up, Gibson and Zodiac managed to escape. He had a feeling that Andrea's body turning up in a grave nearby to his family home on the south coast was more than just a coincidence.

"So, what do we do now?" Blake asked.

"Given that you're familiar with the area, Gordon is sending your team to the cemetery at 0900 hours tomorrow morning to meet with the local vicar and the forensic team later in the day."

Eric Gordon was head of Special Branch and often had inside information that Blake knew he needed if he was to try and untangle what had happened over the past few months.

"Okay, I'll be there but keep me informed about Graham Evans. I need to know everything he does. He could well be the key to all of this," Blake replied.

"Our man in Paris is on his way there now," Joe confirmed. "It's good to see you again Blake."

"Likewise," Blake smiled before returning to his car on the driveway of the remains of his parents home.

Jenny was waiting inside the car for him.

"Well?" she asked as Blake sat in the driver's seat.

"Andrea Smith is back in the UK. Are you still friends with her older sister?" Blake asked.

"We went to uni together but I haven't spoken to Jade for a couple of years. I guess I could message her on social media. Is everything okay?"

Blake wasn't sure how much information he should tell his sister but at the same time, he knew the media would be all over it sooner rather than later. He took a deep breath. "There's been no official ID, however, a body has been discovered in East Boldre Cemetery in The New Forest. There's a strong possibility that it could be Andrea. Alison, Samir and I have to go there tomorrow morning to continue the investigation."

Jenny gasped, holding her hand over her mouth. "No, not Andrea too. He's tying up loose ends!"

"What do you mean?"

"Tom, he's finishing us off one by one. Nicola was murdered near Paris and now Andrea. It's only a matter of time before he comes for me."

"I don't think that's his plan Jen."

"Why?"

"Because if he wanted to kill you, he would have done it at The Rabbit Hole."

The Rabbit Hole was a disused London underground station that Jenny, Blake and a few friends used to go to as teenagers to hang out until the police sealed up all of the entrances. Jenny received a message to go there and that was where she had learnt the truth about Tom Gibson's betrayal. She hated him for it. As she thought about what Blake had said, she soon realised that the hunter had become the hunted.

"What can I do to help?" Jenny asked.

"Contact Jade but do not let her know too many details about the investigation. There has to be a connection with the Smith family and The New Forest. Something we're not seeing."

"We are the connection Blake. Aunt Mary's house at Lepe. The same house that Dad grew up in and it was owned by his parents, our grandparents. We may have grown up in London but our roots are down in Hampshire."

Blake pondered that for a moment. Jenny had gone to Plymouth University with Jade Smith almost fifteen years ago. She knew Andrea Smith after regularly visiting Jade at her parents' home in Putney, south London. Andrea had been to university with Nicola Pew and Tiffany Mason and had often met up for drinks with Jenny in the bars around Kings Cross University over the years. Now that all three women were dead, Blake could understand his sister's fears but he needed her to reach out to Jade to find out if there was any further connections between the Smith family and whoever was in the unknown grave in East Boldre.

"Okay, I'll drop you off at your place, can you try and make contact with Jade and let me know what you can find out. I'll head back to Lepe tonight. If you still feel uneasy about being in London then come and stay with us for a while," Blake replied.

Jenny agreed and they drove back through the busy London streets towards her flat in Kensington before Blake returned to the south coast. A thousand questions flooded his mind as he drove down the rain-soaked M3 motorway towards Southampton but no obvious answers seemed to be coming through. He knew there had to be a connection with his previous assignment, he just needed to figure out how Andrea Smith fitted into all of it.

Blake arrived home just after 9pm. He let himself in the front door and saw a flickering of candlelight coming from the lounge. He slowly pushed open the door and saw Paula curled up on the sofa hugging a pillow and finishing the last mouthful of red wine from her glass. He sat down beside her and placed his hand over hers. She pulled it away.

"I'm sorry I've been preoccupied lately," Blake said as he moved closer to her.

He noticed her eyes, so often bright, were now red and glistened with unshed tears. She stared at the flickering flame of the candle barely acknowledging that he was there.

"Is Michael asleep?" he asked.

"He's at Dexter's for the night," Paula replied.

Blake moved to place his arms around her but she pulled away again.

"Don't."

He moved away reluctantly. "What's wrong?"

Paula didn't respond.

"Did Jenny upset you yesterday? Have I done something?"

She shook her head.

"I need to know what's wrong so I can try and make things right again."

Paula took a deep breath. "That's just it though isn't it?"

Blake looked at her.

"You always need to fix things Blake. Whatever happens you always need to fix it. Never fear, Blake Langford is here!"

"Is that a bad thing?"

"It is when the thing you're trying to fix is the one thing that can't be fixed."

Blake frowned. "You're talking in riddles Paula, what's happened? What have I done wrong?"

"Nothing. You've done nothing."

Blake waited.

"I never asked for this life. To always be looking over my shoulder in case some crazed criminal comes after me. To be the surrogate mother to my nephew. To be in my sister's shadow for the rest of my life."

"Rachael died and nobody could have seen that coming. Yes, I used to love your sister but that was nine years ago..."

"And yet you still slept with me!"

Blake was taken by surprise at her sudden outburst. "We were both in a situation where we needed somebody!"

"Is that how you justify it?"

"My father died that morning. I was up to my neck in aggravation at work. There was a suspicion that Rachael had been sneaking off with one of her college friends and I needed a release. I drank myself into stupidity to escape the reality of my world crashing down around me!"

"So I'm stupid now? Is that what you're saying? That I'm some kind of stupid mistake!"

Blake shook his head. "No, no, I'm not saying that at all."

"If you can sleep with me whilst being engaged to my sister, how can I trust you with anything now?"

"It takes two Paula."

She laughed in disbelief. "That's your excuse?"

"You had just been beaten up by Andrew Broughton and turned up at my flat and practically threw yourself at me. I'd just finished a bottle of Jack Daniels and could barely understand what was happening."

"So it's my fault now then?"

"No, I'll accept my part in it. Yes, we did sleep together. Yes, I willingly made love to you at a time when in the cold light of day we shouldn't have done it. No matter what you think, I cared for you then and I..."

Paula waited.

"And I love you now," he finally replied.

Paula moved towards him and they held each other close. "I'm sorry," she whispered.

"So am I."

"With so many things going on and raking up the past I just don't know what's going on anymore."

They broke the embrace. "There are a lot of things at play here that don't make any sense. But I promise, I will do whatever it takes to keep you and Michael safe," Blake said.

"I don't want to be, just safe, I want time with you. The three of us as a family. Burying so many people lately makes you realise that life isn't that long and you need to make the most of it."

"Andrew's death has hit you hard hasn't it?"

"Have you been talking to Jen?"

"No, but I know you and I know what it's like to lose someone you used to love."

Paula looked at him.

"Rachael will always be in my heart but my life, my future and my love is right here with you. Likewise, I know deep down that Andrew still has a place in your heart but I hope that we can both move on together and create a beautiful future together."

Paula hugged him again. "You're an asshole aren't ya," she laughed into his shirt.

"I'll take that as a complement shall I?" Blake smiled.

They blew out the candles and headed off to bed. Blake knew that he had a lot of things he needed to juggle at the moment but being there for his family was still important. He'd made many mistakes over the years, he just hoped that he had learnt from them and the consequences of his decisions in the future were less than what had gone before.

Chapter Six

Mr Smith

Saturday 21st August 1948

A tall middle-aged man wearing a brown suit, mustard yellow shirt, light brown tie and brown shoes stepped off of the train at Southampton Terminus Station just after 11am. He took a deep breath of fresh air, embracing his freedom, after being stuck in a sweaty crowded carriage for the past couple of hours before taking in his surroundings.

He recognised the road that led towards dock gate number three from a newspaper report he had read from earlier in the year when King George VI and Queen Elizabeth had visited to see Cunard's renowned Atlantic liner, Queen Elizabeth. It was a big event for the city which was still recovering from the after effects of the second world war.

The man carried his brown leather suitcase that had seen better days with a newspaper tucked under his arm. He wandered over towards the ticket office as his train left the station to continue its journey along the coast towards Bournemouth.

"Good morning, sir," the man in the ticket office beamed.

The man in the brown suit noticed a nameplate in front of the ticket office gentleman. It read "Kenneth Bates." "Good morning, could you kindly inform me when the next train to Lymington is scheduled to depart?" he asked.

"You've just missed the morning one. The next train is due at one o'clock," Kenneth replied.

The man in the brown suit let out a sigh. "Oh well, that will have to suffice. May I purchase a second-class one-way ticket for the one o'clock train to Lymington, please?"

Kenneth promptly stamped a ticket before exchanging it for several shillings. "Would you like to store your suitcase in the cloakroom until your train arrives, sir?"

"Yes, that would be greatly appreciated, thank you."

Kenneth picked up a sheet of paper and a pen. "May I take a name, please, sir?"

"Smith, Jack Smith," the man in the brown suit responded.

"Thank you, Mr. Smith," Kenneth smiled as he handed Jack his cloakroom receipt before placing his suitcase in the wooden storage rack behind him. "Enjoy your time in our city."

"I'm sure I will," Jack smiled before turning away from the ticket office.

He placed his newspaper on a wooden bench at the side of the waiting room before heading outside where he noticed two buses had stopped on the opposite side of the road. The midday heat was stifling so he crossed the road and headed towards the bus stop and the shade of some overhanging oak trees.

After the first bus had left, Jack noticed that the remaining bus was heading towards Lepe Beach. He pulled a crumpled piece of paper out of his pocket and read an address that had been scribbled down on it many years ago. He realised that the bus would bring him closer to where he wanted to be than the train would.

As the last passenger at the bus stop climbed aboard, Jack quickly moved to join them, cursing the fact that his luggage was still in the cloak room at the railway station. He would deal with that later. He exchanged a few coins for his bus ticket before moving towards the back of the bus where an open window generated a cool breeze as the bus travelled away from the city centre.

***

Southward Cottage overlooking Lepe Beach with the Isle Of Wight in the distance was the home of Mavis and Edward Langford.

Enjoying a rare day off from the police force, Edward Langford sat in a deck chair reading a newspaper whilst his children, John, Frederick and Mary played in the sand.

"Daddy, come play with us," Mary squealed excitedly.

"Come now, children. Your father's had a demanding few weeks. Let him have his rest," Mavis replied, offering Edward a glass of lemonade.

"Have you heard from Dana lately?" Edward asked.

"She's coming over with Edith soon. It's been a struggle for her since Gerald passed. I wish we could do more," Mavis sighed.

"All we can do is hope for Gerald's military pension to come through, or she'll have a tough time making ends meet."

"I couldn't bear to see her and her daughter without a home."

"We're not a charity, Mavis. Sadly, misfortunes befall good people. Besides, her father does quite well at the bridge club near Portsmouth. He's been swindling those navy cadets for years. I'm sure he's stashed away a tidy sum."

"You're all heart, Ed," Mavis quipped as she wandered back toward the house.

"Ow! Mary, don't flick sand into my eyes!" Frederick shouted.

"Ow! Don't kick me!" Mary responded.

Frederick pushed her out of the way.

"Mummy, Fred kicked me!" Mary cried out, scurrying towards Mavis.

"Frederick, brush yourself off. You know better than to bury yourself in the sand. Go find your brother," Mavis advised.

"He's off collecting shells for Edith," Frederick replied.

"Johnny has a soft spot for her," Mary teased.

"Even if he does, playing in the sand won't set the table for lunch. Frederick, find your brother and Mary, help set the table," Mavis instructed.

"Alright," they both sighed before heading off in opposite directions.

Further down the beach, John Langford gathered shells from amongst the rocks before following a stony path leading away from the shore and toward a small woodland at the top of the hill. At the summit, he spotted his friend Edith and her mother, Dana, engaged in conversation with a man wearing a brown suit and brown shoes. John didn't recognize the man, but it seemed like they were having a heated discussion. He concealed himself behind a tree until the voices quietened down. After a minute, John peeked out and saw the man handing an envelope filled with money to Dana before walking away.

John watched the man as he left before emerging from his hiding spot behind the tree.

"John! Delightful to see you!" Edith called out, rushing over to him. "What are you doing so far down the beach?"

John showed her the red bucket he was carrying. "I was collecting shells..."

Edith quickly sorted through them and selected an intriguingly shaped one. "Oh, I adore this one. Can I have it?"

"Of course," John beamed.

"Thank you, John. You're the best."

"Come along, you two, or we'll be late for Mrs. Langford's luncheon," Dana urged.

The two friends skipped along the beach, with Dana following a few steps behind. John stole a few glances back at Dana, pondering the man who had given her the money. Something didn't seem right, and his father's advice echoed in his mind, prompting him to question the situation if it seemed amiss.

"Who was that gent your Mum was talking to?" John asked.

"What gent?"

"I spied someone leaving your twosome as I arrived," John pushed.

"Oh, I don't know. Someone my Uncle Frank dispatched to aid us."

"I didn't know you had an Uncle Frank..." John began as a damp lump of sand smacked his face.

"Freddie!" Edith giggled, tossing sand back at him.

"Now, now, Edith. Don't get your dress mucked up with sand before luncheon. It'd be most disrespectful," Dana advised.

"What've you got here?" Frederick asked, tipping shells onto the sand after grabbing John's red bucket.

"Hey careful! They're fragile!" John protested.

"The only thing fragile here is you," Frederick retorted, kicking sand in John's face.

"Leave him be, he found this most amazing shell for me!" Edith replied.

John hurriedly placed the shells back into his bucket before rushing on ahead as they strolled back towards the Langford family home.

"Why are you so hard on him?" Edith asked Frederick as they arrived outside Southward cottage.

"He's too soft. If I don't toughen him up then the world will eat him alive."

"Ah, there you are Dana. We were wondering where you'd got to. Mavis has put on a delightful spread," Edward called out before leading them up the wooden steps to the picnic table on the lawn at the back of the cottage.

After lunch, the four children went to play in the sea whilst Edward reclaimed his deckchair and Mavis and Dana sat on a blanket that had been laid out on the sand. At that moment, Edward noticed a man in a brown suit staggering along the beach. He was coughing into a handkerchief and looked extremely hot. As he approached, Edward stood from his deckchair and walked over to him.

"Afternoon Sir, are you alright? You seem a little lost," Edward asked.

"I am rather, I was hoping to find somewhere to have a drink and some shade. It's so very hot today," the man replied, glancing towards Mavis and Dana.

Both women stared warily in his direction.

"Office wear isn't the best for the summer is it?" Edward chuckled. "The old cafe is a couple of miles the other way but Norman, poor old chap, hasn't opened since the war. Why don't you join us for a drink, Mister..."

"Williams, Vincent Williams," the man lied.

"Well Mr Williams, I'm sure my wife may be able to find a cold beer from indoors," Edward replied, placing his hand on the man's shoulder and leading him over to where they were all sitting.

After some awkward conversation, Mavis and Edward went back inside, leaving Dana and the man in the brown suit outside.

"What are you doing here Jack? I told you to leave. If they find out..." Dana began.

"They won't. I need to know that our son is safe. I haven't got long left. Where is he?" Jack asked.

"I told you, I gave him up for adoption at the hospital. I don't know who is looking after him now. The accusing eyes after Gerald's death would have been too much. Everyone would know that I had been unfaithful..."

"I need to see you later."

Dana sighed. "Meet me at Honeypot House, about two miles down the coast on Lepe Road. Now go, before they realise who you really are."

As Jack stood up to leave, Edward wandered back out of the house with a camera.

"My word, I haven't seen one of those cameras in years," Jack beamed as he examined Edward's camera.

"It belonged to my older brother, Robert. He gave it to me just before the war. I thought it would be nice to have a photo to remember this moment by."

"Oh, Mr Langford, I'm sure Mr Williams will want to be getting on his way," Dana tried.

"Nonsense, there's always time for a photograph," Jack replied.

"Come along children, time for a photograph," Mavis called out as the children came running over from where they were playing on the beach.

John looked at Jack suspiciously.

"Can I take the photo? I've got my own camera at home and I've taken some lovely photographs of the birds in the trees," Edith beamed.

"Okay, but please be careful Edith, it's an old and fragile camera," Edward replied, handing her the camera.

The children knelt down on the sand in front of Dana, Edward and Mavis ready for the photograph.

"Come on Mr Williams, join us," Edward called out.

"Oh, I wouldn't want to intrude," Jack replied sheepishly.

"Not at all; it'll be a reminder of the pleasant day we've all had."

Jack walked over and stood next to Dana as Edith took two photographs of them all together. As the day wore on, Dana excused herself and began walking back down the beach with Edith. Edward wandered back inside the house to listen to the radio in the lounge. The three children were building mountains with piles of stones that they had collected from further down the beach whilst Mavis began tidying up the glasses and cups from the picnic blanket.

"Alone at last," Jack whispered to her.

"You shouldn't be here Jack. Edward is no fool. If he ever found out who you really are, he'd kill you," Mavis replied.

"I had to see you one last time."

"It's over Jack. What we had, it's in the past. I'm married to Edward. We have a family and a home together. He's a good man and I'm not willing to give all of that up!"

"I'm not asking you to."

"Then why are you here pretending to be someone you're not?"

"I had to visit the doctor in London. It's not good news I'm afraid."

"What did they say?" Mavis asked.

"They think I have tuberculosis. There's no cure. I have to deal with fever, coughing and I don't have as much energy as I used to. Funny, after being sent home from battle, a damn virus takes me out."

"Why are you telling me all this?"

"You took good care of me when I came home. You helped me get my life back. Proved to me that I could still be a man..."

"Don't."

"Don't what?"

"I made a mistake. A stupid mistake. Now go."

"Or else what?"

Mavis glared at him. "If you break up my family, I'll kill you myself."

Jack raised his hands in mock surrender. "I guess I'll be on my way then."

Mavis watched him as he stood up from the picnic blanket and dusted the sand off of his clothes.

"Nice kids, shame about their mother. Good day Mrs Langford," Jack said before walking away.

Mavis watched him as he staggered down the beach and away into the distance.

"Where did Mr Williams go?" John asked as he rushed over towards his mother.

"He had an urgent appointment," Mavis replied before turning her attention back to the picnic blanket. "Come John, help me clear the cups and plates back to the kitchen, there's a good lad."

"I don't think Mr Williams is a nice man," John commented as he helped his mother carry the picnic items back towards the cottage.

"What makes you think that?"

"I saw him arguing with Mrs Wise earlier today."

"Were you eavesdropping when you shouldn't have been Jonathon?"

"I wasn't dropping any eaves Mum, honest. I was collecting my shells and I heard loud voices and saw it was Mr Williams and Mrs Wise."

"Did you hear what they were saying?"

John shook his head. "He did seem to be angry with her about something though."

Mavis pondered that for a moment. "Let's keep this between ourselves okay? Nobody else needs to know. All right?"

"What about father?"

"Especially not your father. He's got enough to worry about. Tomorrow morning, we will go to Mrs Wise and ask her if everything is okay. Until then, we say nothing more. Am I understood?"

John nodded before following his mother into the kitchen with the plates and cups. His curiosity was still beginning to think up possibilities about the mysterious Mr Williams. Did his mother know something about the man and Mrs Wise that she didn't want him to know about? Whatever it was, he was sure that Edith would have the answer. He just needed to work up the courage to ask her.

Chapter Seven

Uncovering Secrets

Sunday 2nd November 2008

Blake woke up early from a restless sleep and wandered into the study at his beachside house in Lepe. A grey metal box was on his desk. He scrolled the combination lock before opening it. He had spent the previous evening attempting to map out his own family tree to try and figure out some of the answers to the questions the photo of the mysterious man at the beach had created.

As he flicked through some old photos, he found a photo of his mother, Emily, when she was a teenager alongside her mother Dana and her younger brother Jim. There was another man in the photo that was standing behind Emily that Blake seemed to recognise. Blake pulled out the 1948 photo that he had found in Emily's safe deposit box and laid it alongside this new photo that he had found. He studied the faces of the man behind Emily and the mystery man from 1948. There was definitely more than a family resemblance between the two men. Were they father and son? And if so, what connection did they have with Blake's mother's side of the family?

Blake rubbed his hands over his face in frustration. It seemed like the more he looked at the old photographs, the more confusing everything became. He opened his laptop and began looking at the records for deaths in Hampshire from 1984. He scrolled through pages of names until he found what he was looking for.

DANA SYLVIA HANDANOWICZ
DIED 17TH APRIL 1984
AGED 69 YEARS
LOVING WIFE OF WILLIAM DAVID HANDANOWICZ
MOTHER OF EMILY MAY, JAMES HAROLD, EDITH
WINIFRED AND EVELYN JOAN.

BURIAL SITE: RECORD INCOMPLETE

Blake read the obituary before beginning a search on the Special Branch database but there was no record of an Evelyn Joan Handanowicz. He knew his grandmother was married before she met his grandfather William Handanowicz. Her previous husband was Gerald Arthur Wise who had died during the second world war. He found his record and also the record of Edith Winifred Wise. He remembered his mother talking of her older sister Edith who had died of pneumonia when she was only sixteen in 1956 but she had never mentioned anyone called Evelyn.

Blake tried searching for Evelyn Joan Wise and still found no matching records. He racked his brains trying to remember his grandmother's maiden name but it just wouldn't come to him. He searched for his grandfather's death record from 1987 in the hope that he would find Evelyn Joan's name there too but as he read his grandfather's obituary, nothing became any clearer.

WILLIAM DAVID HANDANOWICZ
DIED 22ND DECEMBER 1987
AGED 75 YEARS
LOVING HUSBAND OF DANA SYLVIA HANDANOWICZ
FATHER OF EMILY MAY AND JAMES HAROLD.
BURIAL SITE: CREMATION AT SOUTHAMPTON CREMATORIUM

"What are you looking at?" Michael asked as he wandered into the study.

Blake turned around as his son approached him. "Hey, I thought you were still asleep."

"No, I had a nightmare."

"Oh, what was it about?"

"I dreamed that I woke up and you and Aunt Paula were gone."

"Is that why you didn't want to stay at Dexter's all night?"

"I'm sorry, I didn't mean to call you out late."

"It's okay, I hadn't been home long anyway."

Michael looked at him disbelievingly.

"We're not going anywhere, Michael. We're a team, remember, and we always will be," Blake smiled.

"Don't make promises you can't keep."

"What makes you think that I won't keep them?"

"Mum always promised that she'd never leave."

Blake felt a pang in his chest. His failure to save Rachael after a previous Special Branch case in Miami went wrong still haunted him to this day. "Your mum didn't choose to leave you. I'm sure if there was anything that could have prevented what happened, she would've taken that chance."

"I guess."

"I'm not going anywhere and neither is Paula."

"Then why are you looking for dead people?"

Blake closed his laptop before turning back to him. "It's just something I'm working on for my job. It's nothing to worry about. No one is going to die."

"But Nan did."

Blake bit down on his bottom lip. "I know but your Nan was very ill and unfortunately, when people get old, they will eventually die. She's not in any pain anymore."

"Is that why you're trying to figure out her life story now that she's gone? Why couldn't you ask her about it when she was here?"

Blake thought back to his argument with Paula last night. "Sometimes, we get so caught up in doing our own things everyday, we forget to listen or be curious about our family and friends until..."

"Until it's too late."

"Yeah," Blake sighed.

Michael looked over at the photos that Blake had laid out on the desk. "Is that Nan?"

"Yeah, they were taken a long time ago."

"And is that Uncle Vic?" Michael asked, pointing to the man standing behind Emily in the photo.

Blake looked at Michael. "Do you know this man?"

"Kinda."

"Michael, if you know who he is, it's really important that you tell me. Did Nan go to visit him with you?"

"Only once."

"When?"

"Just after Mum's funeral. You and Aunt Paula were speaking to people who had come along and Nan said that she would bring me back here with Aunt Jenny."

"So Jenny knows who he is too?"

"No, Aunt Jenny drove on ahead and we visited some kind of place for old people, Priestfields, I think it was called. Anyway, we saw an old man with a walking stick and Nan gave him a brown envelope."

"And then what happened?"

"They spoke for a few minutes and then we walked back down the road for a while until one of the men in the big black cars saw us and gave us a lift back here. He gave me some buttercrunch too. They were the best buttercrunch I've ever had since we came to the UK."

"Buttercrunch?" Blake asked.

"Tofu or whatever you call it here. Sticky sweets or candy."

"Toffees."

"Yeah, I think that's what Nan called them."

"Are you sure that guy is the same guy you and Nan went to see at Priestfields?"

Michael looked at the photo again. "Kinda sure, he's a lot older now but he had that mark on his cheek and wore those thick glasses. Nan said his name was Uncle Vic. Does that mean he was Nan's brother?"

Blake pondered that for a moment. "No, your nan only had one brother. His name's Uncle Jim and he lives in Greece."

"If he's her brother, why didn't he come here for Nan's funeral?"

"Michael?" Paula called out. "Is everything okay?"

"Yeah, Dad was just explaining that Nan had a brother and I wondered why I haven't met him yet?"

"Sometimes when people live far away, they can't always get to places that they want to be. Come on, shall we get some breakfast? How about I make us some eggs and toast."

"Only if I can break the shells!" Michael replied as he headed towards the kitchen.

"Deal," Paula smiled as he ran past her. She looked over at Blake who mouthed "thank you" to her. She smiled before following Michael into the kitchen.

Blake's phone cut into his thoughts as a message from his colleague, Alison Pearce, lit up the screen. Two hours later, he parked his silver Ford Mondeo outside East Boldre Cemetery in The New Forest. He stepped out of his car and walked over towards the cemetery gates.

"We seem to be making a habit of meeting in these places," Alison said as she approached him.

"What do we have?" Blake asked as he walked alongside her towards the grave.

"They removed Andrea Smith's body from the grave but the local police are still trying to negotiate with the undertakers regarding the paperwork for the plot."

As they arrived at the graveside, Samir Khalifa was talking to one of the forensics team. He wandered over towards them. "Forensics say she was alive when she was buried and suspect that she died of suffocation when she was covered over with the dirt," Samir explained.

"Drugged?" Blake asked.

"They're still running tests but I'm guessing so. Nobody would willingly let someone bury them alive," Samir concluded.

"What's the deal with the undertaker?"

"Crowther and Jones, apparently, even though the grave has been unmarked, there is a paperwork trail to a family in London. Until they have written consent from that family, they refuse to allow the coffin below where Andrea was buried to be exhumed," Alison explained.

"How long has the body been down there?"

"Twenty-six years," Samir replied.

"For God's sake, the coffin and body would've disintegrated by now. All that's gonna be left is the skeleton, surely," Blake snapped.

"Do you wanna tell them that?" Alison asked. "Whoever is down there is obviously someone's relative. You wouldn't want a member of your family dug up just to complete some paperwork would you?"

Blake ran his fingers through his hair. "I guess you're right. Samir, can you tag along with the investigating officer and let us know what forensics finds out."

Samir nodded and wandered over towards the police officers on the opposite side of the cemetery.

"What are you thinking?" Alison asked.

"We need to fill in the gaps of what Andrea Smith has been up to since we left her in France with Graham Evans," Blake replied as he began heading back towards his car with Alison close behind him.

"The local police have tried to contact her parents already but haven't been able to track down either of them. We'll just be doubling up on their investigation."

Blake thought about that for a moment. He knew Andrea had an older sister called Jade but he wanted to see how much information Jenny could get out of her first. "What about the man with the dog?"

Alison pulled a notepad out of her pocket. "George Harding, retired, lives in Priestfields near Blackfield. He gave the police a statement when he found the hand and after the paramedics checked him over, he went home."

"Then, Priestfields seems like a good place to start. Let's go," Blake replied.

He had driven past Priestfields Assisted Living complex many times and after his conversation with his son, Michael, earlier, it seemed like an ideal time to visit the complex.

***

Jenny Langford walked through Tottenham Court Road Underground Station in London before heading out onto Oxford Street. After a few minutes, she found a cafe called Chequered Flag next door to a huge department store. It had a Formula 1 racing theme throughout with signed photos of racing drivers from over the years alongside metal models shaped like various racing circuits from all over the world. At the corner table at the back of the cafe sat a woman dressed in black with auburn her hair tied back in a large black hair grip. Jenny wandered over towards her before taking a seat on the opposite side of her table.

"I wondered when you'd come out of the woodwork," she said as Jenny sat down.

"I'm sorry Jade, I meant to keep in touch but I..."

"Was too busy leading my sister into trouble."

"It wasn't like that. She knew who she was dealing with in those student bars."

"It doesn't matter now anyway, does it? It's over."

"I'm sorry."

"For what?" Jade asked.

Before Jenny could answer, a waitress approached them. They both ordered latte's and Jade ordered a slice of carrot cake.

"You know, Andrea was always playing with fire," Jade continued. "But somehow, your family, my family, we always seemed to cross swords."

"I don't want to fight."

"Neither do I, yet here we are. Two old friends sharing a coffee and catching up on old times when the people we love are missing or barely cold in the grave."

"I realise this must be hard for you but we need to try and understand what's been happening over the past couple of years if we are going to have any chance of figuring out what happened to Andrea."

"You still don't know, do you?" Jade asked.

"Know what?"

"Your mother's will. Do you know what's inside it?"

Jenny wasn't sure how much Jade knew so decided to play it safe. "She wrote the same will that my father had. Everything goes to the surviving spouse and when they are both gone, it gets split equally between Blake, Steven and myself."

"That's what you were led to believe."

"What do you mean?"

"Did your Mum ever mention Uncle Vic?"

Jenny shook her head.

"Victor Gerald Wise is your Mum's older half brother. Your grandmother had him in 1940 but he was sent away for adoption when the bombing started in London."

"No way, Grandma Dana only had Edith before she met Grandad William, then they had Mum and Uncle Jim. Edith was only sixteen when she died. The dates don't add up."

"Edith died just before her seventeenth birthday. Victor was only a year younger than her but he was practically orphaned by the war. His father was killed and his mother abandoned him."

"How do you know all of this?"

"Because Victor Wise is my grandad."

Jenny gasped. "Wait, are you telling me that we are related?"

Jade nodded.

"You wait over twenty years to spring that one on me! Why didn't you tell me before?"

"I only found out about it myself a few years ago."

"How many is a few?"

"Your Mum, Emily, had been exchanging letters with my grandad, Victor Wise, for a few years. After your father died, she finally decided to meet with him. She told him that she lost touch with her younger brother James and her twin sister, Evelyn, after they disappeared years ago and that he was the only relative she had left from her generation."

Jenny sipped her latte as she processed what Jade was telling her. Her mother rarely spoke of her siblings and whenever they came up in conversation, the subject was quickly dismissed. "I can't believe she never told us about him."

"It was a different time back then. Being a widow with two children in tow tended to leave women in a desperate situation. It was very much a man's world. There was no childcare and she couldn't work to make ends meet either."

"But she kept Edith?"

"Yeah, that's one thing that Grandad couldn't understand. Why not give them both up if she couldn't look after them?"

"Then after the war, Grandma met Grandad, Will, and they married. Mum came along..."

"Four months later," Jade added.

"Yeah. So her and grandad must have conceived Mum and Evelyn before they were married. Given the time, there must have been a rushed wedding to cover up any scandal."

"Except William Handanowicz was only discharged from the military three months prior to their marriage. I checked the records."

"So unless Mum and Evelyn were born very premature, which probably meant that it was highly unlikely that they would have survived, especially being twins back then..."

"There's a chance that William Handanowicz was not your biological grandad."

Jenny ran her fingers through her hair trying to piece everything together. "So, let me get this right, Grandma Dana had Edith and Victor before the war. Victor is given up for adoption, Edith dies in 1956. After the war she had Evelyn, my aunt, Emily, my mother, and James, my uncle who is now living somewhere in Greece. Why would she put herself into a situation with four children around the war and where is Evelyn now that all of this has blown up?"

"Nobody knows. Not meaning to state the obvious here but the rhythm method is no longer a recommended contraception for a reason. It was never a topic of conversation but do you honestly believe all of the women remained faithful whilst their men were out risking their lives for King and country?"

"I guess not," Jenny replied. She had heard snippets from her parents about someone called Evelyn but had never known the full story. "Why would they break up the family like that? Surely there must have been a way to sort their differences out!"

"This was just after the second world war. Every family was struggling on rations and a huge depression so money was tight. Quite often, families had to make a choice. Whatever the differences they had, for some reason, it's taken your mother's death to bring it all out into the open again."

Jenny paused for a moment. "So, Victor Wise is your grandad on who's side?"

"My mother's side. Both of my parents died in a motorbike accident three years ago. I never really understood the family history until we began sorting through all of their things."

"And what did you find?"

"A whole lot of nothing. My grandfather never contacted us after mum died so it was just Andrea and me against the world."

"So what did you do next?"

"What do you mean?"

"I haven't seen you for a few years, do you have a family, boyfriend?"

"Oh, no, nothing like that. I work as an accountant for one of the large firms in the city. Tell me, if Andrea hadn't gone missing, would you have contacted me?"

Jenny suddenly realised that Jade had no idea of what had happened to her sister. "I'm sorry, I've been battling with a few mental health problems recently which has led me to lose contact with a lot of people I care about. Tell me, when did you last speak to Andrea?"

"Around a month ago. She was staying somewhere in France until the heat died down in London. She got kicked out of that student house she was renting with those other two students so some guy offered her a place to stay. I didn't ask what kind of arrangement they had but knowing her..."

Jenny nodded. "Jade, I need you to come with me."

"Why? Where to?"

"Have the police contacted you?"

"No, why?"

Jenny took a deep breath. "There's a chance that your sister is dead."

A smirk of disbelief appeared on Jade's face. "No, no, you're wrong."

"Andrea became involved in a Special Branch operation and was killed by someone connected to Tom Gibson."

A look of realisation crossed Jade's face for a moment. "You're lying. Tom would never touch her. How the hell..."

"How do you know what he would do?"

"I've met him before, he couldn't possibly..."

"Jade, listen to me, Tom is tying up loose ends. Andrea's housemates Tiffany Mason and Nicola Pew are both dead. Now Andrea has disappeared, it's only a matter of time before he comes after us. I need you to come with me to see my brother."

"No."

"Jade, please, your life is in danger if they think you're involved."

"I'm only involved because you've dragged me into something..."

"He's got his claws into you hasn't he? I can see it in your eyes. He's got you running scared."

"Jen, you have no idea what you're getting yourself involved in. Our family history is going to blow up in a big way..."

"Our family history? What are you talking about?"

"Your Mum's will has opened up a can of worms and now none of us are safe!"

"What are you scared of Jade?"

She bowed her head.

"Blake can protect you."

"How?"

"I used to be you. I loved Tom Gibson with all my heart. My love for him blinded me to what was really going on and without Blake's help, I'd be behind bars if not dead by now."

"It's not like that, it's complicated."

"Then uncomplicate it for me. What hold does Tom Gibson have over you?"

Jade stood up from the table. "You're playing a dangerous game Jen. My advice, tidy up your mother's affairs and get the hell out of London."

"And if I don't?" Jenny replied, standing up to face her.

"This thing goes way deeper than you could ever understand. Leave London or you won't live to see the consequences," Jade replied before walking out of the cafe.

Jenny sat back down once again feeling her whole body shaking. She took a few deep breaths to calm the adrenaline that was running through her. She left some cash on the table before heading back outside and following the path towards the tube station.

She knew that she needed to find out exactly what was in her mother's will. The solicitor had been extremely vague when her and Blake had attended the reading. All of the information and this HM25 clause seemed to revolve around some unknown family history that she was struggling to piece together. And where did Evelyn and Jim Handanowicz fit into all of this? She took the train to South Kensington before making her way towards the remains of 124 Alfredson Road, her family home where she hoped that she could find something to help answer the million questions that were clouding her mind.

Chapter Eight

Edward's Discovery

Sunday 22nd August 1948

A loud knocking at the front door woke Edward Langford from a restless sleep. He fumbled for a match and relit a candle that he had placed on the chest of drawers at the side of his bed before going to sleep last night. The knocking became more insistent as he wandered down the stairs.

"All right, all right, I'm coming!" he called out as he unlocked the door.

As he opened the door, he saw his Sergeant, Peter Hastings waiting on his doorstep illuminated by the headlights of a police patrol car on the driveway.

"Sorry to disturb you, Sir, but Honeypot House on Lepe Road went up in flames during the night. It seems like a deliberate act," Peter explained.

Edward gasped, knowing Dana Wise and her daughter, Edith, lived there. "Any survivors?" he asked.

"None Sir. The fire department has only just got it under control."

"What's wrong?" Mavis asked as she began to walk down the stairs towards them.

"Nothing, I just, er, I need to assist Hastings with a case. I'll just get dressed and gather my things," Edward replied as he closed the door on Peter. "Go back to bed, the children will be up soon."

Mavis nodded before returning upstairs. Edward quickly changed into a white shirt, black trousers and black shoes before sliding a black suit jacket around his shoulders. He collected his keys and wallet from the fireplace before joining Peter Hastings outside. As Hastings drove down the Lepe Road and the smouldering remains of Honeypot House came into view, Edward had a feeling of dread come over him. He stepped out of the car and approached the house.

"Good morning Sir," Officer George Wells greeted as Hastings and Langford approached. "Looks deliberate. We have found an oil can and remnants of cloths or blankets near to the front door."

"Any survivors or witnesses?" Edward asked.

"No Sir, in the middle of the night down here, hardly anyone ventures out in the darkness."

"Whoever set the fire must have gained access to the house or at least had some help to feed the rags through the front door," Peter Hastings reasoned.

"We thought it might have been that Sir but there's no sign of a letterbox in the front door," Officer Wells replied.

"So, whoever started the fire must have been inside the house."

"It would appear so, Sir."

Edward looked over towards the fence at the front of the property and saw a metal post box on top of a wooden stick. He walked over to it and opened the flap at the front. Five letters had been placed inside by the postman from a few days ago. As he looked at the first four letters, they all had FINAL DEMAND written on the front of the envelopes but the fifth letter was a handwritten envelope. On the back was a return address for the C.A.S. in London.

"Have you found something Sir?" Hastings asked.

"Possibly. Do you know anything about C.A.S. in London W1?" Edward asked.

"It's the Children's Adoption Service, for war orphans. Why? Who lived here?" Peter inquired.

"Dana Wise and her daughter Edith. How long does it take for a child to be adopted if the mother can't pay her way?"

"It depends. It could be a few days to a few weeks, Sir."

Edward opened the adoption letter, revealing Dana's intent to give up her eight year old son.

"Was she giving up her daughter for adoption?" Hastings asked.

"No, her son," Edward replied.

"I didn't know that she had a son."

"Neither did I. It looks like he has been at the adoption agency since birth and this was a letter confirming that she still wanted this arrangement. We need to find Dana and Edith Wise. When did the fire start?"

"It was called in at around two in the morning," Officer Wells responded.

Edward looked at his watch. It was ten minutes past five and the sun was beginning to rise in the distance as he looked up at the surrounding trees of The New Forest. "They've had at least a three hour headstart but they couldn't have gone far."

***

As the day wore on, the search teams found no sign of Edith or Dana Wise in the surrounding areas. Edward Langford and Peter Hastings returned to the Police Station to file their reports alongside the police officers that had been involved in the search and at Honeypot House.

"Did you find out anything from those letters?" Peter Hastings asked.

"Only that Dana Wise was six months behind on paying her gas and electricity and they were about to cut her off. It's this adoption letter that puzzles me though," Edward replied.

"How so? A lot of single mothers unfortunately have had to put their children into the hands of the adoption services. They would rather let them go than give them a life where they could end up on the streets."

"Her husband, Gerald Wise was one of the first to get drafted and was killed in the war. Dana Wise gave birth to her daughter Edith in 1939. This new child that has been discussed in this letter is only eight years old."

"So she got pregnant whilst her old man was away fighting," Hastings surmised.

"He was already dead. She was working as a military nurse looking after the war wounded."

"It was a tough time for us all, Sir. Most of the men I know sowed a few seeds over the years..."

"I saw Dana Wise with her daughter Edith only yesterday afternoon. She was a good friend of my wife, Mavis, but as far as I am aware, nobody knew about her son. If the adoption was done recently, where has the boy been in the meantime? It doesn't make sense. They joined us for luncheon along with a mysterious well dressed man who was strolling along the beach. Had a bit of a cough and was very sweaty. Not really dressed for the occasion," Edward explained.

At that moment, there was a knock on Edward Langford's office door.

"Come!" he ordered.

Officer George Wells entered the office. "Sorry to interrupt Sir, we may have had a breakthrough with the Honeypot House fire. A gent dressed in a brown suit has been found leant against ol' Norman's beachside cafe."

"Vincent Williams?" Edward asked.

"Do you know him, Sir?"

"Sort of, he stopped by my home yesterday afternoon."

"Well, we might need you to formally identify him Sir as nobody else seems to have the slightest idea who he is."

"What do you mean?"

"He's dead. No identification on him. No wallet. All he had on him was a train ticket for yesterday afternoon, a bus ticket, a comb, a packet of cigarettes and some matches."

Edward pondered Officer Wells' reply for a moment. The bus ticket he could understand but why would he need a train ticket for yesterday afternoon when he was at the beach? "What connection does he have with the Honeypot House fire?" Edward finally asked.

"Harry Partridge, the vicar, apparently saw the man walking nearby the house yesterday evening. Could be nothing but it's quite a trek from Honeypot House to Norman's cafe in the dark if you don't know the area too well."

"Thank you officer," Edward replied, dismissing Officer Wells before standing up and retrieving his suit jacket from the coat stand. "Come along Hastings, we need to go back to the beach."

***

Two police officers were standing guard at opposite ends of the stretch of Calshot Beach near to the building that previously belonged to Norman's Cafe. Edward Langford and Peter Hastings arrived in their car and wandered over towards where the body was laying on the beach.

"What the devil is going on here?" a man's voice called out.

Edward turned around and noticed Norman Whitehouse, the owner of the cafe, was fast approaching them. The police officer attempted to block his way.

"It's okay Jones, let him through," Edward advised as he approached the back of the cafe.

"Good God!" Norman gasped as he saw the man's body leant against the wall.

"Were you here last night Norman?" Edward asked.

"Of course not, the place hasn't reopened since the war. Don't you realise the rent they want to charge me now! Three times what I used to pay and the council won't listen to reason."

"Then why are you here now?"

"One of the villagers said that the police were interested in the place so I thought I'd come down and see what all the fuss was about."

"I see. Do you recognise this gent?" Edward asked.

Norman shook his head. "Never seen him before. Can't be local."

"No, he wasn't dressed for the beach and seemed a little out of place in the countryside."

"Probably worked in the city and took the bus out here for some sea air. You know what those city folk are like."

"Indeed. Do you still have the key to the cafe?"

"Am I under suspicion?"

"Of what?"

"I've got a dead body on my cafe doorstep."

"Should you be under suspicion?"

"No, of course not."

"Then answer the question, do you still have the keys or not?"

"Yes but it's due to be taken over by someone else in a few days so I shouldn't use them."

"Open the door," Edward replied.

"What? Why?"

"Norman, I'm investigating a possible murder here and I don't have time to ask the same question twice. Can you please unlock the door and let us inside your cafe?"

Norman nodded reluctantly before approaching the door and unlocking it. As he opened the door, it was obvious that somebody had been sleeping inside the cafe. Three blankets and pillows made from straw were laid out on the floor with empty tin cans left on the tables.

"I didn't know, I swear..." Norman pleaded as Edward and Peter entered.

"When did you last visit the cafe Mr Whitehouse?" Peter asked.

"About three weeks ago. I received a letter from the landowner telling me that I had to remove all of my things from here by next week or they would be thrown out by the new owners. Surely, you can't think the dead gent has anything to do with that?"

"I'm not ruling anything out," Edward replied.

At that moment, a knock on the door interrupted them.

"Excuse me Sir, forensics have finished and they're ready to move the body," Officer Jones explained.

Edward nodded. "What have they found so far?"

Officer Jones handed over an unused train ticket from Southampton to Lymington dated August 21st 1948, a receipt for the cloak room at Southampton Railway Station, a packet of chewing gum, a packet of cigarettes with matches and a bus ticket from Southampton to Lepe also dated August 21st 1948. Edward opened the packet of cigarettes and found a note folded around three of the cigarettes inside the packet. He unrolled the note and it had one word written on it;

FERTIG

Edward handed the note to Peter before studying the cigarettes closer.

"Any idea what fertig means?" Peter asked.

"It's a German word meaning finished or the end of something. I'm more interested in this though. Who would hide Lucky Strike cigarettes inside an Old Gold packet?" Edward asked.

"A lot of people tend to buy cheaper cigarettes and hide them inside the packet of a more expensive brand to make them look wealthier than they are," Norman explained. "It used to happen all the time."

"Except this time, we have expensive cigarettes inside a cheaper packaging," Peter replied.

"Maybe he was confused," Norman suggested.

"Everything seems peculiar with this gentleman," Officer Jones replied.

"How so?" Edward asked.

"It seems like he was almost trying to hide his wealth. All of his clothes have had the tags removed. He seemed to be a strong, well built man but besides the yellow cigarette stains, he had no calluses on his hands so he wasn't a manual worker. Missing sixteen teeth and it seems he drank some alcohol before he died. When they get him to the hospital, they should be able to tell us more."

"Other than the vicar who I will pay a visit to, do we have any witnesses who saw him on the beach late last night or early this morning?" Edward asked.

"Nobody has come forward yet Sir but we are asking all of the locals for their whereabouts in the past twenty-four hours," Officer Jones confirmed as they watched the man in the brown suit's body being loaded into the ambulance.

"Well, keep me informed. In the meantime, Hastings and I need to visit the church," Edward replied as he headed back towards his car.

As he arrived at his car, he turned back towards the group. "Oh, one more thing, Norman. Clean this place up and keep the door securely locked. You never know who is lurking around here."

As they watched Edward Langford and Peter Hastings drive away, Officer Jones noticed a black car approaching. As he walked over to stop them from parking on the verge, he recognised Officer Wells in the driving seat with a young man sitting beside him.

"Officer Wells, Detective Langford and Sergeant Hastings have just left," Officer Jones said as they stepped out of their car.

"That's okay, Charlie, I heard there were some squatters in the cafe and have come to investigate," Officer Wells replied.

"But Detective Langford..."

"Will continue the investigation so when the body has been loaded into the ambulance, you can stand your men down."

Officer Jones nodded before moving away. Officer Wells' passenger stepped out of the car and they both wandered over towards the cafe. Norman stepped outside and noticed them approaching before swiftly turning back inside again. Officer Wells and his passenger followed Norman back into the cafe and closed the door behind them. A few minutes later, Officer Wells left the cafe alone, closing the door behind him and led the rest of the officers away from the crime scene.

Chapter Nine

A Message From The Grave
Sunday 2nd November 2008

Blake Langford parked his car outside the Priestfields Assisted Living Complex.

"So this is the halfway house," Alison said as they stepped out of the car.

"What do you mean?"

"Halfway between independent and dead. You know, you grow up as a teenager and think you know everything then suddenly the world kicks you in the ass before everything goes in reverse. You lose your freedom and independence and then eventually you're back in nappies again before you return to dust."

Blake laughed. "What's made you so cynical?"

"Life, I guess."

"Well, I suppose you could put it that way. At least with living here they still have some degree of freedom left before they get put into a nursing home."

"It's hard to imagine us in a place like this in thirty years' time."

"Speak for yourself, I wanna slide into my grave on the back of a motorbike shouting "What A Ride!"" Blake laughed.

"Seriously though, we seem to be dealing with a lot of deaths lately. Sometimes I wonder if it's all worth it?"

"It's the job and unfortunately, it can get a bit morbid at times."

"I didn't sign up for exhuming bodies from graveyards and having arms sticking out of graves. I prefer to live with the living and when I'm dead, I wanna stay with the dead."

"At least you can't say we don't have variety in our day, come on," Blake replied before stepping out of the car and wandering over towards the entrance with Alison following close behind.

He pressed the intercom button on a metal plate that displayed the numbers zero to nine. After a few seconds, a crackly voice answered.

"I'm here to see Mr George Harding," Blake said.

"Who?"

"George Harding."

"Then you need to call his room number."

"Look, I work for Special Branch, London, we have a few questions for Mr Harding."

At that moment, Blake noticed a man wearing white jeans, a white shirt and a straw hat approaching the glass entrance door. He pressed a green button on a display panel on the inside before opening the door.

"Do you have any ID?" he asked.

Blake showed him his ID.

"And hers?"

Alison sighed before pulling her ID out of her jeans pocket.

The man studied it for a moment before handing it back to her. "You look different."

"So did you six years ago," Alison quipped.

"Can we see Mr Harding now?" Blake sighed.

"Yes, yes, come in. You can't be too careful these days. Can I get you both to sign into the visitors book and then I'll take you up to him."

Blake and Alison both signed their names into the visitors book before following the man in white upstairs. After negotiating a maze of corridors, they eventually arrived at room thirty-three. They could hear the sound of horse racing commentary coming from inside. The man in white gently knocked on the door and waited. They heard someone shouting amongst the ferocious horse racing commentary as the race reached its conclusion, but nobody came towards the door. The man in white knocked again. Still no response. Blake moved forward and knocked loudly on the door.

"You can't hit these doors that hard, they break very easily," the man in white protested.

At that moment, they heard a latch being unlocked before the door opened and a grey haired man dressed in a white vest and beige trousers was standing there.

"No need to break the door down Ernie, I heard ya the first time!" George Harding said as he looked at Blake and Alison. "Who are these two?"

"Mr Harding, I'm Blake Langford and this is my colleague Alison Pearce, we need to ask you a few questions," Blake replied.

"Well you'd better hurry up, I've got thirty quid on the next race at Newbury," George replied as he turned and headed back inside his apartment.

Alison and Blake followed him in.

"If you need anything..." Ernie began.

"We won't," Blake replied before closing the door on him.

"Where's your dog Mr Harding?" Alison asked as she sat down on the armchair next to his sofa which had a half eaten packet of cheese and onion crisps and two empty cans of coke strewn across.

"Spike's downstairs with Maud. Her and Vic get a bit lonely so I let them look after him when I watch the racing. Made two hundred already today. If this one comes in I'll have enough for that new halogen heater I've been wanting to buy for a good while."

"Mr Harding, when you made your rather gruesome discovery, what were you doing in East Boldre cemetery late at night especially on Halloween?"

"I went to tend my late wife's grave and took Spike for a walk and lost track of time. The bloody mutt ran off and when I found him, he'd discovered the hand sticking outta the grave."

"And what did you do when you saw it?"

"I thought it was some kids playing silly buggers so I went over and grabbed hold of it."

"You grabbed hold of the hand?" Alison asked.

"Yeah, I thought some silly sods had left it there as some kind of sick joke."

"And what happened when you discovered it was real?"

"I put Spike back on the lead and we walked back down the road to the old phone box on the corner and called the police," George replied.

"You don't have a mobile phone?" Alison asked.

"Oh, that bloody thing," George replied, pointing to an old mobile phone on the coffee table. "It keeps bloody losing signal and turning itself off. Even when you try and text someone, it changes the word you type and you have to do it again and again until it gets it right. Tried to tell someone about the duck I saw at the pond the other day and almost got myself into all kinds of trouble. Modern technology is bloody crap these days."

"Did you notice anyone else around whilst you were waiting for the police?" Blake asked.

"No, I told the police officer all of this. Why are you rehashing it all again?"

"Did you tell them that you touched the hand?" Blake pushed.

George paused for a minute. "Come to think of it, no. No, I didn't. Oh Christ, they're gonna think I bloody killed her ain't they!"

"Not if you explain what happened," Alison tried to calm him down.

"It felt warm," George sighed as he leant back on the sofa.

"Warm?" Blake asked. "On Friday night it was raining and cold. Are you saying that she might have still been alive when you grabbed her hand?"

George began to shake and he brought his hands up to his mouth. "Oh my God, I killed her. I killed the poor girl."

"No, you didn't. The people who buried her there killed her," Alison replied. "You found her and with your help, we're going to make sure that whoever did this to her will go to jail for a long time."

At that moment, someone knocked at the front door. Blake wandered over and opened it.

"Oh, you're not George," an elderly man with white hair and a goatee said as a cocker spaniel bounded inside.

"No, you must be Vic," Blake replied.

"Yes, how did..."

"George told us all about you. May I ask you a few questions?" Blake asked.

Vic looked closely at Blake before answering. "Are you the police?"

"Kind of. I wanted to ask you about what happened to George on Friday night and also about Emily Langford."

Vic glared at him. "What about Emily? She has nothing to do with this!"

Blake closed the door behind him leaving Alison and George inside the apartment. Vic's eyes widened as Blake reached inside his jacket pocket.

"What are you doing?" Vic asked nervously.

"You met my son, Michael Langford, a few months ago," Blake replied as he showed Vic the photograph from Emily's safety deposit box. "I'd like to know who this man in the photo is."

A realisation crossed Victor's face. "Blake Langford?"

Blake nodded.

"Not here, come with me," Vic replied as he led Blake down the corridor and down a flight of stairs before stopping at room twenty-one.

Vic fumbled with the key before finally managing to open the door and leading them inside. Blake closed the door behind them as Vic stood in his kitchen. Blake noticed that the apartment was surprisingly spotless and the smell of disinfectant and bleach hung in the air.

"Expecting someone?" Blake inquired.

"I always thought that death would bring a familiar face back into my life. I just didn't think it would be my nephew's," Vic replied.

"I only have one uncle and he lives in Greece."

"Your grandmother had five children Blake. Edith, myself, Evelyn, Emily and James. One with Gerald Wise, one with William Handanowicz and three with Jack Smith. Unfortunately, Emily, Evelyn and I were cursed to be the bastards of the family. I'm just thankful that William stood beside mother in the end. Not many self-made men in those days would have taken on that kind of responsibility but he loved her dearly."

Blake froze. How did this man know about Edith and Evelyn and why had his mother never told him about her older brother? "That's not possible. The war. Gerald Wise was killed fighting in world war two. William Handanowicz is my grandad. He was Emily and Jim's father. And who is Jack Smith?"

"Jack Smith was my father. He was also Evelyn and Emily's father. Your grandmother had two flings with him at opposite ends of the war. I guess she must have loved him or he gave her a bit of excitement that she craved. He is the man in the photo. Take a seat," Vic replied as he wandered over towards a small dining table and sat down on one of the chairs.

"That's not possible. William Handanowicz was my grandad," Blake replied as he pulled out the opposite chair and sat down.

"I was given up for adoption just after I was born in 1940. You have to remember Blake that the war was going on. Your grandmother worked as a nurse helping the war wounded when they came back from battle minus limbs and whatever else had happened to them. Gerald Wise was killed early-on in the war leading my mother, Dana Wise, your grandmother, to send me away for mine and her own safety. It was a different time back then. Things were not as socially accepted as they are these days. If it ever came out that I was her bastard child after Gerald had been killed, she would have been cast aside. A leper. Damaged goods. Being a widow with her legitimate daughter by her side gave her a chance within the community."

"How do you know all of this? You were only a baby when all of this was going on."

"In 1967, I finally met my biological mother, your grandmother, Dana Handanowicz. She told me everything. I was made to stay away from the rest of the family but back in January 2000, I received a letter from Emily Langford, your mother. We began regularly writing to each other from then until the day she died."

Blake shook his head in disbelief. His mother had kept this secret all of her life and he had never known any of this. "So what happened during the war?"

"Your grandmother met a man who had been brought into her care suffering from what they called "shell shock" back then. His name was Jack Smith. She cared for him and helped him back to full health. Knowing that her husband, my father, was dead, my guess is that they ended up having a relationship."

"Why would she have risked being a social outcast back then? Surely any sexual relationship outside of wedlock was frowned upon."

"We're all human Blake. In our younger years we don't always make the right decisions. One night stands were still a thing back in the forties, it just wasn't in the public knowledge as it is these days."

"So, she gave you up but then fell pregnant again with Jack's child, my mother."

Vic nodded. "Children, not child Blake. Your mother had a twin sister called Evelyn. William Handanowicz married Dana Wise knowing that the children she carried were not his."

"So he was my step grandfather and nobody knew. What happened to Jack Smith?"

"He died of tuberculosis. His body was found on Calshot Beach in the summer of 1948."

"Found? Did he just collapse on the beach?" Blake asked.

"Your grandfather, Edward Langford, was the DCI in charge of the case. He managed to piece together who Jack Smith was from a railway ticket found in his pocket on the day he died."

"How do you know all of this?"

Vic stood up from his chair and opened up the top drawer of a metal filing cabinet that was in the corner of the room. He pulled out an A4 ring binder folder that was full of plastic wallets containing handwritten letters. Blake felt a lump in his throat as he recognised his mother's handwriting when Vic opened up the folder.

"Your Mother told me everything," Vic said as he sat back down.

He turned to the back of the folder and in the last plastic wallet was a small blue envelope. Vic removed the envelope from the plastic wallet and handed it to Blake. Blake opened the envelope and removed a letter from inside it. It read;

Dearest Victor,

I feel my time is near and I must pass the burden of truth to you. The Smith secret is safe in Lindos but I fear Dana may yet have a part to play. Jade will leave a white carnation on the grave of the unknown soldier if the secret is out. Only then must you contact Blake. He will know what to do.

May God help us all.

Emily

Blake laid the letter on the table and looked at Victor. "When I came here, you said that you thought death would have a familiar face but not mine. What did you mean by that?"

"Jack Smith was injured during the war and was medically evacuated but that's not the whole story. In 1938, a bank was robbed in Portsmouth city centre. The thieves got away with over three-hundred-thousand pounds worth of gold. After two years of searching, the bank wrote off the gold. Around the same time, a Mr J. Smith was medically evacuated from the front line and disappeared. His last recorded sighting was at a manor house in The New Forest called Holbury Manor. The nurses there assisted with the rehabilitation of soldiers returning from the war. Many people have suspected that the Smith family money is still out there somewhere and they will do anything to uncover its location."

"I gave up looking for buried treasure when I left school. If the money was there, someone would have claimed it by now."

"Your mother seemed to think that James knew where it was located."

"Then he would have spent it by now. Uncle Jim led my father to lose several thousands of pounds on a dodgy investment and when it all went pear shaped, Jim ran off to Greece with the remaining money."

"Blake, there are still people out there that would kill for this money. It's in my family line and it's in yours. Whoever is going after this will know that and it will turn both families into targets."

"How much money are we talking about?"

"Like I said, in 1938, it was estimated to be around three-hundred-thousand pounds in value."

"So, with the rate of inflation, in today's money, it's got to be worth..."

"Over eleven million pounds," Vic finished for him.

Blake took a moment to let it sink in. He struggled to comprehend that his mother would keep this from him and then send him this letter via Victor after she had died.

"In the letter, she said about the grave of the unknown soldier. Was that the grave that George stumbled upon?"

"No, the unknown soldier's resting place is in the shadow of All Saints Church in Dibden, a few miles from here. No one can be certain but it is the suspected resting place of Jack Smith."

"What's stopped you from pursuing this for yourself?" Blake asked.

"I'm an old man Blake. I live a simple life. I have no need for money or possessions anymore."

"What about the rest of your family?"

"My daughter Anne and her husband died in a motorbike accident three years ago and my granddaughters don't come anywhere near me anymore."

"And what about Evelyn?"

Victor looked at him. "You don't know, do you?"

"Know what?"

"Evelyn disappeared on the same day your parents got married. That's why she was wiped from the family memory. There were very few photographs and everyone wanted to forget she ever existed."

Blake bowed his head. "I'm sorry, I only found out about Evelyn after doing some digging through the obituaries this morning."

"That's not a surprise. There was a huge fallout just before your parents wedding in 1977. Evelyn and Frederick left the church and then there was the accident."

"When Dad's brother Fred died?"

Vic nodded. "Nobody knew what really happened but she just disappeared and never spoke to the family again."

"How did Dad fail to find her? He was the police sergeant at the time. There must have been a lot of unanswered questions!"

"He knew what happened but he let her run rather than face the consequences over what happened."

"But there was a chance that she was involved in his brother's death!"

"Not everything is that cut-and-dry Blake. You know that. Remember, she was also your mother's twin sister."

Blake ran his fingers through his hair. "Wait, let me get this straight, Grandma Dana had my mother Emily and Evelyn as twins and Grandma Mavis had my aunt Mary and uncle Fred as twins at opposite ends of the war. That's a massive coincidence."

"Especially as all four of them shared the same father," Vic replied.

"What?"

"Emily and Evelyn were born in 1949. Fred and Mary were only eighteen months older than your father, John Langford who was born in 1939."

"Are you saying both Dana and Mavis had affairs with the same man? Jack Smith?"

"It seems to be that way, yes."

Blake looked at the photo again before turning back to Victor. "That photo seems to show that both of my grandmothers on the Handanowicz and Langford sides were friends in 1948. My father, John, would have only been eight years old by then and Mum wouldn't have been born. Dad was thirty-seven when they married. Mum was only twenty-nine. The two families were somehow connected for over thirty years before then," Blake reflected, shaking his head in frustration. "There has to be a connection and everything is pointing to Jack Smith."

Vic bowed his head. "You have to remember that technology was nowhere near as advanced as it was today and I may be completely wrong with this but I'm going to say it anyway."

Blake looked into Victor's eyes. "You know the real reason why Evelyn disappeared after Fred died don't you?"

Vic nodded. "They were beginning to have a relationship together until..."

"Until what?"

"This is all hearsay as it was never proven at the time and I guess now we'll never know."

"Know what?"

"They discovered that they had the same father."

Blake sat back in his chair trying to process everything that Victor was telling him. What were the odds of one man having twins with two different women eight years apart? Pretty slim even with today's technology. "This can't be right."

"I've questioned it all myself thousands of times."

"All of my grandparents were cremated so there's no way to prove it either way so all of this could just be a wild goose chase."

"If you believed that, you wouldn't have come here to see me today. Your mother sent you a message from the grave Blake. She wanted you to figure out who Jack Smith was and how he links back to you today. There are a lot of people who know about the Jack Smith legacy. They will stop at nothing to get their hands on it. This is your family's genuine birthright. The Handanowicz and Langford families combined."

Blake pondered that. "I guess we'll never know because Dana and William Handanowicz were both cremated over twenty years ago."

"William was."

Blake looked at him. "On the obituary, Dana Handanowicz, my grandmother's file showed, burial site, unknown. I remember being at my grandparents house after her funeral as a child with my brother and sister because Steven ended up in hospital after hitting his head on the fireplace."

"Dana Handanowicz was not cremated on that day. She had a separate funeral with the Smith/Wise side of the family and was buried in East Boldre cemetery in The New Forest."

Blake shook his head. "No, no, that's wrong..."

Victor didn't reply.

"Then who the hell did we cremate in 1984?" Blake snapped.

"I don't know," Vic replied. "If you find that out, you may find the missing piece of the puzzle."

At that moment, a knock at the door interrupted them. Victor wandered over and answered it. After some muffled conversation, Alison walked through into the kitchen area where Blake was sitting at the table.

"Everything okay?" Alison asked.

"Just another line of inquiry but I think we're done here," Blake replied.

"You'll have to forgive ol' George, he is one for the melodrama," Vic chuckled.

"Thank you for your time Mr Wise, I'll be in touch," Blake replied as he shook Victor's hand.

"Be careful Blake, they know you're coming," Vic replied as they headed towards the door.

Just as Victor was about to close the door, Blake turned to face him again.

"One more thing," Blake asked.

Victor looked at him.

"Who are your two granddaughters?"

"You'll never get anything out of them."

"But I may be able to protect them."

Victor sighed. "Jade Lucy and Andrea Louise."

"Jade and Andrea Wise?" Blake asked.

"No, Smith," Victor replied before closing the door.

Alison looked at Blake. "He doesn't know?"

"No, and for now he doesn't need to," Blake replied as they walked away.

"If she's his granddaughter, he has a right to know. It's only a matter of time before it all comes out anyway."

"I think I may have found the link to all of this but we need to speak to the undertakers first."

"Joe came up with nothing from them."

"But I may have an angle that Joe didn't," Blake replied as he climbed back into his car.

Alison joined him in the passenger seat. "And what angle is that?"

"That grave that Andrea Smith's body was found in may belong to my grandmother."

Alison looked at him. "What? How?"

"That's what I need to find out, let's go."

Chapter Ten

Forgive Me Father For I Have Sinned
Sunday 22nd August 1948

"Lovely service Vicar, much obliged," one of the parishioners said as she left St David's Church in Lepe.

"You're most welcome Mrs Brown," Harold Partridge, the local vicar replied.

Mavis Langford hurriedly walked up the stone path towards the entrance of the church.

The vicar noticed her heading towards him. "Ah, Mrs Langford, I thought I missed you at morning worship, is everything all right?" he asked.

"Please Vicar, I don't have much time. I need to confess to you to help myself get past this awful tragedy."

Harold looked at her for a moment. He had always looked out for Mavis and seeing her in such a muddle gave him cause for concern. He nodded. "I'll meet you there in ten minutes."

Mavis rushed into the church whilst Harold continued to say goodbye to the remaining parishoners as they continued on their way out of the church. After the last parishioner had left, Harold closed the doors of the church and walked over towards the confessional box. He sat in his seat and took a deep breath. Thoughts flooded his mind. What on Earth could have made Mavis so worried that she needed to speak to him so urgently? He carefully removed the wooden slate on the wall next to him and through a wire mesh window, he saw her sat in the opposite side of the confessional box, her hands shaking on her lap.

"Forgive me Father for I have sinned," she started, her voice shaking with emotion.

"May God grant you forgiveness and peace," Harold replied.

"I don't think what I have done will find forgiveness, Father."

Harold waited a moment until she was ready to continue.

"I fear I may have contributed to the death of my friend."

Harold took a deep breath. "In what way do you think you contributed?"

"There was a gent who visited us yesterday. Someone who I thought I would never see again."

"An old friend?"

"No, no, just... Just someone I used to know," Mavis sighed.

"Someone from the village?"

"He was brought to our medical tent during the first attacks eight years ago."

Harold bowed his head. "When the bombings started at the beginning of the war."

"Yes, he had a broken arm and was struggling to focus on anything. The nurses thought he suffered shell-shock. He was in our care for six months before disappearing."

"Did he go back into battle?"

"Nobody knows. I never saw him again until yesterday."

"What happened yesterday?"

"We all had luncheon out on the beach. The sun was shining and the children were playing in the sand. Everything felt like it was going to be all right again until he showed up."

"What did he do?" Harold asked.

"He pretended to be someone else."

"Why would he do that?"

"He must have realised that Ed would work it out. He's a police detective, not much gets past him."

"And yet he failed to notice this man was not who he claimed to be."

"Dana and I covered it up well."

"Why would you not want your husband to know who this man really was?"

"My husband is a good man, Father... I never... I never meant to do it but... Oh dear Lord, what am I saying?"

"Take your time," Harold reassured her.

"He was such a strong, friendly character and we were out in the tents everyday trying to help. Our children were kept in bunkers, watched over by a select few who couldn't wrap bandages or were sick at the sight of blood. It was a silly, stupid mistake..."

Harold didn't respond.

"You understand that, don't you, Father? We didn't know if our husbands would make it back or not. It was a difficult time for us all."

"The Lord has no judgement Mrs Langford. If you have sinned then you have the right to repent."

"I don't want my sins to flow down to my children, Father. They are innocent. They love Ed so much. He is their father in almost every sense of the word."

"If you confess your sins before God, He will guide you on the path to righteousness upon hearing your confession."

"But will he forgive adultery, Father?"

Harold took a deep breath. "Is this your confession Mrs Langford?"

"I was weak. I know I shouldn't have been but Edward had been gone for weeks. We never knew if we would survive and..."

Harold waited.

"It just happened and now I have to live with the consequences. I have the reminder everyday of what I've done and I can't even begin to tell Edward what happened. I'm so ashamed, Father."

"You should not torture yourself Mrs Langford. The start of the war was a trying time for us all. If you can admit and repent for your sins, God will grant you his forgiveness. Let yourself be free of this burden and ensure that you never sin again."

"But how can I look into my children's eyes and tell them their father is dead?"

Harold paused for a moment. "Edward Langford has died?"

"No, Jack Smith is dead. He is Mary and Fred's father," Mavis admitted.

They both sat in an uncomfortable silence for a moment before Harold finally spoke again.

"Are you sure Edward Langford is not their father? Could you have become pregnant before he left for the war?"

Mavis sobbed. "I've worked out the dates, the twins were born exactly nine months after Jack and I..."

Harold nodded. "Do you believe that your secret has been discovered and that is why Mr Smith has died?"

"I... I don't know. He looked ill yesterday. Very pale and sweaty."

"It was a hot summer's day yesterday, Mrs Langford. Did he have any health problems?"

"He claimed that the doctor had told him that he had tuberculosis and that there was no cure. He said that he wanted to see me one last time before he died."

"Did you tell him that he was the father of two of your children?"

"Of course not."

"Why?"

"It was none of his business."

"It is if it was ever proven that he was their father."

Mavis shook her head. "I shouldn't have come here, I'm sorry."

"Mrs Langford, I'm sorry, I didn't mean to pry," Harold replied.

Mavis sighed deeply. "I made a stupid mistake, Father, and because of that, he came back to Lepe and lost his life."

"He would have died anyway without the right medical care. At least you were able to give him some kind of closure before he passed on. If you truly repent your sins and ensure that from this day forward, you will never sin again, you may find forgiveness in the love of God."

"And if he was murdered because of our secret?"

"That is not for us to judge unless you were the one who ended his life. If that proves to be true then you need to be honest with your husband. He is a good detective and he will find out the truth one way or another."

Mavis thought about that for a moment before stepping out of the confessional booth. Harold followed her back towards the nave of the church. They both knelt before the cross and said a silent prayer together before heading for the exit. As Harold opened the door, Detective Edward Langford and Sergeant Peter Hastings approached the church.

"Mavis, what are you doing here? Who's looking after the children?" Edward asked.

"After everything that happened this morning I missed morning worship so I came down to say a few prayers with Father Partridge before picking up some bread and oats whilst Frances from Thyme Cottage next door is watching over them for me. What are you doing here?"

"Just continuing our inquiries into the fire and the man on the beach. Frances? Is that Arthur and Iris' daughter? The one with the mole on her chin. She's only just finished school!"

"She's seventeen Ed, I was running the family home at that age. I'm on my way home now. Good day Father," Mavis snapped before walking away.

Harold watched her leave momentarily before turning his attention to Edward and Peter. "What can I do for you both?"

"What was the real reason she was here?" Edward asked.

"She came to say a few prayers at the altar, just like she said, Mr Langford. It's such a terrible thing isn't it?"

"What is?" Peter asked.

"Well, the house fire... Everyone is talking about it," Harold stammered.

"News travels fast. What else are they talking about?" Edward asked.

"I'm not at liberty to say."

"Why don't we step inside and have a conversation about it," Edward replied as he walked into the church with Peter and Harold following closely behind.

"You must hear a lot of things in your confessional Father," Peter began.

"Anything that is shared before the presence of God shall be kept within the confessional. I have taken a vow of trust..."

"And I've taken a vow to keep the people of this village safe! I have a suspected arson attack on a friend's house and a potential murder victim on our local beach so if you know anything about either of them, I'd be glad to hear it," Edward replied.

"Can you tell us your whereabouts yesterday evening, Father Partridge?" Peter Hastings asked.

"I was here until around four o'clock and then I went to visit Jim Gibbs. He's recently had a few health problems and I dropped off a basket of fruit to him and his family."

"And where did you go from there?"

"After that I walked down the old Lepe Road as I was going to visit Sheila and Derek Johnson at Sundial House."

"You said you were going to see them. Did you?"

"No, I saw a gent in a brown suit and yellow shirt wandering down the road. I don't think he was local. He was leaving Honeypot House and took the old dirt path through the woods up towards the shops."

"Did you follow him?" Edward asked.

"Yes, he went into Tom Allan's fruit and veg shop."

"And then what?" Peter asked.

"He disappeared."

"What do you mean he disappeared? He must have gone somewhere."

"I waited for a few minutes and then I carried on my way back here."

"Were you suspicious of him?"

"You can't be too careful these days."

"Meaning?"

"The war changed a lot of people."

"So, after he went into Tom Allan's fruit and veg shop, you never saw him again."

Harold shook his head.

"Did you go back to Mr and Mrs Johnson's house after your detour?" Edward asked.

"No."

"Why not?"

"I changed my mind. It was getting late and I wanted to get some tea before having an early night."

Edward and Peter looked at each other seemingly satisfied with Harold's explanation of events.

"If you think of anything else, please give the station a call," Edward said before heading towards the door with Peter Hastings following closely behind him.

Harold released a breath he hadn't realised that he was holding as they walked away.

"Oh, one last thing, Father," Peter said as he arrived at the door.

Harold looked at him warily.

"Have you heard about anyone camping out in the cafe on Calshot Beach recently?" Peter asked.

"Norman's old cafe?"

Peter nodded.

"No, nothing. Isn't that meant to be closed down? Norman hasn't reopened since the war. Why?"

"Just a thought, good day, Father," Peter replied before following Edward Langford out of the door.

Harold rushed into his vestry and watched as Edward and Peter walked down the path towards the church gate. He knew he needed to keep the vow of his confessional to God but his hands began to shake uncontrollably as he thought about the events of the past 24 hours. He knew he needed to be careful who he spoke to. One wrong word could open up a lot of secrets that a lot of people would rather keep hidden.

As Edward and Peter arrived back at their patrol car, Peter unlocked the drivers door and climbed inside before leaning across to unlock the passenger door. Edward sat alongside him and closed the door.

"Do you trust him?" Peter asked.

"Do you?"

"He seemed nervous."

"I know."

"Do you think Mavis had something to do with it?"

"To do with what?"

"His nerves. I've seen better liars in the courthouse."

"I don't know. Why would he follow a gent that he'd never met before towards the shop and then not even speak to him or follow him into the shop?" Edward asked.

"You know how nosey some of the locals can be, Sir. You only have to change your hairstyle and the whole village knows about it."

"You're right Hastings, maybe I'm overthinking it. Let's call it a day, hopefully tomorrow will give us a better idea of what's happening."

Peter started the car and drove away from the church and down the Lepe Road towards Edward Langford's house. As the car disappeared out of sight, a man wearing black trousers and a white shirt stepped out from an alley behind two houses that were on the opposite side of the road from the church. He walked up the pathway and knocked on the church door. After a couple of minutes, Harold opened the door.

"Hello Father Partridge," the man smiled.

"Officer Wells, George," Harold smiled. "I've already spoken to your superior. I've got nothing more to say."

"Forgive me Father for I have sinned," Officer George Wells replied before pushing past Harold and closing the door behind him.

Chapter Eleven

Dana Handanowicz
Sunday 2nd November 2008

Blake Langford knocked on the front door of Crowther's Funeral Services on Sunday evening. A man dressed in a white shirt with a black waistcoat, black trousers and polished black shoes answered the door.

"We're closed, nobody's here," he said as he opened the door ajar.

Blake flashed his ID. "Blake Langford, Special Branch, London, is your boss here?"

"I told you, no one's here. Come back tomorrow."

Blake put his foot in the way of the door to stop the man from closing it. "I'm sorry, I didn't catch your name Mr..."

"No, you didn't," the man snapped.

"Well, Mr "No, you didn't," if I need to file a report that you have obstructed an investigation into your funeral home, I'm sure that would be a major problem for the locals looking for an honest and reputable funeral director to assist them in their time of grief. Do yourself a favour and open the fucking door."

The man looked over Blake's shoulder at Alison before letting out a sigh and opening the door.

"There you are, it's amazing what you can do when you try," Blake smiled as he entered the funeral home with Alison following close behind.

"What do you want?" the man asked as he closed the door behind them.

"The unmarked grave at East Boldre cemetery," Alison began.

"There's several..."

"The one that had the arm of a young woman sticking out of it on Friday night!" Blake snapped.

"We had nothing to do with it!"

"I'm sorry, Mr..." Alison began.

"Anderson, Chris Anderson," the man replied.

"Mr Anderson, our investigation shows that your company was the funeral director when the grave was originally occupied in 1984. Is that correct?" Alison asked.

"If you say so."

"Can you check for us please?" Blake asked.

Chris walked over and turned on a desktop computer in the corner of the room. After tapping on a few keys, he brought up the record.

"It seems that the original owner of the plot, Miss Patricia Smith, is no longer active so we need to follow the family line. She had a sister Dorothy, who is deceased so the next in line would be her daughter, Jade Smith of Arlington Grove in Ealing, West London. She's the person you need to speak to regarding the identity of the deceased as she still has seventy-six years on the plot," Chris explained.

"Mr Anderson, can I ask you, if for argument's sake, the arm of that young girl who had been buried alive in one of your graves happened to be your own daughter, or your own sister or mother, what would you do if an undertaker was pulling your chain rather than helping the investigating team solve the case?" Blake asked.

"I would make sure that I followed the relevant channels correctly and not display threatening behaviour towards the one person that could potentially help me solve the case," Chris smirked.

Blake approached the desk but Alison stood in his way.

"Let's go," she said as she ushered Blake towards the door. "Thank you for your help Mr Anderson."

Chris Anderson watched them leave before pulling his phone out of his pocket and typing out a text message. He looked out of the window and watched Blake's Ford Mondeo kick up some of the gravel at the front of the funeral home before sending the message. He looked out at the traffic on the main road for a moment before heading back over to the desk. He opened the report once again before deleting the file and closing the PC down. He waited for the screen to turn black before picking up his coat and heading out of the door.

***

"You know the one thing I hate about this job..." Blake complained as they headed back towards his home at Lepe Beach.

"The wonderful travel opportunities it presents?" Alison smirked.

Blake half smiled. "Some bureaucratic jobsworth who thinks he's being clever by impeding an investigation by using the red tape to his advantage. Client data protection crap, what a load of..."

"Okay, I get it, he's being a dick but not everything gets sorted out with fighting either," Alison countered.

"I guess you're right. Did you get much out of George Harding?"

"Apart from the winning horse at Newbury this afternoon, not much. Took his dog out for a walk, discovered a dead body and called the police. No idea who the grave belonged to or who Andrea was. Seems to be someone who just keeps himself to himself and doesn't want any fuss."

"They're usually the ones you need to watch out for."

"What about you? Did the other guy tell you much?" Alison asked.

"A lot more than I ever expected," Blake replied as he told Alison about his conversation with Victor.

As they arrived outside Blake's family home at Lepe Beach, his phone lit up with Joe Knight's number displayed on the screen. Blake turned off the ignition and answered the call.

"We have a breakthrough!" Joe said as Blake answered.

"So have we. The grave seems to be registered to Jade Smith," Blake replied.

"Correct but I've managed to dig through the paperwork, unofficially of course, and it's brought up something interesting. The occupier of that grave was thought to have been cremated by the family and in 1984 with the ashes scattered in the memorial garden in South Kensington. However, there was a rift between the families and a Miss Patricia Smith and Mrs Dorothy Farlington paid Leonard Crowther of Crowther's Funeral Services a substantial amount of money to have the body transported to The New Forest and have her buried in that unmarked plot."

"If they were so hell bent on having the body in the cemetery in East Boldre then why not have the gravestone memorial too?" Blake asked.

"No one except for certain members of the immediate family were meant to know of the location of the grave."

"So they paid Leonard Crowther for the anonymity," Alison added.

"Precisely."

"Who is the body in the grave Joe?" Blake asked.

"Dana Sylvia Handanowicz, died 17th April 1984," Joe replied.

Blake felt a shiver run through his body. "No, it can't be!"

"I've got the paperwork right in front of me."

"There has to be some mistake."

"The only way to be sure is to exhume the body and take DNA tests with her surviving relatives but so far, Jade Smith has been unresponsive."

"She's not Dana Handanowicz's relative."

"The paperwork claims that Dana would be her aunt," Joe replied. "What makes you so sure that she isn't?"

"Because Dana Handanowicz is my grandmother. She was Emily Langford's mother," Blake replied.

At that moment, Alison's phone rang. She pulled it out of her pocket and saw a coded message from Special Branch.

"We'll call you back," Alison said as she cut off Blake's phone and answered her own phone.

"Scrambler D, F, Twenty-Seven, Nine, G," she said into her phone.

The screen flickered pink and grey before connecting to a secure line.

"Alison, is Blake with you?" Eric Gordon asked.

"I'm right here," Blake replied.

"I need you both on the first plane out of Gatwick tomorrow morning flying to Diagoras in Rhodes."

"With all due respect Sir, we may have had a breakthrough in the East Boldre graveyard case," Blake replied.

"Samir and Joe can hold it until you come back. There was a mass shooting at a villa near Monolithos this evening. Greek authorities seem to believe that they were targeting one of the patients from a mental health facility called Kolopsia House until someone gunned them down."

"Do they know who the gunmen were?" Alison asked.

"Zachary Zhal and Ian Bleeker."

Blake looked at Alison in disbelief. Zachary Zhal, better known as Zodiac and Ian Bleeker, better known as Reaper, had escaped after an attempt to traffick young students out of London and into Europe was intercepted by Blake and his team.

"That can't be a coincidence," Blake replied.

"No, and neither are the others involved which is why you need to head out to Rhodes as soon as possible. One of the people involved who the Greek authorities arrested asked specifically for your help."

"Who was the person involved and who were Zodiac and Reaper targeting?" Blake asked.

"The patient was Evelyn Joan Handanowicz and the person protecting her was her brother, James William Handanowicz."

Blake couldn't believe what he was hearing. The Handanowicz family had suddenly reappeared from all angles and now it seemed that they had somehow become involved in a criminal organisation.

"Are you still there Blake?" Eric Gordon asked.

"We're here," Alison replied for him. "We'll be at Gatwick first thing in the morning."

"Angela will send over the details. This body in the cemetery seems to hold the key to all of this. You need to tread carefully as there is no telling how deep this organisation is involved and we can't let the media get hold of any more than they already have," Eric Gordon replied.

"Agreed, thank you Sir," Alison replied before ending the call.

She turned to Blake. "We need to start figuring out what the hell happened in your family's past."

Blake nodded.

"What relation are Evelyn and James Handanowicz to you?" Alison asked.

"They are my mother's brother and sister. I've never met Evelyn as she disappeared in 1977. James took a loan off of my father in 1984 to help set up a hospice, I guess you could call it, to help people with mental health difficulties. Obviously, back then, it wasn't as widely talked about as it is today but Dad saw that Uncle Jim wanted to make a difference and gave him fifty-thousand pounds to set it up."

"Then what happened?"

"I was only a child when it all went down but for some reason, he couldn't get the hospice or the support that he needed so he abandoned the idea. When Dad asked for his money back, Jim fobbed him off until Dad and another police officer turned up at Jim's home to collect the money. When they entered, they realised that he had disappeared and Dad discovered that he had flown out to Athens the day before. They never spoke or saw each other again."

"I'm sorry."

"For what? Dad learnt a big lesson that sometimes your family can screw you over more than your enemies. He was advised not to give Jim the money but he did it anyway."

"Did it affect your parent's marriage?"

"I guess so. Dad was a lot more guarded around financial matters and anytime Mum wanted us to spend time with anyone on her side of the family, he would always have other plans so he never had to socialise with them as often."

"So when Paula gave her father that money, you saw history repeating itself?" Alison asked.

"You can't hold a grudge with someone just because they were blinded by their love for a relative can you? Jim put a wedge between my parents and their relationship. I'm not going to let Graham Evans do that with mine and Paula's."

At that moment, the outside light turned on by the front door and they noticed Paula standing in the doorway.

"Come on, let's go in. I have a feeling tomorrow is going to be a long day," Blake sighed as he stepped out of the car and headed towards the house with Alison following close behind.

***

It was getting late and Jenny Langford was still picking through the remaining debris of her parent's house at 124 Alfredson Road, Kensington by torch light. She found an old red and grey metal case that contained some paperwork. The lid had buckled in the explosion but somehow, the contents were undamaged.

As she searched through the paperwork, she found some old solicitors letters, some handwritten letters still in their opened envelopes, tied together with string and an old photo album. As she sifted through them, she couldn't help but feel a sense of intrigue. These were fragments of her family's history, pieces of a puzzle she had never known existed. One particular letter caught her attention. It was addressed to her late grandfather, William Handanowicz, dated decades ago. Jenny's heart quickened as she read its contents, a plea for help from someone named Evelyn Handanowicz. The letter spoke of danger and an impending threat to their family.

Realising the significance of her discovery, Jenny decided to dig deeper into her family's past. With each photograph and letter, a clearer picture emerged. The story unfolded like a gripping tale of secrecy and betrayal. She learned that Evelyn Handanowicz, her aunt, had disappeared in 1977. She had uncovered something dangerous, something that powerful people sought to keep hidden. But what was it? What was the big secret?

She opened an A4 brown envelope and pulled out a sheet of paper that had turned yellow over time. As she read the print on it, things began to fall into place. She had found the death certificate of Jack Walter Smith, who died August 23rd 1948. The same day the photo that her mother, Emily, had left in the safe deposit box had been taken. Whatever secrets were hidden in these letters and photos, Jenny was convinced that Jack Smith was the one who linked it all together.

As she collected up her things, she heard the metal front door creak open and clank against the remains of the hallway downstairs. Jenny froze. She knew she shouldn't have been in the building whilst it was still unstable but something in her gut told her that whoever had just entered the house shouldn't have been there either. She placed her hand over her torch giving her just enough light to see where she was walking but not enough to give away that she was there. Her senses were going into overdrive. She heard footsteps as someone walked through the debris downstairs. A drawer opened followed by the rustling of some keys.

Jenny's heart raced as she strained to listen to the sounds below. Who could be in her family's old house? And what were they looking for? She clutched the stack of letters and photographs tightly, her mind racing with possibilities. Her instincts told her to stay hidden, but curiosity compelled her to investigate further. She cautiously descended the creaking stairs, each step careful and deliberate. The beam of her torch pierced through the darkness, revealing a figure hunched over a dusty desk in what used to be her father's study.

As Jenny approached, she noticed the stranger rifling through papers and files. Their back was turned towards her, obscuring their face. She could hear laboured breathing, a mixture of excitement and urgency.

Determined not to let fear paralyse her, Jenny took a deep breath before stepping forward. "Who are you?" she demanded, her voice steady despite the adrenaline coursing through her veins.

The intruder froze, before slowly turning to face her.

Jenny gasped. "Jade?"

"Guilty as charged," Jade replied.

"What the hell are you doing searching through the remains of my family home?"

"The same thing as you. Looking for clues to the family secret."

"I don't understand, what is your interest in my family's past?"

Jade leant against the doorframe of the lounge. "Jack Smith."

"Who's Jack Smith?"

"The man who started this whole deception. Why do you think Tom was at that bar in Soho when you two got together? Why were your parents so against your relationship together? Why was your father so eager to cover up your involvement in Tom's misdemeanour with the Russian agent?"

Jenny thought back to ten years ago when her relationship with Tom came to an end. He had told her that he was in trouble and that he needed her to go to Salisbury to meet a Russian agent called

Ivan Stepanchikov. Unbeknown to her, she had handed him a dossier containing the details of Tom's regiment's next assignment in Afghanistan. The regiment were ambushed and were all killed. Jenny was led to believe that Tom Gibson was amongst the dead until he returned to London six months ago.

"My father was a good man and a brilliant police detective. He did what he needed to do to protect his family!" Jenny replied.

"But he left one final detail out of that story."

"What?"

"Tom Gibson is your second cousin. Andrea and I are too," Jade admitted.

Jenny sat down on the arm of an ash covered armchair. "No, how? What are you talking about? You have no connection to my parents or grandparents. They never spoke of it."

"Jack Smith is our mutual great-grandfather. Your mother left clues. Photos, letters, none of it leads us to the location of the family's inheritance though."

"What inheritance? Tom destroyed this house! There's nothing left but a charred hollowed out shell!"

"Jack and his wife Ada robbed a bank in Portsmouth in 1938. They got away with the money and were never caught. All that we know is that it's buried somewhere in Hampshire. The map of where he hid the money was split into several pieces and hidden. If we can find the pieces of the map, we'll find the gold."

"Don't you think we're both too old for fairytales. Next you're going to tell me that a dashing prince is going to come along and sweep me off my feet and take me away to an enchanted land," Jenny replied.

"Both of our families have been keeping this secret for generations. Your mother has given you the opportunity to uncover the truth. Don't waste it Jen. There's people in the shadows willing to kill for it."

Jenny sighed. "Come with me to The New Forest tomorrow. We might be able to find out more there."

"So you believe me?"

"I don't know what or who to believe anymore but Blake and his team are dealing with a case in The New Forest and it could lead to helping us find out what the hell is going on."

"I received a letter and a phone call about a grave plot in East Boldre cemetery. I didn't even know anything about it," Jade admitted. "Apparently, they want to exhume the body for DNA testing and it belongs to a distant relative."

"Do you know who?"

"No, they won't tell me unless I actually go there in person."

"Meet me here tomorrow morning at 10am. We'll go down and see what we can find out."

Jade nodded. "I'm sorry."

"For what?"

"Intruding in your family home."

"Hopefully we can get some answers tomorrow," Jenny replied.

Jade smiled awkwardly before making her way through the debris and out of the front door. Jenny watched her leave. She felt bad for not telling her what she knew about her sister, Andrea's, whereabouts but deep down, she knew that Jade couldn't be trusted. She just hoped that when the coffin was exhumed from the unmarked grave in East Boldre cemetery, the identity of the body would give them some answers.

Chapter Twelve

Secrets Of A Sinner

Sunday 22nd August 1948

Police Officer George Wells pushed past Father Harold Partridge and entered the church. Harold watched as the last couple of parishoners walked away towards the main road before closing and locking the church doors. As he walked back into the church, Officer Wells was standing in front of the altar.

"It is a tad unusual for a police officer to come to my confessional. I did not realise you were catholic," Harold said as he approached him.

"Let's cut the small talk Harold, we both know why I'm here."

"I'm not sure that I understand."

"The young men at Norman Whitehouse's Cafe on Calshot Beach."

"I know nothing about them."

"Indeed. I had an interesting conversation with one of them. His name was Maximillian Friedrich Ekkehard. Is this ringing any bells Father?" Officer Wells asked.

Harold bowed his head. "Weakness of the flesh is a sin that I am unfortunately guilty of."

"This is not a straightforward sin though is it Father? Are you aware of the Criminal Law Amendment Act of 1885? Any act of male to male sexual activity shall be seen as gross indecency! I should take you in and throw you into jail right now!"

"Then why won't you?"

"Because you can still be useful. You may have betrayed the trust of those young men but whilst Detective Langford is investigating the death of the man on the beach, it has cast a shadow on Norman's dealings with the Germans."

"Meaning what?"

"Langford and Hastings won't stop until they discover who that man really is and what connections he has to the area. If they attempt to blame the Germans for his death then it blows that case wide open."

"One of them is already making eyes with a young lady in the village. They're not exactly being discreet."

"Arthur King knows what to do. He's keeping a close watch on his daughter and Christoph knows what will happen if he steps out of line."

"So why do you care so much about these men?" Father Partridge asked.

"A fellow officer identified the man on the beach as Jack Walter Smith. He was a defector during the war. He helped those four men get into the country undetected and used the local women to ensure that he never went back into battle."

"If you know who the man is then you can close the case."

"My fellow officer knew Mr Smith before the war. He helped him rob a bank in Portsmouth ten years ago. Smith then ran off with the gold and no one heard from him again until he turned up injured in a hospital in Fareham in 1942."

Harold Partridge began making the connections in his mind after Mavis Langford's confession earlier but he said nothing.

"New money is coming into the area. Someone is buying Whitehouse out of the cafe. The men need somewhere safe to stay. I'm sure you can make room in your little cottage to accommodate them," Officer Wells continued.

"But, what if they are seen? What about my parishioners when they come to visit?"

"What would happen if your parishioners knew that you were having sexual activity with a young gent that has recently come to the area? I don't think they would ever trust you again and I have a big mouth Father."

Harold bowed his head. "Indeed."

"Cheer up Father, you still have your freedom," Officer Wells smiled before heading towards the door.

"You won't get away with this George. Sooner or later, fate will cross your path."

Officer Wells stopped by the door and looked back at him. "Yours too Father, yours too," he said before leaving the church.

***

Later that day, there was a loud knocking on the front door of Harold Partridge's cottage, a short walk away from St David's Church. He ignored it at first as he furiously rushed to pack a suitcase full of clothes, handkerchiefs, talcum powder, a comb, a notebook and a couple of pens. As the knocking became more intense, he made his way to the front door.

"Finally, I thought you'd never answer," Norman Whitehouse said as he entered and closed the door behind him. "We don't have much time."

"What do you mean?" Harold asked.

"Bad news travels fast. I'll explain more as you pack."

"Pack for what?"

"Do you want to remain a free man?" Norman asked.

"Of course but..."

"Then listen to me. Those men at the cafe are getting restless. Rumour has it that one of them is courting Miss King at Thyme Cottage. It's not going to take long before the whole village is questioning where they all came from. One of them has been able to live at the institute in Totton but if the others follow, their cover will be blown."

"What does all of this have to do with me?"

"We all know as men it can be awfully lonely at times..."

Harold Partridge bowed his head.

"I met briefly with Max at the cafe earlier," Norman continued. "I told him that it was over. That he needed to leave the village and you would never see him again. If news gets out that you have been, you know..."

Harold nodded.

"I don't trust that copper, Wells, I think his name is. He's been sniffing around too much. The sooner I can sell that cafe, the better. For now, you need to come with me."

"Where are we going?"

"Somewhere safe. Somewhere where nobody can get to us. My driver will be here in twenty minutes so you had better hurry up and pack whatever you need."

"Why are you helping me?"

Norman sighed. "When Audrey passed away, I did some stupid things. Things that I'm not proud of. I found comfort in a bottle of whiskey and in a young man called Hans. I broke it off. Now he's threatening to tell everyone everything unless I help him settle here in England. You're not the only one with secrets that should never be told."

Harold nodded before heading back upstairs to continue packing. When the car stopped outside his cottage, he took one last look around it before heading out of the front door. Norman took his seat behind the driver whilst Harold opened the passenger door. As he was about to climb inside the car, he noticed a young man with blonde hair and blue eyes standing by the edge of the woodland that led up to the church. He was wearing a green shirt with baggy trousers and scuffed trainers. Harold made eye contact with him and the young man raised his hand and made a sign of the cross across his chest. Harold nodded before sitting in the car and the driver drove them away from the village.

***

Police Officer Charlie Jones stood behind a large oak tree nearby the vicar's cottage. He watched as Norman Whitehouse and Harold Partridge left in a car he didn't recognise but his attention was caught by a young man who was watching from the woods on the opposite side of the clearing. Jones waited and watched as the young man approached the cottage. He recognised him from when he had attended Norman's cafe on Calshot Beach when Jack Smith's body had been discovered. The young man removed a key from his pocket and unlocked the door before disappearing inside. Jones waited. He'd grown suspicious over Officer George Wells' involvement in this case and the young man coming here had confirmed his suspicions. He waited. Ten minutes. Twenty. Thirty. He was beginning to think that the young man would never leave until a car's headlights cut into the darkness.

Jones stayed out of sight as the car stopped on the gravel driveway. The driver stepped out of the car all dressed in black. He approached the front door of the cottage and let himself inside. Jones moved to try and get a better position. He looked at the car registration number but it was not one that he recognised.

At that moment, the silhouette of a man appeared in the bedroom window illuminated by candlelight behind him. He looked directly at Jones who felt a shiver run down his spine. The man looking back at him was Officer George Wells. He closed the curtains and moved away from the window. Jones waited a moment longer in case either one of the men left the cottage but there was no sign of any further movement from inside the cottage. Jones headed back through the woods towards the shops and returned to his car.

"Evening Officer," a woman's voice called out from behind him.

Jones spun around. "Oh, good evening Miss King," he stammered.

"I'm sorry, I didn't mean to give you a fright."

"No, no, I'm sorry, I, er, I had my mind on other things."

"Nothing too worrying I hope."

Officer Jones took his chance. "Has the young gentleman you've been courting with been around recently?"

"As a matter of fact, he has. He was tending to father's rose bushes earlier. Why?"

"Has he been staying locally?"

"How should I know?"

"Miss King..."

"Frances, please Charlie. No need to be so formal. Is he in trouble?"

"Should he be?"

"Not that I'm aware of."

"Then he has nothing to worry about."

"I'm confused, why all of the questions?" Frances asked.

"Has he been visiting the vicar recently?"

"No, why?"

"Just following up on some inquiries, that's all."

"If this is to do with that gent who was found on the beach then you can forget it. Christopher is a good man and he wouldn't hurt anyone."

"How can you be so sure?"

"Because I am."

"Do you know where he goes each night?"

"I don't stalk him if that's what you mean. He's free to come and go as he pleases."

"So where was he on Saturday night?" Jones asked.

"With me."

"All night?"

"All night."

"And your father's okay with that?"

"I know where your mind is going with that and the answer is no, we didn't. We sat out in the garden looking at the stars and talking so if you're trying to pin this murder on anyone, leave Christopher out of it!" Frances snapped.

"Who said it was a murder?"

Frances looked at him for a moment. "What else could it be?"

"People die from natural causes all the time."

"I don't like coincidences Officer Jones and I'm sure you don't either. If you want to look for clues about what happened to the gent on the beach, I suggest you begin looking closer to home."

"Meaning?"

"George Wells is one of the most untrustworthy people I have ever had the misfortune to meet. If you're looking for a scapegoat, I suggest you begin with him. Good evening to you Officer Jones," Frances snapped before walking away.

"Good evening Miss King," Jones smiled before sitting inside his car.

As he started the engine, a thousand thoughts flooded his mind. He knew that Frances King had information about who was living out of Norman Whitehouse's cafe and their connection to Officer George Wells. He just needed to find out what that connection was.

***

Edward Langford sat on a wooden chair in the back garden of Southward Cottage looking up at the moon as it shone down and glistened on the waves of the sea in the distance. His children had long gone up to bed and he was savouring the last few drops of

Johnnie Walker whiskey that he had been swirling around his glass for several minutes. He hated coincidences and too many of them had been happening recently. Mavis Langford walked up behind him and placed her arms onto his shoulders. He moved his head slightly towards her.

"Did you find out who did it?" she asked.

"I'm working on it. Whoever he was, he was certainly a complicated character."

"What do you mean?"

"Most people try to increase their social standing, he was looking to decrease his."

"I don't understand."

"He was a wealthy man and he tried to hide it."

Mavis felt a shiver run through her. She knew that Edward would eventually discover Jack Smith's true identity and she would have a lot of explaining to do.

Feeling her tense up, Edward turned to face her. "What did you need to see the vicar for earlier?"

"I told you that already."

"Tell me again."

"I missed morning service so I rushed down at the end so we could say a few prayers together."

"Without the children?"

"You know how restless they get..."

"So you left them with the girl next door."

"Frances is seventeen, she's old enough to be responsible..."

"Did Father Partridge seem nervous to you when you were with him?"

"No, not that I noticed."

"He didn't have anything on his mind."

"Even if he did, I doubt that he would discuss it with me."

Edward nodded. "I guess you're right. I suppose I should be focusing more on Norman Whitehouse anyway."

"What's Norman done wrong?"

"Nothing as far as I'm aware but the body was discovered outside his cafe and when we entered the building, it looked like some people had been camping inside it."

"You shouldn't judge people for that Ed. A lot of innocent folk lost their homes and their families during the war. Who knows what the poor souls have been through."

"I don't begrudge any man an honest living Mavis. If he is willing to put in the hard graft to earn his crust then he should be able to have a roof over his head and food on his table. It's these freeloaders I struggle to deal with expecting everything to be given to them. Anyway, I've left it up to Wells and Jones to move them on. Hopefully with new owners coming into the village we won't have to deal with this calamity for much longer."

"You're all heart Ed."

"Don't you want our children to grow up in a safe environment?"

"Of course I do but just because someone has fallen on hard times does not mean they are suddenly bad people."

"What about Dana Wise?" Edward asked.

"What about her?"

"Did you know she had an eight year old son?"

Mavis opened her mouth but no words came out.

"Did she give birth whilst you were both in service at the hospital? And if so, where is that child now?" Edward asked.

"I don't know."

"You don't know where the child is..."

"I don't know if she was pregnant or not. Gerald was one of the first enlisted when war was announced so..."

"It's not uncommon for war widows to cling onto the first man that they find to give themselves some kind of future security and prospects," Edward persisted. "If she had indeed given birth, there would surely have been some obvious signs of that."

"I guess so but I never noticed it. If she was, then she managed to hide it very well."

"And what about Edith?"

"What about her?"

"Where was she during the war? She was obviously too young for service..."

"She stayed with the elderly maids who looked after the children whilst their mothers worked in the hospitals treating the wounded. Why suddenly all of these questions?"

"Did Dana Wise know this gent before he arrived at our home on Saturday afternoon?" Edward asked.

"Not that I'm aware of."

"You're not aware of much are you dear? Are you sure he wasn't treated at some point in your hospital?"

"We saw hundreds of gents with all kinds of injuries coming back from the war. How am I meant to remember one out of many hundred who passed through."

"The vicar seems to believe that he was loitering around outside Honeypot House last night before it caught fire. You know how much I hate coincidences."

"Then perhaps you should be interrogating the vicar rather than me."

Edward stood up and walked back inside the house. "Indeed," he sighed as he placed his glass in the kitchen sink before heading towards the stairs. "Maybe a good night's sleep may answer a few questions. Are you coming?"

"I'll be there soon," Mavis replied as she locked the back door and tidied up the kitchen area.

Edward nodded and continued on his way upstairs to bed. He knew Mavis was withholding some information that he needed. He just needed to figure out why.

Chapter Thirteen

Murder In Monolithos
Sunday 2nd November 2008

A red Vauxhall Cavalier entered the gates of Eurydice Villa overlooking Monolithos Beach and parked on a driveway lit with solar powered stick lights at either side of it creating a landing strip for its owner. Jim Handanowicz stepped out of the driver's seat and walked around to open the passenger door allowing his sister, Evelyn, to step out of the car before closing it behind her. He collected a bag of groceries from the boot of the car and they headed towards the front door. As they entered, Jim headed towards the kitchen to prepare some food whilst Evelyn wandered over towards the lounge. At that moment, he heard her scream. Jim dropped the groceries on the kitchen sideboard and rushed into the lounge. Ian Bleeker and Zachary Zhal were standing in the corner of the room dressed in black. Zachary held a gun to Evelyn's head.

"I wondered how long it would be before you turned up," Jim said calmly as he entered the room. "Let her go, this doesn't concern her."

"It concerns your whole family Jim," Ian replied.

"You know these people..." Evelyn gasped but Zachary hardened his grip on her shoulder.

"What do you want, Reaper?"

"The map."

"What map?"

"The map your sister gave you to hide as part of the Jack Smith inheritance."

"I don't know what you're talking about."

"Tom Gibson was denied a huge inheritance by your family. He owes a lot of money to a lot of influential people in Moscow."

"If Gibson was so concerned about his inheritance, why did he send you?"

"Paper trails tend to get messy. I can glide across Europe and not even cause a ripple."

"Give them what they want Jim," Evelyn said.

Jim glared at her.

"Where is it?" Zachary asked.

"In my handbag over there," Evelyn nodded towards a black bag that was on the coffee table.

Zachary pushed her towards the bag. "Then get it!" he snapped.

Evelyn walked over to the bag, placed her hand inside it, picked it up and turned to face the two men. She fired two shots in quick succession through the bag before removing the gun from it and standing over them. Ian looked up as she stood over him. "No one threatens my family," she said before shooting him in the head.

Jim rushed over towards Zachary as he took his last breath. "How the hell did you do that?" he asked.

"Shooting tin cans in the garden at Kolopsia House," Evelyn replied calmly.

"We need to get you out of here. If anyone heard those gunshots, the police will be here in no time."

Evelyn calmly placed the gun back inside her handbag before heading out of the front door towards the car. Jim swung the car around and headed out of the main gate before taking the coastal road along the western side of the island towards Kolopsia House.

"Who were those men?" Evelyn asked as they travelled.

"Zachary Zhal and Ian Bleeker, also known as Zodiac and Reaper, two killers who work for a Russian mafia boss that I had dealings with back in the day."

"You told me you left all that behind you."

"I have, mostly."

"You're a terrible liar."

"You haven't exactly covered yourself in glory either."

"Are you angry with me?"

"No, of course not but where did you get that gun?" Jim asked.

"Under the sink."

"What sink? At the care home?"

"No, Father kept his old revolver under the sink behind the toilet bleach. I've been looking after it. It's one of the few things that I managed to bring with me from home."

"Eve, that was in 1977. Are you sure you haven't bought another one since then?"

Evelyn pulled the gun out of her handbag. "It still has the WS on it. It's our father's old Webley And Scott revolver."

"We need to get rid of it," Jim said as he pulled into a layby overlooking a stony beach far below the cliff-face. "If they find the gun, the police will know what's happened."

"Maybe they should."

"What do you mean?"

"I'm tired of running Jim. Mother's affair cost me a life with Fred Langford and I will never forgive her for that betrayal."

"But what about everything we've achieved? The new life we created out here..."

"The life that you've created."

Jim bowed his head. "I did what I thought was right."

"I know you did and I appreciate that. Take me back to the home Jim. I'm tired and it's been a long day."

"The police will come for you."

"Let them and if they do, call your nephew. He'll know what to do."

"Blake? We haven't spoken since he was a child. Why would he help us?"

"Because you have what he needs. Take him to the map and let him figure it out."

Two police cars sped past them as they sat in silence for a moment. Finally, Jim restarted the car and continued on to Kalopsia House. Evelyn placed the gun back inside her handbag and headed inside. Jim watched her leave before turning the car around and heading back home.

***

Back in London, Jenny Langford stepped out of her family home at 124 Alfredson Road and headed back to the main Fulham Road past the Picturehouse towards Redcliffe Road. The white pillared porches brought back memories of when she used to visit her mother's friend, Sandra Hayes, when she was a teenager. She approached the front door of number 24 and a doorbell echoed inside the building as she pressed it. A few moments later, an elderly man answered the door.

"Can I help you?" he asked, looking at Jenny over his black rimmed bi-focal glasses.

"Yes, I was hoping to see Mrs Hayes."

"Who?"

"Mrs Hayes, Sandra Hayes. I am Emily Langford's daughter."

"Hayes? Don't know no Hayes."

"She used to live here..."

"Who is it Albert?" a woman called out from somewhere inside the house.

"Someone looking for Greys!" Albert replied.

"No, no, Hayes, Sandra Hayes," Jenny corrected.

"Okay Albert, you go finish watching the snooker," the woman said as she approached the door from behind him. She had a blue and white striped tea-towel draped over her shoulder and was wearing a yellow and blue apron. She looked at Jenny up and down for a moment. "Sorry about him, he gets easily confused. Who were you looking for?"

"Mrs Sandra Hayes," Jenny replied. "She was close friends with my mother, Emily Langford."

"Ah yes, terrible business. I'm afraid you're out of luck if you want to find Sandra."

"Why's that?"

"Because she died three weeks ago."

Jenny's mouth opened but no words came out.

"She had moved in with her daughter and they were renting this place to us. With only our pensions to live on, it's almost impossible to acquire any real estate in the city these days so we took the opportunity to look after this place until such times..."

"What happened to Sandra?" Jenny asked.

"The police are still investigating."

"The police? Why? Did somebody kill her?"

"They don't know, it's just..."

"Just what?"

"She froze to death."

Jenny looked at her confused. "How?"

"Her son-in-law owns a restaurant in Chelsea. They were under the impression that she was meeting an old friend for dinner. After closing time, he locked up as normal and went home but Sandra wasn't there. His wife had received a text message that she was going back to her friend's house after they had eaten and would be staying the night. When the son-in-law's colleague opened up the following morning, they found her frozen to death inside the walk-in freezer at the back of the restaurant."

"Oh my God, that's terrible. She was locked inside overnight."

The woman nodded.

"Who was the friend that Sandra met that night?"

"Nobody knows her real name but the reservation for the meal was made under the name of Frances King."

***

Back in Monolithos, Jim Handanowicz drove up the incline of his driveway towards his villa before rushing inside and locking the doors behind him. He used a rug from the lounge and rolled Ian Bleeker up in it before dragging his body out of the back door and across the patio towards a small vegetable patch on the right side of his back garden. He rushed upstairs and removed a rug from the landing area and repeated the same treatment for Zachary Zhal. Thousands of thoughts flooded his mind as he furiously cleaned the marble tiles of his lounge with bleach and a mop until he was satisfied that all traces of blood had been removed. As he stepped out onto the patio outside, he noticed a red smear of blood had created a ghoulish pattern on the paving slabs. Hosing the patio down with water and scrubbing hard with a brush gave him a sense that he was finally getting things under control. He picked up a petrol can from his garage and doused the two rugs that contained their victims inside with the liquid before striking a match and setting them alight.

Standing on a soaked patio, Jim Handanowicz drank a generous glass of whiskey as the bodies of Ian Bleeker and Zachary Zhal burned in front of him. He looked at the fire burning menacingly and relentlessly. He felt nothing. No guilt. No shame. No emotion. To him, this was just business. He had spent many years evading the attention of many who had crossed his path. He heard sirens in the distance and soon, the telling flash of blue lights illuminated his front garden. As the flames began to recede and turn into ashes, Jim walked down the side of his villa and down towards his front gates. As he opened the gate, a police detective followed closely behind by a male and female officer approached him.

"James William Handanowicz?" the detective asked.

"That's what the birth certificate says," Jim replied.

"Is that meant to be funny?"

"I don't know, is it? Who are you and why are you invading my property."

The detective removed a sheet of paper from his pocket and unfolded it before handing it to Jim. "I'm Detective Aris Sotiropoulous Stathakis, there were gunshots heard coming from your property earlier this evening followed by smoke caused by a significant fire in your garden."

"I was shooting cans and it's not illegal to burn off excess garden waste last time I checked."

"So you won't mind if my officers take a look around."

"Do I have a choice?"

"Not really."

Jim Handanowicz moved aside and allowed the police to enter the villa.

As night gave way to day, Detective Stathakis stood opposite Jim in his lounge. "Mr Handanowicz, my officers have found the partially cremated remains of two men in the vegetable patch of your back garden."

Jim didn't reply.

"James William Handanowicz, I'm arresting you on suspicion of murder. You have the right to remain silent, anything you say can and will be used against you in the court of law."

Jim stood up and stared into the eyes of Detective Stathakis. "Get Blake Langford," he said.

"Who?"

"Blake Langford, Special Branch, London. I will not make any comment until he is here."

"You're not in the place to make demands, do you realise the seriousness of these allegations Mr Handanowicz."

Jim nodded. "Call Blake Langford," he said before walking out of the villa and heading towards the waiting police car outside.

***

A nurse entered room 215 at Kolopsia House and saw Evelyn Handanowicz sitting on the edge of the bed with her back towards her.

"Is everything okay, Evelyn? I've just bought some hot cocoa here for you," she said as she placed a mug on the side table. "Did you have a good evening with your brother?"

Evelyn didn't reply.

The nurse walked around the bed towards her and noticed the gun in her hands. "Maybe I should take that," she said.

Evelyn shook her head. "No, it's all that I have left of home."

"Guns are dangerous Evelyn. Maybe I should put it away until we start shooting cans again."

"Guns aren't dangerous. It's the people who pull the trigger that are the problem."

The nurse looked at her uneasily.

Evelyn placed the gun under her pillow before laying down on the bed. The nurse walked back around towards the door. "You're not planning on using that gun are you Evelyn?"

She didn't respond.

"Do I need to be concerned?" the nurse asked again.

"I murdered two men tonight."

The nurse froze. "What did you say?"

"I just squeezed the trigger and pop, pop, they were gone," Evelyn smiled.

"Evelyn, you know if this is true, it could cause a whole lot of trouble."

"Call Blake Langford."

"Who?"

"Blake Langford, he'll know what to do," she said before closing her eyes and falling asleep.

The nurse watched her for a moment before leaving the room. When she returned to the nurse's station in the hall, she told her colleague what Evelyn had said.

"Evelyn Handanowicz hasn't said a word in four months," her colleague said.

"I know but she told me she has killed two people and she has a gun under her pillow."

"Evelyn has schizophrenia and serious psychological issues. She probably dreams of killing someone every day. That gun is merely a family heirloom. Do you honestly think her brother would take her out for days away if he thought she was dangerous?"

Evelyn's nurse nodded noncommittally.

"Relax, Evelyn Handanowicz is harmless," she replied before walking away.

Chapter Fourteen

A Suitcase With A Secret
Monday 23rd August 1948

Edward Langford left Southward Cottage, his family home overlooking Lepe Beach, just after six o'clock on Monday morning. Peter Hastings was waiting for him in their patrol car and began driving them into the city centre.

"We may have had a development in the case of the man on the beach," Peter said as they began driving down the Lepe Road.

Before he had a chance to continue the conversation, a tall blonde haired man talking to the eldest daughter of Edward's nearest neighbour at Thyme Cottage caught their attention.

"Stop a moment," Edward said before stepping out of the car and walking over towards the gate.

"A bit early for a stroll Frances," Edward commented.

Frances King was walking around the front garden with a young man he didn't recognise. "No strolling this morning Detective. Christopher is doing some gardening for us whilst father recovers from a bad back," Frances smiled. "Is Mrs Langford all right? She seemed rather flustered when she arrived here to pick up the children yesterday."

"Flustered? In what way?"

"Oh, I didn't mean any disrespect Sir, she just seemed to be in a hurry. Like she had been running or something."

"You know Mavis, she often is rushing around doing things at the last minute," Edward replied before turning his attention towards Christopher. "I don't think we've been formally introduced, I'm Edward Langford, I live in Southward Cottage, just up the hill from here."

Christopher walked towards the gate and shook his hand. "I've heard of you Detective Langford. You're a village hero."

"Well, I wouldn't go that far," Edward smiled. "Your accent isn't local..."

"No, I was born in Amsterdam, raised by my grandmother after my parents died during the first war."

"I'm sorry to hear that."

"Don't be, my grandmother was a wonderful woman. She taught me well."

"You'd better not be trying to recruit my gardener Mr Langford!" Frances' father, Arthur, called out from his front door.

"Well our hedge could do with a trim," Edward replied.

"Maybe Christopher could call round and take a look..." Frances suggested.

"Our flower beds and lawn have never looked so good," Arthur added.

"If you wouldn't mind I'd be..." Edward began.

"Of course, I have a couple of jobs to do for the vicar and then I'll call round this afternoon if that suits?" Christopher replied.

Edward nodded. "Perfect, we'll see you then."

Edward returned to the patrol car and Peter continued to drive into the city centre. Frances and Arthur watched them leave before turning towards Christopher.

"You need to be careful what you say to the Langfords," Arthur advised. "His father was a police officer before the war and if they get a hint of anything, they'll be on you like a tonne of bricks."

"I don't understand why people would turn against Christoph, he's done nothing wrong," Frances argued. "If anything, he's helping the community with their gardening, mending Mr Baker's bike, Mrs Holder's mangle and fixing the shelves in Mr Wallis's shop."

"That counts for nothing if they find his passport. You can stay in our barn until you find somewhere else to live but only you. The rest will have to go elsewhere, am I understood?" Arthur asked.

"Understood, thank you Mr King," Christopher replied as he wandered around to the back garden to start tending to the flower beds.

***

Detective Edward Langford stared out of the window of the patrol car as Sergeant Peter Hastings drove them into Southampton City Centre. Christopher's comment about him being a local hero began nagging at Edward's mind. His father Alfred was also a police officer before the war and had helped many of the people of Portsmouth to get justice against those who had suffered at the hands of others. He could cut through the years to the night in 1942 when the bombs rained down on Portsmouth's Naval Base. Although he was too old to be called up for battle, Alfred Langford was heavily involved in motivating the troops until one of the German bombs landed on the building where he was stationed. Edward never had the chance to say goodbye to his father and his mother had died of a heart attack last year. If he could become half the police officer his father was, Edward Langford knew that he would have made him proud.

As Peter Hastings parked the car outside Southampton Railway Station, Edward's mind returned to what Hastings had previously mentioned before their meeting with Christopher.

"What are we doing here?" Edward asked as he stepped out of the car.

Peter Hastings joined him in front of the station. "The train ticket that Officer Wells and the forensic team found on the body of the gent on the beach had a locker number on the back of it."

Edward nodded. "And..."

"That locker number belongs to the cloakroom here at the station. Mr Kenneth Bates was working at the ticket office on Saturday and his boss has arranged for him to meet us here this morning so we can take a look at whatever was stored in the locker."

"Did Mr Bates take a name when our man dropped off his luggage?"

"The name in the book was Mr Smith, Jack Smith."

Edward thought about that for a moment. He recognised the name Jack Smith. He had read over some old paperwork recently about a Jack and Ada Smith who disappeared after a bank robbery in Portsmouth in 1938. They had left a newborn baby behind who had been adopted by a couple near London.

Edward and Peter entered the bustling train station, their eyes scanning the sea of people making their way through the station. Spotting a man with thinning hair and a worn-out suit standing near the cloakroom area, they approached him.

"Are you Mr. Bates?" Edward asked, extending his hand for a handshake.

The man nodded nervously, wiping his palms on his trousers before shaking Edward's hand. "Yes, that's me. Are you the police officers investigating the locker?"

"We are," Peter replied, introducing them both. "We'd like to take a look at what was left in there."

Mr. Bates fumbled through his pockets for a key and handed it to Edward. With a quick nod of gratitude, Edward made his way to the cloakroom whilst Peter stayed with Mr. Bates, engaging him in small talk to put him at ease. As Edward turned the key and unlocked the locker, he felt a rush of anticipation. The door swung open, revealing a worn brown leather suitcase.

Edward lifted the suitcase out of the locker and laid it on a wooden bench. He carefully unfastened the rusty clasps before opening the case. The musty smell of mothballs hit him as he opened it. Inside he found a pair of scissors, a dressing gown, a laundry bag with an unused flannel and soap inside, underpants, slippers, trousers, shirts, toothbrush, handkerchiefs, envelopes, coat hangers, a cigarette lighter, two ties, a shaving brush, a razor, a towel, pencils, scarf and a coat. Nothing unusual at first until Edward took a closer look and noticed that all of the labels and tags had been removed from the clothing. There was nothing to identify who this mysterious Mr Smith was and it seemed as if he had covered his tracks very well.

The lack of progress frustrated Edward and he slammed the lid of the suitcase closed. As he did though, he noticed that the top of the suitcase was lopsided. It felt heavier on the right corner than on the left. He opened it again and ran his hands over the inside of the case. He traced with his fingers what seemed to be the outline of some kind of book or paperwork.

Edward removed his penknife from his pocket and cut the inside covering of the suitcase. Inside, he found a collection of old photographs, letters and newspaper clippings. The photographs revealed a young couple with striking features, Jack and Ada Smith. They were smiling in some pictures, while others captured them in intense discussions or far-off contemplation. Edward studied their faces, feeling an uncanny familiarity that stirred his curiosity. The letters were filled with affectionate words, describing the deep love shared between Jack and Ada. They spoke of dreams, aspirations, and their desire for a better life outside the constraints of society. Edward's eyes widened as he read one particular letter from Ada, describing their plan to flee to America after the bank robbery. Looking back at the young dreams from before the war gave Edward food for thought. The war had left devastation in its wake in so many ways.

The newspaper clippings told the story of the bank robbery in vivid detail, revealing how Jack and Ada had managed to escape authorities despite a nationwide manhunt. The articles praised their cunning and audacity, labelling them as modern-day Robin Hoods. Edward couldn't help but admire their resourcefulness and determination, even if their actions were unlawful. Realising that he was onto something significant, Edward meticulously examined each photograph and scrutinised every word in the letters. As he delved deeper into the contents of the suitcase, a puzzle began to form in his mind. The pieces fit together with uncanny precision, painting a picture of an extraordinary story waiting to be unravelled. If this was indeed the same man who had joined them for luncheon two days ago, it was absolutely extraordinary how he had kept his identity a secret for so long.

It became clear to Edward that Jack and Ada Smith's disappearance wasn't merely a case of fugitives eluding capture; it was a carefully orchestrated vanishing act. Their trail had gone cold, leaving the world to believe they vanished without a trace. But now, with the discovery of this old suitcase, Edward knew that there was much more to this story than met the eye. As he continued to look at the papers, he then found an obituary notice cut out from a newspaper in 1940. Ada May Smith, died 22nd December 1940, aged just 24 years. Edward sighed. All of the hopes and dreams of a young couple just two years before came to an end at the start of the war. As he was about the close the suitcase and take the items back to his office, a yellow official looking form fell out of the bundle and onto the floor.

Being an ex-military man himself, Edward Langford recognised the form immediately. It was the discharge papers for a Mr J Smith, medically discharged on September 30th 1940 after suffering shell-shock from artillery and mortar fire. He was cared for by the red cross in Fareham, Hampshire. This piqued Edward's interest. During the war, his wife Mavis and her friend, the missing Dana Wise, both worked in Fareham's red cross hospital as volunteer nurses helping injured servicemen and those affected by the war to recover. Yet, when Jack Smith visited them on Saturday afternoon, neither of them seemed interested in him or acknowledged knowing him.

Edward pondered that for a moment. Perhaps he was reading too much into it but it was definitely a line of inquiry that he would keep in mind. He placed the paperwork inside the suitcase before closing it and taking it back to the police station for further investigation. Dana's disappearance with her daughter was completely out of character and Edward felt that Jack Smith may have had something to do with it before his death. Whatever happened next, he knew he needed to talk to his wife, Mavis Langford and find out if she remembered anything about Jack Smith from their time together in Fareham.

Chapter Fifteen

All Rhodes Lead To The Langfords
Monday 3rd November 2008

In a two bedroom rundown flat in south-east London, cigarette smoke lingered in the lounge as Tom Gibson looked over some old letters and photos from his past. His mother, Patricia, had kept a diary from his birth in 1970 through to 1987 when she had decided to move to Greece. There had been no warning. No conversations took place. All that was left was a letter telling him that the family home was being repossessed and he had two weeks to find somewhere else to live.

Tom found himself scared and alone at seventeen years old. With no father-figure to look after him, he found a new kind of brotherhood when he joined the Royal Air Force. It became his escape route from the harsh reality of how his life had changed since his mother's disappearance. The training was hard. The days were long. But they made him into the man he was today. Despite everything he had gone through, he still kept this metal box of memories with him. Still searching for the day he could find redemption and take back what he felt was his family's legacy.

"You're up early," Jade called out as she stood in the doorway of the lounge.

"I couldn't sleep," Tom replied as he collected up the diaries, letters and photos and placed them back inside the metal box.

"I met up with an old friend at the Chequered Flag cafe yesterday."

Tom looked over at her as she walked towards him and sat on the opposite end of the sofa.

"She said that you may know where my sister is," Jade continued.

"And who might this friend be?"

"Jenny Langford."

Tom glared at her. "Why were you talking to her?"

"Tell me Tom, where is Andrea? I know she was involved with one of your friends. Is she still alive?"

"She was the last time I saw her."

"What's that supposed to mean?"

"Trust me, your interest in the Langford's is just as great as mine. Andrea got too involved in a Special Branch operation and she's hiding away in the south of France until the heat dies down. Until then, I want you to stay away from Jenny Langford. Is that understood?"

"What hold does she have over you? Whenever her name is mentioned you get all defensive."

"A lot of people don't want to discuss failed relationships from their past."

"No, it's more than that. You and Jenny were over years ago. What are you not telling me?"

"It's complicated."

Jade moved towards him. "If we're going to work together on this, I need to know what you're thinking. If one of us is on the wrong page, we could both end up in trouble."

Tom sighed deeply. "My mother once told me about stories she had been told when she was growing up in foster care in London. There was a rumour that my grandparents robbed a bank in Portsmouth back in 1938. They got away with everything. From what I've found out by doing some research, it could be worth over a million pounds in today's money. She told me that Ernest Hughes, who would have been my great-grandfather, was involved in my mother being given up for adoption."

"So, where do the Langfords fit in?

"Ernest was influenced by a close friend. That friend was Blake's great-grandfather, Alfred Langford. He was the first officer on the scene after my great-grandfather, Ernest Hughes, committed suicide."

"Do you believe he committed suicide?"

Tom shook his head. "Neither did my mother. Whenever she tried to get more details about that time, everyone clammed up. Didn't want to talk about it. They changed the subject."

"Your mother was given up for adoption. How did she know about her biological parents or grandparents? Also, not a lot of people like to talk about suicide."

"It was the talk of the town throughout my mother's childhood. There were always whispers about the girl that Ada and Jack left behind. If Alfred Langford hadn't convinced Joan and Ernest Hughes to give up their granddaughter, my mother, for adoption, then I'm convinced that Ernest wouldn't have died the way he did."

Jade sighed. "What proof do you have of that?"

"None. Just a feeling, deep down inside. Why else would they just give up their granddaughter? Their daughter Ada had just run off with Jack leaving them with a baby to look after. Surely they would have still wanted some kind of connection to Ada through my mother."

"The war was about to start. Maybe they thought she would be safer elsewhere."

Tom shook his head. "My mother felt that it was important enough to look into her past before she left and I'm going to do all that I can to make sure I claim what's rightfully mine."

"This all happened seventy years ago Tom. A lot of water has gone under the bridge since then."

Tom stood up and walked over towards the window to look out at the dawn skyline over London. "Don't you see... The Langfords have always been there. I was never good enough in John Langford's eyes for his precious daughter Jenny. When she was meant to go down for helping a Russian spy, Blake and his father, John Langford, covered it up. When Blake's brother Steven woke up to a house full of murdered students, Blake once again was there to make sure that the charges went away. And now, we find out that their family history isn't so pure after all. When Emily Langford's true identity comes out, Blake will have nowhere to run. Our families are all intertwined whether he likes it or not. That shadow will follow him everywhere. His reputation will be ruined and I will finally claim my birthright and disappear from this drab and dingy city forever."

Jade sighed as she walked back towards her bedroom. "I hope you're right."

As he heard the bedroom door close, Tom opened his laptop and logged into his secure network. Special Branch had seized control of funds tied up in The Crystal network that he had been building but so far, they hadn't found the loophole on the dark web where he had built his own secure application and thousands of users were trading money for crypto-currency. He smiled to himself as the current user profiles stood at four hundred thousand and rising rapidly. Soon, he would have enough money to investigate his family's legacy and this time, he won't let anyone stand in his way. He checked his phone. No messages. Thoughts rushed through his mind. Surely Ian Bleeker and Zachary Zhal, two of his closest allies would have made contact by now. As he logged off of the secure network, a newsflash appeared on his search engine.

GREEK POLICE DISCOVER TWO DEAD BODIES AT THE VILLA OF A WEALTHY BUSINESSMAN ON THE ISLAND OF RHODES

As he read the report, Tom swore under his breath. He had sent Reaper and Zodiac, to trace down and kill two beneficiaries of the stolen money who had emigrated to the Greek islands. He closed the laptop and tossed it onto the sofa in disgust before heading towards the bathroom for a shower. He knew that if the identities of the two dead bodies came out, Blake would not be too far behind to chase up a lead and he needed to be ready.

***

Alison Pearce and Blake Langford landed at Diagoras Airport in Rhodes just after 1pm that afternoon. As they cleared customs and walked through the small and rather basic looking airport, they saw a man with grey hair and moustache, wearing a pale blue shirt and jeans holding up a piece of cardboard with the words Langford/Pearce written on it.

"So much for being discreet," Blake sighed as he wandered over towards him.

The man looked at his phone briefly before turning his attention to Blake and Alison. "Ah, Mr Langford, Miss Pearce, welcome to Rhodes. I am Christos Antonopoulos Papadopoulos but my friends call me Cap. I work with Detective Aris Sotiropoulos Stathakis. He told me to meet you here and take you straight to Kalopsia House in Monolithos. Follow me please."

Blake and Alison followed Cap out of the airport towards a rusting Vauxhall Astra that had seen better days.

"If he's Cap, does that mean we're working with Detective Ass?" Blake whispered.

Alison slapped his chest. "I'd rather call him Cap than his full name. Anyway, it sounds like you're going to be in the firing line when you see your uncle again."

"I can't wait," Blake replied as he climbed into the front passenger seat alongside Cap whilst Alison sat behind them.

As they drove through the busy streets towards Monolithos, Blake noticed a lot of the local people carrying large sacks and placing them on to the backs of trucks at the side of the road.

"What are they carrying in those sacks Cap?" Blake asked.

"Now the tourist season is mostly over, the locals help the farmers to collect all of the olives from the olive trees around the island. They are then used to make olive oil, soap and all kinds of different things."

"It still feels quite warm here compared to a lot of places in Europe," Alison added.

"We have very mild winters. Sometimes we only have a few days of rain each year. Most British people choose to retire here as they are fed up with the weather in London or they want to get legally stoned," Cap smirked.

"Really?" Alison gasped.

"It's one of the few places where you can legally buy cannabis for whatever you need it for. My brother Steven once brought some sun cream back to London without realising that it had cannabis oil in it," Blake explained.

"What happened to him?"

"He gave it up but was fined and had a suspended sentence for it. Luckily Dad was able to smooth things over but he gave him hell for it for years after."

"Just another reason why Faliraki is the party capital of the island," Cap replied. "Here we are."

Cap drove the car up a narrow gravel track which climbed up a steep hill towards a large house overlooking the beach and sea in the distance. As they stepped out of the car, there was an elderly lady sat on a stool with a wooden table in front of her selling locally produced honey for three euros per jar. She was muttering something in Greek that they struggled to hear.

Blake looked over at her and noticed her calloused hands were shaking as if she was shivering yet it was still relatively warm in the afternoon sun. As he was about to approach her, he heard someone call his name. Blake turned to see a tall middle-aged man with short black hair, clean shaven, wearing a white shirt with black trousers and shoes approach him with a young woman with brown hair tied back in a severe clip wearing a similar black and white suit following close behind.

"Blake Langford, so glad to finally meet you. I'm Detective Aris Stathakis, this is my assistant Lauren Prince, she will deal with the admin for us," Aris said as he shook Blake's hand completely ignoring Alison. "We have a most delicate matter inside, Miss Handanowicz is refusing to speak to anyone and we thought a family member may help to encourage her cooperation."

Blake stepped back for a moment. "Well I'm sure with the help of my colleague, Special Branch Agent Alison Pearce, we will try and assist wherever we can."

"Splendid, let's go inside," Aris replied before turning and heading back towards the entrance.

Blake and Alison looked at each other briefly before Lauren Prince walked towards them.

"Careful what you say to Aris, he's a bastard," she said before swiftly following him inside.

"I gathered that already," Alison replied.

***

Dark rain clouds gathered above The New Forest as Samir Khalifa and Joe Knight arrived at East Boldre cemetery. Two black estate cars filled with equipment and four gravediggers arrived soon after them. Joe and Samir led them through the cemetery to the unmarked grave where the body of Andrea Smith had been discovered. The gravediggers quickly moved to get their tools and pulleys into position to begin exhuming the coffin.

"I can think of better places to be on a Monday morning," Joe said as he watched the men begin digging.

"Unfortunately, the job isn't always glamorous," Samir replied.

"Have you sorted out your phone yet?"

"What do you mean?"

"I messaged you this morning to meet for breakfast but it never went through."

Samir removed his phone from his pocket and noticed that it had been turned off. He tried to turn it on but nothing was happening. "Battery's dead, I'll see if I can use the in-car charger."

Joe nodded in acknowledgement before talking to one of the gravediggers. Samir rushed back to the car and plugged his phone into the charger. He started the engine to get some power from the car's battery and his phone lit up. After a couple of minutes, a text message came through. It read:

YOUR FRIENDS ARE GETTING TOO CLOSE.
MEET ME AT THE SECOND ISLAND TREE AT HATCHET
POND, 10AM MONDAY.
Z

Nothing made sense. Samir and Joe had both seen the reports coming out of Greece that Zodiac and Reaper had been murdered. So how was Zodiac still messaging him and arranging to meet? Samir checked his watch. It was already 9.20am. He had forty minutes to get to the pond and find the second island tree. A thousand thoughts flooded his mind. He recognised the phone number and Zodiac always signed off his messages with the letter Z.

During a previous case, Zodiac had threatened to uncover Samir's past indiscretions and cost him his job in Special Branch if he failed to co-operate. After chasing him away from Kings Cross station in London, Samir had him cornered in an alley. He knew he should have taken him down then but he let Zodiac get away. What he couldn't work out though was what did he have to do with this new case? Where was the connection?

Samir checked the time of the message. 7pm last night. That was around the same time that Blake and Alison had been at the funeral home. Around the same time that the report had come through from

Greece about Zodiac and Reaper's deaths. He hated coincidences but couldn't shake the feeling that the two could be linked.

He reversed off of the grass verge and headed back into The New Forest towards Hatchet Pond. He knew he needed answers and the only way he was going to get them was to face it head-on. When he arrived at Hatchet Pond, there were a lot of people out walking their dogs and he noticed three fishermen had taken up their positions on the left side of the lake. He looked around for any obvious signs for the second island tree. It began to rain and several people immediately pulled on a see-through plastic mack over their clothes.

Samir smirked to himself. He always found it amusing that companies could sell what was essentially a rubbish bag with holes cut out of it for the arms and people would actually pay for it.

"Nice weather if you're a duck," a lady's voice called out from behind him.

Samir turned around and saw a grey-haired lady with rosy red cheeks wearing a thick black coat with her hood up to keep the rain off of her hair. She had a dog lead wrapped around her wrist and Samir noticed a Spaniel sniffing the grass a few steps behind her.

"You're not from round here are you?" she asked.

"Is it that obvious?"

"Unless you're fishing or dog walking, no one comes out here in the winter. The summertime, my word, you can barely find a space to lay a picnic blanket down."

"Maybe you could help me," Samir smiled at her.

"If it's money, all I have is a roll of dog poo bags on me..."

"No, no, nothing like that. I'm supposed to be meeting someone here at the second island tree..."

"Ah yes, such a romantic spot for young lovers. You picked a rubbish day for it though..."

"No, no, nothing like that. I was meant to be meeting a man about something."

The lady looked at him sceptically. "Well it takes all kinds in this modern world I guess. It's just over there," she replied, pointing towards a tree that stuck out on what looked like a small island on the right side of the pond.

"Thank you and enjoy the rest of your walk," Samir smiled as he began walking towards the right side of the pond.

The lady watched him for a moment before continuing on her way. Samir checked his watch again. He had ten minutes to get to the island. He began jogging along the muddy gravel path that circled the huge pond. As he jogged around the first set of trees and hedges, he misplaced his foot and sank into a quagmire of mud and stagnant water. He swore loudly as he pulled himself out of the bog. His shoes had filled up with water and his trousers were filthy and soaking wet. He dusted himself off before carrying on.

As Samir approached the tree on the small island, he saw a figure standing under it, their back turned towards him. The rain intensified, creating a curtain of droplets between them.

"Zodiac?" Samir called out, his voice slightly echoing across the water.

The figure turned slowly, revealing a man in his mid-forties with sharp features and steely eyes. He smirked at Samir before speaking. "Samir Khalifa, always so punctual. I knew you wouldn't be able to resist my little invitation."

"You're not Zodiac, who are you? And why drag me out here in this weather?" Samir asked.

The man laughed. "My name is Chris Anderson. Your colleague called in for a friendly chat at the funeral home yesterday afternoon and then suddenly, Zodiac and Reaper are dead. Which begs the question, if you knew Z was dead, why did you come?"

"I don't like loose ends."

"And yet you let Zodiac, a known criminal go when you had him cornered. Interesting..."

"What do you want and what is your connection with Zodiac?"

"Ah, you see, I've stumbled upon something that might interest you. Something that could change everything."

"What could you possibly have that would interest me?"

Chris pulled out a burgundy urn from inside his jacket and handed it over to Samir. "Zac wanted to give it to you himself. Kind of a parting gift from his employer but he asked me to keep hold of it in case anything happened to him and lo and behold..."

"It did," Samir finished for him.

He turned the urn around and noticed a small gold plaque on the front of it. He looked closer at the inscription. It read:

JACK WALTER SMITH
DIED: 21st AUGUST 1948
Aged 41 Years

"When you uncover the secrets of the unmarked grave, you'll realise its significance," Chris said before turning and walking away.

"That's it?" Samir asked.

"That's it for my part. Good day, Mr Khalifa. Don't cock it up."

Samir carefully opened the urn and looked inside. There were the ashes of presumably Jack Walter Smith but amongst them was a gold key and a small business card. He looked at the card. It had a tracing of some kind of map on it. He placed the card and the key inside his back pocket before closing the urn again. The rain was still falling heavily and the tree was no longer giving him much shelter. He closed the urn and held it inside his coat before heading back to the car.

When he sat back inside the car, he placed the urn in the passenger footwell. His phone had several missed calls and messages on it. Samir ignored it and headed back to East Boldre cemetery, determined to figure out the connection between Jack Smith and the unmarked grave.

Chapter Sixteen

Mistaken Identity

Monday 23rd August 1948

On Monday afternoon, Detective Edward Langford arrived home just after 4pm. As he approached the house, he noticed his neighbour's gardener Christopher collecting up the hedge trimmings into a wheelbarrow.

"Ed, come and take a look at this!" Mavis called out.

As Edward walked into the front garden, his son, Fred, kicked a football that flew through the air towards them. Christopher moved forward and headed the ball back in Fred's direction.

"Wow, that was amazing. Do you play football Mister..." Fred called out.

"A little, when I was younger," Christopher replied.

"Be careful with that ball, if you break anything there will be big trouble!" Edward said as he joined them. "Well Arthur wasn't wrong, fabulous job Mister..."

"Fischer, but please call me Chris."

Edward pulled out a wad of notes from his pocket and handed over ten pounds to Chris.

"Thank you so much. Are you sure?" Chris asked.

"You've done a mighty fine job there and I don't mind paying for good work. I'm sure the vicar will be most satisfied too."

"I didn't get to see the vicar..."

"Oh, why was that?"

"The church was locked up and there was no answer from his cottage so I came here to work for Mrs Langford and yourself."

"How peculiar, was Harold okay when you saw him yesterday?" Edward asked, turning his attention to Mavis.

"He was fine. You saw him after I did. Did he seem okay to you?" she asked.

Edward hesitated for a moment. "Yes, he seemed perfectly fine when I saw him," he replied slowly. "But if Christopher here couldn't find him today, that's certainly odd."

Mavis exchanged a worried glance with Edward. "Perhaps we should go check on him ourselves," she suggested. After their discussion yesterday, Mavis knew that the vicar would have had some concerns over her involvement with Dana's disappearance. "I'll stay with the kids, you two can go."

"Yes, let's do that," Edward agreed. He turned to Christopher. "We'll try his cottage again. Maybe we can find him there."

Christopher nodded and the two men set off through the woods.

As they walked, a sense of unease settled over Edward. He couldn't shake the feeling that there was something he was missing. As they arrived at the cottage, he noticed that the front door was slightly ajar. He exchanged a glance with Christopher before cautiously pushing the door open and stepping inside. Christopher followed closely behind.

The interior of the cottage was dimly lit, with a sense of abandonment hanging in the air. Edward's eyes scanned the room, quickly noticing that something was amiss. Books were strewn across the floor, furniture was overturned and there were signs of a struggle. Edward moved further into the cottage, his heart pounding in his chest. He approached the study. The door stood partially open, revealing a scene of chaos within.

The room had been ransacked, papers scattered everywhere and the shelves were emptied. A broken photo frame lay on the floor, its shattered glass reflecting light from a nearby window.

At that moment, they heard a noise from the hall. Both men turned around and saw someone run out the front door. Christopher chased the man into the woodland behind the cottage. Christopher was gaining steadily before he leapt and tackled the man to the ground.

He rolled the man over to face him. "Stefan?" he gasped.

"Christoph?"

"What are you doing?"

"Surviving. The police killed the man on the beach."

They heard footsteps in the distance.

"Go, I'll cover you," Christopher said as he groaned and rolled onto the floor.

Stefan ran into the woodland as Edward caught up with Christopher.

"What happened?" Edward asked.

"Sorry, I tripped."

"Did you see where he went?"

Christopher shook his head. "No, sorry," he gasped.

"Are you okay?"

"Yes, just winded, that's all."

They both walked slowly back towards the cottage. Inside the hallway, Edward found a set of keys with one long black key on it. After the police arrived to check over the house, Edward and Christopher walked up to the church. As they arrived, they noticed a man sitting next to the entrance dressed in black shorts and a black t-shirt.

He looked up at them as they approached. "Christoph?" he called out.

"I'm Christopher, do I know you?" Christopher asked.

"What do you mean? We were at the..."

"I'm sorry, I don't know who you are," Christopher interrupted.

At that moment, Officer George Wells arrived. "Sorry I'm late Max, here, on your way," he said as he handed the man five pounds.

Max looked at the three of them before walking away. Edward and Christopher exchanged a puzzled look, unsure of what just transpired. Officer Wells approached them with a hint of embarrassment on his face.

"Sorry about that," he said, scratching his head. "Max is a bit confused lately. Claims to know people he's never met before. Helped the vicar out a few times with odd jobs and such."

Edward narrowed his eyes at Officer Wells. "Is this related to the vicar's disappearance?"

The officer hesitated for a moment, then sighed. "I can't say for certain, it was rumoured that the vicar had been spending a lot of time with the young lad for, shall we say, unorthodox purposes, but our investigations proved fruitless. Who knows, there's a suspicion that it might be some sort of memory loss or confusion going around in the village. Everyone seems rather strange at the moment. We're investigating it, but it's been quite baffling so far."

"We just chased someone from the vicar's cottage, could it be connected?" Edward asked.

Officer Wells nodded. "It's possible. We don't have all the answers yet, but we're looking into every lead we can find."

"Why did he claim to know me?" Christopher asked.

Officer Wells looked at Christopher. "Like I said, he is a confused young man," he replied.

Edward glanced at the black key he found at the vicar's cottage. He slid the key into the lock and turned it. The lock clunked as it unlocked before Edward twisted the handle and allowed the door to creak open. A strong musty smell hung in the air as they entered. Edward and Christopher cautiously stepped into the dimly lit church, their footsteps echoing through the empty pews. Officer Wells followed closely behind them. The air inside was heavy with silence, broken only by the occasional scurrying of small creatures or the distant rustle of wind outside. As they made their way further into the church, Edward's eyes were drawn to a flickering candle at the front altar. It cast dancing shadows upon the walls, creating an eerie ambiance that made his skin prickle.

"Hello?" Edward called out tentatively, his voice swallowed by the vastness of the space. There was no response, only a faint echo that bounced back to him.

As they moved towards the vestry, Christopher noticed scratch marks on the floor leading towards the door. He nudged Edward and pointed to the floor. Edward nodded before cautiously approaching the vestry door. He carefully turned the handle and opened the door.

All three of them gasped when they looked inside. A man dressed in the vicar's robes was sitting in a chair with a metal candlestick holder impaled into his chest. As they looked closer, they could see burn marks where the lighted candles had singed the clothes as they entered the man's body. There was a hood covering the man's face. Edward moved closer and lifted the hood expecting to see the face of Harold Partridge but as he revealed the face, the vacant eyes staring back at him were of a man he had never met before.

Christopher struggled to stop himself from vomiting and rushed out of the church. Edward placed the hood back over the face of the victim.

"Officer Wells, please call the station and ask Sergeant Hastings and the forensic teams to get here as soon as possible," Edward said as he stepped away from the body.

"Yes Sir. Do you know who he is?" Officer Wells asked.

Edward looked down and noticed a significant amount of blood in the groin area of the body as well as the chest. "No, I've never seen him before," he sighed. "Do you think the rumours were true about Harry and the young lad?"

"Nobody could be certain and no complaints were made. He was just acting rather odd."

Edward thought about that. Was this murder meant for Harold Partridge and if so, had the killer murdered the wrong person? "We need to find Harry as soon as possible."

Officer Wells nodded and rushed away to find a telephone. Edward walked back through the church and out of the main entrance. He looked around at the empty cemetery but there was no sign of Christopher.

One hour later, Sergeant Phillip Hastings and the forensics team arrived at the church. Officer Wells and Edward told them what had happened earlier and how the body was discovered. After his colleagues had taken over, Edward Langford began walking away from the church and back through the village towards Lepe Road. Christopher hadn't returned since the gruesome discovery had been made and it had raised a suspicion in Edward's mind. A lot of people struggled with the sight of a dead body but to run away from a police investigation completely made him question whether it was just fear or something more.

Guiding his way through the country roads by torchlight, Edward made his way to Thyme Cottage, his neighbour's house. He walked up the main path and knocked on the door. He heard footsteps approaching followed by the sound of several bolts unlocking. Eventually, the door opened ajar allowing a slither of light to escape onto the porch.

"Yes?" Arthur answered.

"Arthur? It's me, Edward."

"What are you doing calling round this late?"

"I was concerned about young Christopher and wondered if you had seen him?"

"No, haven't seen him since he went to your place and trimmed your hedge. I hope you paid him well. He does a marvellous job."

"Of course I paid him," Edward sighed. "So, you haven't seen him?"

"No, not since lunchtime."

"Okay, thanks anyway. My apologies for disturbing you."

Arthur closed the door shrouding the porch in darkness once more. Edward turned on his torch once again before continuing on his way home. He still had some nagging questions in his mind from earlier that he wanted to speak to his wife, Mavis, about. He had a suspicion that she knew more about this, Mr Smith, who had visited them yesterday than she was telling him. When he arrived home, the whole house was in darkness.

Edward let himself inside the house as quietly as he could. He made his way upstairs and peered inside the bedrooms. Everyone was sleeping. He knew he needed answers but they would have to wait until morning. He got himself changed in the dark before stumbling into bed. Mavis stirred momentarily before turning over and going back to sleep.

Edward stared up at the ceiling. Thoughts swirling in his mind. Too many weird things were happening and he needed to find some answers and fast. He eventually drifted off, hoping that he would have a clearer focus in the morning.

***

A black Ford Anglia crunched across a gravel courtyard near Portsmouth Naval Base just after midnight. A man stepped out of the driver's seat before springing the seat forwards to allow Reverend Harold Partridge to exit from the back seat.

"Where are we?" Harold asked as he looked up at a tall stone building illuminated only by the light of the moon.

"You will be safe here," the driver said before leading Harold towards the front door.

The driver rang the doorbell which chimed like an old church bell echoing around the courtyard. A few moments later, the front door opened and a nun stood in the doorway.

"Harold Partridge," the driver said.

The nun stepped aside allowing them both to enter. The main hall was illuminated with candles placed in holders every few metres. Harold looked up and noticed three levels of accommodation above them.

"I'm sister Mary Chamberlain," the nun said as she led them further inside the building. "You will be under our protection until it is safe to return to your parish."

"Safe? What do you mean, safe? I haven't done anything," Harold protested.

Sister Mary raised her eyebrows. "We all know that is not true don't we, Harold."

Harold bowed his head. "He was just some company. Oh Lord, what have I done?"

"That will be all Sidney," she replied.

The driver turned and left as Sister Mary led Harold towards a room on the ground floor of the building. She stopped outside room twenty-three and handed him a key.

"Am I a prisoner here?" Harold asked.

"You can take walks in the grounds and interact with others in a similar position to you here. We do have children living in this facility so be mindful of that wherever you go. I shall see you in the morning. Good night, Mr Partridge," she said before walking away.

Harold watched her leave and looked at the door of his room. He placed the key into the lock and turned it. The door creaked open. Inside was a single bed, a bedside table with a lighted candle illuminating the room. Next to it was a small glass with a jug of water beside it. To the left of the room was a bathroom which had a toilet, a small sink and a bathtub inside it.

Harold closed the door behind him and sat on the edge of the bed reflecting on what had happened in the past twelve hours. Mavis Langford's confession, the visit of Detective Edward Langford and

Sergeant Phillip Hastings, Officer Wells' warning to stop associating with the three young men who had recently arrived in the village and then this. Norman Whitehouse had persuaded him to go for a drive with his friend Sidney. After a drive through Portsmouth city centre, Norman had been dropped off at The Kings Hat and Sidney continued on to wherever this place was and now it seemed as if he was to be a prisoner in this concrete tomb. He walked over towards the window and found a postcard on the window sill. He brought it over towards the candlelight. It was a black coloured card with a gold crucifix on it. As he turned the card over, it read:

ST. ANNE'S CONVENT, PORTSMOUTH

Chapter Seventeen

Evelyn's Secret
Monday 3rd November 2008

Blake Langford stood outside room number 215 in Kalopsia House in Monolithos. As he stepped inside, he saw an elderly lady sitting in an armchair looking out at the garden with a jungle of trees leading down towards the beach and sea in the distance. Aris, Lauren and Alison waited in the doorway as Blake approached her. He noticed a wooden stool in the far corner of the room. He picked it up and placed it near to where the lady was sitting before sitting on it next to her.

For a moment, she ignored his presence before slowly turning her gaze towards him. Blake felt a pang of adrenaline running through him and his heart skipped a beat as he looked into her eyes. He felt as if his late mother was suddenly staring back at him and it caught him off-guard.

She nodded as if reading his mind before turning her attention back towards the window. Blake took a couple of deep breaths to compose himself before speaking.

"You don't know me and unfortunately, I never had the opportunity to get to know you," Blake spoke softly, barely above a whisper.

She looked directly at him but still never spoke a word.

"I am Emily Handanowicz's son and I believe your life may be in danger since her death four months ago," he explained.

"Just you," she said before turning back towards the window.

Blake stood up and walked over towards the door. "She'll only speak to me alone."

"That's not going to happen, I'm investigating a double murder here..." Aris protested.

"The nurse who looks after her has said that she hasn't spoken to anyone other than her in four months. If Blake can get her to open up and tell us what's going on, let him talk to her," Lauren replied.

Aris glared at her before turning back to Blake. "All right but I want a full report..."

"You'll get one," Alison interrupted.

Blake smiled at her before closing the door on them and returning to the stool next to the elderly lady.

She continued to look out of the window. "What day is it today?" she asked.

"It's Monday the third of November," Blake replied.

She lifted a necklace from underneath her jumper which had a gold ring attached to it. "Do you know it's thirty-two years today since Frederick Langford asked me to marry him?"

Blake gasped. Frederick Langford was his father's brother. He had died in 1977 shortly after his parents were married but he never knew the full details about his Uncle Fred's relationship with Evelyn. "I'm sorry, I wasn't aware of that," he admitted.

"Not many people were. It lives on now only in my memory. You have your mother's eyes."

"Aunt Evelyn, I'm sorry that things turned out the way that they have. Until recently, I never knew that you were here. When Mum died four months ago, she left a photograph in a safe deposit box in London. I think it holds the key to a family secret. One that those men came after you for."

Evelyn nodded. "Emily knew everything. I was very much ignorant to what our parents were up to. All I knew was that I had been cruelly tricked out of being with the love of my life. Fred was my soulmate. He was everything to me. When I was admitted here in 1984, my brother, James, made sure that I had everything that I needed but he refused to supply the one thing I yearned for, the truth. I was kept in the dark for so long until a distant cousin came to see me."

"Who was it?"

"Ada and Jack Smith's daughter, Patricia. She came here in 1987 and told me everything. As usual, these family reunions never last and we lost touch but suddenly, everything began to make sense."

Blake took a moment to take in what Evelyn had told him. "When mum's will was read, we discovered that after her estate was split between myself, my brother and my sister, there was something left called Harvey Matchbox Twenty-Five. This was left to you, Victor Wise and James Handanowicz. What is Harvey Matchbox Twenty-Five?"

"Jack Smith's legacy," Evelyn replied.

"Who is Jack Smith?"

"Did you know on January 6th, it will be twenty-nine years since they took me away?"

"Away from where?"

"Not now Jim, I'm tired."

"Aunt Evelyn, who is Jack Smith?"

"Jack Smith? Ah, yes, Jack Smith was your grandfather. Mine, Emily's and Victor's father. Your grandmother began a wheel of deception during the war. I guess someone wants to take back what's rightfully ours."

Blake shifted in his stool as he noticed a gun hidden underneath Evelyn's jumper.

"I'm not here to take anything from you. I just want to help. I need to understand what is going on here."

"That's what that bastard said at Jim's house right before I put a bullet through his head. He never saw it coming. Zodiac, he called himself, pah! Who really believes all that bullshit!"

"You killed him, not Jim."

"Of course I did. No one suspects a mental old hag do they."

"How? I thought you never left this place."

"I'm not a prisoner. Back in 1989, I remember Victor came with Anne and we sat in the garden drinking and reminiscing. That was twenty-one years ago last July. That was the last time I saw my brother."

"How did you get to Uncle Jim's Villa?"

"He took me there yesterday. After it all happened, he brought me back here and left. Then that dosey copper started poking his nose into my affairs and I hear that Jim's been arrested."

"Give me the gun and I promise I will take care of everything."

"How do I know I can trust you? The last Langford I trusted ended up dead."

"Because I am your twin-sister's son. I may be half Langford but I am also a Handanowicz or Wise or Smith, whatever you call yourself. I am half of your blood line. You trusted Emily to do the right thing. Even after her death, she sent me a clue to figure out the truth. Let me do that and tidy up this mess, not just for me but for you, for Uncle Jim, for Mum's memory."

Evelyn reluctantly removed the gun from under her jumper and handed it to Blake. "Now what?" she asked.

"I need to help Uncle Jim but I need to know why Zodiac and Reaper came after you. What is their connection? Is it me or does it involve Tom Gibson?"

"How do you know Tom Gibson?"

"He came up in a previous case."

"Is that all?"

"Yes."

"You're a terrible liar."

"Okay, he used to be in a relationship with my sister. We recently stopped him from trafficking young women and weapons out of London."

"Why did they break-up?"

"He faked his own death. He used my sister to enable a Russian task force to kill his entire regiment in Afghanistan."

"Looking out for himself. Like father, like son."

"What do you mean?"

"It was the 3rd of September 1938 when Jack Smith and his wife Ada abandoned their child. The bank robbery was more important to him than the life of his daughter who then spent most of her childhood being passed around foster parents and orphanages during the war."

Blake stared at her in shock. "How many children did Jack Smith have?"

"Six that I know of."

"Did Mum know?"

Evelyn nodded. "Emily knew. We all did. Our mother Dana admitted it all before she died. William Handanowicz was not your biological grandfather, Jack Smith was."

Blake sat there struggling to process what Evelyn was telling him. There was a good chance that the man in the photograph that his mother had put in that safe deposit box was actually Jack Smith, his grandfather.

"So where does Tom Gibson fit into all of this?" he finally asked.

"His mother was Patricia Smith. The child that Ada and Jack gave up in 1938. The same Patricia Smith that came to see me in 1987."

"Dad knew..."

Evelyn didn't reply.

"That's why he never wanted Jenny and Tom together. It had nothing to do with him being in the military. Tom and Jenny were cousins!"

Evelyn nodded. "If you've recently crossed swords with Tom, you've kicked the hornet's nest. Emily's will uncovering heirs to Jack's money will create a storm that nobody is going to come out of unscathed."

"I spoke to Victor Wise yesterday. He told me that he wanted no part of the will. If Tom feels like there is an inheritance for him, he'll try and remove anyone who opposes him for it."

"Which is why I had the gun. I knew they would come sooner or later. Jim and I are the final two pieces of the puzzle. I may have been locked up in this place for nearly thirty years but my memory is as sharp as a packet of pins. They are coming for the money and they won't stop until they find it."

"Something that happened to a baby girl seventy years ago has triggered a fight for inheritance today..." Blake shook his head in disbelief. "Don't worry, I'll make sure he gets what's coming for him."

Evelyn glared at him. "Don't be a fool Blake."

It was the first time that she had said his name ever since he walked into the room. "You knew I was coming didn't you. You knew I wouldn't let this go."

"You're my sister's son. You have that fighting spirit. What Jack Smith did was wrong and many people have died chasing the money, the legend of it. All I'm saying is don't be an idiot. We don't need any more family in the graveyard yet."

Blake handed her back the gun. She looked at him warily.

"I will make sure that Tom can't hurt you and I'll smooth things over with Uncle Jim. He came out here in 1984 for a reason and I think that reason was to make sure that you were okay. Now I'm making that same promise. Until then, look after yourself and don't trust anyone."

"You too. If Jim asks about me, tell him to check the right foot."

Blake looked at her confused for a moment.

"He'll know what you mean," she reassured him. "Good luck."

Blake smiled before leaving the room. Finally things were beginning to form in his mind. He struggled to believe how Jack

Smith had fathered six children around the time of the second world war. He had four names, Patricia, Victor, Evelyn and Emily. Blake had a feeling that the identities of the final two could help him piece the rest of the puzzle together. For now, he needed to find out where Jim Handanowicz was being held and fight for his release. He knew he needed to tread carefully. Jim had betrayed the Langfords in the past but this time, Blake was sure that he held the key to figuring out Emily Langford's will.

***

Back in the UK at East Boldre Cemetery in the New Forest, Jenny Langford and Jade Smith joined Special Branch agents, Samir Khalifa and Joe Knight as a coffin was lifted up by a small crane out of the unmarked grave.

"What happened to your trousers?" Joe asked.

"I got splashed by a passing car," Samir lied.

"Must've been quite a puddle."

"It was," Samir replied before approaching the coffin.

"After so long, I'd have thought that the coffin would have disintegrated by now," Jenny said.

Jade nodded, her eyes fixed on the old wooden coffin. "It's a miracle it's still intact," her voice barely above a whisper.

The agents carefully opened the lid, revealing the skeletal remains inside. Jenny felt a chill run through her as she gazed down at the bones. A nagging doubt in her mind made her feel uneasy about what was about to be uncovered. She couldn't help but wonder who was buried here and what was their connection to her family, if any? Or was it someone else entirely? The mystery was like a dark cloud hanging over them and now they could hopefully uncover the truth.

Samir Khalifa had previously worked with forensics teams and he carefully examined the bones, his gloved hands prodding and inspecting each fragment. After what felt like an eternity, he finally spoke up. "These remains appear to be that of a woman in her late sixties, perhaps early seventies," he said, his voice steady.

Joe Knight frowned. "Something doesn't add up here."

Jenny noticed a metal plaque had fallen off of the side of the coffin as they removed it from the grave. She knelt down and picked it up. When she read the name inscribed on it, she felt a shiver run down her spine. "Oh my God!" she gasped.

Everyone turned to look at her as she turned the plaque towards them.

"It's my grandmother, Dana Sylvia Handanowicz," she said.

The revelation stunned everyone. Jenny's grandmother, Dana Handanowicz, buried in an unmarked grave where Andrea Smith's body was discovered. How could this have happened and the Langford family knew nothing about it? Questions began to swirl in Jenny's mind. Why would her own family go to such lengths to hide the truth? How did her grandmother's remains end up here?

"Could that plaque have been planted in the grave?" Jade asked.

Joe looked at the coffin lid. "No, it was originally screwed on the coffin or at least an identical plaque was before it came loose over time and fell off."

Samir carefully examined the plaque. "This changes everything," he muttered under his breath. "We need to find out why Dana Handanowicz's body was hidden here without any official records. We'll take the body back to the lab and check the dental records just to be sure but if it is Dana, we need to find out the connection."

"Do you think Tom Gibson had something to do with this? Could he have orchestrated this entire cover-up?" Jenny asked.

Samir nodded. "It's certainly a possibility he was either involved or knew who was. Tom is desperate for the inheritance and we know he'll stop at nothing to get it. But we can't jump to any conclusions just yet."

Jenny clenched her fists in anger and frustration. "We can't let him get away with this!"

Joe placed a comforting hand on her shoulder. "Don't worry, we won't rest until we uncover the truth and find who's responsible."

"And what about Blake?"

"I just hope he's finding out the answers he needs in Rhodes."

Samir looked at the remains once more before closing the lid of the coffin. He had seen many dead bodies during his career but it never became any easier. "We need to take these bones back for further analysis," he said. "I'll get our chief of forensics, Kevin McCoy, to take a look. Maybe there's something more we can learn from them."

As they prepared to leave the cemetery, Jenny's mind raced with questions. Why would her grandmother be buried in an unmarked grave after the rest of the family had believed that both her and her husband, William, had been cremated? Nothing made sense anymore. And what secrets did Dana Handanowicz hold that someone was willing to kill for? And not only kill but also place the victim in the grave they knew potentially held secrets to the past. She knew that finding answers would not be easy and she knew that she couldn't completely trust Jade, but she was prepared to do whatever it took to uncover the truth. As they arrived back at the car, Joe Knight called after them. Jenny and Jade both turned to face him.

"Can you both join me at the mortuary for the identification?" Joe asked.

"What identification?" Jade asked. "We've already seen the corpse."

Joe looked at Jenny who turned to face Jade. "The reason Special Branch got a court order for this grave to be dug up was because a young woman had been buried alive in it," Jenny explained.

"The missing woman on the news, oh my God! Why didn't you tell me? Wait, why do we have to go and identify her?" Jade asked.

Jenny bowed her head.

"There is a chance that she may be your sister, Andrea," Joe replied.

The colour drained from Jade's face. "No, no, you're wrong. She's in France."

"If you could come with us then we will know for certain," Joe insisted.

"You knew didn't you!" Jade snapped.

Jenny nodded.

"Why didn't you tell me?"

"I tried but you didn't want to listen. At least now we can be sure either way. It's only a possibility at the moment."

"Bullshit! You led me here under false pretences!"

Jenny didn't reply.

Jade ran her fingers through her hair in frustration. "Hang on, I need to make a call," she replied as she walked away from them.

She scrolled through her phone to find Tom's number. It went straight to voicemail.

"If my sister is dead then you are too!" she said before cutting off the call.

She turned back towards Joe and Jenny who were standing by the car waiting.

"I honestly thought I could trust you!" Jade snapped. "What am I doing here? This is madness!"

"We don't know for definite that it is her," Jenny replied.

"Have you seen her?"

Jenny shook her head.

"Please Miss Smith, come with me and we can hopefully answer all of your questions there," Joe replied.

Reluctantly, she climbed into the back of Joe's car. Jenny followed them in her car away from the cemetery and along the single-track forest roads towards the mortuary. Jenny knew that when Jade discovered Andrea's fate, things would blow up very quickly. She just hoped that Tom wasn't the one who put Andrea in the grave but she had a nagging doubt that he was.

Chapter Eighteen

A Letter From The Dead

Tuesday 24th August 1948

Edward Langford was awake early on Tuesday morning and headed down towards Norman Whitehouse's cafe on Calshot Beach. Something was bothering him ever since his visit on Sunday evening. He needed to take a closer look at the cafe before trying to piece together Jack Smith's final few hours. He parked his car next to a brown Austin before heading down onto the beach. As he arrived, he was surprised to find Officer Wells already there supervising a group of men who were removing the remaining fixtures and fittings from inside the cafe.

"Good morning George," Edward called out as he approached.

Officer Wells turned around to face him. "Oh, hello Sir, I didn't expect to see you down here today."

"I always find that an early morning walk helps me focus on things a little better. What brings you down here? Aren't you supposed to be following up on the postmortem of Jack Smith?"

"Officer Jones is taking care of that. Ol' Norman Whitehouse called me up late last night, he's been caught up with some business in Portsmouth so he gave me the keys to let the lads in this morning to empty the cafe out."

"I never knew you and Whitehouse were that close."

"We're not. Just doing my bit for the community, Sir."

"Would you mind if I had another look inside?"

"No, no, of course not. I'll join you," Officer Wells stammered as he led him towards the entrance.

"So who is taking the place over from Whitehouse?"

"Don't really know, some guy called William Handanowicz. He works at the City Bank in Southampton. Some kind of genius with investments or something like that."

"If he's working in the city, why does he want to buy some old cafe out here?" Edward asked.

"Who knows? He made Norman an offer he couldn't refuse so he sold it."

As they entered the cafe, Edward watched as the men worked methodically removing the remaining tables, benches and work surfaces from the cafe. One of the men lifted up a bench and carried it on his shoulder towards the exit. He had short brown hair and wore a beige buttoned-up shirt with matching trousers that looked as though they had mud or dirt splattered across one of the legs.

"Excuse me, do I know you?" Edward asked the man.

He nervously looked at Officer Wells before turning back to Edward. "No, no, I'm from out of town."

"Where out of town?"

"Tooton," he replied.

"Tooton, not Totton?"

He didn't reply.

"What's your name?"

"Steven."

"Steven what?"

"Steven Thomas."

Edward smiled. "Sorry, my mistake. You reminded me of someone I used to know. On your way."

Steven quickly continued on his way out of the door.

Edward turned back to face Officer Wells. "Do you know any of these guys?"

"No, the new owner sent them in. Why?"

"That guy I just spoke to looks a lot like the guy Christopher and I chased out of Harold Partridge's house yesterday."

"Are you sure? Did you get a good look at him?"

"No, it all happened so fast. I need to find Christopher. He would recognise him."

"Christopher, is he the gardener?" Officer Wells asked.

"Yes, do you know where he lives?"

"No, sorry. My rhododendrons need some pruning though so if you find him, send him my way."

Edward stepped outside with Officer Wells close behind him. "If you hear anything from Norman Whitehouse or if this, William Handanowicz, makes an appearance, will you let me know."

"Of course, good luck with the case," Officer Wells replied as he watched him leave.

Edward Langford looked all around the beach and the field that led towards the woodland in the distance as he left but there was no sign of the man who called himself Steven. He was about to turn back towards his car when he noticed something black on the road. He walked over and picked it up. It was a man's wallet. As he opened it up, he found some banknotes, coins and a membership card for 101 Casino in Portsmouth. What really intrigued Edward though, was hidden amongst the banknotes. As he removed them from the wallet, he found a military discharge paper folded up inside. It confirmed that the owner of the wallet was Stefan Thomas Weber, who was recently discharged from the German Armed Forces.

***

Mavis Langford was hanging some washing out on the clothesline when the postman arrived.

"Good morning Mrs Langford!" he called out.

"Good morning Terrance! If it's bills you can keep it!" she replied as he handed her several letters.

"If I had a shilling every time I'd heard that..."

"You'd never have to work again, I know. What's new?"

"Nothing much. Shame about Mrs Wise's house down the road..."

"I know, it's so out of character for her to just disappear like that."

"Are the police any closer to discovering where she went?"

"Not as far as I know but Ed doesn't tell me anything."

"What about that man on the beach?" Terrance asked.

"What about him?"

"Well he turned up dead didn't he."

"Oh, yes, yes, he did."

"Did you know him?"

"No. Well, not really. Oh, listen to that, the kettle's on, must dash," Mavis replied before rushing back inside the house.

Terrance watched her as she rushed back inside before continuing on his way. When she was inside, she quickly sorted through the letters until she came to an envelope with handwriting that she recognised.

"No, it can't be," she said to herself.

"We're off to the beach!" Fred said as he rushed past with fishing nets and buckets followed by John carrying a bowl of crabs.

"Don't go too far, remember Mary has her dance class this evening," Mavis called out.

"How could we forget..." John sighed before heading out of the back door.

Mavis sat on the chair and opened the letter. As she read it, tears fell from her cheeks down onto the envelope in her lap. It was from Dana. Her and Edith had left during the night and fled to Portsmouth where they had been looked after in a convent. She explained about her affair with Jack Smith when she was caring for him during the war. The son that she gave birth to, named Victor, who she then had to give away to the nuns to look after and how she hoped to be reunited with him once more. After their meeting on the beach on Saturday afternoon, Jack had told her that it was no longer safe to stay in the village and had given her two gold bars, worth over three hundred pounds each, to help her start a new life.

Mavis sat in stunned silence, the letter clutched tightly in her hand. Her mind raced with a whirlwind of emotions as she tried to process the shocking revelations from Dana's confession. The familiar sounds of her home faded into the background as she delved deep into the memories of the past.

She remembered the war vividly, the uncertainty that shrouded their lives and how Dana's kindness had touched so many hearts in the village. But this revelation of betrayal and clandestine love shattered the image she held of her dear friend. The weight of secrets buried for years now bore down heavily on Mavis's shoulders.

Every time she looked into the eyes of her twins, Mary and Frederick, she saw Jack staring back at her. Just like he had done on the beach only a few days ago. How could she tell her friend, the man who gave her her son, Victor, was also the father of Mary and Frederick. It had been a stupid fling. A one night stand. Edward had been working nights for over a month and he was just some company for her. She never expected to see him again, let alone, care for him during the war and now the story of his relationship with Dana, her best friend, cut her anew.

She knew if Edward ever discovered this secret that she held, their marriage would be over and what then? What about the children and the family home they had built up over the years. All gone due to one moment of weakness. She folded up the letter and wandered upstairs into the bedroom. There was a loose floorboard in the corner next to the ottoman. She removed it and placed the letter and its envelope under the floorboard before replacing it once again.

"Hello!" a voice called out from downstairs.

The shout startled Mavis. She stood up quickly and hit her head on the side of the bedpost. Cursing quietly to herself, she wandered back downstairs.

"Hello?" the voice called out again.

"Hello Christopher," Mavis replied as she walked down the stairs. "Sorry for taking so long, I had to spend a penny."

Christopher looked at her confused.

"Use the toilet," she elaborated.

"Oh, right, okay, sorry."

"What brings you here this morning? Is everything okay?"

"I was looking for Mr Langford, is he home?"

"No, he went out early this morning and hasn't been back yet."

"Oh, okay. Maybe I'll call back later."

"Is something wrong? Anything that I can help with?"

"No. It's just... After seeing the vicar in the church yesterday, I thought that I should mention that I often saw him and a young man visiting the institute just outside the village. There may be a connection between them."

"The vicar visits many of us regularly to spread the word of God, that's not unusual. Did you ask him who the young man was when you saw him yesterday?"

"I couldn't."

"Why?"

"Because he was dead."

Mavis gasped as the front door opened and Edward Langford entered. "Did you know and you didn't tell me?" she asked.

"Know what?" Edward replied.

"The vicar is dead."

Edward gave Christopher a stern look. "You were asleep when I arrived home last night and I needed to follow up on an investigation at first light so when did I have the chance to tell you anything?"

"Is it true?"

"There was a murder at the church last night but it wasn't Harold Partridge."

Both of them looked at Edward.

"It was someone else who was locked in and murdered in the vestry. Harold's disappeared and I found this by the beach this morning after I scared away someone at Norman Whitehouse's cafe."

Edward dropped the wallet on the kitchen table. Christopher felt a shiver run through him. He knew who the wallet belonged to but tried not to let it show.

"Where did you go yesterday after you ran out of the church?" Edward asked.

"I went home. Sorry, I'm not very good in those situations. After what I saw, I had to get away. I'm not used to seeing dead bodies like that," Christopher replied.

"And where is home? Nobody in the village seems to know where you live."

"I'm staying at the institute about three miles from here. Just until I can earn enough money to buy a home of my own."

"Why all the questions Ed? Surely you can't suspect Christopher of being involved in all of this," Mavis replied.

"The man who dropped this wallet this morning whilst running away from the cafe on Calshot Beach looked very much like the man who managed to get away from us in the woods yesterday. Do you think you could recognise him again?"

"I didn't get a clear look at him. I was running through the woods and caught my foot on a tree stump. I fell and winded myself and he got away. You saw that because you were behind me."

"I saw the guy disappear into the woods whilst you were on the ground but I didn't see you fall. Where did you say you were from again?"

"Amsterdam in the Netherlands."

"And how did you end up here?"

"I came here after the war to find work."

"Do you have your papers?"

"Not with me, why?"

"Where are they?"

"Back at the institute. Have I done something wrong?" Christopher asked.

"Ed, what's going on? Christopher came here today to tell you about the vicar visiting a young man at the institute," Mavis replied.

Edward held open the discharge papers he had found inside the wallet. "Discharge papers for Stefan Thomas Weber from Dusseldorf, Germany. Either someone is housing the enemy or he was one of the squatters in the cafe where Jack Smith's body was found."

Mavis froze. How did Edward discover Jack's real identity so fast? "Who's Jack Smith?" she asked nervously.

"The gent that we were meant to believe was Vincent Williams. The man who shared luncheon with us at the weekend and who old Harold Partridge saw with Dana Wise on the evening before she disappeared who then turned up dead on the beach!" Edward replied.

"Did she have a daughter with her?" Christopher asked.

"Yes, why?" Edward asked.

"Because I saw a man in a brown suit lead a woman and her daughter to a car late on Saturday night. He handed over a lot of money to the driver and then they drove off."

"Where was this?"

"Outside the house that burnt down. Well, it was still okay when they left."

"And where did the man in the suit go after they drove away?"

"He walked back towards the house."

"Was he alone?"

"He was and then a car arrived. An Austin, I think it was."

"Did you see who got out of the car?"

"No, I wasn't paying much attention. I didn't even think about it until Frances, sorry, Miss King, told me about the house fire."

"What about the car?"

"What do you mean?"

"What colour was it? Anything unusual about it?"

"How's he meant to remember that? There's hardly any streetlights down there," Mavis interrupted.

Edward glared at her.

"I think it was brown or black but it was very dark. I only had my torch to light the way."

A loud knocking at the front door interrupted their conversation. Edward walked over and answered it. As he opened the door, they saw their neighbour, Frances King, holding a brown envelope.

"Ah, Frances, we were just talking about you," Edward said.

"Nothing bad I hope. Chris, I've been looking for you. Is there any chance you could help with my bush later, it needs trimming?"

"I'll call round in a while after I've finished helping Mr and Mrs Langford," Christopher replied.

"What brings you here dear?" Mavis asked.

"Oh, Terrance delivered this to the wrong house. It's addressed to you Mrs Langford. I don't know what's gotten into him lately. How difficult is it to put some letters in a mailbox or post them through the right doors?" Frances sighed.

Edward took the letter from her. "Well, thank you for delivering it to us Miss King, I'm sure you have a busy day ahead so run along now."

Frances looked at Mavis and Christopher for some support. Finding none, she swiftly turned and walked away as Edward closed the door behind her.

"That was rather rude," Mavis said.

"She'll live," Edward replied, looking at the envelope. "Since when have you been using the CityBank in Southampton? Have you been hiding money away from me?"

"No! I don't know anything about CityBank," Mavis snapped as she snatched the letter out of Edward's hand and opened it.

She removed the letter from the envelope and read it. On CityBank headed paper, it was a statement of earnings from a gold depository in the bank which was opened in 1940. It showed the measurement of four pounds and four ounces of gold deposited on 31st December 1940 which had now been valued at three hundred and one pounds, placed in a trust fund for Mavis Joan Langford by Mr J. Smith.

The colour drained from Mavis' face. She dropped the letter and raced to the kitchen sink to be sick. Edward picked it up and read it. He walked over to Mavis and gave her a cup of water. After a few minutes, she turned to face him.

"I want the truth this time, who is Jack Smith?" Edward asked.

Mavis began to cry. "He was someone Dana and I cared for during the war."

"Did you recognise him on Saturday?"

"Not at first. I didn't want to embarrass Dana so I just played along with her that we thought he was a stranger."

"A stranger doesn't leave you that kind of money Mavis and now Dana has disappeared with Edith. How long before whoever is behind this comes after you?"

"Maybe I should leave," Christopher said as he headed for the door.

"Yes, I'll speak to you soon," Edward replied before turning his attention back to Mavis. "I need to know what happened during the war. It may give me the answer to who killed him on the beach."

Mavis wiped her eyes. "After we heard that Gerald had died. Dana felt very lonely. She was struggling. Her sister couldn't look after Edith anymore so she had to send her to the chapel where the nuns were looking after the children whilst we looked after the wounded. John, Mary and Fred were there too so it made sense that they were all together. Dana was a marvellous stitcher. She saved a lot of the men who would have bled to death if she hadn't helped them."

"What's the connection between Dana and Jack Smith? Does it have anything to do with the boy she sent into foster care?"

"How do you know about that?"

Edward didn't respond.

"Dana had a short romance with Jack Smith. When he found out that she was pregnant, he left. As far as I know, she never saw him again until Saturday. Dana continued to work in the medical tents and buildings for as long as she could and then her sister, Enid, looked after Edith whilst she had the baby and then..."

"Then she took care of that," Edward finished for her.

"Yes, she took care of that," Mavis sighed. "Within a week, she was back in the medical tent acting like nothing had ever happened."

"You know this gives Dana Wise a reason to kill Jack Smith don't you?"

"She wouldn't. She couldn't. She loved him."

"And he left her. A widow. Pregnant and alone. A broken heart can sometimes be a dangerous thing to have. I have witnesses to say that she was seen with Jack on Saturday evening. Then, suddenly, her and Edith disappear and Jack Smith ends up dead on the beach. You know how much I hate coincidences."

"Did it look like Jack was murdered?"

Edward sighed. "To be honest, no. The postmortem will tell us more but it looks like he died naturally."

Mavis bowed her head.

"The bank would have sent this letter after they had discovered that Jack Smith had died. He must have left that gold in his will but why leave it to you and not Dana?"

"I don't know."

A knock at the front door interrupted them. Edward wandered over and as he opened the door, he found Sergeant Peter Hastings waiting for him.

"Sorry to bother you Sir, there's been another body found in the woods," Hastings said.

Edward ran his fingers through his hair. "Any idea who it is?"

"No Sir, he was found hanging from a tree with no wallet or identification on him."

Edward turned back to Mavis. "We'll continue this later," he said before heading out of the door.

Mavis sat on the chair at the kitchen table looking at the letter once again. Reading the numbers over and over again. Trying to figure out why he had decided to put the gold in trust. She had never told him about Mary and Fred. She knew she needed to keep Edward away from the truth but letters from the departed were becoming a major problem.

Chapter Nineteen

The Right Foot
Monday 3rd November 2008

Blake Langford and Alison Pearce followed Detective Aris Stathakis into Lalysos Police Station. He whispered something to the officer at the reception desk before leading them down a corridor to a room at the back of the station. As they entered, they noticed a table with two chairs either side of it and an old style cassette tape recorder had been left on the table.

"Am I under interrogation or something?" Blake asked.

"No, no, of course not. We just need to make sure that we have everything correct before we proceed. Please, take a seat," Aris replied before taking a seat on the opposite side of the table with Lauren Prince sitting alongside him.

Blake and Alison reluctantly took their seats opposite them.

"You know they have CD's these days too," Alison quipped.

"I don't think this is the appropriate time for jesting Miss Pearce," Aris snapped.

"And I don't think this is an appropriate time for wasting our time. We came over here to find out why two men involved in a Special Branch operation tried to kill two of your local residents," Blake replied.

"I agree. I'm just as eager as you are to find out why this has happened but I was unaware that both of the people in question are in fact related to you. Don't you think that is a conflict of interests that needs to be addressed?" Aris asked.

"Work with me or against me, I don't care. I just want to find out what's going on with Jim Handanowicz and then I'm outta here. I've got bigger fish to fry than some up-tight detective on some map dot in the Mediterranean having an ego trip!"

Aris looked at Alison. "Is he always this aggressive? No wonder the family fled the country."

Blake was about to respond but caught a stare from Lauren which told him otherwise. "Fine, have it your way but you have the wrong man in custody."

Aris glared at him. "What do you mean? My officers arrived at James Handanowicz's villa and found two dead bodies. When we arrived, he had blood on his clothes which matched the victims."

"But what if he didn't trust the Greek police?" Alison asked.

"And why wouldn't he..."

"He's not a Greek national," Blake interrupted. "He was born and raised in England before moving here in 1984. Sure, he's worked here for the past twenty-five years and looked after his sister, Evelyn, whilst she was locked away in that facility in Monolithos but he is still a British citizen in a foreign land. You arrested him on the flimsiest of evidence so you can either charge him in the next few hours or he is a free man. You decide."

Aris sat back in his chair. "Okay, you managed to get Miss Handanowicz to talk when no one else could, maybe I should give you some rope here. I will let you talk with James Handanowicz but if you try anything to get him or Evelyn out of the country whilst this investigation is going on, I swear, I'll track you down."

Blake leant forward towards Aris. "Bring James Handanowicz to me, press record on your little tape recorder then piss off and let me do my job."

Aris glared at him. Blake held his gaze. Neither of them flinched for a moment before Aris stood up and stormed out of the room. Lauren gave Blake a little smirk before following Aris out of the door.

"Smooth Langford, real smooth. I don't want to come all the way out to Greece to get myself thrown into jail," Alison snapped.

"You won't, he's clutching at straws, he knows nothing," Blake replied.

After a few moments of silence, the door swung open and James Handanowicz was escorted into the room by two uniformed officers. His face carried a mix of confusion and apprehension as he glanced at Blake and Alison.

"You called for me?" James asked, sounding slightly nervous.

Blake nodded, gesturing towards the empty seat next to him. "Please, have a seat."

James hesitated for a brief moment before complying and taking the offered seat. His eyes darted around the room, clearly aware of the tension in the air. "I often wondered when the Langford juggernaut would roll into my beautiful island. For some reason, I didn't expect my nephew would be the executor of my downfall."

"Whatever dealings you had with my father are irrelevant, James. Or do I call you Uncle Jim?"

"Jim is fine. No need for false sentimentality. We all know that John Langford would have poisoned his family against us anyway. Emily was too weak to speak up. Scared of losing her privileged lifestyle."

"My mother, your sister, Emily Langford, is dead!" Blake snapped.

Jim bowed his head. "I know, I'm sorry. She was a wonderful woman."

Blake let that hang for a moment before continuing. "You underestimate my father. He told us the whole truth about what happened in 1984 and let us decide for ourselves what we thought of you."

"And?"

"Initially, I thought you were a callous bastard who had taken my parents for a ride on some sob story to extort money from the family but, when looking at the facts, you came over here and supported your sister, Evelyn Handanowicz, with her medical needs and looked after her for the past twenty-five years. For a man to give up his life to help his sister with her mental health issues, he can't be all bad."

Jim sighed. "So I assume you're here to interrogate me about those bodies they found at my home."

"Partly yes," Blake replied, his tone softer than before. "We're trying to get to the bottom of this. But before we dive into it, there's something you need to know."

Jim raised an eyebrow curiously. "What is it?"

Blake leaned forward, fixing him with an intense gaze. "You're not the only one who's been keeping secrets, Jim. There's more to this case than meets the eye. We suspect there's a connection between those bodies found at your villa and a powerful criminal organisation operating across Europe."

Jim's eyes widened in surprise. "I-I had no idea about any criminal organisation. I've been minding my own business, taking care of Evelyn. I wouldn't get involved in anything like that."

Blake nodded sympathetically. "I believe you, Jim. But sometimes, circumstances force us into situations we never anticipated. We need your help to uncover the truth."

Jim took a deep breath, his shoulders sagging with the weight of the ordeal he found himself in. "Alright, what do you need from me?"

"We need you to tell us everything you know about your sister's time at the Monolithos facility," Blake said, leaning back in his chair.

As Jim recounted the years from when he arrived in 1984 and found Evelyn crying on the floor in her rundown shack that she was living in at the time, the ups and downs of her care whilst he also attempted to earn a living as a bricklayer, there was nothing obvious there that stood out to Blake as being significant to the case. He waited for Jim to finish before playing his trump card.

"Does the name Jack Smith mean anything to you?" Blake asked.

He saw the colour drain from Jim's face.

"Not here," Jim replied.

"We don't have much time Jim," Alison spoke for the first time. "Emily's will has opened up a lot of questions and we think it may have been linked to why those men came after you."

"Get me out of here and I'll tell you everything," he replied, looking at Alison.

"What about the right foot?" Blake asked.

"Get me out of here and I'll tell you everything," Jim repeated.

Blake sighed as he leant back in his chair. "It might not be as easy as that right now. They still suspect that you murdered two men in your home."

"Circumstantial is all they have, come on Blake, you know the drill," Jim pleaded.

At that moment, Detective Aris Stathakis burst into the room. Blake and Alison immediately stood up, about to argue with him but he raised his hand in anticipation of their response.

"He's free to go," Aris said.

All three of them looked at Aris confused.

"We've had a confession and currently have no grounds to hold Mr Handanowicz any longer but don't leave the country, this is not over," Aris continued.

"I doubt it is," Jim replied.

"Does the deal still stand?" Alison asked.

"What deal is that?" Aris asked.

Jim nodded. "You two only."

Alison and Blake both nodded in agreement.

"What deal?" Aris asked again. "I told you Langford, if he even looks at an airport or boat I'll..."

"You'll what? You had your chance and failed, now let the Special Intelligence Branch of Great Britain help a British citizen to get justice for a crime he didn't commit!" Blake snapped holding Aris' gaze.

"You have no right to speak to me like this!"

"Then do your job, detective and find out as much as you can about Reaper and Zodiac!"

"And what good will that do?"

"At least you'll be earning your pay."

Aris glared at him. Both men stood unflinching for a moment.

Blake's face broke out into a smile. "You know what, you've been wasting my time. Ever since we arrived on this island, we've been tidying up your mess..."

Aris's face turned scarlet. "I'll have you thrown off the case!"

"Aris, listen, I've got five fingers and guess what, the middle one's just for you," Blake replied.

"Get him out of my sight!" he snapped before storming out of the interrogation room.

"That went well. I guess it's time to go," Alison replied as she led them out of the room and after Jim had collected his belongings, out of the police station.

As they wandered down the road, Blake heard a woman call after them. They turned and saw Lauren Prince rushing to catch up with them. Alison approached her as she handed over some paperwork.

"The confession came from Evelyn Handanowicz. She told them she killed the men and Jim had nothing to do with it. With her mental state, the judge will probably rule on her being mentally incapacitated," Lauren explained.

"Why are you helping us?" Alison asked.

"I'm not a Greek national. I moved here from London ten years ago. I want to help you get the answers you need but Aris is a bastard. Once he realises that Evelyn's confession won't hold, he'll come after Jim again."

Blake took the paperwork and quickly flicked through it. "What part of London were you from?" he asked.

"Sutton, just off the old Cheam Road," Lauren replied.

"I know it well."

"You helped my uncle with that arson attack on the church back in '97."

Blake thought for a moment. "The First Church Of Christ? Albert Prince?"

Lauren nodded. "You helped my family catch the ones responsible for the fire, it's my turn to help you."

Blake smiled. "Albert was a good man. Thank you. To be honest, we could use a car..."

Lauren reached into her pocket and pulled out a car key. "My red Fiat is parked near the gate at the side of the station, I won't need it until later."

Within minutes, Jim was driving them along mountainous roads across the island heading towards Lindos. "What did Evelyn tell you about Jack Smith?" he asked.

Blake repeated the conversation he had with Evelyn at the care home about her and Emily being fathered by Jack Smith and the fall-out it caused when it all came out.

Jim shook his head. "Evelyn never got over Fred," he sighed.

"Uncle Fred? Dad's brother?" Blake asked.

Jim nodded. "It was your parent's wedding day back in 1977 when it all happened. There had been rumours that Evelyn had found herself a man and that he would be at the wedding. Nobody realised until the week before that it would be Fred Langford."

"So what happened? It's not unusual for two sisters to marry two brothers," Alison asked.

"That's the problem, Fred was her brother. Well, half-brother at least."

Blake shook his head. "I don't understand. My grandmother on mum's side, Dana Handanowicz, had a fling with Jack Smith during the war and he fathered my mother Emily and her twin sister Evelyn. Mavis Langford, my grandmother on dad's side, had Fred, Mary and John with my grandad Edward Langford."

"Was Edward Langford called up during the Second World War?" Jim asked.

"Yes, he was always showing us his medals when Jenny, Steven and I were kids."

Jim nodded. "William Handanowicz and Edward Langford were both called up and fought for their country and when they came home, there were new babies waiting for them."

Blake shook his head. "You mean Jack Smith slept with both Dana and Mavis whilst..."

Jim nodded. "It was all covered up, you know how taboo sex outside of marriage was back then."

"So were my parents related?"

"No."

"How can you be so sure?"

"John Langford was Edward Langford's son. Mary and Fred were Jack's. That's why Evelyn and Fred couldn't be together. They shared the same father."

The pieces of the puzzle were finally falling into place for Blake. "My father said that Fred sped away from the church after a huge argument."

Jim nodded. "He lost control of the car and hit a tree somewhere near Winchester. He was dead on impact. Evelyn never forgave herself."

"Did she know about Jack?" Alison asked.

"She found out when they had the argument outside the church before Emily and John's wedding. Fred gave her the ring that he was going to propose with before speeding off and having his accident. Unbeknown to him, Evelyn was also pregnant with his child at the time."

Blake gasped. "What happened to the baby?"

"She had a miscarriage, two months after he died. From that moment on, her mental health has been in decline. The services back in the late 70's and early 80's were nothing compared to what's available today. They thought she was mad. Hallucinating. Schizophrenic even. At one point, they had her in a straight-jacket and kept her isolated for three weeks. That was why I needed the money. To help her get the support she needed. Nobody in England was willing to help. The doctors here had given up on her. I found out about a man on the island called Stelios Christodoulopoulos who ran wellness clinics and helped people with deep mental health problems. He was the one who opened the care facility in Monolithos where Evelyn stays now."

Blake bowed his head realising his anger towards Jim had been misdirected. "Is he still running the facility?"

"No, he died three years ago. The place has been going downhill ever since."

"Is she too ill to live outside of the care home?" Alison asked.

"She comes out on day trips and stays the occasional night with me but she gets overwhelmed and very reactive if she's away from the facility for too long. They have her on a strict timeline for her medication and I don't think she would be able to organise that for herself in the outside world," Jim explained.

As they turned a corner, they saw a beautiful bay far below the cliff and the road that they were travelling on. To their left was the deep blue sea lapping against a small sandy beach and in front of them was a huge rock with a stone footpath twisting its way from the base all the way to the top. Jim parked the car on the top of the cliff and handed some Euros to the parking attendant before leading Alison and Blake down a steep hill at the side of the cliff.

"Where are we going?" Blake asked as families rushed past them heading towards a market at the base of the cliff.

"You wanted to know about the right foot. First, we have to climb to the top of the acropolis," Jim replied.

As they followed Jim down towards the base of the cliff, they discovered cobbled paths that snaked their way between hundreds of market stalls selling everything from olive oil, traditional greek alcohol, souvenirs of the local area, cheaply produced football shirts, sponges from the mediterranean sea and various greek salads and moussaka. The smell of the freshly cooked food made Blake feel hungry. They had barely eaten anything since they had left London almost twelve hours ago.

Relentlessly, Jim led them out of the market and up the stone steps and pathways that circled the huge rock several times before they arrived at the summit. A couple of times, Alison lost her balance and Blake helped her up to the next section. There was no handrail or anything to guard somebody falling over the side and plummeting hundreds of metres onto the rocks and shallow sea below.

Jim looked at his watch. "We need to be quick, the sun sets in one and a half hours and you don't want to climb back down in the dark."

Blake looked around at the top of the acropolis. There were several well preserved ancient statues standing tall on top of the rock. Behind them was the cliff face that led back up to the main road but in every other direction was deep blue mediterranean sea. If he hadn't been so involved in the case, Blake thought it would be an idyllic place for a family holiday in the summertime.

"So what are these statues and how are they relevant?" Alison asked.

Jim looked around and noticed the final few tourists were beginning to leave and make their way back down towards the market. "These statues signify the Greek Gods and rulers from thousands of years ago. Come with me."

Alison and Blake followed Jim over towards the statue on the far side of the acropolis. They stopped at the feet of the statue. Jim looked around once more before removing a chisel from his pocket.

He picked up a rock and used it to hammer and chisel away the stone of the right foot of the statue.

"What are you doing? This statue is thousands of years old. You're destroying history!" Alison gasped.

Jim hit the rock onto the chisel a few more times before the side of the right foot shattered and revealed what looked like a bronze pipe. It was around an inch wide and about three inches long. He removed the pipe and handed it to Blake.

"Inside there is part of the map of where Jack Smith left his fortune," Jim smiled. "Find Dana's part and you'll locate the family inheritance. This is what those men were after but Stelios and I completed some patch work for the acropolis in 1985. Before we cemented it over, I hid the pipe inside hoping that nobody would ever find it."

"So why have you given it to me?" Blake asked.

"Emily took her secret to the grave before entrusting you to figure it out. Too many people are dying because of Jack Smith's mistakes Blake. You have a chance to end it all."

Blake looked down at the pipe and then back at Jim.

"Ti kaneis ekei?" a man shouted out from behind them.

"Go! I'll take care of them!" Jim said, handing Blake the car key and ushering them away.

"I'm not leaving you here," Blake replied.

"Na stamatisei!" the man shouted as he lunged towards Alison.

Jim moved between them and caught the man with a strong punch to the right side of his face. The man turned and took a swing at Jim who dodged before landing another blow on the man's jaw.

"Don't argue! Go now!" Jim shouted.

Two more men appeared and began rushing towards Jim. Blake took his opportunity and shoulder barged one of them against one of the statues. The man fell to the ground winded.

He handed the pipe and key to Alison. "Get back to the car. I'll catch up with you," he said as the third man launched a kick towards Blake's ribs.

Blake blocked it before following up with a kick to the man's standing leg that sent him down momentarily. He quickly got up and charged at Blake who ducked down and flipped his attacker over his shoulder. The man's momentum took him off-balance and over the side of the acropolis. They heard a scream followed by a sickening thud below. Blake looked over at Jim as the remaining two men were lining up to bring him down. Jim looked at Blake before turning and jumping off the edge of the rock.

Blake rushed to the edge and saw Jim land in the sea below and begin to swim away. He shook his head in disbelief before turning and realising that the two men were now heading his way. Blake turned and quickly rushed back down the cobbled stone steps back into the market below. As he rushed past a stall selling traditional Greek Ouzo, someone grabbed his shirt and pulled him inside. He was about to lash out before realising that it was Alison who had pulled him in. The two men rushed past the stall and into the market.

"Kalispera," the owner of the stall called out.

"Yamas," Blake replied before heading back towards the main path.

"You English?" the stall owner asked.

"Yes, how did..." Alison began.

The stall owner handed over two shot glasses of ouzo. "Take this and there's a shortcut behind here that takes you back to the hill."

They both drank the ouzo and thanked the stall owner before rushing down an alleyway filled with rubbish bags and a couple of children playing with a football before heading back up the hill.

"Where's Jim?" Alison asked as they arrived back at the car.

"He went for a swim."

"Seriously?"

"He leapt off the rock and swam away."

"So what do we do now?"

Blake looked over and noticed the two men that had been chasing them halfway up the hill. He took the car keys and climbed into the car. Alison joined him in the passenger seat. Blake calmly reversed the car and headed out of the car park following the road that Jim had driven them down earlier.

"There seems to be a lot of people protecting whatever it is that mum's will has opened. We need to find out what's inside that tube and get it back to London," Blake replied.

"Where are we heading?"

Blake pulled over to the side of the road and searched for Monolithos on the satnav. "The only place we can go, Jim's villa."

Chapter Twenty

A German, A Police Officer And A Woman Scorned
Tuesday 24th August 1948

Sergeant Peter Hastings led Edward Langford down the mud path into the woods between the church and Harold Partridge's cottage. Officer George Wells was speaking to Christopher whilst the forensic team worked on securing the area.

"You're turning up like a bad penny today George," Edward commented as he looked up at the body hanging from the tree. "Wasn't he the guy who ran away from the cafe this morning?"

"Never seen him before," Officer Wells replied.

"Come on George, you were supervising the workers for Norman Whitehouse at the beach cafe this morning. You must have had some idea of who they were!"

"I told you, the new owner sent those men in to empty the place out."

"Who sent them? Who did they work for?" Sergeant Hastings asked.

"William Handanowicz, the guy who paid Whitehouse for it. Why am I suddenly getting questioned?" Officer Wells asked.

"Because this man has discharge papers from the German military so either you or this Handanowicz guy have been helping a German or those squatters we discovered are being killed off," Edward replied.

"How dare you suggest that I'd help a Kraut!" Officer Wells fumed. "Those bastards killed my parents!!"

"Which gives you a motive! Go back to the station Officer Wells, I'm relieving you of your command," Edward replied.

Officer George Wells glared at Edward, then at Sergeant Hastings before storming away towards the church.

Edward wandered over towards Christopher who was still looking up at the body hanging from the branch. "Do you recognise him?"

Christopher nodded. "I'm almost certain he was the one I chased..."

"I thought you were going to see Frances after you left my house. What brought you down here?"

"I was heading towards the bus stop when I saw what had happened."

"Where were you planning to go?"

"Back to the institute."

Edward sighed. "I'm sorry if I made you feel uncomfortable earlier but I need to look into every possible lead I can find."

"I understand."

"What did Officer Wells say to you?"

"Just asked if I knew who the man in the tree was."

"Did you tell him?"

"No."

"Why?"

"Because I don't trust him," Christopher replied.

"You don't trust a police officer?"

"Like you said, he keeps turning up like a bad penny."

"Have you got something to tell me Christopher?"

He looked at Edward. "The man in the church we saw yesterday..."

Edward nodded. "The one who was murdered..."

Christopher nodded. "His name is Hans Schwartz. He stayed at the institute for a while and then disappeared. When I recognised him yesterday, I panicked. I thought you'd think that I was helping them if I told you who it was."

"Did Mr Morris, the head of the institute, know?"

"No. He claimed to be someone else but, like you, I discovered who he really was."

"And what did you do?"

"I asked him to tell me the truth. He did and I told him I would report him unless he left straightaway."

"And did he?"

Christopher nodded. "He said he needed to see someone in the village first and then he would leave."

"Do you know who it was?"

"He went to the vicar's cottage."

"You followed him?"

"I didn't trust that he would do what he said."

"So what happened?"

"I met Frances King."

"What was she doing at the vicar's house?"

"She wasn't. She was walking back from the grocery store when her bags split open. I helped her carry her groceries back to her house."

"And then what?" Edward asked.

"I met her father and began helping around the village."

"You didn't think about going back to check if Hans had left?"

"Frances was very persuasive."

Edward nodded. "I'll need you to come to the station with me so we can complete the paperwork."

Christopher nodded. "I'll be there later."

***

Officer George Wells climbed into his car and slammed the door. As he started the engine, he felt a cold blade against his neck.

"Langford knows about us!" a man's voice said.

"Max, calm down. He knows nothing," Officer Wells replied.

"Stefan and Hans are both dead. How long before he finds out about Christoph and me?"

"He won't. Christoph won't tell them anything."

"I know Christoph won't but what about you?"

"What about me?"

"Remember, I know what you did at Honeypot Cottage. If Langford finds out that you helped Smith before he died, you will be finished. I can destroy your career anytime I want to."

"It doesn't matter now. Langford has taken me off the case."

"Then you're of no use anymore," Max replied before slashing the knife across George's throat.

Blood covered the steering wheel and dashboard of the car as George frantically tried to stop the bleeding. Max calmly stepped out of the car and walked away.

*****

Frances King stepped out of the grocery store carrying two bags of shopping. She noticed Christopher standing at the bus stop on the opposite side of the road.

She wandered over to him. "Going somewhere?"

"I need to go back to the institute," Christopher replied.

"You don't need that place..."

"I do. Mr Langford knows about Stefan and Hans. It won't take him long to work out the rest."

"You seem to forget I have something of yours. If father finds out, he'll kill you."

"That's your problem now."

Frances raised her hand to slap him around the face but he grabbed her wrist. "You need to remember who saved you from being thrown into prison. I can end you anytime I want to."

The sound of a diesel engine interrupted them. Christopher looked over her shoulder at the bus approaching in the distance. "Let me go, Frances. It's better for everyone if I'm gone."

"Not everyone, just you," she cried before rushing away towards the woods.

The driver stopped the bus as Christopher watched her leave. He climbed on board and paid his fare before taking a seat halfway down on the left hand side of the bus. As he watched the village pass by in a blur, he knew this was far from over.

***

It was just after 6pm when Detective Edward Langford and Sergeant Peter Hastings returned to the police station. Officer Jones was at the front desk as they entered whilst a flurry of activity continued in the offices behind him.

"I have the forensic reports regarding the man on the beach for you Sir," Officer Jones said as they arrived.

"Thank you Jones, any sign of Officer Wells or Christopher Fischer yet?" Edward asked.

"Have you not heard about Officer Wells Sir?"

Edward looked at him. "No, what's he done now?"

"He's dead."

"What?"

"He was found dead in his car with his throat cut outside St David's Church this afternoon."

"What time was this?" Sergeant Hastings asked.

"It was reported at three o'clock."

"Around an hour after we found the body in the woods," Edward replied. "Do you have any idea who called it in?"

"Frances King," Officer Jones replied.

"We need to bring Miss King in for questioning," Sergeant Hastings said.

"She's only seventeen years old. We can't interview her without her father here too," Officer Jones replied.

"Then bring them both in. She could help us answer a lot of questions," Edward said before heading into the back offices.

***

Later that evening, Officer Stone brought Arthur and Frances King into the police station. Sergeant Peter Hastings led them towards an interrogation room near the cells at the rear of the station. After a few minutes, Detective Edward Langford joined them.

"What is the meaning of all this Edward? You drag us down here in front of the whole village like we're some kind of criminals!" Arthur fumed.

"I apologise for that Arthur but we think there may be some links between the cases of the man on the beach, the fire at Honeypot Cottage, the three recent murders and the men working at ol' Norman Whitehouse's cafe," Edward explained.

"How the hell are we meant to know anything about all that? I'm laid up most of the day whilst Frances keeps the house tidy and keeps an eye on the gardener."

"It must be difficult," Sergeant Hastings said.

"What?" Arthur asked.

"For Frances, I mean. Not having your mother around at such a young age."

"We get by."

"Frances," Edward spoke this time. "I want you to know that you are not in any kind of trouble and whatever you tell us here will not leave this room."

"Pah, you've got others listening in who love a good story Langford. Whatever we say will be round the village by sundown," Arthur replied.

Edward kept his focus on Frances. "Trust me to make things right. Tell me what you know about Christopher Fischer."

Frances began to cry.

"What is the meaning of this?" Arthur snapped. "He's just a gardener trying to make an honest living for Christ's sake! What are you suggesting Langford? That my daughter would frolic with the likes of him? How dare you degrade my family! This meeting is over."

"Mr King, I suggest you either take a seat next to Frances or leave the room and I will find another appropriate adult to be with her," Edward replied.

"Oh, it's Mr King now is it? Well, let me tell you this Detective Langford, my daughter is not some cheap tart who sleeps with anyone she can get..."

"Will you stop it both of you!" Frances shouted.

Both men turned to face her.

"Father, I think you should leave," Frances said, her voice barely above a whisper.

"What are you talking about?" Arthur asked.

"Please, I need to do this alone."

"But he'll twist everything you say. You'll have to watch every word in case you say something wrong."

"You can wait outside Mr King," Sergeant Hastings replied as he stood to lead him out of the room.

Reluctantly, Arthur followed him out of the door and down the corridor towards the waiting room.

"We do have a female officer, PC Joan Barnes, working here today. Would you like her to be with you?" Edward asked.

Frances nodded.

Edward sent Officer Stone away to find PC Barnes before leaving them alone to talk for a while. When Edward left the room, he could hear Arthur King arguing with Sergeant Hastings in the waiting room. He walked down the corridor to join them.

"Go home Arthur. I will make sure that Frances is driven home and taken right up to your front door after we have finished our meeting," Edward said.

"No you won't. You'll plant something on her. You'll make her confess to some kind of crime she didn't commit and then what'll happen to me? I'll be in that house all alone!"

"I think you need to realise that Frances is your daughter, not your slave. Not your late wife, Maud. She is your daughter. She has her own life and can make her own decisions."

"Pah, she wouldn't last five minutes out in the real world. She's just a kid and you're keeping her here illegally!"

"She is free to go whenever she wants to."

"Then let her go, now!"

"When we have spoken to her in a civilised manner and answered a few questions, she will be taken home by one of my officers so if you want to help your daughter, go home and wait for her," Edward replied.

Arthur considered arguing for a moment before bowing his head, turning and walking out of the station. Sergeant Hastings followed Edward back to the interview room.

"Thanks for that," Hastings said as they arrived at the door.

"It's not over yet," Edward replied before they entered the room.

***

Meanwhile in Lepe Village, Mavis Langford was tidying up the back garden of Southward Cottage whilst Mary played on the swing at the bottom of the garden and John and Fred kicked a football around.

"You make sure you don't damage your father's rose bush or there will be trouble!" Mavis called out to them.

"Of course we won't mom," Fred replied as he tackled John once again.

As Mavis entered the house, she heard somebody knocking at the front door. As she opened the door, she noticed a short man with brown hair, unshaven and wearing black shorts and a black t-shirt. "Can I help you?" she asked.

"Is Mr Langford home?" he asked.

"No, he's at work at the moment, you can..."

"Good!" the man snapped before pulling a knife out of the pocket in his shorts and pointing it at Mavis.

Mavis stepped back. "Now, don't do anything you might regret."

"Your husband killed two of my friends. He chased the vicar away. He chased Christoph away. Now he's going to know what it's like to lose everyone he cares about!" the man replied as he stepped forward and closed the door behind him.

"There's no need for violence. I'm sure whatever has happened, there must be a simple explanation for it. What's your name?"

"Name's not important."

"You're a friend of Christopher's. The gardener? Maybe he can help you."

At that moment, they heard a squeal and then some laughter from the back garden.

"Who else is here?" the man asked.

"No one, no one, it's just kids next door. Please don't hurt them," Mavis replied.

The man moved forwards. Mavis grabbed a vase and threw it at him. It hit his arm before dropping and smashing on the floor. He dropped the knife momentarily before quickly picking it up again.

"That was stupid!" he said before launching himself at Mavis.

Out in the back garden, John heard the vase smash. Fred and Mary were playing tag by throwing the ball at each other. Whilst they were distracted, John headed back inside the house. He heard someone arguing with his mother in the hall. He crouched down on his knees and crawled into the kitchen.

"What do you want from us?" Mavis shouted.

"I told you, he's taken everything and everyone away from me. Now I'm going to show him what it feels like!" the man replied.

John managed to crawl towards the cupboard under the kitchen sink. His father, Edward, had shown him where he hid a revolver in case there was ever an emergency. He opened the cupboard and removed the revolver that had been stuck to the underside of the sink.

John could hear the man shouting in the next room. He took a deep breath, pulled the hammer back to load the bullet and then walked from the kitchen into the hall. The man was slashing wildly at Mavis who blocked him firstly with a wooden chair and then a coat stand. He caught her arm and drew blood from a deep cut. John took a deep breath, aimed and fired. The gunshot echoed inside the house as the bullet hit a mirror on the wall shattering it into hundreds of small pieces that fell to the floor like confetti.

The man laughed and turned towards John. "You're dead, kid!" he smirked.

John quickly pulled the hammer back and fired again as the man rushed towards him. This time the bullet hit him in the centre of his chest sending him to the floor. Mavis froze as she saw what had happened. John walked over towards the man and kicked him. Suddenly, the man's arm came out and grabbed his ankle. John fell to the floor furiously kicking out at the man with his free foot in an attempt to get away. The man held onto John's ankle before Mavis picked up a wooden clock from the mantlepiece and smashed it over the man's head. He released the grip on John's ankle and Mavis moved him away. Fred and Mary quickly arrived to see what all of the commotion was about. Mavis moved them all into the kitchen and closed the door behind her.

"Mum, you're hurt!" Mary cried.

"It's just a scratch, it's fine," Mavis replied as she quickly picked up a towel, soaked it in water and applied it to the wound on her arm.

"What were you doing John!" Fred shouted.

"Freddie, leave John alone. I want you and Mary to go and tidy up your things in the garden and then go and read in the dining room until we can contact your father. Come along, hurry up," Mavis insisted.

Mary and Fred reluctantly wandered back outside before Mavis turned her attention back to John.

"How did you know that gun was there?" she asked.

"Dad showed me. He said if there was an emergency, then I should use it," John explained.

"You could have gotten yourself killed, you silly boy."

"You're welcome," John replied.

Mavis glared at him for a moment before softening her stare. "Thank you. How did you know how to use it?"

"You don't think father and I only go fishing for twelve hours do you?"

"I guess not. This is strictly between us, okay. Do not mention any of this to the other two."

John nodded in agreement.

"My purse is on the side by the stove. Take some coins, go to the telephone box and call your father. Don't speak to anyone. You go there and you come straight back, you hear?"

John nodded before picking some coins out of his mother's purse and heading towards the telephone box. He walked out of the back gate and around the house to the front garden. As he stepped outside the gate, he saw Arthur King walking down the road from the bus stop.

John began walking up the hill towards the telephone box. "Good evening Mr King," he said as he passed Arthur in the street.

Arthur ignored him and didn't reply.

John turned around and watched him walk back down towards his house. Something wasn't right. He ran the rest of the way to the telephone box. He needed his father to come home fast. Things were getting out of hand.

Chapter Twenty-One

The Dead Can't Talk
Tuesday 4th November 2008

A loud knocking on the front door of Jim Handanowicz's villa in Monolithos woke Blake from a restless sleep. Alison slept soundly on the sofa whilst Blake had pulled two armchairs together to create a makeshift bed for himself however the stiff neck he was experiencing this morning made him regret that decision. She stirred as the knocking became louder.

"What time is it?" she asked.

Blake looked at his watch as he headed towards the front door. "Quarter-to-six," he replied.

Alison groaned and forced herself to wake up as Blake answered the door.

"Detective Stathakis, what an unpleasant surprise," Blake quipped.

"Where is he, Langford?" Aris Stathakis snapped.

"Who?"

"Don't play games with me. You had that all planned didn't you? Take James Handanowicz to Lindos and then let him jump down into the sea and swim away to a waiting boat that will take him out of the country where we can't touch him!"

"I'd like to take the credit for such an amazing story but I don't have a clue what you are talking about! James took us to Lindos because he was convinced that we would find something important at the Acropolis!"

Aris pushed past him and walked into the villa closely followed by Lauren Prince.

"Shouldn't you be invited in unless you have a warrant to search the premises?" Blake asked as he closed the door behind them.

"Don't play dumb with me Langford, where is James Handanowicz?"

"I don't know."

"What's going on?" Alison asked as she joined them in the hall.

"Detective Ass here thinks we had something to do with Jim's disappearance yesterday," Blake explained.

"We're as much in the dark as you. He led us to the acropolis and then dived off the edge. I'm amazed he didn't kill himself in the process," Alison explained.

"James Handanowicz is a well known scuba diving instructor on the island. He's a very good swimmer and he knew we were onto him for the murder of Ian Bleeker and Zachary Zhal," Lauren added.

"I didn't want to do this but you leave me no choice," Aris replied as he handed Blake some papers.

Blake scanned his eyes over the fine print. "You're deporting us?"

"Yes. You've aided a fugitive and blown this murder investigation wide open. If you weren't working for Special Branch, I'd arrest you both and throw you into the cells right now but I've been overruled," Aris admitted.

"Overruled my ass, you don't have any evidence that proves we helped Jim Handanowicz escape. We settled his bail and he led us to Lindos to find something," Blake replied.

"And what were you looking for?"

"Something valuable to our family."

"In a prehistoric acropolis? What on Earth did you expect to find there? The report said that the three of you damaged one of the ancient ruins before being chased away back through the market."

"Okay, let's say for example that we did help Jim leave the country, why did your colleague, Miss Prince, lend us her car to get to Lindos in the first place?" Alison asked.

"All police officers have trackers on their cars," Lauren admitted. "We tracked the car to Lindos and then the head of security at the acropolis saw James climb aboard a boat a mile or so off-shore. The coastguard tracked the boat all the way to Marmaris in Turkey where they lost him."

"James Handanowicz didn't kill Reaper or Zodiac. They were looking for something that they thought James had in his possession. The piece of the puzzle that would lead them back to the UK to uncover some kind of mysterious secret. Both men were involved in a human trafficking investigation in London earlier this year that went wrong for them. I'm starting to think that it was a cover for something bigger that is yet to happen," Blake replied.

"What do you mean? James Handanowicz had the blood of those men on his clothes. They were killed right here in this villa! And this whole puzzle story, this isn't some kind of kids fairytale, this is a real murder investigation and I won't tolerate mistakes!" Aris snapped.

"James Handanowicz wasn't alone when those men came here and you never found the gun did you?" Alison replied.

"No," Aris admitted.

"So how can you prove that James Handanowicz is the murderer?" Alison asked.

"Because we found the gun yesterday."

Blake felt a shiver run down his spine. Had Evelyn been searched and they found the murder weapon on her? "Where?" he asked.

"At the nursing home but you already knew that, didn't you, Langford?"

"What's that supposed to mean? Evelyn Handanowicz was visiting Jim when the men broke in and she admitted to shooting them. Given her mental health condition, there's no way that any of this would stand up in court. She would be acquitted due to diminished responsibility and would continue to need psychiatric care for the rest of her life!" Blake replied.

"Yes, the wheel of deception turns quite conveniently to get James Handanowicz out of trouble and she gets away with a murder she was incapable of doing."

"What are you talking about? She admitted to Blake that she had done it and Jim tried to hide the evidence! Ask her yourself," Alison replied.

"We can't," Aris admitted.

"She won't talk to you or any of your team because she doesn't trust you. Says a lot for your police force on the island," Blake said.

"She won't talk because she's dead!"

The whole room fell silent for a moment before Blake launched himself towards Aris. "You son-of-a-bitch! What did you do to her!" Blake shouted as he grabbed Aris's shirt.

Alison dived in between them. "Blake! Stop! He's not worth it!" she shouted at him.

After a moment, Blake released his grip on Aris's shirt before stepping away running his fingers through his hair in frustration.

"Evelyn Handanowicz committed suicide an hour after you left the home in Monolithos," Lauren admitted.

"So, who did she confess to?"

"She spoke to me after you left."

"After being mute for so long? No, no, she wouldn't..." Blake began.

"She had the murder weapon inside her clothes when you were talking to her. She knew she was either going to be caught or James would be arrested. Either way, she would be forever alone. She put the gun in her mouth and fired it before anyone could stop her," Aris replied.

Blake stood in the doorway leading towards the lounge. He'd placed both hands on the doorframe and stared down at the floor, struggling to comprehend what Aris had told him. His mother's twin sister. The woman he had never known apart from the occasional mention in conversation during his childhood. There had to be a connection to the piece of the map they had found at the acropolis and his family but for now, he knew he needed to keep that information to himself. "So, what now?" he asked.

"Now I need you both to leave Rhodes and never come back. Your participation in this investigation has caused a lot of unrest between us and Turkey and we will do everything we can to bring James Handanowicz back to the island to face justice," Aris replied. "You have twenty-four hours."

Blake nodded. "And what about Evelyn?"

"She is a Greek citizen with no immediate family. She will be given a traditional Greek funeral and will be buried on the island."

"Like hell she will. I'm not letting my aunt's body be tossed into an unmarked grave in some island ghetto for paupers who have nothing!"

"You seem to forget that you are no longer welcome here Mr Langford so you have no say in what happens to the citizens of this island."

"She does have a family and I will pay for her body will be flown back to London and she will be buried in the same cemetery as her twin sister!"

"Very well, I will make the arrangements and when our investigation is complete, we will release the body," Aris replied before heading towards the door. "Oh, by the way, did you find what you were looking for at Lindos?"

Blake shook his head. "No, but I'm sure it's only a matter of time."

"You don't have much time left," Aris replied as he opened the door and walked out.

"Neither do you pal, neither do you," Blake said softly as he closed the door behind them.

***

Meanwhile, at a rundown two bedroom basement flat in south-east London, Jade Smith rushed towards the front door and inserted her key. She tried to turn the lock but it wouldn't budge.

"Tom! I know you're in there, you lying son-of-a-bitch! Open this door!" Jade fumed as she hammered on the door.

She tried her key again before attempting to shoulder-barge her way in. The door refused to move.

"Gibson! I'm gonna kill you!" she shouted as she kicked the door.

"Are you okay dear?" an elderly woman asked.

Jade looked up and saw her at the top of the stairs that led down to the basement flat. "It's okay, sorry. My partner has locked me out of our flat and I can't get back in."

The elderly lady carefully made her way down the stairs towards her. "Why don't you let me try? Sometimes these old wooden doors just need a little jiggle."

Jade stepped back and allowed the lady to try. She wiggled the key and then gave the door a firm hit with her forearm and surprisingly, it opened.

"How did you..." Jade began.

"Just need to know the right combination that's all," she giggled as she moved aside.

As Jade stepped forwards, she felt a sharp prick on her arm and then suddenly everything went black.

"Get her inside quick!" the lady said as she closed the door behind them.

Two men quickly manoeuvred Jade into a seat in a glass cell on the left side of the room. They strapped her arms and legs to the chair with leather restraints before injecting her again to wake her up. The two men then left the glass cell and stood by the door next to the elderly lady.

When Jade woke up, she realised where she was and immediately noticed Tom in a similar glass cell next to her. The flat had been emptied and what looked like a sprinkler system had been fitted to the top of the glass cells they were now trapped inside.

"Did you honestly think you could betray me and get away with it?" one of the men said.

"I told you Dmitri, I'll get you the money," Tom replied. "Just let her go."

"Money isn't as important as knowing who to trust and why would we want to let you go, the fun has only just started?" the elderly lady replied.

"Who are you and what the hell is going on?" Jade asked.

"You mean he didn't tell you? He's been banking all of this money in the hope that he'd uncover the location of Jack Smith's treasure whilst ripping off my family."

"Wait, you're Dmitri's Mother?" Tom asked. "What has any of this got to do with you?"

"My name is Frances Vasilievich but your parents knew me as Frances King. I believe you had some dealings with my ex-husband, Vladimir. You already know Dmitri and this is my eldest son, Timmy. John Langford took away Timmy's birthright when he chased after that Handanowicz family and now we will get what's rightfully ours!"

"I don't know what you're talking about! I have nothing to do with the Langfords!" Tom replied.

"Of course you don't. Patricia never had the guts to follow her instincts even after I gave her the information she needed."

"You poisoned my mother's mind with tales of her family before she was adopted?"

"She was already poisoned and now you have the chance to prove your loyalty to the cause. I have two pieces of the map. Jack Smith's treasure is buried somewhere near to Holbury Manor in The New Forest. During the war it was a place of recuperation for injured war heroes. Jack stayed there during the war after he deserted before returning to London. It's only a matter of time until the secret is out."

"You seem to have all the information so why do you need us?" Jade asked.

"You two share the Smith bloodline," Timmy replied.

"Fortunately we only need one of you. Tom, with his guilt over his mother's legacy and Jade, the one cast aside from the Handanowicz line by a grandfather who disowned his side of the family," Frances continued.

"Enough of this bullshit, why are we tied to these chairs?" Jade asked.

"You've heard of the phenomenon of snakes shedding their skin to remove parasites," Dmitri explained. "The same can be said here. I had dealings with a snake who failed to deliver the goods a few months ago. In the sprinkler system on top of these glass cells is sulphuric acid. On the table in front of you are scalpels and a tube that opens out onto a set of scales beneath the cells. In a moment, your restraints will be released and you will have two minutes to shed your skin. The one of you who places the most skin on the scales below will be saved and will join us on our quest for the gold."

"And the loser?" Tom asked.

"Our sprinkler system will cover them in sulphuric acid leading them to a slow and painful death."

"What kind of sick mind comes up with this?" Jade asked.

"A mind similar to the one that led his military colleagues into an ambush for a huge Russian pay-off. Isn't that right Thomas?" Frances asked.

Tom bowed his head. Seventeen years ago, he was in a relationship with Jenny Langford. He asked her to pass a dossier onto a Russian informant who she met over lunch in Salisbury, unaware that it contained details of the RAF mission into Afghanistan. The Russians used the information to murder Tom's entire regiment whilst Tom was safely smuggled into Moscow on a fake passport.

"In any case, it's got to be better than being buried alive," Frances added, breaking Tom's thoughts before leading Dmitri and Timmy out of the flat.

As they shut the door, the restraints on the chairs released. They both leapt out of their seats, shouting and hitting all sides of the glass prison they found themselves in but nothing seemed to work. A digital clock illuminated on the wall in front of them counting down the two minutes.

"You bastard, what the hell have you done!" Jade shouted.

"Stop complaining and find a way out of here!" Tom replied as he frantically hit every piece of glass in an attempt to escape.

Jade watched the clock ticking down for a moment before looking at the knives and scalpels on the table. She took some deep breaths before walking over and picking up the scalpel. She looked at the clock. Only one minute left. She rolled up her sleeve and began to cut her skin. Clenching her fist as pain ripped through her arm. She systematically removed chunks of her skin in a pool of blood. Dropping each piece into the tube.

Tom watched her trying not to vomit. He looked at the clock counting down. He looked at the knives. He picked one up. Then he placed it back down again. He screamed. He punched the glass cell wall. He picked up the knife again. Thirty seconds remaining. He began slicing chunks of skin from his arm screaming with every cut. Twenty seconds. Fifteen. Ten. Nine. Eight Seven. He frantically began cutting himself as it counted down. Six. Five. Four. Three. Two. One. Zero.

Deathly silence. Both Jade and Tom looked at each other. It was as if time had stood still. Pools of blood and skin were spread over the metal tables.

"No, no, this was a fucking setup?" Tom raged.

At that moment, the sprinkler systems began spraying inside both cells. They both screamed as acid poured down burning their skin. The sounds of sirens outside caught their attention for a brief moment before it was all over.

Two police officers stepped out of their car outside the flat. A concerned neighbour had heard screams and had called the police to investigate. When they barged open the flat door, a gruesome discovery awaited them. Amongst the blood and the acid, a putrid stench hung in the air as the burnt and scarred bodies of a man and a woman laid inside two glass cells. Jade Smith and Tom Gibson were dead.

Chapter Twenty-Two

Hello Old Friend

Wednesday 25th August 1948

It was just after midnight in the early hours of Wednesday morning when Sergeant Peter Hastings joined Edward Langford outside Southward Cottage. An ambulance had arrived to remove the body and a paramedic tended to the cut on Mavis Langford's arm. Edward was by her side as the paramedic wrapped a bandage around the cut.

One of the forensic team members handed Sergeant Hastings a wallet. When he opened it, he found a German passport folded inside it with the name Maximillian Friedrich Ekkehard displayed next to a photo of a much younger man in it. He walked over and handed the passport to Edward.

"So Officer Wells knew who he was..." Edward said as he looked at it.

"It seems to be that way, Sir. Whatever Wells, Harold Partridge and Norman Whitehouse were trying to cover up, it looks like they were trying to house the enemy."

"We need to find Partridge and Whitehouse. We were lucky this time but they might be the Germans next target. We need to find Christopher Fischer too. Ask Officer Jones to assist the forensics in tidying this place up. Where are the children?"

"Upstairs in their bedrooms. Do you want me to call in PC Joan Barnes to be with them?" Hastings asked.

"No, it's okay, I'll do it," Edward replied before climbing the stairs up to the children's bedrooms.

Meanwhile outside, the paramedics had finished bandaging the wound on Mavis Langford's arm and Officer Jones walked over towards her.

"The forensic teams are almost finished Mrs Langford and then we can let you and your family get back to normal," he advised.

Mavis nodded in acknowledgement.

"Do I remember seeing you in the red cross tents in Fareham during the war?" Officer Jones asked.

Mavis looked at him. "Most of us were."

"I seem to remember you..."

"My husband..."

"And his father were very good police officers. Alfred Langford caused a lot of heartache for a mutual friend of ours."

"I don't know what you're talking about."

"I was there the night Ada Hughes gave birth to Jack's first born. It was old Alfred Langford that convinced Ada's mother to give the baby up and made it look like her father committed suicide."

"I don't know anything about that."

"Your twins look a lot like him, Mavis. Jack told me stories of how he had his fun during the war after Ada died. Never believed it until now. I know your secret. You keep your old man off of my case and I'll keep my mouth shut. By the way, did Jack tell you where he buried the gold?"

"What gold?"

"Come on, he said he'd make sure that you and Dana were all right but then he died before anyone else knew where he'd hidden it."

"You're Charlie Jones aren't you? You helped him rob the bank in Portsmouth in 1938."

Officer Jones smiled.

"How did the police overlook that?" Mavis asked.

"It's amazing what money can buy you these days isn't it."

"Forensics are done, Detective Langford wants you to finish up here and then meet us back at the station to file the report," Sergeant Peter Hastings said as he approached them.

"On my way Sir," Officer Jones replied before heading back into the house.

Mavis bowed her head.

"Is everything okay Mrs Langford?" Hastings asked.

She nodded quickly trying to avoid eye contact. "Yes, everything's fine Peter. Everything's fine," she replied before heading back inside the house to find Edward and the children.

***

Eight Years Later...
Saturday 25th August 1956

John Langford stepped off of the bus and headed down the Lepe Road walking past his parent's home at Southward Cottage before entering Thyme Cottage where Frances King was finishing hanging some washing out on the line.

"John!" a seven year old boy shouted before charging towards him and wrapping himself around John's legs.

"Let him come into the house Timmy, for goodness sake," Frances smiled as she kissed John on the cheek.

John ruffled Timmy's hair and attempted to walk whilst Timmy held onto his leg. They heard loud coughing and spluttering coming from inside the house. "Is he still no better?"

"You know what he's like. Doesn't want to see a doctor even though he's coughing up blood."

"Frances! Where's my tea?" Arthur shouted.

"On the way Dad," she replied, rolling her eyes as she finished hanging the clothes on the washing line.

John wandered into the kitchen and began preparing three cups of tea. As Frances hung the last pair of shorts on the line, she noticed the postman approaching the gate.

"Good afternoon Terrance, Anything for us today?" she asked.

He glared at her and threw three letters over the gate and onto the grass.

"There's no need to be like that! What have I done?" Frances asked.

"You gave birth to a kraut's child," Terrance snapped before continuing on his way.

Frances crouched down and picked up the letters before heading inside. She placed them on the dining table as John came over with the cups of tea. He handed one of them to Arthur before turning back towards her.

"Are you okay?" John asked.

"They'll never forget will they?" Frances sobbed. "We'll have to move away. The stares. The whispers. Timmy's never going to be able to play with the other kids in the village."

"Terrance Trilby again? He should keep his bloody nose out of other people's business!"

"He's right though isn't he?"

"Christopher did a lot of things to help people in this village. He helped father find out who murdered the man on the beach. He tended everyone's gardens and he helped uncover old Harry Partridge's secret. People in this village have very short memories when they want them."

"And long ones too!" Arthur shouted out. "She should've kept her bloody legs shut!"

Frances began to cry and ran up the stairs towards the bedroom.

Timmy came rushing into the kitchen. "Is mummy crying?" he asked.

John crouched down in front of him. "She's just a little bit upset, that's all," he explained. "Are you going to show me your stick collection?"

"Yes!" Timmy replied as he led John back outside.

As they were building wigwams with sticks in the garden, John noticed a truck heading down the road towards the rebuilt Honeypot Cottage on the corner of the woods. The truck stopped outside the cottage and a husband and wife stepped out alongside their teenage daughter, two younger daughters who John guessed were around eight years old and a small boy who looked a little younger.

There was something about the teenage girl that John recognised. Her shoulder length brown hair, her dark features and the way she was ushering the children towards the house.

"It's another demand letter," Frances called out, interrupting his thoughts. "What are you looking at?"

"Oh, just the new family moving into the new Honeypot Cottage. Who is the letter from?"

"Dad hasn't been able to make the rent payment for the past three months. If we don't repay what we owe, they're going to move us out of the house."

John dug around in his pockets and pulled out some notes.

"Where did all of that money come from?" Frances gasped.

"I had an advance on my wages at the police training school. I have three pounds here. Use it to keep the housing officer happy for now and I'll get the rest as soon as I can."

Frances wrapped her arms around his neck. "I don't know what I'd do without you John Langford. You're the only one who never turned their back on me."

"Frances! What's for dinner?" Arthur shouted out.

Frances reluctantly broke the embrace.

"I'd better call in at home. I'll see you later tonight," John smiled as he left the front garden.

As he turned to walk back up the hill towards Southward Cottage, he heard someone call his name. He turned around and saw the teenage girl he'd noticed earlier rushing towards him. She was coughing and looked pale as she approached him but John recognised her immediately.

"Edith?" John asked.

"Yes, it's me. It's so good to see you again. You've changed so much," she replied before wrapping her arms around his neck.

John reluctantly returned the embrace before stepping back. "It's been over eight years, what happened to you? Where did you go?"

Edith coughed and held her chest momentarily.

"Are you okay?" John asked.

"Yes, just a bit of a cough, that's all. We went to a convent in Portsmouth where a group of nuns looked after us. I was able to finish my education there and mother met William. They've been married for four years now and I have two younger sisters and a younger brother. William owns that cafe down on the beach so we thought we'd move back here so he can keep a closer watch on it now that Norman Whitehouse is retiring. But enough about me, what about you?"

"I finished school and Father pushed me through the police training program so I can become a police officer if I pass my exam next year. His dream was to have three generations of Langfords in the force and now he's got it."

"But what's your dream John?"

"What do you mean?"

"You said it was your father's dream to have three generations of Langfords in the police force but is that really what you want?"

"Of course it is. I wouldn't have signed up for it if it wasn't."

"What about girlfriends? Or moving out into your own place."

"I'm sure that will happen in time."

At that moment, John noticed Frances standing at the front gate watching them.

"Anyway, nice to catch up. I guess I'll be seeing you around," John said before rushing away towards his parents house.

"Yes, I guess so," Edith sighed as she watched him leave.

As she turned to head back home, she noticed Frances standing at her gate.

"Edith Wise isn't it?" Frances called out.

"Yes, and you're Frances King, the woman who gave birth to a German's child out of wedlock."

"Good news travels fast."

Edith coughed again before continuing. "Not really. My stepfather owns a business in the area so he needs to know who he is dealing with."

"Just stay away from John Langford if you know what's good for you."

"Or what? John's an old friend. We grew up playing on the beach and making memories together."

"Right before your mother burnt the house down and fled the village like some criminal!"

"My mother did what she had to do to protect her children. If your father had done the same you might not have ended up in the situation you're in!"

"My situation has nothing to do with you. Just stay away from us and stay away from John!"

"You seem to forget that John and I have history together."

"From when you were ten years old, you're both fully grown adults now."

"I know, that's what makes it more exciting doesn't it. I'll be seeing you Frances," Edith smiled before heading back towards Honeypot Cottage.

"Frances! Where's my bloody medicine?" Arthur shouted from inside the house.

Frances waited at the gate for a moment watching Edith walk away before reluctantly heading back inside. She didn't trust her or her family and their return to the village would only mean trouble for her relationship with John.

***

John entered Southward Cottage just as his mother, Mavis, was serving the evening meal.

"Ah, perfect timing John. Can you take the cutlery and lay out the dining table for me?" Mavis asked.

"Of course, is father home yet?"

"No, you know him. He won't be home for hours. I'll leave him a plate of stew on the stove."

"Where are the others?"

"Fred is outside building a treehouse with his friend Sean and Mary is in her bedroom finishing some homework. Can you call them in on your way through, there's a good lad."

When the family sat down at the table to eat their evening meal, they were interrupted by someone knocking at the door. Mavis stood from the table and wandered over to answer it. When she opened the door, she gasped in surprise.

"Hello old friend," a woman's voice said.

"No, it can't be," Mavis replied.

John rushed over to join his mother at the front door. Standing in front of them was Dana Wise.

Chapter Twenty-Three

Blake Makes The Connection
Wednesday 5th November 2008

Samir Khalifa was waiting at Gatwick Airport when Alison and Blake returned from Rhodes. As they walked through the arrivals gate, he approached them with two police officers beside him.

"What have we done now?" Alison sighed.

"Samir, what's going on? I thought you and Joe were tying up loose ends in East Boldre," Blake asked.

"We'll come to that. This is Sergeant John Burrows and Officer Kingsley Amos," Samir replied.

"Mr Langford, Miss Pearce, could you please follow us this way?" Burrows asked as he led them towards a room near to the exit.

When they were inside, Blake turned to Samir. "What the hell's going on?"

"Mr Langford," Burrows began. "We understand that Special Branch has an ongoing investigation into a Mr Thomas Edward Gibson."

"Amongst others, yes."

"Official records show that Mr Gibson is currently residing in the south of France with his cousin, a Miss Jade Elizabeth Smith."

That took Blake by surprise. "Cousin?"

"Second-cousin to be precise," Amos added.

"Is this the same Jade Smith who's sister Andrea was found in the grave in East Boldre?" Alison asked.

"The same. Formal identification was completed by Mr Khalifa and his partner, Joe Knight, when they attended the mortuary with Jade Smith and a Miss Jennifer Eleanor Langford on Monday evening," Burrows replied.

"What's Jenny got to do with this?" Blake asked.

"Nothing as yet, Mr Langford, however, after the identification, Miss Smith returned to south-east London and visited a rundown flat on Tuesday morning around 11am according to eye-witnesses."

"There's no crime in that," Blake replied.

"No, except a neighbour heard screams coming from the flat a few minutes later. When Officer Amos and his colleague arrived on the scene, they discovered two mutilated bodies trapped inside glass cells covered in acid."

Blake shook his head. He had heard about some torture methods that had been used after an alleged betrayal of Russian informants but this was the first time he had come across it in his own line of work. "Was it Tom Gibson?" he asked.

"We're still trying to identify the victims from dental records but it seems to be Gibson and quite possibly Jade Smith," Burrows confirmed.

"So, where do we come into this?" Alison asked.

"Jade Smith was involved in your investigation into the woman, Andrea Smith, who was buried alive. Our team also found evidence that led them into investigating a hidden inheritance involving the Smith, Handanowicz and Langford families. The laptops have been seized and are being analysed as we speak. There were also links to the dark web, more specifically, a program known as The Crystal."

"The Crystal was shut down after Tom Gibson and his men were stopped from trafficking students and weapons out of London six months ago," Alison replied.

"Officially it was closed down but there have been continued investments on the dark web to fund terrorism," Amos explained.

"This inheritance that you're talking about," Blake replied. "When was it discovered?"

"Its whereabouts were unknown until recently when a safety deposit box was reopened at Goodman, Parker & Knowles inc. on Regent Street."

Blake took a deep breath. The day after his mother's funeral, he received a letter in the mail containing a key to a safety deposit box at Goodman, Parker & Knowles inc. When he went to open it, he had uncovered some photos of people he didn't recognise alongside his grandparents from 1948. There had to be a connection.

"Is something wrong Mr Langford?" Amos asked.

Blake shook his head. "No, just thinking about things. Safety deposit boxes are rarely used these days so if one is opened, how is that information used?"

"Usually no information is shared however, when you opened the box belonging to the late Emily Avis Jane Langford, it automatically sent out letters to all beneficiaries of the Jack Smith legacy," Burrows explained.

"And do they all know each other?" Alison asked.

"No, but it wouldn't take a genius to work it out if you were involved in the families," Amos replied.

"If you already knew that I opened the box then why all this cloak-and-dagger bullshit?" Blake asked.

"Because more and more people connected to that box have died or had an attempt on their life!" Burrows replied. "We need to find out who is behind this and stop them before they strike again."

"Hang on, back up a minute here," Alison interrupted. "You said that the bodies you suspect belong to Tom Gibson and Jade Smith were found locked in glass cells covered in acid. Obviously they didn't encase themselves there of their own free will so did your so-called eye-witnesses notice anyone else coming or going from the flat around the time the screams were heard?"

"Only an elderly lady who was walking past with two middle aged men, probably her sons," Amos replied.

"And have you traced them?" Blake asked.

"Not yet, no."

"Well don't you think that's a good place to start?"

"We don't tell you how to do your job Mr Langford so please refrain from telling us how to do ours," Burrows replied.

"Maybe it's time to pool our resources," Samir suggested.

"What do you have in mind?" Amos asked.

"Alison and Blake headed out to Rhodes after someone tried to murder Evelyn and James Handanowicz. If what you say is true about the Jack Smith legacy, there's a good chance that Evelyn and James would stand to inherit something."

Amos nodded.

"Therefore, it seems that somebody is trying to kill off those who stand to inherit to take the money for themselves."

"Yes, we realise that Mr Khalifa. The Greek police have already informed us of Mr Langford's involvement in their case..." Burrows snapped.

"The two men sent to kill Evelyn and James worked for Tom Gibson!" Blake replied. "Ian Bleeker and Zachary Zhal, also known as Reaper and Zodiac, were big players in the trafficking of young students in the capital. If you took more care of the vulnerable people in your city, we wouldn't have to keep tidying up your mess!"

"Our mess? We weren't the ones who let a murder suspect escape a Greek island during an investigation!"

"James Handanowicz was innocent! The men who came after him were shot by Evelyn Handanowicz!"

"Who conveniently committed suicide after telling you what you needed to know. Almost like it was planned..."

"What are you insinuating?" Blake asked.

"Oh stop it, both of you!" Alison snapped. "The reality is, we have a serial killer who is somehow manipulating the system and targeting anyone who stands in their way. Does anyone know who would have some kind of vendetta against the families now that Zodiac, Reaper and Gibson are dead?"

"The Smith family were linked to the murder of several of Zodiac's acquaintances which could have made Andrea and Jade targets," Samir replied.

Blake glared at him.

"How do you know this?" Burrows asked.

"A previous investigation."

Burrows turned his attention to Blake. "Jade and Andrea were close friends with your sister, Jennifer."

"Meaning?"

"Her life could be in danger. They've already taken out both of her friends and their grandfather."

"What about their parents?" Alison asked.

"Both Smith parents were killed in a motorcycling accident three years ago. Victor Wise was their only living relative remaining," Amos replied.

"What do you mean, was?" Blake asked. "I spoke to him at the weekend!"

"Victor Wise was found dead yesterday morning in his assisted living complex near The New Forest. Early reports show that he took an overdose," Burrows confirmed.

Blake held his head in his hands.

"If you know anyone who has a vendetta against your family, now is the time to tell us Blake."

"I come from four generations of Langfords who have worked in law enforcement in one way or another. We've been responsible for putting hundreds of people away. It could be any of them," Blake admitted.

"We have advised your sister to stay with your family on the south coast. Eric Gordon has doubled up your security. Frank Jackson will be supported by Andre Park until things calm down. In the meantime, I suggest you work out who is coming after your family and stop them," Burrows replied.

When they left the airport terminal, Samir led them towards the car park. "Joe managed to track a signal from Special Branch to Goodman, Parker & Knowles inc. yesterday. Someone has inside information and we need to shut it down."

"I didn't mention it in there but my father once spoke of a woman named Frances King. She lived next door to my grandparents when my dad was growing up. Before he married my mother, he had a brief relationship with her. After he broke it off, she was borderline schizophrenic, stalking him, calling him, leaving him letters, she was obsessed with him. She was part of the reason why the family moved to London just to get away from her," Blake explained.

"Do you think she could be involved?" Alison asked. "Your parents were married for a long time."

"They married in 1977 but when I was fishing with my father one night off of Lepe beach when I was a teenager, I remember he told me how he had avoided going there for so long. It was one of the best fishing spots on the south coast but he was scared to go back in case Frances showed up and saw him there."

"So how did you come into possession of the cottage?" Samir asked.

"My grandparents died in the late 80's under suspicious circumstances which were probably connected to the King family. My father's sister, Mary, bought his share of the house and stayed there until she died in 2004. In her will, she left the house solely to me which pissed off my siblings to the extent that we didn't talk for three years."

"Why wasn't it split between the three of you?" Alison asked.

"I guess it was mine and my father's escape from the pressures of work and life. Several times per year we would go and stay with Aunt Mary and spend many nights fishing off of Lepe Beach. He told me that the beach somehow made him feel closer to his parents. I never really knew my father before then. He'd always been a private man. Much like my grandfather. They never shared their thoughts and feelings. Whatever difficulties you had in life were your own and it was a sign of weakness to show them to others."

"A lot of older people were like that."

"But when it was just the two of us, we had deep conversations that we'd never have had if we were at home or at work. I really got to know him as a man as well as a father."

"And this is when he told you about Frances?" Samir asked.

Blake nodded. "I may be completely wrong but not much unsettled my father, John Langford, but she really got under his skin."

"Did they have a serious relationship together?" Alison asked.

"Briefly, I think. She was ten years older than my father and was the next door neighbour whilst he was growing up. She had a child out of marriage, I think the father was German, and dad kind of took on the father role after leaving school, even though he was only nine years older than the child. I guess he felt sorry for them as the family became social outcasts."

"Having any kind of a relationship with the Germans after the war was frowned upon so I can see why he tried to help. What happened? Was the social stigma the reason they split up?"

"No, father's childhood girlfriend who moved away eight years earlier returned and a love triangle developed and he ended up leaving Frances for his old girlfriend."

"No wonder she was pissed then," Samir replied as they arrived at the car.

As they sat inside, Alison began logging into Special Branch's internal network to begin searching for the connection. "What was the woman's name back then?" she asked.

"King, Frances King," Blake replied. "Although there's a chance she may have been married."

"Who was the girl your father left her for? Was it your mother, Emily?" Samir asked.

"No, her older sister, Edith..." Blake paused for a moment. "Of course."

"What?" Alison asked.

"Edith Wise. Dana Handanowicz was originally married to Gerald Wise. Victor Wise told me about Edith breaking up Dad and Frances when she returned to Lepe. If Frances knew about the huge inheritance then she would have felt cheated out of the money. If it's not her then it's got to be her relatives."

"Blake, if that's true and she had this German's child in 1948, she must have been at least late teens, early twenties then, that makes her almost eighty years old! How the hell can an eighty year old arrange a coup like this?" Samir asked.

"Do you know the name of the child?" Alison asked.

"Tommy or Timmy, something like that," Blake replied. "She was seventeen when the baby was born. Her mother was killed during the war and she had to look after her father and a newborn baby at that young age. I guess that's why Dad tried to help her."

"That would still make her late seventies now. When my grandmother was in her seventies it took her all her effort to fart," Samir said as he joined the motorway heading back into London.

"That explains why you're full of hot air then, it's hereditary."

Samir gave a sarcastic laugh. "Whatever that deposit box contained, it seems to have created a shitstorm that nobody seems to be able to work out."

"You said Joe found a signal coming out of Special Branch to Goodman, Parker & Knowles inc. Any idea who made contact?" Blake asked.

"It's bouncing off of the firewalls but it seemed to come from one of the main offices. Joe has based himself in The New Forest in the hope that he can rattle the undertaker and the locals and try and get some answers there. We'll head in to see Gordon and find out if we have anything new," Samir replied.

"I think I may have found something," Alison said as she leant forward from the back seat to show Blake her phone.

"Obituaries?" Blake asked.

"Arthur Stafford King, died 5th September 1960, from Lepe, Hampshire. Beloved father of Frances Irene King and grandfather of Timothy Mark King. His grave is at All Saints Church cemetery in Hythe. That must be the same family."

"He's buried in the next village so that makes sense but as far as I'm aware, she was still there until at least 1977."

"Maybe she took over the house after her father died?" Samir added.

"How can you be so sure on dates?" Alison asked.

"My parents got married on August 12th 1977. From that date on, dad never heard from Frances again."

"Maybe she realised that now he was married, she was fighting a lost cause and moved onto someone else," Samir replied.

"It's possible but if she was that much of a stalker, a marriage certificate isn't going to stand in her way," Alison reasoned.

They soon arrived at Special Branch headquarters. Samir parked his car in the underground car park and the three of them headed up in the lift to the eighth floor. They walked along the corridor and entered the second from last door on the left.

"We thought you'd never get back," Angela, Eric Gordon's secretary, said as they entered the office.

"We had a welcoming committee at the airport," Blake replied. "Any news from the undertakers?"

"Not yet but we've traced your family tree through records back to 1882 to highlight any connections with the infamous Jack Smith."

Blake walked over and looked at Angela's screen.

"It seems that both of your grandparents, Dana Handanowicz and Mavis Langford both gave birth to Jack Smith's children as well as someone called Ada Hughes," Angela explained.

"Are you suggesting my parents could have been siblings!"

"No, John Langford was born in 1938 and was Edward Langford's biological son. Mary and Frederick Langford were fathered by Jack Smith in 1942."

"That's what Victor Wise said," Blake replied as he ran his fingers through his hair. "My grandfather was fighting in the war in '42."

"I'm sorry Blake."

"What about the Handanowicz side?"

"It seems that Dana Wise as she was originally known had two children, Edith and Victor. Edith's father was Gerald Wise who she was married to but he died in the war. Victor Wise was born in 1941. A year after Gerald Wise was enlisted."

"So Jack Smith fathered Victor in '41 and then Mary and Fred in '42."

"The photograph you discovered in the safety deposit box was from 1948. The man in that photo is Jack Smith, twenty-four hours before he died," Angela explained.

"So he was still with the family in 1948. How the hell did my grandfather not make the connection, he was a police detective for Christ's sake!"

"Sometimes, if we're too close to the subject, we become blind to things. You of all people should know that."

Blake nodded. "Point taken."

Angela clicked onto some old newspaper reports from 1948 of a burnt out house in Lepe. "The report says that Honeypot Cottage had been destroyed in a suspected arson attack on 15th July 1948."

"The day after the photo was taken."

"Dana and Edith Wise had disappeared, presumed dead, until they returned to live in the rebuilt house eight years later. Dana had a new husband, William Handanowicz, a successful businessman and two seven year old daughters with her, Emily and Evelyn Handanowicz and a four year old son, James Handanowicz."

"And there's nothing to suggest that Emily and Evelyn were William's children?" Blake asked.

"The timings don't add up. It wouldn't have been possible as Dana and William were not married until 1950."

"Even back then there was still the chance of sex before marriage," Samir reasoned.

"When your mother passed away Blake, a DNA test was done on the order of Eric and it proved a match for Jack Smith being her father," Angela admitted.

"How did Special Branch get DNA from Jack Smith? He's been dead for sixty years!" Blake snapped.

"He died in 1948 but his eldest daughter is still alive in witness protection."

"Who is she?"

"I'm not at liberty to say."

"Angela..."

At that moment, the buzzer sounded and the light above Eric Gordon's room changed from red to green. Alison, Samir and Blake reluctantly entered, more confused than ever.

Chapter Twenty-Four

Edith's Secret

Saturday 22nd September 1956

John Langford entered Southampton Hospital just after 6pm on Saturday evening. Dana was waiting outside a treatment room as they approached.

"What happened?" John asked as they arrived.

"The doctor thinks she has pneumonia. She's been coughing and struggling to breathe for weeks."

"And you've only just decided to bring her to the hospital now?"

"There's been a lot of things going on in the past few months, John. We thought coming back to the village and being in familiar surroundings would help Edith recover."

"But it didn't, did it?"

"She asked for you to be here. Going in there angry isn't going to help anyone."

"If you hadn't run away all those years ago..."

"We'd be in the same situation we're in now," Dana replied. "Don't make this any more difficult than it already is!"

"What do you mean?" John asked.

At that moment, the doctor came out of the room where Edith was being treated. They both approached him.

"She's stable for now but her breathing is very shallow. We will need to run some more tests before we know how bad the pneumonia is," the doctor explained.

"Can we see her?" John asked.

"Yes but keep it brief. She needs as much rest as possible."

John looked at Dana. She nodded. She had spent the past month rebuilding her friendship with John's mother, Mavis, and knew that he still held a close bond with Edith.

John entered the room and was immediately greeted with wires and tubes coming out from all angles and making all kinds of noises. Edith smiled briefly before coughing once again.

"It's okay, don't try to talk," John said as he held her hand. "The doctors are doing all that they can to help you."

"It's too late for that," Edith sighed.

"Don't say that."

"It's true. I've been ill for so long now. It's just a matter of time until..."

John bowed his head. Edith squeezed his hand. He looked up at her. She was staring directly at him.

"I want you to do something for me John," she said.

"Anything, what is it?"

"In my bag, over there, is a brown envelope. Can you get it for me?"

John picked up the bag and brought it over to the bed before sorting through its contents. He found the brown envelope and removed it from the bag.

"Keep it safe for me. Don't let anyone else read it or know about it."

"What is it?" he asked.

"Our family's legacies. The truth about why we had to disappear in '48," Edith replied before coughing again.

John handed her a tissue which she coughed blood into. "What do you mean, our family's legacy?"

"No matter what, our families will be entwined forever. If anything happens to me, I want you to open the letter and then keep it hidden forever."

"Edith, you're not making any sense."

"Please John," she coughed again. "If you ever loved me, promise you'll do this one thing for me."

John nodded. "I promise."

He stayed at the hospital for a while longer before heading back home. As he walked up the hill towards Southward Cottage, he noticed Frances standing at the front gate of her house waiting for him.

"Where have you been?" she asked as he walked by.

"Working."

"Until this late?"

"It's a big case. Where's Timmy?"

"Inside, father's reading him a story. I heard Edith got rushed into the hospital."

"Did she?"

"But you already knew that didn't you!"

"What's your problem Frances?" John snapped.

"My problem John is the fact that my partner is spending more time with that tart down the road than me!"

"Don't ever call her that again! We've been close friends since we were children and if I want to catch up with an old friend from time to time then I will!"

"And what about us," Frances cried. "What about Timmy and me?"

"What about you?"

"Don't you care about us too?"

"Of course I do, it's just..."

"You care for Edith more."

John bowed his head.

"Just go John," Frances snapped. "Go. Be with her, just get the hell out of our lives!"

John turned and began to walk away. Frances called out his name but he ignored her. He carried on walking until he arrived at Southward Cottage, his family home. He walked up to the front door, let himself inside and closed it behind him.

***

Two days later, John was attending a call with his colleague, Officer David Oldman, from someone who discovered a pile of rubbish that had been dumped down by the river near Beaulieu. As they were collecting statements from the local residents, Edward Langford parked up next to them. Sergeant Hastings stepped out of the car and wandered over towards them. He took over the line of questioning from John and urged him to go over to the car.

John opened the passenger door and sat inside the car alongside Edward. "I thought you were avoiding me?"

"Just trying not to interfere," Edward replied. "We need to go."

"Go where? I'm in the middle of an investigation."

"Hastings can cover it until you get back."

"No Father, what's going on?"

"We had a phone call from the hospital, Edith Wise died this morning."

John sat back in his chair. A shiver ran through his body and tears stung his eyes. He took a couple of deep breaths. "When? How?" he asked.

"She died peacefully in her sleep this morning. Her lungs just couldn't go on anymore. I'm sorry, I know you and Edith were close for a long time. Dana and William Handanowicz are still at the hospital if you want to see her."

John nodded.

Edward started the car and drove away to the hospital. Both men never spoke another word on the journey there. When John walked into the hospital ward, he felt a feeling of emptiness he had never experienced before. People were rushing around him going from place to place but it all seemed to disappear into the background as he became consumed in his own little zone.

"John?" a woman's voice interrupted his thoughts.

He turned around to see Dana Handanowicz looking at him.

"Are you sure you can do this?" she asked.

John nodded.

Together, they walked along the corridor and entered a small side room at the end of the hospital ward. Laying lifeless but this time without all of the wires and tubes he had seen before was the one girl he knew deep down, had stolen his heart from when he was just a young boy. Now, at nineteen years old, he looked at Edith's body, at peace in the hospital bed and his heart broke anew. He felt a pain deep within that he knew he could never explain. So many dreams, so many memories together came flooding back but he knew, no matter what he did, there was no way to bring her back. Edith Wise, his first love, had gone.

John spent a few minutes at her bedside before leaving the hospital once again. He walked for what seemed like an eternity, not meeting the glances of anybody or acknowledging any kind of conversation or distraction. He walked into the city centre before sitting down on a wooden bench outside a pharmacy.

He looked around watching everybody else rushing to wherever they were headed, carrying on as if nothing had happened and to them, nothing had happened. Life goes on as normal. Nobody stopped to consider the wishes and dreams of those who had died and John felt a bitterness deep inside. He felt like he and Edith had been cheated out of a life they had always dreamed of and his anger burned deep inside him.

As he leant on the arm of the bench, he felt something in his inside jacket pocket. He reached inside and found an envelope. His heart panged anew as he recognised Edith's handwriting on the front of it. He opened the envelope and read the letter inside;

Dearest John

If you're reading this, it means I'm no longer with you and though it makes me sad to think of this, I know you will go on and live those dreams we had together for me.

I know we will never be able to reclaim those missing years. I never expected to have to flee my home for the safety of my family but the war should have taught me that nothing is ever certain anymore. Not even the love of a family. You see, I have three siblings who share the same father as your siblings too. Our mother's, no matter how much they deny it, could not resist the charm of a serviceman in their care during the war.

Jack Smith was a scoundrel. He made his fortune robbing banks from before the war and used the gold to charm his way into the arms of the lonely willing women who stayed at home when their husband's went off to war.

Mother could never live with the shame of having a child out of wedlock and my elder brother has found a new life in London. She was not done there though and now Evelyn and Emily will carry on his family genes to the next generation too. If William had not been so understanding, who knows where we would have ended up?

Jack gave mother two gold bars to disappear from Lepe and never return. When I became ill, I asked her to give me one last wish and that was to see you one last time. At least we had the chance to say goodbye and I will always love you John Langford.

Take care of Evelyn, Emily, Fred and Mary. They must never know how deep the family ties run but our love will live on forever.

With all my love, now and forever,

Your Edith

xx

John read the letter several times, barely believing the words that Edith had written. Both of their mothers had had affairs during the war and it was with the same man that his father, Edward, had discovered on the beach, the day after he had joined them all for luncheon. It all made sense now. Seeing Jack Smith handing over money to Dana before she had come along to join them on the beach. Their disappearance. How he longed for those missing years now. There must have been a way for them to have resolved the situation.

He placed the envelope back inside his pocket and headed towards the railway station. He stopped at the bank just outside the station and withdrew enough money to see him through for a while before buying a one-way ticket to London Waterloo. As he climbed aboard the train, only taking with him the clothes he was wearing, John Langford knew he needed to get away, he needed somewhere to start over again. As the tall buildings and busy streets of Southampton disappeared into the distance, he took a deep breath and relaxed for the first time in a long time. He felt at peace with his life. Edith had wanted him to live his life and dreams like they had imagined when they were young and now John was determined to do just that.

***

"Open the door! I know you're in there!" Frances shouted as she hammered on the door of Southward Cottage. "Come out and face me you coward!"

"What on Earth is going on?" Edward Langford asked as he approached his front door.

"Your son has been ignoring me!"

"I'm not surprised with the way you are acting. When you decide that you can act like a lady, you can come in. Until then, be on your way."

"But..."

"No buts. My son has been more than kind to you considering your situation."

"He gets compensated for it!"

"Indeed, what I mean is there are a lot of people in this village that have very long memories."

"Just because some people are prejudiced doesn't mean I should live my life in fear!"

"Of course not but likewise, hammering on the door of a man ten years younger than yourself demanding his attention isn't a good look for a young lady either."

"This is not over!" Frances fumed before storming away back down the driveway.

"I doubt it is," Edward replied before heading inside.

As he entered the cottage, an eerie silence greeted him.

"Hello!" Edward called out but there was no reply.

He walked through the cottage and into the kitchen where there was a note left on the dining table.

GONE TO CHURCH.
DINNER IS IN THE OVEN.

Edward frowned. Ever since old Father Harold Partridge had been discovered frolicking with two young German men, most of the villagers had left the congregation in their droves. Harold had since moved on and a new vicar by the name of Rupert Bradley had taken over from him. He thought of Edith Wise and her untimely death. Since leaving John at the hospital, he hadn't heard from him for the rest of the day. He reheated his dinner before settling down to read the newspaper and enjoying some time alone. Around an hour later, the family all returned home. Mary and Fred rushed off to get ready for bed whilst Mavis made a pot of tea.

"Have you seen John this evening?" she asked.

"No, I haven't seen him since I dropped him at the hospital at lunchtime," Edward replied.

"You didn't go in with him?"

"He's not a child anymore, Mavis. There are some things that a man should do on his own."

She didn't reply.

"How was church? Has the new reverend managed to convince the naysayers back?"

"It's not like that and you know it. However you dress it up, what Harold did to those poor men was illegal."

"Is it illegal to love somebody?"

"You know what I mean!"

"Times are changing, Mavis. Maybe the world needs to too."

"Too much is changing if you ask me. That blasted Frances turned up at the church looking for John again. Caused quite a stir."

"Well she's desperate isn't she. I told him she'd be nothing but trouble. He's too caring for his own good."

"Can you have a word with her?"

"I tried earlier when she was trying to break the door down."

"She was here too?"

Edward nodded. "If John doesn't report in, she goes loopy. No wonder Christopher left her."

"You really can be heartless at times!"

"If a woman is going to put herself in that situation then she needs to deal with the consequences."

"She lost her mother during the war, her father uses her as a slave and the gardener took advantage of her and left her pregnant and alone. I hardly call that a situation she created on her own."

"So you think John is right to keep going around there and helping her?"

"Oh, I don't know. I'm worried about him. He was very close with Edith. Her death could take its toll on him and he should be concentrating on his career rather than women."

"I'm sure he'll make the right decision in the end," Edward replied before heading out towards the back garden.

Meanwhile next door at Thyme Cottage, the doorbell echoed around the house.

"Frances!" Arthur shouted from the living room.

"Don't shout, I've just got Timmy settled," she replied as she headed towards the front door.

"If it's that Langford lad you can tell him to get lost! Calling round at this hour. Only one thing he's after..."

Frances slowly opened the front door and saw a man dressed in black waiting there.

"Father Partridge, I thought you had left the village," Frances said.

"I had, I did, I mean, well, I heard you needed some help so I thought I'd call by."

"How thoughtful," Frances smiled ruefully.

"Who is it?" Arthur asked.

"Just a friend," Frances replied as she stepped outside.

"I heard about Edith Wise. Terrible situation," Harold continued. "Have you heard from John?"

"No, not today."

"It must be tough, being cast aside for a teenager like that."

"What do you mean?"

"Oh, John and Edith were always so close. It was obvious when her family returned that she would turn his head."

"Is that so?"

"Oh, don't get me wrong, you really are a most wonderful woman Miss King, I just, er..."

"Just what?"

Harold didn't reply.

"Actually, there is something you can help me with," she said as she led Harold towards the garden shed.

"Oh, right, okay, what is it?"

"I've been having a bit of trouble with a clamp in the garden shed. It seems to be a little stiff."

Frances opened the door and picked up the torch that had been left on a workbench inside the shed. "After you," she insisted.

Harold stepped inside and in one quick movement, she struck him on the back of his head, sending him falling to the floor inside the shed. She shone the light on him briefly to check that he was unconscious before locking the door and returning to the house. As she closed the front door, she heard her father calling out again.

"It's okay, no one will disturb us anymore," she replied.

Chapter Twenty-Five

Misplaced Trust

Wednesday 5th November 2008

"In forty-three years of working for the British Government, I don't think I've ever come across a case where my lead investigator has risked everything for a fairytale!" Eric Gordon snapped as Alison, Blake and Samir entered his office and sat down. "Where is James Handanowicz?"

"Escaping an unfair justice system in the Greek Islands when all he was doing was protecting his sister," Alison replied.

"Yes, this family affair of the Langfords seems to have thrown up a history of betrayal and red herrings."

"I didn't realise my family tree was public knowledge," Blake replied.

"Don't you think we fully vet every operative that ever enters this room Blake? This is threatening to blow up into something that could seriously undermine Her Majesty's Government!"

"I don't follow Sir, how does a body sticking out of a grave and a double murder in Rhodes constitute a problem for the Government?" Alison asked. "Blake and I were just following a lead."

"When the coffin was exhumed from the cemetery, there was a noticeable difference to how the corpse was expected to be," Eric explained.

Alison and Blake both looked at Samir. "When I examined the body, it was remarkably well preserved," he explained.

"The coffin was lead lined, therefore preserving the body and its hidden contents which was discovered when it was brought to the undertakers for further examination."

"What was hidden in the coffin?" Blake asked.

Samir removed the card he found in Jack Smith's urn earlier and placed it on the desk. "I removed this when I examined the body," he lied.

Blake picked it up. "It's a piece of the map. How was it so well preserved?"

Samir shrugged.

"Dana Handanowicz, the woman whose body was in the coffin was used by her husband to hide a secret. William Handanowicz had the access codes to a nuclear bomb that was buried just after world war two in the UK. When Joe Knight went back to the undertakers to inspect the coffin and retrieve the codes, they were gone. Today, we received a letter demanding the gold that was hidden in Holbury Manor as payment for not setting that bomb off," Eric Gordon explained.

"Where is the bomb?" Alison asked.

"Underneath an oil refinery on the south coast near to The New Forest."

"The same refinery that pumps gas across the entire south of England," Blake gasped. "If that goes off, it'll kill millions and wipe out the whole of London and half of the country!"

"Indeed," Eric Gordon nodded.

"How the hell did William Handanowicz have the codes?" Samir asked.

"Because he was my senior officer in Special Branch until he retired in 1982. When I took over the office, there was no mention of it until after his death in 1987. An internal investigation discovered that he had indeed taken the codes to the grave with him."

"Was William Handanowicz's grave searched?" Alison asked.

"He was cremated," Blake replied.

"So was Dana Handanowicz," Samir added.

Blake glared at him. "So how do we stop this bomb?"

"There is an underground bunker inside the refinery that goes five hundred metres below ground. If you can access that, you could find the bomb and defuse it but you need to find those access codes."

"That's like looking for a needle in a haystack. Where do we even start?" Samir asked.

"Our friend the undertaker would be top of the list. Where's Joe Knight now?" Blake asked.

Eric Gordon pressed his intercom. "Angela? Angela?"

No response.

Eric checked his watch. "That's odd," he said as he walked towards the door.

As he opened it, the office was empty. Eric walked through and checked the toilet area before coming back to his office.

"Where is Ada Hughes' daughter?" Blake asked as Eric returned to the office.

"What do you know about the Hughes family?"

"Angela had been doing some digging before we arrived but clammed up when Blake asked where she was," Alison replied.

"Please Sir, she may be our missing connection," Blake replied.

"Patricia Hughes is in witness protection for her own safety."

"Yet Angela knew all about the Jack Smith connection. Who is Patricia hiding from?" Samir asked.

"The same people who killed her son and her niece."

"Patricia Hughes is Tom Gibson's mother," Alison replied.

Eric nodded.

Blake felt a shiver run through him. If his father John knew about the Jack Smith connection, that was why he did everything in his power to break up Tom and Jenny. He knew there was a chance that they were cousins. He rushed into the outer office and began tapping away on Angela's laptop.

"What are you doing?" Alison asked.

"If we can pick up the signal from Angela's mobile phone, we can find out where she's going!"

"You mean this mobile phone," Samir replied as he lifted up a phone that had been left by the coffee machine.

Blake swore under his breath. "Where is she going Sir? There was a signal from here to Goodman, Parker & Knowles inc. Who sent the message to release all of the information?"

"Angela released the information to the solicitors as per the freedom of information act," Eric admitted.

"In doing that, my family is now at risk. Whoever killed Gibson will now be heading for Southward Cottage!"

"Your family have protection Blake. Frank and Andre are there. They will know that and won't attack. They want the gold that Jack Smith robbed from CityBank in 1938. Tom Gibson would have had a section of the map, you have the pieces from Victor Wise and James Handanowicz, the final piece would have been left with Mavis Langford."

"But Mavis has died," Alison replied.

"Her belongings were moved after she died. Aunt Mary took over the house and Grandma's things were donated to Francesca Audrey's Hospice in Lymington," Blake said.

"That's where you'll find Patricia," Eric Gordon replied. "She will have the final piece."

***

A red FIAT 500 pulled up outside Francesca Audrey's Hospice in Lymington. Frances Vaselievich stepped out of the passenger seat and closed the door. She walked around to the drivers' side and as the window wound down, the driver handed her a small vial with clear liquid inside it.

"Make me proud," she said before walking towards the entrance.

The car drove away leaving an eerie calmness outside the home as day gave way to night time. She pressed the doorbell and waited at the door until a nurse came and answered it.

"Can I help you?" the nurse asked.

"Yes, I'm here to see Patricia Hughes," Frances replied.

"Are you a relative?"

"An old friend."

"I'm afraid visiting time is over for today."

"Oh, I've come a long way and you wouldn't see an elderly lady out in the cold in this weather would you?"

The nurse looked at her quizzically for a moment before sighing and stepping aside. "I guess thirty minutes wouldn't hurt," she said as she closed the door behind Frances.

"Bless you dear," Frances replied as she slipped off her coat.

"If I could get you to sign in for me..."

Frances picked up the pen and signed a false name in the book.

"May I take your coat?" the nurse asked.

"No, no, it's okay, I'll keep hold of it. Where is Patricia?"

"This way," the nurse replied as she led Frances through the hospice.

When they arrived at the day room, there were two elderly women and an elderly man sat in armchairs watching snooker on the TV whilst two other women were standing in, what looked like a kitchen area, making themselves a drink. Frances recognised one of the women in the kitchen area and she in turn, recognised Frances.

"Mrs Hughes, you have a visitor," the nurse called out.

Patricia kept her eyes firmly on Frances whilst fiddling with something in one of the drawers. "I thought visiting time was over."

"Is that a way to greet an old friend Pat?" Frances asked as she approached her.

The second lady in the kitchen area moved away leaving them alone.

"What do you want, Frances?" Patricia asked.

"I just came to see an old friend as I was in the area."

"Don't you live abroad now?"

"I did until my divorce and then suddenly, I no longer felt welcome behind the iron curtain anymore."

Patricia watched her as she approached the work surface where she had placed her coffee cup. "I came here to end my days in peace. Whatever Thomas has done is on him now. I've washed my hands of it all."

"You see, that's where you're wrong," Frances whispered.

"What do you mean?"

"You have something I need."

"I gave up the family legacy long ago. We're both too old for fairytales."

"Tom died for that fairytale..."

In one quick movement, Patricia removed a dinner knife from the drawer and stabbed it through the top of Frances's hand impaling it to the wooden work surface.

"Mrs Hughes! What on Earth?" the nurse gasped as she rushed over to attend to Frances's bleeding hand.

"Miss King was just leaving," Patricia replied as she began to walk away.

Frances stuck out her leg and tripped her up sending her down to the floor, hitting her head on one of the cupboards. Two more nurses rushed in to attend to Patricia whilst the knife was removed from Frances's hand and a bandage was wrapped around it to cover the wound.

"That woman is the devil!" Patricia shouted as she was led away.

The nurse who had attended to Frances picked up her handbag from the floor but as she did, a small vial of clear liquid fell out of it. "What's this?" she asked as she picked it up.

Frances raised her uninjured arm and hit the nurse in the throat with the side of her hand in a vicious karate chop. The nurse staggered backwards, dropping the vial of liquid on the floor which shattered on impact. Frances rushed towards the exit before being confronted by two men who grabbed hold of her arms and led her into a side room, closing the door behind them.

***

Joe Knight was waiting in his blue Vauxhall Astra outside Crowther's funeral home as Paul Crowther locked the front door and began heading towards his car.

Joe stepped out of his car and walked towards him. "Mr Crowther?"

"Who wants to know?"

"Joe Knight, Special Branch, may I have a word?"

Paul looked at him up and down. "I hope they paid you well for that."

"For what?"

"Looking like that in the name of Queen and country, I'd be amazed if your wife ever looked at you in the same way again."

"My appearance has nothing to do with this case. When Dana Handanowicz's body was exhumed, there was something hidden in the lining of the coffin. Something of importance to national security. When we returned to inspect the coffin, it had been removed so either you or one of your work colleagues have the information that we need."

"What information? All we received was a rotting corpse."

"We both know that's not true."

"Prove it," Paul smirked.

"Interfering with a Special Branch investigation will cost you a lot."

"Listen, all that was in that coffin was a rotting corpse of a woman who died almost thirty years ago. To be honest, her face looked in better condition than yours."

Joe grabbed his shirt and pinned him against the side of his car. "No, you listen to me you piece of shit, I know you're hiding something and you're looking to sell it to the highest bidder but this goes way deeper than you could ever understand."

"Everything all right Paul?" a passer-by asked.

"All good, just a misunderstanding..." Paul replied, "...Ain't it cop?"

Joe reluctantly released his grip on his shirt.

"As long as you're all right," the passer-by replied, looking at Joe and then back at Paul.

"You lot need to get your priorities right here. A young woman has been left buried alive and all you and your colleagues are doing is harassing me and my staff! If you don't back off, I'll get a restraining order put on the lot of ya!" Paul snapped.

"It's because a young woman was buried alive in a grave that your company was responsible for that we are investigating you in the first place. Dana Handanowicz was believed to have been cremated by her family and then her body turned up in an unmarked grave at the centre of an investigation!" Joe replied.

"Families are always at war during a time of grief. Money changes people. Even the most placid and laid-back individuals would chase a fiver in force ten gale if they thought it would give them status over someone else."

"So is this a regular occurrence amongst undertakers then? Kind of a buy one get one free on the funerals?"

"I don't know what deal they cut with my father and I don't want to know. As far as the records show, Dana Handanowicz was buried in that plot but a headstone was never ordered. If the family didn't have the money to pay for one, it wasn't unusual for there to just be the small metal plaque in the ground and any sod can pull that up and nick it. So until you have concrete evidence against me or my company, why don't you piss off and do some real police work scarface and stop wasting my time," Paul snapped as he stepped inside his car.

Joe wanted to react but forced himself to calm down. He knew Crowther wanted a reaction from him so he could get him thrown off the case. He reluctantly headed back towards his car as Paul drove away. As he climbed inside, he found a message from Alison. It read:

GO TO FRANCESCA AUDREY'S HOSPICE IN LYMINGTON, WE MAY HAVE FOUND JACK SMITH'S DAUGHTER, PATRICIA SMITH.

***

A red FIAT 500 pulled up outside Southward Cottage overlooking Lepe Beach. Dmitri and Timmy walked up the driveway past a blue Nissan Note with a spherical dent in its rear bumper and a green Volkswagen that had shiny alloy wheels reflecting the moonlight. As they arrived at the front door, they heard the crackle and bangs of fireworks coming from the back garden as a rainbow of colours illuminated the sky above the cottage. Dmitri pointed for Timmy to head around to the side gate whilst he headed towards the front door. As Dmitri reached for the doorbell, the front door opened and a tall man of African descent with wide shoulders and strong arms dressed in a navy blue shirt and jeans answered.

"Can I help you?" Frank asked.

"Yes, I was looking for Mr Langford," Dmitri replied.

Frank stepped forward and closed the door behind him. "I'm sorry, he's not home right now."

"Oh, that's a shame," Dmitri replied before pulling a knife from out of his sleeve but Frank was too quick for him, aiming a kick to his stomach before landing a right uppercut underneath his chin to send Dmitri to the floor.

At that moment, Michael came rushing out of the side gate and was immediately grabbed in a headlock by Timmy who was waiting by the gate. Michael struggled as much as he could but Timmy held a knife to his neck as he stepped back towards the front garden.

He saw Dmitri laying on the floor with Frank standing over him picking the knife up. "Drop it! Or the kid gets it!" he shouted.

Frank dropped the knife and began slowly walking towards Dmitri. "Let the kid go," he said.

"Where's Langford?" Timmy asked.

"Not here, let the kid go!" Frank replied as he continued to slowly move closer to them.

"Stop! Don't come any closer. I'll kill him, I swear!"

At that moment, Andre charged from the back gate knocking Timmy and Michael to the floor in a rugby tackle. Michael managed to free himself and ran back towards the gate. Timmy kicked, punched and scratched with all of his might and managed to wriggle free of Andre's grasp. Andre leapt on him again but missed as Timmy began running back down the driveway.

"Stay with the family!" Frank shouted as he gave chase down the driveway before heading up the hill and into the woods.

***

Meanwhile, at Francesca Audrey's Hospice in Lymington, the two men who had escorted Frances into the side room locked the door before turning to face her. Frances reached inside her bag for a small spray bottle that looked like a bottle of perfume.

"Is it here Hugh?" she asked.

The man on the right walked over to the mantlepiece and picked up a small gold clock and handed it to her.

"What's going on here?" the second man asked as he approached Frances.

"The less you know, the better," she replied before spraying the man in the face with the contents of the perfume bottle.

The man stepped back before falling to the floor.

"You weren't meant to kill him!" Hugh snapped.

"It's chloroform, it'll wear off," Frances replied before smashing the clock on the floor.

Amongst the pieces of plastic, metal and screws was a small folded piece of yellow paper. Frances carefully picked it up and opened it.

"Five down, three to go," she smiled. "Take his keys and let's go."

Hugh knelt down and removed the second man's keys from his belt before opening the fire exit and leading Frances out into the car park.

Chapter Twenty-Six

Rats

Sunday 23rd September 1956

In the early hours of Sunday morning after Frances's father, Arthur King, and her son Timmy were in bed, Frances wandered into the kitchen and picked up a knife, a jar of honey and a packet of sesame seeds before quietly sneaking out of the back door. Shining her torch on the ground, she walked down the garden path and unlocked the shed door. Squeaking and rustling noises came from the back of the shed as she entered and closed the door. Harold Partridge was still laid out cold on the floor.

Frances tossed a few sesame seeds into the cages at the back of the shed and several rats scurried to collect them. Her father had built a metal workbench around the edge of the inside of the shed where he used to craft wood and metal before he became ill. The legs of the workbench were cemented into the ground giving it a solid base for completing heavy work.

Frances picked up some rope and tied Harold's arms and legs securely to each of the legs of the workbench before waking him up. She splashed his face with some water a few times. When he opened his eyes, he saw a silhouette of a woman standing over him and realised he had been restrained.

"What's happening? What's going on?" Harold asked frantically.

"You took something away from me and somehow, you got away with it," Frances replied.

"What do you mean?"

"You know what I mean."

Harold tried to move his head and grimaced at the pain from the blow he had received to knock him out. "What do you want, Frances?"

"I want you to suffer like I have. Why did you come here?"

"I wanted to help you."

"Liar."

"I'm not proud of what I did..."

"Sleeping with those young men, you should be rotting in jail."

"I know, I know what I did was wrong. I want to make it up to you. Let me help you."

"If you'd just left them alone, Christoph would still be here and my child would have had a father."

"I can help you find him," Harold replied.

"How? After you were exposed by the police and his three friends were killed, there's no chance that he would come back. He's probably back in Germany if not dead by now!"

Harold didn't reply.

"It doesn't matter anyway," Frances sighed as she picked up a handkerchief and used it as a gag.

"What are you doing?" Harold gasped before she forced the material into his mouth.

"You destroyed my life and now I'm going to destroy yours," she replied as she picked up the knife.

Harold's eyes darted everywhere as he groaned and tried to talk through the gag. Frances used the knife to cut open his shirt before undoing his belt and removing his trousers and underwear. She then opened the jar of honey and used the knife to spread the honey over his stomach and down towards his genitals.

Harold tried to wriggle himself free from his restraints, kicking and pulling as hard as he could but he could not break free. After she had finished with the honey, she sprinkled a whole packet of sesame seeds over him. Harold watched with a mix of fear and confusion until he heard the squeaking and rustling coming from the back of the shed. One by one, Frances opened the seven cages that housed the rats. They scurried down onto the floor and climbed over

Harold's body, feverishly attacking the honey and seeds. Frances soaked a blanket in a bucket of water before placing it over the top of the rats as they gorged on the honey and seeds. The wet blanket created a weighted covering that kept the rats contained on his stomach and they slowly ate him to death. Frances watched for a moment as Harold thrashed against the rats before quietly leaving the shed and locking him inside before returning back into her family home.

Later that morning, Sergeant Peter Hastings arrived at Southward Cottage as Edward Langford was building a wooden bench in the garden.

"Good morning Sir," Hastings called out as he approached the house.

"Good morning, what brings you here today?"

"Sorry to bother you on your day off Sir, I just wondered if you have seen John this morning?"

"No, he didn't come home last night, have you tried next door?"

"Yes, no answer there either."

"That's odd, Arthur rarely leaves the house these days," Edward replied as he began walking towards the driveway with Hastings following him.

"Perhaps he needed some time to himself after yesterday."

"I'd have thought that would be the last thing he wanted. In times of grief, a man needs his family's support around him."

"What's that?" Hastings asked as he jogged down the hill towards Thyme Cottage.

A plume of black smoke rose into the air with a decaying smell lingering on the breeze. Edward and Hastings rushed towards the side gate of the house.

"Mr King! Mr King! Are you all right?" Hastings shouted.

They tried the gate but it was locked. Hastings attempted to climb over and reach the latch on the opposite side but kept sliding down.

"Stand clear!" Edward shouted before shoulder barging his way into the garden.

The wooden gate splintered open and bashed hard against the side wall of the house as Edward stumbled into the garden with Hastings following close behind. Inside the garden, they saw Arthur King sitting on a garden chair drinking a cup of coffee as his garden shed burned to the ground.

"Arthur! What the hell are you doing?" Edward gasped. "Hastings, get some water from the outside tap!"

"No, leave it!" Arthur replied.

"You're going to set fire to the hedges and the fence!"

"The shed must be destroyed!"

Hastings filled a bucket of water and threw it over the fire. Flames continued to engulf the shed as a fire engine siren echoed in the distance. Between them, Hastings and Edward threw buckets of water over the hedge, fence and shed, in an attempt to control the blaze, before the firemen came to put it out completely. Edward and Hastings led Arthur back inside the house.

"What on Earth were you thinking, setting your shed on fire like that?" Edward asked. "You could've killed someone or created a bush fire!"

"Rats!" Arthur replied.

"What?"

"Rats. We had rats everywhere. Tons of them."

"Where's your daughter and grandson Mr King?" Hastings asked.

"They went to church earlier this morning. They are too pure to have death for breakfast."

At that moment, one of the firemen walked over towards them. "Excuse me Sergeant, I think you should see this!"

Edward looked back at Arthur. "Don't go anywhere," he said as he followed Hastings back out into the garden.

The fireman picked through the charred rubble of the shed with a metal pole before poking something solid. As Hastings and Edward arrived, he used the pole to move charred pieces of wood and hidden beneath the rubble was a partially cremated skeleton of a man.

Arthur approached from behind them. They turned and faced him. "I'm sorry," he said as he bowed his head.

Hastings walked over towards him and placed handcuffs onto his wrists. "Arthur King, I am arresting you on suspicion of murder. You do not have to say anything but anything you do say may be used in evidence."

Edward and Hastings led Arthur away whilst the firemen finished off what they needed to do. When they arrived back at Hastings's car, he called in the incident and waited for his colleagues to arrive before taking Arthur to the police station. As Hastings drove away, Frances and Timmy began walking down the hill towards their home.

"What's going on?" Frances asked as she approached.

"Your father has been arrested," Edward replied.

"What? Why?"

"For suspected murder and attempting to conceal the body by setting his shed on fire with the body inside."

Frances gasped. How had he known that Harold Partridge was in there? Her father was still asleep when they left for church earlier this morning. "No, no, there must be some mistake!"

"My advice to you is to find a good solicitor, you're going to need one," Edward replied before walking back to his house.

21 Years Later...

Saturday 30th July 1977

John Langford drove his black Ford Cortina back down the old
Lepe Road towards his parents' house for the first time in over 20
years. His fiance Emily Handanowicz, was by his side as they parked
their car on the driveway of Southward Cottage. His parents, Mavis
and Edward, a little greyer but still full of life, greeted them as they
arrived with his sister, Mary, following them closely behind.

"It's so good to see you here again," Mavis said as she embraced
them both. "Come in, I've made some cake for you."

As the three women headed inside, John remained outside with
his father. "Is she still here?" he asked.

"She's become a recluse since Arthur was convicted of murder
and died in jail. Her sons have moved away and nobody sees her
anymore," Edward replied.

"Sons?"

"She had a brief relationship with some foreign fella but he's
hardly ever here. No surprise really. She always manages to scare
them off eventually."

"I still don't think it's a good idea for us to be married in the
village, Dad. There's so many bad memories here for so many of us."

"You and Emily were brought up here. It means a lot to her that
you're getting married in the local church and I've made sure that
Frances King will be kept away so nothing can ruin your big day."

John nodded. "How are you keeping these days? Leaving the
force is a big change."

"Retirement isn't too bad. I get to go fishing more and your
mother has a grocery list of jobs she wants doing everyday so it keeps
me busy. But enough about me, this is about you and Emily, so come
on, stop worrying and let's go inside."

When they were inside the house, they discovered that Mavis
had put on a huge spread of cakes, sandwiches and drinks for them.

"Has anyone heard from Fred?" John asked as he sat alongside
Emily.

"He's coming down next weekend with his girlfriend from London. It's so exciting, our boys beginning their own families," Mavis replied.

"Where did he meet her?"

"The same place you and Emily met up again, she goes to Kings Cross University. Fred has a new plumbing business that keeps him busy all over London. He's just signed a contract for the new football stadium at Wembley."

"The difference is we already knew each other from childhood," John replied.

"So did they," Emily laughed.

"You know who she is?" John asked.

"I should do, she's my twin sister Evelyn."

John felt a shiver run down his spine as Emily told him. "What? When? How long have they been together?"

"A couple of months now but it seems to be going well," Emily replied. "Are you okay? You look a little pale."

"I'm fine, just a little tired, that's all. Probably from the long drive."

Emily nodded before continuing to chat with Mary, Mavis and Edward but John knew he needed to speak to his brother as soon as possible.

Later that day, John stood out in the back garden looking out at the deep blue sea with the Isle Of Wight in the distance.

"You didn't say much at luncheon. Is everything okay?" Mavis asked as she approached him.

John turned to face her. "Did you love him?"

"Who?"

"You know who, Mum, Jack Smith."

Mavis gasped. "How did..."

"We need to stop Evelyn and Fred from being together."

"You knew this whole time and you didn't tell me."

"Why do you think I never came home? There's so many secrets hidden here. In London, Emily and I have our own little bubble where no one can hurt us. We come back here and all hell breaks loose."

"That's not fair. Emily knew they were together and decided to tell you today to keep it as a surprise. I take it she doesn't know..."

John shook his head. "It would break her heart to find out that William was not her real father."

Mavis placed her hand on his shoulder. "I love your father very much John. You're living proof of that. When the war broke out and Ed went off to fight, I thought I'd never see him again. I was convinced it was a fool's errand and he would be killed in battle. I had one moment of weakness and from that, we gained Mary and Fred. Your brother and sister who have been there for you through thick and thin. Kept in touch with you when you ran away after Edith's death. And who supported you when you began dating Emily."

"But you kept the wheel of deception going."

Mavis nodded. "I'm not proud of what I did, John. God knows if I could turn the clock back, I would. As luck would have it, they were born premature and survived. Your father believes that I fell pregnant just before he left for the war. Don't destroy that one piece of hope that he held through the battle and what inevitably led him home after. He's been their father in all but blood throughout their lives. Don't destroy that now."

John took a deep breath as he looked out to sea. Hundreds of thoughts clouded his mind. "What about Dana?"

"That's her story to tell, not ours. When Frances began making trouble for them after Edith died, they sold up and moved away again."

"Edith told me everything before she died."

"So what brought you back into the Handanowicz family? Do you see Edith in Emily?"

John shook his head. "Nothing will bring Edith back and Emily is her own person. She's special and she was there when I needed someone to be there. She never gave up on me and I'll never give up on her."

"Then there's nothing more to be said."

John turned and walked down the side of the house and out into the front garden. He continued down the driveway and up the hill towards the woods. He looked up at the remains of the old treehouse that he used to play in with Mary and Fred as a child, the little stream that ran through the woods down to the sea, the old oak tree where lovers and friends carved their names into its trunk. It all felt like a lifetime ago that he used to run through the woods carefree and alone.

He came to the cut-through that brought him out next to St David's church. The same church that he would be marrying Emily inside in two weeks time. He wandered into the cemetery that led up to the church before walking down towards the far side near to where the honeysuckle grew and found a small grey marble headstone. He crouched down next to it and read the inscription:

IN LOVING MEMORY OF
EDITH HILDA WISE
DIED SATURDAY 22ND SEPTEMBER 1956
AGED 17 YEARS
WHEN ALL OUR DREAMS TURN TO ASHES
THE LORD WILL LEAD US HOME

John felt tears sting the backs of his eyes as he read the words. For so long, he had wanted to visit her grave and had always found excuses to not come here. Now reading the stone in front of him, Edith's loss had a sense of finality to it.

"I hope you understand," he said softly as he kissed the tips of his fingers on his left hand and placed his hand on the stone as he walked away.

As he arrived at the church gate, he took one last look back towards where Edith's grave was.

"John?" a woman's voice called out.

He spun around towards where the voice came from and he saw a middle-aged woman wearing black walking towards him.

"Long time no see," she smiled at him.

John recognised her smile immediately and wished that the ground would swallow him whole. Walking towards him was Frances King.

Chapter Twenty-Seven

Secrets From The Past
Wednesday 5th November 2008

Frank Jackson chased Timmy through the woods towards the open field next to St David's Church in the distance. Fireworks crackled in the night sky and a huge bonfire in the centre of the field gave the sky an eerie glow as they rushed through the woods. A crowd of people had gathered to see a firework display as Frank weaved his way through the crowd trying to find Timmy.

He heard someone shouting out up ahead and saw Timmy dart out of the crowd and head towards the church. Frank chased him through a narrow cut-through in the hedge and across the cemetery towards St David's Church. A lady holding a tray of Remembrance Poppies stood in the doorway. Timmy hit the tray out of her hands sending poppies and badges falling like confetti all over the floor. Frank quickly manoeuvred and leapt over them as he entered the church.

A curtain on the far side of the altar swished in the breeze and Frank immediately headed towards it. At that moment, he heard the clunk of a door closing and the vicar entered the church from his vestry.

"Can I help you at all?" the vicar asked.

Frank flashed his pass. "Frank Jackson, Special Branch in pursuit of suspect. Did you see anyone come in here?"

"No, I didn't. What..."

"Where does this door lead to?" Frank asked, pointing towards the curtain.

"Up to the bell tower and the balcony, why?"

Frank didn't reply and rushed through the door climbing round and round the spiral staircase. The bells began to ring out for eight o' clock and the sound was deafening as it echoed around the tight space but he continued to climb. Eventually, he made it to the top of the church. He rushed towards the left side, noticing the crumbling brickwork at the edge of the balcony. The church was in need of serious repair and he knew he needed to be careful. He stopped and listened.

Fireworks crackled and banged in the distance and he could hear the muffled tones of people talking and celebrating in the next field around the bonfire. He slowly continued moving around the edge of the balcony, listening for any kind of noise until Timmy came charging at him. Frank quickly ducked back behind the corner as Timmy made contact with his arm almost knocking him off balance. He placed his foot on the crumbling wall and launched himself at Frank once again. Frank caught him with his right arm diverting his face into the wall. Timmy staggered back momentarily stunned as blood began gushing from his nose. He charged at Frank once again but Frank dodged him. His momentum took him towards the edge. As he reached down, one of the bricks came loose and fell to the ground around fifteen metres below.

"You don't have to do this!" Frank shouted.

"Langford took everything from us!"

"What's your name? I'm sure we can sort something out."

"Timmy!" a voice called out from behind him.

Timmy turned and saw the vicar at the top of the staircase. As he turned the brickwork on the wall his foot was on, crumbled away. His foot slipped and he fell backwards.

"No!" the vicar shouted.

Frank leapt forward and managed to grab hold of his hand.

"I'm slipping!" Timmy screamed.

"Hold my legs!" Frank shouted.

The vicar rushed over and held Frank's legs as he tried to grab hold of Timmy with his second hand but he was just out of reach. He could feel Timmy's hand slipping from his grasp.

"Help me!" Timmy shouted.

The vicar held on to Frank as he took one last chance, he reached as far down as he could and managed to get his second hand onto Timmy's wrist. With all of his strength, Frank pulled as hard as he could and managed to pull him back up onto the balcony. Frank rolled over onto his back before standing up again as Timmy got back on his feet.

"Why did you save me?" Timmy asked.

"No one deserves to die that way," Frank replied. "What did the Langfords do to you?"

"John Langford walked out on us when I was only a child. He used my mother and then threw us away like a piece of rubbish!"

Frank turned to the vicar. "How did you know who he was? Is he local?"

"No," the vicar replied.

"So how did you know me?" Timmy asked.

"Because my name is Christoph Fischer. In 1948, I had a brief relationship with your mother, Frances King, before foolishly running away from my responsibilities. I'm not proud of what I did and I hope you can forgive me."

Timmy looked at him in disbelief.

"I'm your father," Christoph admitted.

"No, no, that can't be right. Mum said you were dead!"

"Maybe I was to her. I came here as a prisoner-of-war. I managed to escape with three friends and we hid out in the old cafe down on the beach in 1948. The local vicar at the time helped us out along with the owner of the cafe until one day, a police officer killed a man on the beach. Suspicion suddenly came upon us and one by one, my friends were killed. I ran away because I thought I would be next but

I was spared. I discovered a convent in Portsmouth where I was able to train as a vicar and was placed in this parish ten years ago."

"So you must be, what... eighty years old now?" Timmy asked.

"Eighty-one. I'm afraid I'm not as sprightly as I used to be."

"No, no, this is wrong, everything is wrong. We were meant to uncover the Langford's treachery and we've uncovered our own instead."

"What do the Langfords have?" Frank asked.

"The map to Jack Smith's gold!" Timmy replied.

"You don't honestly believe that old fairytale do you?"

"It's there, I know it is!"

"It's not Tim. I met Jack Smith. He was nothing but a lying, cheating scoundrel who used women to get his own way in life," Christoph replied.

"Then all this was for nothing. The deaths, the constant searching, all for nothing," Timmy gasped.

"What deaths?" Frank asked.

"It doesn't matter now. It's over for us."

"It doesn't need to be," Christoph replied. "You can repent your sins. You can be born again."

"You may believe that old cobblers but mother will never let it go. It's consumed her life and in turn it has consumed mine," Timmy replied before walking towards the edge of the balcony.

"Timmy, what are you doing?" Christoph asked.

"She'll never let it go! Never! Forgive me, father," he replied before throwing himself off of the balcony.

"No!" Frank shouted as he launched himself towards him but he was too late.

Screams echoed from the cemetery below as Timmy's body fell to the ground.

***

Meanwhile, Hugh, the security officer from the hospice and Frances were driving along the country roads towards Lepe Beach. Two ambulances and a police car overtook them in a blur of flashing blue lights. Frances felt a feeling in the pit of her stomach that something wasn't right. She pulled out her phone and called Timmy. No answer. She tried to call Dmitri, no answer.

"What's wrong?" Hugh asked.

"Follow that ambulance!" she replied.

"What about the Langfords?"

"We'll get to them later!"

As they arrived at St David's Church, a large crowd had gathered in the cemetery and surrounded the right side of the church. Paramedics rushed through the crowd with a stretcher as police attempted to clear the area. Frances climbed out of the car and waited near the ambulance. After what seemed like an age, the paramedics wheeled the stretcher down the path before lifting it into the back of the ambulance. As they lifted the stretcher, she managed to get a glimpse of who was laying on it, it was Timmy.

***

Joe Knight arrived at Francesca Audrey's Hospice accompanied by two police cars. He saw a forensic team dusting for fingerprints on a side fire exit door and two nurses talking to one of the police officers at the front door.

He walked over towards them and flashed his ID. "Joe Knight, Special Branch, what happened?"

"Someone came to visit one of the residents but ended up getting her hand stabbed with a knife and then assaulting a member of security before leaving with another security guard," the officer replied.

"Do we know who she was?"

"She signed the book as Rose Wilton but the resident she came to see said her name was Frances King."

"Who was Frances King coming to see?"

"Patricia Hughes."

Joe thought about that for a moment. Frances had obviously made the connection between Tom Gibson's family and the Langfords and was looking to tie up some loose ends. "Was Mrs Hughes the one who stabbed her with the knife?"

"Yes, why?"

"I think I may know where she rushed off to. What about the security guard, who was he?"

The officer turned towards the nurse.

"Hugh Johnson, he'd only been working here for a couple of months," she replied.

"Does he live locally?" Joe asked.

"He used to help the vicar at St David's Church near Lepe chop wood for the locals to use for their fires in the winter."

"Would the vicar know where he lives?"

"No, they had a falling out quite a few years ago. The cutting shed at the back of the vicar's property is rented out by a local businessman who oversees it now."

"Who's the local businessman?"

"Andre Lewis, he bought Thyme Cottage on the old Lepe Road, next door to where old Mary Langford used to live a few years back but he's struggled to find any residents to live there."

Joe rushed back to his car and headed towards Lepe. Andre Lewis had recently been recruited by Special Branch and was being trained by Frank Jackson. If he had brought the old King family home next door to the Langfords, Blake and his family were likely to be the next targets.

***

A police car was parked outside Southward Cottage as Andre led Dmitri towards the car and pushed him into the back seat. He finished talking to the police officers who then left and drove Dmitri away. As they left, a red Vauxhall Vectra pulled up outside the house. Andre wandered over towards it as the driver's window rolled down.

"Get in, we don't have much time," Angela Barnes said.

"What about Frank?"

"Leave him, we have to go now."

Andre walked around towards the passenger side and climbed into the front seat before Angela sped away into the night. A few minutes later, Blake arrived and parked his car on the driveway. He rushed up to the front door and headed inside the house. As he opened the door, Paula, Jenny and Michael all rushed towards him.

"What's happening? What's going on?" Paula asked.

"Where's Frank and Andre?" Blake asked.

"They both went after two men who turned up at the house. One of them grabbed Michael!" Jenny explained.

"And they both left you all alone!" Blake fumed. "Where did they go?"

"Frank chased one of them into the woods whilst the second one was knocked out in the garden. The police have just taken them away," Paula explained. "What the hell is going on Blake? We've had more police and ambulances down here tonight than I've ever seen!"

Blake was reluctant to tell them the full story and just held them close. Suddenly, the front door opened and he immediately spun around pulling his gun from his belt before stopping himself from firing. "Frank, you scared the hell out of me!"

"We've got bigger problems, where's Joe and Alison?" Frank asked.

"Joe's gone to Francesca Audrey's Hospice and Alison and Samir have gone to the oil refinery. Where were you? Why did you leave my family alone?"

"Timothy Vasilievich has just tried to commit suicide by jumping from the balcony of the church after discovering the vicar is his father. Turns out he was on a revenge mission that his mother has spent his and her entire life masterminding against your family."

"Who's Timothy Vasilievich?"

"Before his mother got married to Vladimir Vasilievich, he was known as Timothy King, Frances King's son."

Blake felt a shiver run down his spine. Frances King was the woman who had stalked his father throughout his teens and twenties before finally giving up on him when he married Emily Handanowicz. "That's our connection! Where is he now? Is he still alive?"

"Barely, paramedics have taken him away but it doesn't look good."

"Where's Frances King now?"

"Nobody knows. Police were called to Francesca Audrey's Hospice so maybe Joe can fill you in on that."

Blake thought about that for a moment. It all made sense. The vendetta that Frances King had against the family because his father left her after they had briefly been in a relationship back in 1956. "The map! It's got to be!" he said before rushing upstairs.

"Blake! What are you talking about?" Paula asked as she rushed after him.

Blake grabbed a pole from the bedroom and opened the loft hatch before pulling a metal ladder down and climbing up into the attic. He used his phone for a torchlight and quickly rummaged through some boxes before he found an old leather briefcase. He carried it back down the ladder before heading back downstairs and placing it on the dining table.

"Who keeps briefcases anymore?" Jenny asked.

"This is what Aunt Mary kept after Dad moved out and after our grandparents died," Blake explained as he moved the dials to the right combination before opening the case.

"How did you know..."

"Dad's date of birth. He told me about this when we used to go fishing."

"How do you remember that? It must have been fifteen years ago!"

Blake pulled out a handful of envelopes and handed some to Jenny, Paula and Frank before opening one himself.

"What are we looking for?" Paula asked.

"Our Grandfather kept all of these letters hidden from Dad so he wouldn't have to deal with them when he married our mother. Frances sent him letters constantly from 1956 until 1977. We're looking for the letter from 12th August 1977," Blake replied.

"There must be over two hundred letters here! It's a needle in a haystack!" Jenny complained.

"And I found the needle," Frank replied as he handed Blake the letter.

Paperclipped to the letter was a receipt for the transfer of two 6lb gold bars transferred to Miss Francis King as well as a small folded piece of yellow paper.

As Blake opened it and placed the two pieces of paper he had recovered in Rhodes, he noticed a familiar outline. "It's in Holbury Manor. Of course," he said. "This is Mavis Langford's piece of the map."

"Where's Holbury Manor?" Jenny asked.

"It's a residential area now but the old Manor House was used as an emergency hospital during the war. The same place where little Frances King, who was only a teenager when the war broke out, helped out with her mother, Dorothy King, before she was killed in the bombings. Jack Smith buried it right under her nose. If we find the rest of the map, we'll find the gold," Blake replied.

"Gold? What gold?" Paula asked.

"The Langford and Handanowicz family legacy. Jack Smith robbed a bank in 1938 and stashed the gold away in The New Forest. For the past seventy years, no one has known where it was hidden and it's been written off."

"So, if it was worth a lot in 1938, it's got to be worth..."

"Millions," Frank replied. "And Frances King is willing to kill whoever gets in her way of claiming what she believes to be hers after she was rejected by Blake's father."

"So, how do we find the missing pieces of the map?" Paula asked.

"Are we millionaires Dad?" Michael asked excitedly.

Blake shook his head. "No, people have died for that gold. It's blood money. It's not ours or anyone else's to keep. We need to find Frances King."

"She'll kill you as soon as she lays eyes on you," Frank replied. "It's too risky."

"That's why we need to come at it from a different angle. Where's Andre?"

At that moment, there was a knock at the door. Frank drew his gun and cautiously approached. He carefully opened it ajar before relaxing and opening it fully and letting Joe Knight enter the house.

"We've got trouble," Joe said as he walked over to Blake.

"I know, we need to locate Frances King and Andre," Blake replied.

"Have you met your next door neighbour whilst you've been living here?" Joe asked.

"No, the place has been empty for the past couple of years, why?" Paula asked.

"The ID we've got from the Hospice of the security guard that helped Frances King escape is Hugh Johnson. He works for a local businessman chopping wood in the cutting shed located on the back of the vicar's property up near the church however he has been recently seen coming in and out of your neighbour's house Thyme Cottage."

"So this Hugh owns the cottage next door?" Paula asked.

"The same cottage where Frances King lived until 1977," Blake replied.

"And according to records, the property was bought for four-hundred-and-seventy-thousand pounds three years ago by Andre Lewis."

Chapter Twenty-Eight

Forbidden Love

Saturday 30th July 1977

"What do you want, Frances?" John asked as he began to walk away from the church.

"Is that any way to greet an old friend?"

"Our friendship was over a long time ago."

"I hear you're now with Edith's sister. How does she feel about being the consolation prize?"

"Better than having a murderer as a father and a son by a kraut."

"You never complained when you were getting your leg over."

"We were different people back then. Some of us move on whilst others stay trapped in the past."

"The past will always haunt you, John Langford. Every time you look into her eyes you'll see Edith staring back at you. If you'd given us the chance, I could've made that all fade away for you."

"I'm sorry to hear about your father and I hope whoever the new guy is makes you happy. Now do yourself a favour and stay away from me and my family."

"You know father wasn't a big loss anyway. He was a liability for the last few years of his life and then became useful in the end."

"What do you mean?" John asked.

"He went down for a crime he didn't commit. Ironic really that it was your old man who convicted him. Made our family even more of an outcast than before until I met Vladimir."

"I don't understand, your father killed someone and then tried to burn the body before it was discovered in the shed at the bottom of your garden."

"That's what the official report said but in the end, a father will do anything to protect his children won't he. I made sure that the old vicar paid for past crimes. Vlad said I even have a knack for getting what I want. I'll be seeing you John," Frances replied before continuing on her way.

***

The following weekend, Mary, Mavis, Edward, John and Emily all gathered outside Southward Cottage as Frederick drove his car onto the driveway before stepping out with Evelyn by his side. John stood back as they all smiled and greeted each other. He knew he needed to tell Fred the truth but he also knew it would break the family apart. As they all headed inside, the postman stopped and leant his pushbike against the hedge before handing John three letters.

"Looks like quite a party," the postman smiled before continuing on his way.

"That's an understatement," John replied as he flicked through the letters and noticed one addressed to him.

He walked down the side of the house and headed into the back garden where Edward was beginning to start the barbecue.

"Ah, there you are John, could you please give me a hand with this? Blasted thing doesn't seem to want to light," Edward asked as he looked over at him. "What have you got there?"

John handed him two of the letters and Edward took the third one from his hand too.

"She's at it again, I warned her," Edward said.

"Warned who? The letter was addressed to me," John replied.

"Yes, and so have dozens of others too. Your mother said she was going to put a stop to all of this."

"A stop to what?"

"Frances King or whatever her name is now. Every week we would receive a letter from her declaring her love for you and how you broke her heart. Even after she went off with that foreign bloke."

"She's definitely persistent."

"Yes. Awful woman. First a German and then a Russian. Probably because no English gent would put up with her antics. No, you're well rid of her."

"I saw her."

"What? When?"

"Last week after I visited Edith's grave. She was in the village walking back from the shop."

"But she's moved away. What on Earth is she doing back here?" Edward asked.

"Probably heard about the wedding," Mary replied.

"It's rude to eavesdrop into others conversations, young Mary," Edward snapped.

"Then you shouldn't be talking loud enough for others to overhear. Come on, this is meant to be a celebration of the family being back together again. You're not going to let some village idiot ruin it are you?" Mary asked.

"I agree," Edward replied before placing the letters in his back pocket. "Now, can you help me light this?"

John lit a small piece of balsa wood on fire and managed to get the barbecue burning before Edward began cooking sausages, burgers, bacon and corn on the cob.

Later that evening, Emily and John walked down the wooden stairs from the back garden before wandering along the stony beach as the sun began to set.

"What are you thinking?" Emily asked as they walked hand-in-hand.

"Nothing much," John sighed.

"You've been distracted today. What's wrong? Surely, you're not still thinking about work."

"No, no, nothing like that."

"You've worked tirelessly for years John, you deserve some time to relax."

"I know," he smiled. "I guess I'm so used to being on the go all the time and always looking over my shoulder, it's a hard habit to break."

"It's this place isn't it?"

"What do you mean?"

"I know I was only ten when we left here but our families have been tied to this place for so long, it almost seems like there's a curse when we come back here."

John nodded. "I always enjoyed fishing off of the beach when I was a nipper. Now I just feel detached from it."

"Is that why you went to London rather than following Edward through the police academy down here? You just needed to get away."

"Something like that. I've always wanted to face up to my problems and I guess in this case, I ran away from them."

"But we don't have to run anymore. Everything's going to be fine. We'll have a lovely wedding and we can finally be Mr and Mrs Langford," Emily smiled.

John smiled back at her. "You're right. I'm overthinking things."

As they watched the sun set over the waves of the sea, John knew that he needed to let go of the past for the sake of his marriage however, a nagging worry still troubled him. When they climbed the wooden steps back up to the back garden of Southward Cottage, Frederick was waiting for them.

"John, I'm glad I caught you, can I have a word?" Fred asked.

Emily looked at John who nodded. "I'll see you inside," he said.

As Emily headed into the house, John leant against the back gate. "Is everything okay?" he asked.

"Dad told me about Frances."

"What about her?"

"She's still sending those letters."

"You knew about them?"

Fred nodded. "She just won't let you go."

"That's all in the past now Fred. As soon as we're married, Emily and I will put as much distance between us and this place as we can."

"Her parents were pretty adamant that they wanted the wedding here."

"I know and we will do what they ask but the sooner we can get away, the better. What did you want to speak to me about anyway?"

Fred reached inside his pocket and pulled out a small burgundy box. He opened it and showed John a huge diamond ring. "I'm going to ask Evelyn to marry me," Fred smiled.

"Don't you think it's too soon? You've only been together a few months," John replied.

"I thought you'd be happy for me. She's going to be your sister-in-law next weekend anyway and we've known each other most of our lives."

"I am happy for you Fred, honestly, I am but..."

"Worried I may steal your thunder next weekend?"

"No, it's not like that..."

"Of course it is. Same old John Langford, always thinking about himself."

"No, Fred, there's a lot of things to consider..."

"Like what, your feelings. Can't have your little brother stealing some of your spotlight whilst you and Emily get married. Does she know she's only got you because her sister died?"

John grabbed Fred's shirt. "You know that's not true! I love Emily and I'm going to marry her and spend the rest of my life with her. She is not a consolation prize!"

"Let go of my shirt John," Fred said calmly.

He took a deep breath before releasing his brother's shirt.

"You've got issues John. Issues that you need to get a hold on before you put that wedding ring on or your marriage is doomed before it even gets started," Fred replied before walking away.

One Week Later...

John Langford was standing in front of a mirror in his old bedroom at Southward Cottage. His grey suit, white shirt and navy tie with a white rose in the lapel of his suit jacket gave him the confidence boost he needed. He took a deep breath before heading towards the door.

At that moment, Fred walked in. "All set?" he asked.

"As I'll ever be," John smiled.

"Look, John, I'm sorry about what I said about Edith and Emily last week. I was out of order."

"Fred, I need to tell you something," John said as he walked over and sat on the edge of the bed.

Fred joined him. "What's wrong? Feeling nervous?"

"A bit but there's something you need to know."

"What?"

"You can't marry Evelyn."

Fred smirked. "Why? You're marrying her sister?"

"That's because we have different parents."

"What do you mean?"

"You share a father with Evelyn Handanowicz," John replied.

"What are you talking about? No, Edward Langford is our father and William Handanowicz is hers."

John shook his head. "No Fred, Evelyn's mother Dana and our mum both had affairs with a man called Jack Smith during the war. He is father to both of you."

Fred stared at him without saying a word.

"I'm sorry Fred," John said as he placed his hand on top of his brother's but he moved it away.

"No, no, this can't be happening. How long?"

"How long what?"

"How long have you known?"

"Edith told me."

"She must have been mistaken. That's over twenty years ago! You knew and you never said anything! Does Dad know?" Fred asked.

"I don't think so."

"You're lying."

"Mum admitted it to me when I came back here two weeks ago. Evelyn is your half-sister."

Fred shook his head. "No, no, this can't be happening. Mum would have told me! She knew we were..."

"Let's get through today and we can sort things out."

"I can't do this," Fred replied before rushing out of the room

"Fred!" John called after him but he ran out of the house.

Edward Langford rushed upstairs to the bedroom. "Is everything okay?" he asked. "What's up with Fred?"

"He had to rush off to see somebody."

Edward looked at his watch. "He's cutting it a bit fine."

John took a deep breath. "It's fine Dad, let's go," he said before leading his father back downstairs and out towards the waiting car.

***

Meanwhile, at St David's Church, Mavis Langford rushed inside to make sure that all of the last minute arrangements had been made and people were beginning to arrive. As she walked down the aisle however, she noticed a woman dressed in red with a black hat sat near to the exit. She walked over towards her and grabbed her arm, leading her away from the crowd towards the vicar's vestry.

"What the hell are you doing?" the woman snapped.

"I could ask you the same thing Frances. You are not welcome here so why don't you do us all a favour and leave!" Mavis snapped.

"I'm not leaving your family until I get what I'm owed."

"We owe you nothing."

"I know about Jack Smith and I have a big mouth. You know I'll use it if I have to."

Mavis felt a shiver run down her spine. "Who?"

"Don't play dumb with me Mavis. He had half the village back in the forties. Wouldn't it be a shame if it all came out in front of everyone here today. Your precious little family. A pillar of the community. You'd be ruined. No one would ever trust you or your family ever again."

"No one would believe a two-bit whore like you!"

"Do you want to take that chance?"

Mavis looked around at the crowd of people entering the church. "What do you want?"

"The gold of course."

Mavis bowed her head.

"How much do you value your pride?" Frances asked.

"Okay, I'll give it to you."

"And the map."

"What map?"

"Don't give me that rubbish. The map of where the rest of it is."

"I don't have any map. I don't know what you're talking about."

"That's a shame. Maybe I need to tell everyone out there about your little affair."

"Frances, listen to me," Mavis sighed. "Leave now and never contact John again and I'll give you what you want. Meet me at the vicar's cutting shed at 6pm today."

"I have your word on that?" Frances asked.

Mavis nodded.

"You'd better not back out..."

"I won't."

"I'll see you at six then," Frances replied before turning and heading out of the church.

Mary saw her mother in the corner of the church and rushed over towards her. "Are you okay? What was that about with Frances?"

"I will be," Mavis smiled. "Nothing to worry about. Come on, they'll be here soon."

Mavis wandered back outside the church once more as Mary watched her from the altar. She knew something wasn't right and was determined to find out what it was.

Chapter Twenty-Nine

Suspicion

Wednesday 5th November 2008

A red Vauxhall Vectra parked outside 391 Hampton Lane as Paul Crowther climbed into the back seat.

"Do you have it?" Angela asked.

"Do you have the money?"

Andre handed over a briefcase from the front seat. Paul opened it and flicked through the notes before reaching inside his jacket and pulling out a brown envelope. As he handed it to Angela, two silenced gunshots popped inside the car. Paul slouched down on the back seat as Andre pulled the suitcase back into the front seat.

"I do hate seeing good money go to waste," Andre smiled as they continued on their way towards the oil refinery.

Meanwhile, at the refinery terminal, Alison Pearce and Samir Khalifa arrived in their green Land Rover and were met with armed guards at the entry gate.

"Authorisation to see Colin Sanderson," Alison said as she showed her ID. "Alison Pearce, Special Branch."

"And him?" the guard asked.

Samir showed his ID. The guard studied it before handing it back and waving a hand to his colleague.

"Report to the first office on your left," he said as the barrier raised and they were waved through.

As Alison drove into the grounds of the refinery, she had a suspicion that something wasn't quite right.

"Did you notice something back there?" she asked.

"Like what?"

"The guards on the gate. I asked to visit Colin Sanderson and yet he didn't even check my name against the daily log. This place could be a major coup for any terrorist plotting to cause chaos and yet he let us through with barely a passing glance. Something's not right."

"Do you think they know about the bomb?" Samir asked.

"Doubtful but we need to be alert. I did notice their accents though."

"In what way?"

"Normally people on the south coast have that country farmer twang. I don't think their accents were necessarily local or even English."

"We do live in a multicultural country, Ali. I'm living proof of that. After 9/11 I couldn't go for a piss in peace without someone inspecting it but it's calmed down a lot lately."

Alison parked the car in a parking space numbered thirty-six. "I guess you're right. All this running around chasing undertakers and older generations is making me paranoid."

Samir placed his hand on hers. "As long as we're together, it'll be fine."

She pulled her hand away. "Don't make it complicated."

"What do you mean?"

"I don't want us screwing up because you've got one eye on my ass rather than the terrorists," Alison smiled before stepping out of the car.

"I'd never dream of it," Samir smirked as they headed towards a metal container that housed an office.

Alison knocked on the door and waited for a moment until a middle-aged bald headed man with tufts of grey hair at the sides wearing navy overalls that struggled to contain a huge beer gut answered the door.

"What?" he asked.

"Colin Sanderson?" Samir enquired.

"He's with the foreman, be back in about half hour. Whadda ya want?"

"To stop a nuclear bomb from exploding but I see you have other priorities so we'll make our own way down to the workshops," Alison replied as she turned to leave.

"Wait, wait, hold on a minute. You from the asbestos department?"

"Should we be?" Samir asked.

"They found some asbestos on the far side of one of the units down there. Foreman went ape-shit as they had to close two of the units down."

"No, we need to speak to the foreman and Colin Sanderson as we believe there is a nuclear bomb hidden inside one of your chimneys down here," Alison explained.

"Yeah and I'm Elvis Presley. Jeez, who let you clowns in here?"

"Pietro on the gate," Samir replied.

"We don't have anyone called Pietro on the gate."

"I'm sorry, what was your name?" Alison asked.

"Stanley, Stanley Froggatt."

"Well Mr Froggatt, I suggest you check your security, you may well already have a leak."

Stanley glared at her for a moment before backing up and lifting some navy overalls and two hard hats from a coat stand in the corner of his office. "You'll need these," he said as he ushered them inside the office.

When they had changed into the overalls, Stanley pressed an intercom. "Lurch, take these two new recruits down to the heat exchanger and radio Sanderson to meet them there," he said.

A minute later, a tall man with short black hair and thick dark rimmed glasses arrived at the door and led them away from the office and down through a metal tunnel towards a larger building further down the hill. After a few minutes, they arrived on a platform overlooking a workshop where at least twenty men were adjusting metal clamps and hydraulic machinery that was then passed onto a conveyor belt that led somewhere else.

"Looks like a mad scientist's tea party," Samir whispered as they continued on their way through a maze of metal corridors.

Eventually, they stopped at a noisy substation where there were two channels of liquid moving in opposite directions.

"This is the heat exchange," Lurch said as he pointed down towards the two channels of liquid. "The machine separates oil from the water and then it is pumped out of here, through the system and eventually, after it has been treated, into the pipeline."

"And any excess is burnt off through the chimneys at the far end of the site," Samir replied.

"Indeed. Ah, Mr Sanderson," Lurch smiled as a man with short blonde hair in tight curls, piercing blue eyes and flushed red cheeks came towards them.

"You two must be the two agents that have been sent on a wild goose chase from London," Colin Sanderson replied as he shook both Alison's and Samir's hands.

"If this place goes up, I'm sure it won't be a wild goose chase then," Alison said, looking at Sanderson's perfectly starched light blue shirt collar that poked out from his overalls.

"Thank you Lurch, I'll take it from here," Colin said dismissing him before leading Alison and Samir onward through another maze of corridors. "As you can see we have the most stringent procedures in place and we are equipped for any kind of attack."

Colin stopped at a metal door and tapped a code into a keypad before removing a large metal bolt that held the door shut. As it creaked open, he removed a metal bar from inside his overalls and hit Samir on the back of his head. Samir fell forwards into the darkness. Alison swung around attempting to land a punch on him but he avoided it and bundled her inside the darkened room too before closing the door once again.

***

Meanwhile at Southward Cottage, Joe and Frank rushed out into the woods in search of Andre Lewis whilst Blake remained at home with Paula, Jenny and Michael.

"You need to tell us everything Blake. What have these people got against us?" Jenny asked.

"When Dad and I used to go fishing off of the beach, he used to tell me about how he had to move away to get away from Frances King. She was obsessed with him. They had a fling when Dad was eighteen but after he left her, she never let it go. Years later, just before grandma Mavis died, she told him that she had given Frances two gold bars worth hundreds of thousands of pounds in 1977 to keep her away from Dad so he could have a chance of making his marriage to Mum work."

"And it did. They were married for twenty-two years until he died in 1999," Jenny replied.

Blake nodded. "The problem is, I think Frances King believed that Mum only had the two bars. When Mum's will was read, it proved that the map of where the rest of the gold was hidden had been split into eight different pieces. We have three of them and I'm guessing that either Frances King or her family have the other five pieces. They need our three pieces to find out where the gold is."

"But we've already worked out that the gold is in Holbury Manor," Paula added. "Surely, even with a partial map, they would have worked that out too."

"Holbury Manor backs onto The New Forest. Back in 1938, the Manor spread a lot further than it does now. Basing it on that, there are over a hundred trees in that Manor that it could be buried under or near."

Michael looked at the map. "Roman numerals," he said.

"Where?" Jenny asked.

"On the map."

Blake picked up the map and looked at it. "You're right. The trees all have roman numerals by them on the map. It has to be some kind of key."

"I've got a Forestry Encyclopedia upstairs," Michael replied as he rushed up to his room and searched for the book.

A few minutes later, he returned with the book open on a page that showed a black and white photo of an old Manor House.

Blake looked at it. "There it is. It's been changed a lot since 1938 but there used to be an arrangement with the previous landowners that all trees had a number engraved in their trunk."

Jenny pieced the sections of the map together. "You're right, the section we are looking for is between LXXIII, LXXIV and LXXV."

"Seventy-three, seventy-four and seventy-five," Michael replied.

"So if we find those trees, we'll find the gold," Paula gasped.

"It seems like it," Jenny replied.

"Hang on a minute, this gold has been buried for over seventy years. Surely someone would have found it by now," Blake said as he looked at the map.

"Only one way to find out," Paula replied.

At that moment, there was a knock at the front door. Blake pulled his gun from its holster and carefully approached the door. Rain was tapping away on the window and irritated Blake as he attempted to listen for any kind of noise from the other side of the door. As he carefully opened the door, he saw an elderly woman in a long navy blue coat standing in the doorway.

"Hello dear, I'm sorry it's so late, I was looking for Mary Langford," she said.

"I'm sorry, Mary Langford died six years ago," Blake replied.

"Oh my, I feel so foolish. I didn't know."

Blake replaced the gun in his holster but still remained in the doorway. "How did you know Mary?"

"We were old friends from when I used to live in the village. I don't suppose I could trouble you for a hot drink could I? It's so cold out tonight."

Paula joined Blake in the doorway. "I'm sure that would be okay," she said.

Blake glared at her for a moment before turning back to the woman in the doorway. "Yes, come on in Mrs..."

"Wilton, Rose Wilton, thank you dear," she said as she entered the cottage. "My, my, this place has changed over the years."

"Dad!" Michael called out as the woman slipped her coat off and removed a gun from her inside pocket.

Blake turned to face her and as she opened her coat, there were three pieces of C4 explosives and wires strapped to her chest.

"Don't do anything stupid Langford," she said.

"Frances King, we finally meet," Blake said.

Paula rushed over towards Michael and moved him away.

"Don't! I press this button on my chest and we'll all be pieces of debris in the ocean behind us," Frances snapped.

"What do you want?" Jenny asked.

"My inheritance of course. Mavis Langford convinced me that there were only two gold bars from Jack Smith's raid on the bank and then I met Tom Gibson and his mother, Patricia Hughes. We had a very enlightening conversation. And in one of life's little ironies, when Emily Langford died, the floodgates opened."

"What connection do you have to my mother?" Blake asked.

"She took John and the inheritance that was owed to my family away from me. I was always there in the background Blake. I took the opportunity to gain vengeance on Edward Langford and I knew that all I needed to do was wait. Wait for the opportunity to face you and your family once again."

"What do you mean?"

"My ex-husband, Vladimir Vasilievich was expecting a consignment of weapons and young students in Moscow until you interfered with Gibson's plan to smuggle them out of London."

"Gibson's still on the run," Blake replied.

"Not any more. He paid his debt and now it's your turn."

"If I'm the one you want then let my family go."

"It was your family who sent me on this vendetta that has consumed my entire life Blake. Your family don't know what it's like to have to fight for everything. What us normal folk have to do so the pound and the clock on the wall doesn't own them and drive them into an early grave. I'm here to give my children what they missed out on and you're going to take me to it."

"You seem to be forgetting something. One of your children are in the hospital after trying to commit suicide and the other is in a police cell."

"Liar! He was pushed! And when I'm finished with you, I'll find out exactly who was responsible and take care of them too!"

"This vendetta of yours needs to end. Not just for my family but for the sake of your own as well."

"You're just like your father, smug and think you're better than everyone else."

"My father was a good and honest man. He worked hard all of his life and provided for his family. The only reason he moved us to London was to escape a psychopath like you!"

"He could never face up to his responsibilities."

"More like you were looking for a meal ticket after your German lover ditched you!"

"Don't make this harder on yourself and your family Blake. I know you have the rest of the map and if you want your family to live, you will join me at Holbury Manor and uncover the gold."

Blake looked over at Paula, Jenny and Michael.

"Give her what she wants Blake," Jenny said.

Blake sighed. "How the hell are we meant to find a coffin full of gold in the middle of the night in The New Forest. It's pitch black for Christ sake!"

"Focus Blake!" Frances snapped. "If you want your family to live, you'll do whatever it takes."

Blake looked over at them again before picking up his keys and heading out of the door with Frances following closely behind.

Chapter Thirty

The Truth Hurts

Saturday 12th August 1977

As the bridal car arrived outside St David's Church, Edward Langford rushed up the path towards the entrance and then scurried down the aisle towards John.

"Fred's still not here!" Edward gasped. "What did you say to him back at the house?"

"Nothing that he didn't need to hear."

"You can't get married without a best man."

"Then I need you to do it Dad."

"Me? I don't have a speech ready or anything."

"You don't need to. Just being here is enough," John replied as he placed the ring in his father's hand. "Please Dad, I need you for this."

Edward looked around at everyone entering the church before nodding. "Okay, I'll do it," he said as he stood alongside his son facing the altar.

Meanwhile outside, Emily Handanowicz stepped out of the bridal car with her sister Evelyn and mother Dana by her side. She looked up at the church and took a deep breath.

"Are you ready for this?" Dana asked.

Emily smiled. "Definitely."

As they were about to walk up the path, they heard someone call out Evelyn's name. As they looked down the path towards the woods, they saw Frederick Langford running towards them.

"Fred, what are you doing out here? You should be inside with John," Evelyn asked as she approached him.

"Is it true?" Fred asked.

"Is what true?"

"Is Jack Smith your father?"

Evelyn looked at him confused. "Of course not, you know who my father is. What's brought this on? Have you been drinking?"

"Tell her the truth Dana!"

"Fred, what are you talking about?" Dana asked.

"John told me what happened with you and my mother and a young soldier during the war!" Fred snapped.

Evelyn turned and faced her mother. "What happened during the war?"

"Nothing!"

"Tell her the truth Dana!" Fred shouted.

"You have to realise, it was a difficult time for all of us. We didn't know if we would survive."

"Mum! What happened?"

Dana bowed her head. "I met a man called Jack Smith. He helped me after Gerald passed away."

"Gerald passed away in 1940. That was eight years before Emily and I were born."

"Yes, you have an older brother called Victor who was born in December 1940. Jack was his father too."

"What?" Emily asked this time. "I have an older brother and you never told me!"

"The bombs were raining down on us. We were scared and didn't know if we would survive from one day to the next. I did what I had to do," Dana cried.

"You gave him up," Evelyn replied.

Dana nodded.

"But this was eight years before we were born so William Handanowicz is our father isn't he?" Emily asked.

Dana didn't respond.

"Mum?" Evelyn asked.

"Tell her Dana!" Fred snapped.

"Can we do this after the wedding?" Dana asked.

"No, Emily and I have a right to know and I want to know now!" Evelyn replied. "Is William Handanowicz our father?"

Dana shook her head. "No, Jack Smith is."

"Are you saying that John Langford is my half-brother?" Emily asked.

"No, he was born long before Mavis had anything to do with Jack. He's definitely Edward Langford's son. It's the twins, Fred and Mary, who are Jack's but she managed to convince Edward that he got her pregnant just before he left for war."

"You've both been living a lie this whole time! Jack Smith fathered two sets of twins, me and Emily and Fred and Mary!" Evelyn snapped. "Why didn't you tell us!"

"I couldn't. It would hurt too many people!" Dana replied.

"And what about us? We're your daughters!"

Fred turned and walked back towards his car. Evelyn ran after him.

"Fred, wait!" she shouted.

"It's over Evelyn," Fred sighed as he arrived back at his car.

"We can work this out. There has to be a way."

Fred reached inside his pocket and handed her a small burgundy box. "I was going to give you this later but it seems irrelevant now."

"Don't say that! It's got to be a mistake! There has to be a way around this. Emily is marrying John so we can make it work. Please Fred, don't do this!"

Fred sat in the driver's seat. "The difference is, John is a true Langford. He's the only true bloodline in my family. Whatever anyone says now, we can't be together. I can't marry my half-sister."

Evelyn stepped back as he slammed the car door shut and sped away down the road into The New Forest. She held her stomach as a pinching pain rolled through her body. As she watched the car disappear into the distance, she opened the box and found a huge diamond ring inside. Tears stung her eyes and she felt an anger rise up inside her. All those dreams. All those promises they made to each other. Gone. In a moment of weakness, her parents had lived a lie that had cost her the love of her life.

Emily rushed over towards her. "Are you okay? What the hell just happened?"

"Mother knew and she didn't tell me," Evelyn sighed through her tears. "She knew and she didn't tell me! How could she do this to us?"

Dana rushed over to join them. "Evelyn, calm down, we have a wedding to get through first. We'll talk it over later."

"Talk it over? Talk it over! You knew I'd fallen for Fred. You knew things were getting serious between us and you didn't tell me! What kind of mother does that to her children!"

"We need to call off the wedding," Emily replied.

"No we do not. You and John will be married today, come what may. We'll deal with this misunderstanding later," Dana said as she began to lead Emily back towards the church. She turned to Evelyn; "If you had any loyalty to this family, you'll tow the line and be there for your sister and not try to ruin her special day."

Evelyn froze as she watched her mother usher Emily towards the church. "You don't care about us at all do you. All you care about is your bloody reputation!" she snapped.

"Evelyn, drop it. We'll deal with it later!" Dana replied.

Evelyn turned and walked away.

"Where are you going?" Dana asked but Evelyn kept walking away.

"Evelyn!" Dana shouted but she ran into the woods and disappeared between the trees.

At that moment, William Handanowicz came rushing down the path towards them. "Come on, quickly now, you're running late and everyone is getting worried," he said.

As he took hold of Emily's arm, he noticed that she had been crying.

"Are you okay? What's happened?" he asked.

"Nothing Dad, everything is as it should be. Let's go," Emily replied as she walked into the church with William holding onto her arm and her mother, Dana, walking close behind her.

As the wedding march rang out around the church, the people from the village, the family and friends that had gathered for the wedding, seemed to fade into the background as Emily focused on John standing by the altar. As they took their vows, Emily knew that there was a lot more happening behind the scenes than her smile let on to the world. She just hoped that her and John would be strong enough to survive it.

***

At quarter-to-six that evening, Mavis Langford left the local community hall where the wedding reception was being held for Emily and John Langford's wedding and headed down the dirt track through the woods towards the vicar's house. As she made her way through the woods, she kept checking behind her to make sure she wasn't being followed until someone calling out her name startled her.

"Mrs Langford!" a woman's voice called out.

Mavis swung around quickly, almost losing her balance and putting her hand out onto a tree trunk to steady herself.

"Sorry, I didn't mean to give you a fright."

"That's okay Elsie, it's been a pretty busy day all told."

"Well congratulations to the young couple. I hope they are very happy together. Tell them to come by my shop when they get back from their honeymoon. I have some lovely fruit cake that they can have for half the price."

"I'll be sure to tell them that, thank you," Mavis replied.

"Shouldn't you be at the wedding reception yourself?"

"I was, I just, er, needed to pay the vicar for the service and then I'll be heading back."

"Ah, that explains it. Well, mind how you go Mrs Langford and I'll see you soon," Elsie replied before continuing on her way towards the shops.

Mavis released a deep breath that she hadn't realised she was holding. She needed to remain calm. She pulled out an envelope from her handbag which confirmed the transfer of ownership of the gold that Jack had left her in 1948. She had wanted Emily and John to have it as a wedding gift and felt guilty that they would no longer have any claim on it but if it meant keeping Frances King out of John's life for good, it was worth it. As she approached the vicar's cottage, she noticed a tall man, in his twenties, walking down past the side of the house. He was wearing a blood-stained apron and a scruffy pair of grey trousers and a black t-shirt.

Mavis stood at the end of the garden path looking at the cottage unsure of what to do next. She slowly approached the front door before she noticed a rustling in the hedge at the side of the house. As she approached the hedge, a black cat darted out in front of her and sprinted across the lawn and into the woods. She took a deep breath to calm her nerves before walking around the side of the house. As she turned into the back garden, she saw the man again but this time, he was standing next to Frances King.

"I didn't think you were going to show up," Frances called out as Mavis approached.

"Who's he?" Mavis asked.

"You don't recognise my son, Timmy?"

"I haven't seen him for a few years. Looks a lot like his father doesn't he?"

Frances glared at her. "That's irrelevant."

"What have you been doing to get all of that blood over you Timmy?" Mavis asked, dreading the answer.

"Helping the old vicar out. The farmer gave him one of his cows so I helped him slaughter it so he can sell the meat."

"I see. Where is the vicar?"

"Indisposed so we won't be interrupted. Do you have the gold?" Frances asked.

Mavis handed over the envelope to her.

"What is this?" Frances asked.

"Transfer of ownership to you of the two gold bars invested in CityBank since 1948 by Jack Smith. Now I want your word that you will leave my family alone and get the hell out of this village."

Frances read through the paperwork before folding it and replacing it back inside the envelope. "A deal's a deal. Come along Timmy, we have a long journey ahead of us," she said as they pushed past Mavis and walked away.

"Where are you going?"

"I don't think that's any of your concern is it?"

"I guess not," Mavis replied as she watched them leave.

When they were finally out of sight, Mavis fell to her knees. She wondered if it truly was over. If Frances really would stay away from John. She had no guarantee but she knew she had done what she needed to do. As the sound of a car engine fired up in the distance before driving away, Mavis stood up and walked over towards the cutting shed. The previous vicar, Harold Partridge, had a wood saw installed inside the shed and would often collect wood from the forest and cut it down to manageable sizes before distributing it to the local residents for their fires in the winter. Something about Timmy's demeanour didn't sit right with her and his explanation about a cow hide seemed fanciful to say the least.

She tried the door of the old cutting shed but it was locked. She moved around to the side to try and look through the window but it was covered in green algae and moss.

"Mr Black! Dennis?" she called out as she walked all the way around the shed.

When she arrived at the back of the shed, there was a crack in the window on the far side with a small hole in the bottom right corner. The moss and algae had blocked out any chance of seeing what was inside but a strong potent smell seemed to be wafting out from the small hole in the window. Mavis looked around and found a small rock on the ground. She picked it up.

"Sorry Father," she said before hitting the damaged window with the rock.

The remaining glass smashed and opened just enough of a gap for Mavis to see inside the shed. The smell was horrendous and made her gag and step away for a moment. Taking a deep breath of fresh air, she risked one more look inside and then screamed. On the wood saw bench laid the vicar and the wood saw had cut through his skull and had sawn his head in half.

***

Three hours later, Emily and John Langford were waving to their family and friends as they headed off to The Grand Hotel overlooking Bournemouth beach for their first night together as husband and wife. As Edward Langford was about to head back inside the community hall, a police car pulled up outside. Mavis froze as she saw Edward's old sergeant, Peter Hastings, who had taken over as detective after Edward's retirement, step out of the driver's seat with a new sergeant following close behind.

"Peter, what a pleasant surprise. I'm afraid you've just missed the happy couple, they've just left," Edward beamed.

"Congratulations on your son's marriage Ed but that's not why I'm here," Hastings replied.

Mavis rushed over to join them. "Is everything okay?" she asked.

"When did you last see your son, Frederick?" Hastings asked.

"Just before we left the house for the wedding around lunchtime. John said that they had a few words and Fred rushed off to do something but didn't elaborate on what," Edward replied.

"We haven't seen Evelyn either come to think of it," Mavis added. "Did they leave early for some reason?"

"There was a road traffic accident this afternoon on the main road through Winchester. A Ford Cortina registered to Frederick Langford flipped up-side-down and hit a tree. I'm sorry Ed but I'm going to need you to come down to the station to identify the driver who I think may be your son Frederick," Hastings replied.

Edward sat on the step outside the community hall holding his head in his hands. "No, no, this can't be happening. The boys only had a few words this morning. What the hell is going on? And where's Evelyn?"

"She ran off with Fred just before the wedding," Dana replied as she joined them outside.

"Was Fred the only one in the car?" Mavis asked.

"Yes, he was on his own," Hastings confirmed.

"You need to find your daughter Dana!" Mavis snapped. "If she's been involved in the death of my son, I'll be coming for you."

"If your son wasn't so hell bent on revealing the truth, none of this would have happened!"

"What's she talking about?" Edward asked.

"Tell him Mavis! Tell everyone!" Dana snapped.

Mavis glared at her. "There's nothing to tell!" she snapped before turning towards her daughter. "Mary, finish up here for me, your father and I need to go with Detective Hastings to sort out whatever this misunderstanding is."

As Edward joined Hastings and his sergeant in their car, Mavis approached Dana. "You need to be careful what you say. You're not as pure as you think you are."

"If you had told me that Fred and Evelyn were together in London, maybe I could have put a stop to it before it got this far."

"Where is your daughter?"

"She ran off after Fred confronted her about Jack just before the wedding."

"How did he know?"

"John told him."

"Why would he do that right before his own wedding?"

"Because Fred was about to propose to her."

Mavis bowed her head. "We need to find her before she blows the lid on all of this."

"It's too late for that. Frances King already knows. If she lets it slip..."

"Frances won't be a problem anymore," Mavis replied.

"How can you be so sure?"

"Trust me on this."

Dana looked at her warily before nodding. "Okay, I'll find Evelyn. She's probably gone to cool off for a while."

"Mavis!" Edward called out.

"I've got to go. Let me know when you find her."

Dana nodded as Mavis rushed over towards the waiting police car and they drove away into Southampton City Centre.

Chapter Thirty-One

Holbury Manor
Thursday 6th November 2008

The fireworks had finished long before Joe Knight and Frank Jackson headed up to St David's Church. A police officer walked away from the vicar as they approached.

"Mr Fischer!" Frank called out.

"Can this wait? It's very late and I'm behind on everything," the vicar replied.

"I'm sorry the attempted suicide of your illegitimate son has inconvenienced you..."

The vicar walked up close to Frank. "I'd prefer it if that information was kept quiet if you don't mind. Mud sticks around here."

"So you won't mind if I ask you a couple of questions and then I'll let you get on with your business," Frank continued.

The vicar nodded.

"Do you know Mr Hugh Johnson?

"Should I?"

"He recently bought a fair amount of property in your parish," Joe added.

"Ah yes, he rented Thyme Cottage for a short time I recall."

"Mr Fischer, I believe you and the previous owner of Thyme Cottage were more than friends."

"That was a long time ago and I've repented my sins for that!"

At that moment, Joe's mobile phone rang. He wandered out of the church to take the call leaving Frank alone with the vicar.

"Does Frances know you're back in the parish?" Frank asked.

"Of course not. She's rarely here anymore. When Andre bought that cottage, he rented it out to workers down at the oil refinery."

"Did Hugh Johnson or Andre Lewis work at the refinery?"

"They both did, I believe. They were both temporary workers down there for a while. Why do you ask?"

"Thank you for your time Mr Fischer," Frank replied but as he was about to leave, Joe came rushing back in.

"That was Paula. Frances King has taken Blake by gunpoint to Holbury Manor. She's wearing a suicide vest and is threatening to blow herself up if Blake doesn't help her find the gold," Joe explained.

Frank turned back to the vicar.

"Oh no, no, no, no, I left that life a long time ago," the vicar said.

Frank walked towards him. "Father, we need your help here. Mr Fischer. Christoph. You were her first love. You are the father of her oldest child who is fighting for his life in hospital. You're the only one she'll listen to."

The vicar pulled out a crucifix from underneath his robe, held it in his hand and closed his eyes. He muttered a few words to himself before looking at Frank once again and nodding. Joe led Frank and the vicar out of the church and back towards the main road where they had parked the car. They knew they only had a small window of time to get to Holbury Manor before Frances did something crazy.

***

Blake had picked up a shovel and torch from the garden shed and placed them into the boot of his car before moving around to the driving seat. Frances sat in the passenger seat alongside him keeping the gun pointed at him at all times. He looked at the explosives strapped to her chest and felt a shiver run through his body. He knew he needed to tread carefully and think before he spoke or she could easily kill them both.

"I think we'll get on a lot better if you put that away," Blake said as he started the engine.

"Ah yes, the typical Langford wit. I'm sorry but I gave up trusting your family a long time ago."

"What did my father do to you that was so bad? When the entire village turned their back on you because you had a child with a German prisoner-of-war, he helped you. Gave you his first wages when he started working. Tried to help you look after your sick father."

"I made sure he was well compensated for it."

"Not many eighteen year old men would put their lives on hold like that but my father cared about others who were struggling."

"He was a manipulative selfish man who only ever looked out for himself. As soon as Edith Wise came back to the village, he couldn't drop us quickly enough. Then when she died, he ran away to London because he couldn't face up to what he did. He never came back to Lepe again until he married Edith's sister and the only way her parents would go to the wedding was if they married in the local church."

"But you never stopped pursuing him did you?" Blake asked.

"Your grandmother made a deal with me that she would sign over her share of Jack Smith's gold if I left and never came back. I'd already planned to move out to Moscow with Vladimir anyway so that was a nice little sweetener to add to the deal."

"And when the police discovered what happened to the vicar and how you had blackmailed my grandmother, Mavis Langford..."

"They stopped the transfer. I'll never forget the smug look on Mavis's face when I saw her a few years later. That didn't last for long though."

"Both of my grandparents died in 1984," Blake replied as he parked the car in a small gravel car park at the side of Holbury Manor.

"I know, I was there," Frances smiled.

Blake felt an anger rise up inside him and he had to force himself to hold it deep within. John Langford had been convinced that his parents' deaths had been linked to Frances King but there was never enough evidence and the case had gone cold.

"I see the apple hasn't fallen far from the tree. That same red mist that John had when he discovered my involvement in that little accident."

"He knew you killed them," Blake snapped.

"Prove it! There was never enough evidence to convict. You see Blake, I have ways of getting what I want and no one is going to stand in my way. Not even you. Now get that shovel and start counting trees."

As Frances stepped out of the car, Blake weighed up his options. If he drove away, she could potentially shoot the car or blow something up that would harm the local residents. If he went into the Manor, he risked her either shooting him when they found it or blowing him up too. He stepped out of the car, hoping that Paula or Jenny had called Joe or Frank for back up. For now, he knew he just had to stall Frances for as long as he could.

He turned on the torch and carried the shovel into Holbury Manor. There was a small children's playground near the car park made out of reshaped tree trunks. As they continued into the manor, Blake shone the torch around the trees but couldn't find any kind of markings or numbers on them.

"How the hell are we meant to find the right tree in the pitch dark. We don't even know for sure if they had numbers on them," Blake said as he continued to look at the tree trunks.

"There are significantly less trees now than there were when the gold was buried in 1938," Frances replied.

"Was there any kind of markings to signify what kind of tree it was on your part of the map?"

"What do you mean?"

"Did it show oak trees, ash, willow trees, anything that's going to help us here?"

Frances looked at the photo of her section of the map on her phone. "It looks like they are next to some kind of stream or pond."

"The fishing pond on the northern side of the manor?" Blake asked.

"It's possible."

Blake continued on down the mud paths deeper into the woodlands of Holbury Manor with Frances following closely behind. He knew his best chance of survival would be to get them away from the main road and the car park and hope that whoever came looking for them could disarm the explosives. They eventually arrived at the fishing pond which was surrounded by tall oak trees.

"If my research into this was correct, the numbers were scratched into the trunks of the trees after they had been planted and grown for twenty years," Blake said as he shone the torch at the oak trees.

"So?"

"So, the majority of these trees around the pond would have been planted around 1900, therefore they would have been numbered around 1920. The average oak tree grows between four and five centimetres per year. It's now 2008 so the piece of trunk that was inscribed is now at least four metres higher than it was in 1920," Blake replied.

"Then you'd better get climbing!"

"There is no way that we are going to be able to identify all these trees. It's going to take all night!"

"Focus Blake! You give me my inheritance and you can carry on living with your family."

He shone the torch up at the tree before then beginning to climb. The wind and rain made it difficult to climb and Blake slipped a couple of times before making it onto a strong branch. He used the torch to look for a number but couldn't see anything. He continued to climb as the wind blew the branches back and forth making each manoeuvre harder than the last. He finally made it over halfway up the oak tree when he saw some roman numerals carved into the trunk.

"LXX, seventy," Blake smirked to himself. "Michael was right."

"Have you found anything?" Frances called out.

"It's not this one," Blake replied as he carefully climbed back down.

"What do you mean?"

"This is number twenty!" Blake lied. "We need to keep moving."

Frances looked at the map on her phone. "This doesn't make sense. The gold was buried within the triangle of trees near to the pond and the stream."

At that moment, Blake slipped and fell the last couple of metres landing onto the mud path and rolling away into a hedge that had grown in a semi-circle around the pond.

He swore loudly as he hobbled back to his feet. "I think I've twisted my ankle."

"You'll live. Come on, this way," Frances demanded as she continued towards where the pond became a stream deeper into the woods.

Blake hobbled along behind her flashing his torch into the trees above in hope that someone would notice them.

Meanwhile, at the car park on the opposite side of the Manor, Joe, Frank and Christoph stepped out of Joe's car and began heading into the woods. Joe used a GPS tracker to try and log on to Blake's phone signal but it was very weak amongst all of the trees around them.

"Up ahead!" Christoph said as they followed the path.

As Frank looked across an open section of field, he saw torchlight flickering through the trees ahead of them. "Put that away," he said to Joe. "The old war hero found them the old fashioned way."

Christoph smiled as they followed the stream and the mud path towards the fishing pond. When they came to a clearing, they saw Frances and Blake on the opposite side of the pond.

"It's here!" she called out.

"What is? You can't even read the numbers down here," Blake replied.

Frances shone the torch from her phone onto the trunk of a tree next to the pond. "LXXV, you lied to me Blake. If this is tree seventy-five then there is no way in hell that the one over there is twenty!"

"Roman numerals are not my strong point."

"Bullshit Langford! You're just like your father, doing everything you can to stop me from getting what's rightfully mine!"

"Okay, okay, just calm down Frances. It's okay. But think about this logically, how do you know that this wasn't engraved into the trunk more recently by someone. Lovers often engrave their initials into trees."

"Who has the initials LXXV? Quite a stretch wouldn't you say?"

Blake didn't reply.

"This is it. Look at the trees around us. A perfect triangle. This is where he buried it. In the centre of this triangle. Now dig!"

Blake looked at her for a moment.

She shot a bullet into the darkness but Blake held her gaze.

"Next time it won't miss, now dig Langford!"

Blake picked up the shovel and began to dig into the mud.

"Ich liebe dich, meine Prinzessin," a man's voice called out.

Frances turned around and shone the torch from her phone in the direction of the voice. "Who's there?"

"I always said that to you back in the day, Frances."

"Christoph?" she gasped.

Christoph walked forward and held his own torch to light up his face. "Hello Frances. It's been a long time."

"No, no, you were..."

"No, I survived, despite your best efforts. And I met our son, Timmy."

"What did you do to him?"

"Nothing, he fell from the church balcony, he's in hospital but he's alive. You need to let the past go Frances," Christoph said as he slowly walked towards her.

She pointed the gun at him. "No, no, stay away from me. Don't come any closer!"

Blake slowly backed away as Christoph continued to walk towards her.

"This isn't your fight Frances. It never was. How many more lives are you going to destroy chasing the gold?" Christoph asked.

"You know nothing about me or my family. You ran out on us. You never saw the abuse and neglect my family had because you were a kraut!"

"I know and in my pain and guilt, I found God and have come back to the parish to repent my sins. Ich liebe dich, meine Prinzessin," Christoph said as he placed his hand over Frances' hand on the gun. "Let love in and let the pain go."

She stared at him for a moment before embracing him. As he held her close, a loud buzzing sound echoed around the Manor followed by a huge flash and a mighty explosion that boomed all around. Five trees uprooted and fell in all directions. A huge sonic boom radiated from the Manor. Car alarms rang out in the distance interrupting the silence of the night and all of the streetlights from the main roads short circuited out. In a few seconds it was over as shards of tree branches, leaves and hedges settled in the woodland but there was no sign of life in the darkness.

Chapter Thirty-Two

The Russians Are Coming
Sunday 13th August 1977

Mavis and Edward Langford arrived home in the early hours of Sunday morning. Southward Cottage, what once was a loving family home suddenly felt cold and lonesome. Edward picked up a bottle of malt whiskey and poured himself a generous glassful before sitting down in the armchair.

"You shouldn't blame yourself," Mavis broke the silence.

"I should've followed my gut. I knew something had happened between Fred and John and I should have gone looking for him."

"And what would that have done? John would've been left standing on his own on his wedding day in front of everyone. His whole family, running off on a wild goose chase."

"How can you act like this?"

"Like what?"

"Our son is dead, Mavis! Fred has died and I could have stopped it!"

"How? He had a few crossed words with his brother, ran off in a huff, had a few drinks and wrecked his car. Even if you had gone after him, would he have listened to you?"

"What did he find out?" Edward asked.

"How should I know? I'm not a mindreader."

"No, no, John said he told him what he needed to know and then Dana went for you at the hall. What was so bad that Fred went off in a rage and killed himself?"

"His girlfriend was his half-sister!" Mavis snapped. "Call yourself an ex-police detective and you never saw what's right in front of your eyes!"

Edward stood up and walked towards her. "Run that by me again."

"Evelyn and Emily have the same father as Mary and Fred."

"You had an affair when I was fighting for our lives in the war!" Edward fumed.

"It was a moment of weakness. We didn't know if you were all coming back. Gerald Wise didn't!"

"And that's supposed to make things right is it? Don't worry about poor old Ed getting himself blown up for King and country as long as ol' Mavis can take one for the team!"

"It wasn't like that and you know it! The war was a stressful time for all of us!"

Edward turned away from her for a moment before spinning around and punching her in the face with a fierce uppercut. Mavis fell backwards against the wall before sliding down to the floor.

"You slept with another man whilst I was risking my life for our freedom! You've made me live a lie for over thirty years!" Edward shouted.

"Dad! What the hell are you doing?" Mary shouted as she rushed down the stairs towards her mother.

"Maybe you should ask the village whore down there!" Edward snapped. "Is our marriage a goddamn joke to you? For pity's sake Mavis!"

"Dad, what the hell is going on? Why are you acting like this?" Mary pleaded.

Edward picked up the whiskey bottle and looked down at Mavis. He threw the bottle at the wall. It shattered on impact before leaving its contents behind. He picked up his coat and stormed out of the house, slamming the door as he left.

Mary helped Mavis back to her feet and into the armchair.

"What happened? I've never seen Dad so angry," Mary asked.

"He found out about Jack and your brother has died in a car accident," Mavis replied before bursting into tears.

Mary held her mother close, unsure of what, if anything, she could say to make sense of anything. Her mother had confided in her and now she felt a sense of duty to protect her from the fallout with her father. She just needed to figure out how.

Meanwhile, Edward Langford stormed through the woods in a rage hitting branches and reeds out of his way as he pushed his way through towards a clearing nearby to the vicar's house. As he arrived, he noticed two young men loading items into the back of a truck. As he approached them, they stopped and looked over at him.

"Can I help you?" the taller man asked.

In the half-light, Edward struggled to see his face clearly. "Is the vicar moving out?"

"He asked us to help move some things for him."

"At this hour?"

"Early bird catches the worm and all that."

"Where is the vicar? I'd like to speak with him."

"He's not home."

"So he's not home but he's allowed you two to empty his cottage for him," Edward replied before he felt a sharp pain in the back of his head and everything went black.

In the half-light, the second man had moved behind Edward and struck him on the back of his head, sending him down to the floor.

"Quick, move him inside," the second man said.

"You idiot Dmitri, he's Edward Langford, people will come looking for him!"

"Relax Timmy, we'll be long gone before they find him. Mother has already sorted out the cargo for us so take those last few bits and let's go."

Later that morning, the local parishioners along with Dana, William and James Handanowicz arrived at St David's Church but there was no sign of the Reverend Dennis Black. As the locals began to ask about the vicar's whereabouts, Dana, William and James wandered back through the woods. As they arrived at the vicar's cottage, they noticed tyre tracks on the front lawn and the door was left open ajar.

William approached the front door and as he opened it he saw a body laying on the floor.

He turned back to Dana and James. "Call the police and an ambulance, quick!" he shouted.

They rushed away towards a phone box as William entered the house. As he turned on the lights, he realised who the body was.

"Edward?" William gasped.

Edward began to stir and tried to move.

"Stay still, the police and ambulance are on their way."

"What happened?" Edward asked.

"It looks like you've had a severe head injury. Just stay as still as you can until the ambulance arrives."

Edward tried to move again but groaned in pain.

"What were you doing here? Where's the vicar?" William asked.

"I don't know. Someone was emptying the cottage last night. I tried to speak to them and ended up like this."

"What time?"

"I don't know, around midnight."

After a few minutes, blue flashing lights reflected around the hall of the cottage as the police and ambulance team arrived. The paramedics rushed in to help Edward whilst the police looked around the cottage for any significant clues as to what happened on the previous night.

Detective Peter Hastings arrived with Sergeant Stuart Newman soon after the ambulance had left with Edward Langford inside it. The police officer leading the investigation walked over towards them.

"Good morning Sir, looks like a burglary gone wrong," he explained.

"I'll be the judge of that, Harris. Edward Langford lost his youngest son yesterday and is now found at the vicar's house unconscious. Have they discovered the whereabouts of Evelyn Handanowicz yet?" Hastings asked.

"Not yet, we are still investigating."

"What's the story with the Handanowicz family?"

"Dana, William and their son James attended morning service. After the vicar failed to attend, they came here looking for him and that's when they found Edward Langford's body in the hall," Officer Harris replied.

"From what I heard from the wedding reception yesterday, the Langford's and Handanowicz's had a rather heated discussion over money and their children courting together," Sergeant Newman added.

"Surely you don't think William Handanowicz had anything to do with this, do you Sir? He's a wealthy local businessman," Officer Harris asked.

"I'm not ruling anything out at the moment. Ask forensics to check the place over, particularly by the hall and front door," Hastings replied.

At that moment, a second officer rushed over towards them. "Excuse me, Sir, I think you need to take a look at this," he said.

Hastings, Newman and Harris all followed the second officer around the side of the house and into the back garden. The shed door had been broken open by one of the officers and a strong pungent smell hung in the air. Hastings removed a handkerchief from his pocket to cover his nose and mouth as he entered the shed. Laying on the workbench in front of them was the body of Reverend Dennis Black. The mechanical wood saw had sliced through his skull and cut right through to his neck leaving a huge ghoulish bloody mess where his head had once been.

Sergeant Newman rushed out of the shed and began vomiting into the rose bush outside. Harris and Hastings followed him out.

"Officer Harris, arrest William Handanowicz and take him in for questioning. We now have a murder investigation on our hands," Hastings said before heading back towards the front of the house.

As Sergeant Newman and Officer Harris continued closing off the vicar's cottage to the public, Peter Hastings walked up the mud path through the woods towards Lepe Road. He looked across the road at Thyme Cottage, the former home of Arthur King and his family for many years.

His father used to be a member of the Dibden Golf Club, a few miles down the road from Lepe, and most Sundays, he would play a round of golf with Arthur before going into the clubhouse to join the rest of the family for an afternoon cup of tea and a cucumber sandwich. Then the war came and everything changed. The bombing cost the lives of Peter's father Joseph and Arthur's wife Anita whilst Arthur had shards of metal in his right leg after an explosive device had blown up nearby leaving him with shell-shock and needing a walking stick to maintain his balance.

Arthur never spoke to Peter again after the war until he was taken into custody in September 1956 by Officer Charlie Jones. He had set fire to his garden shed in what he had said was an attempt to kill a rat infestation that had gotten out of control. When the flames were put out, the half cremated skeleton of Harold Partridge, the previous vicar before Dennis Black was appointed, was found amongst the debris.

Arthur died in prison three months later but right up to his death, he pleaded his innocence. Now looking at the empty shell of a house that remained since his daughter and her two sons had emptied it out into a removal van yesterday, Peter couldn't help but wonder where it all went wrong for the King family and if he could have helped them in any way.

He walked up the hill towards Southward Cottage and knocked on the front door. After a few minutes, Mavis answered.

"Oh no, Peter, what's happened? Is Edward okay?" Mavis asked

"You manipulative bitch!" Dana Handanowicz shouted out from the road as she stormed up towards the house. "It wasn't enough to take my daughter away, you had to take my husband too!"

"What are you talking about?" Mavis asked.

Dana launched herself at Mavis but Peter stepped in between them. "Please ladies, calm down. Fighting between each other won't get us anywhere!"

"How dare you come around to my house shouting at me after what's happened!" Mavis snapped.

"What do you mean, my husband has been arrested for a crime he didn't even do!" Dana replied.

Mavis looked at Peter.

"We're just making inquiries at the moment!" Peter said as he tried to maintain a distance between them.

"So where's Fred?" Dana asked. "My Evelyn has disappeared without so much as a single word of goodbye!"

"Fred didn't come home," Mavis replied.

"Oh that's right, stormed off in a huff did he, after he found out his mother was a whore!"

"Frederick Langford is dead, Mrs Handanowicz," Peter replied.

Dana froze. "What?"

"He died in a road traffic accident yesterday afternoon," Mavis replied. "Peter, where is Edward?"

"In hospital. He was discovered unconscious at the vicar's cottage this morning by Mr and Mrs Handanowicz," he confirmed.

"What did you do to him?" Mavis shouted as she launched herself at Dana.

Peter once again stood in between them. "Calm down you two. Nothing is going to be solved by trying to rip each other to pieces. We need to find out what happened to Edward, Evelyn and the late Reverend Black and Frederick Langford. Mavis, when did you last see Edward?"

"Around midnight last night after we came back from identifying Fred," she replied.

"What happened after you arrived home?"

"We had a fight and he stormed out of the house."

"Is that how you received those bruises on your face?"

Mavis bowed her head. "My husband is a good man, Peter. You know him well enough to know that."

"When he left here after your fight, was he still angry?"

"I guess so. He usually goes for a walk to cool off and then comes back an hour or so later but last night..."

"He didn't," Peter finished for her.

Mavis shook her head.

"Did Edward have any kind of disagreement with Reverend Dennis Black that you knew of?"

"No, none at all. Why?"

"Reverend Black was found murdered this morning in his cutting shed at the bottom of his garden. We're trying to figure out if it is connected to Edward being knocked unconscious in the hallway of the vicar's cottage."

Mavis felt a shiver run through her body. She had seen the Reverend's body yesterday evening and hadn't reported it. Now the police were suspecting that Edward had a role to play in it. She felt tears sting the backs of her eyes. "Ed had nothing to do with it!" she cried.

"Mavis, you said yourself that Edward was angry and in a foul mood last night," Peter persisted. "Could he have potentially lashed out last night as he did to you?"

"I know he's not a murderer and deep down, so do you!"

"But he was out late last night and then the body was found this morning," Dana added.

"The reverend was already dead before Edward went there!" Mavis confessed.

"What?" Peter asked.

"I met Frances King or whatever her name is now at the cottage yesterday evening. I was looking for the reverend and when there was no answer at the cottage, I went to his shed and found his body on the workbench."

"Why didn't you call the police?" Peter asked.

"Because I was being blackmailed by Frances. The only way I could get her away from John was to sign over my share of the gold."

Dana gasped. "You did what?"

"What gold?" Peter asked.

"The gold given to Dana and myself by Jack Smith, the father of our children. It was the only way to get rid of her and from the looks of it, she packed up and cleared off overnight."

"How did she get another house so quickly?" Dana asked. "Was this all planned?"

"She's married to a Russian millionaire called Vladimir Vasilievich," Peter replied. "I believe she was planning to leave the village anyway, with or without your money."

Both women looked at him. "How did you know that?"

"He's the father of her youngest son, Dmitri. He has his own yacht anchored off the coast in Weymouth. Chances are, that's where she's headed but she never wanted to give up the family home until recently."

"When William and I went to the vicar's cottage this morning, there were tyre tracks on the front lawn. It looked like some of the furniture had been taken. Perhaps Edward interrupted them and got knocked out before they left," Dana replied.

"It's certainly a possibility. Did Frances say where she was going?" Peter asked.

Mavis shook her head.

"Either way, I'm going to need you both to come down to the station to make statements and if what you say is true, we need to find Frances King."

Chapter Thirty-Three

The Frogman's Hatch
Thursday 6th November 2008

Blake opened his eyes to discover that he was covered in a shower of wood chippings, leaves and mud. His hearing sounded like he was under water and the flashing blue lights from the car park on the opposite side of the manor created a disorientating glow. As he staggered to his feet, he noticed the destruction around him. Frances had pressed the detonator and had taken the vicar, Christoph Fischer, with her. Joe Knight and Frank Jackson rushed over towards him.

"Are you okay?" Joe asked as he helped Blake to his feet and brushed off the debris from his clothes.

"I think so."

"You have more lives than a cat!" Frank laughed. "She could have easily killed you."

"She almost did," Blake replied as he looked at the roots of one of the uprooted trees. "What's that?"

As the three men approached the tree, they discovered a metal box that looked like an old treasure chest.

"No, it can't be," Joe gasped.

Frank grabbed hold of one side of the chest and Blake held the other side. As they lifted it out of the hole, they were surprised how light it was and almost overbalanced and fell backwards onto the mud.

"I thought treasure chests were meant to be heavy," Frank commented.

"We need to get it out of here before the police discover what we've found," Joe replied.

In the distance, they could hear the barking of police dogs and shadows of police officers appeared across the open field of the manor with their torches as the blue flashing lights illuminated several silhouettes rushing towards them.

"Come on, this way," Frank said as he led them down a mud path towards a road at the back of the manor.

When they eventually made it back to the car park, there were two police officers standing in between Frank's and Blake's cars.

"You two stay out of sight, we'll get Langford's car later," Frank said as he left Joe and Blake with the chest and walked over towards his car.

"I'm sorry Sir, this area has been closed off due to a possible terrorist attack," the police officer said as Frank approached.

"A what?" Frank asked, raising his hands in mock disbelief. "Do you honestly think a terrorist would strike out in the middle of the sticks out here when they could blow the shit out of London only an hour or so up the road?"

"We had reports of an explosion in the forest and we have to investigate."

"So how does that stop a brother from driving home?"

"How do we know that you weren't the one who set off the explosive device?"

"Would I honestly be dumb enough to come and talk to you if I was out here blowing stuff up?"

"Then what were you doing out here in the middle of the night Mr..."

"Hardy, Ivor Hardy, well if you must know, there's a young lady over in the next street and she needed some attention if you know what I'm saying and it's not going to look good if I'm heading home with a police caution after tending to her needs shall we say..." Frank replied.

The officer looked at him for a moment before smirking. "On your way Mr Hardy," he replied.

"Thank you Officer, I'll remember you when I write my memoirs," Frank smiled as he let himself back into his car.

"I hope you won't," the officer replied as Frank shut his door and drove out of the car park.

As he turned the corner, Blake and Joe climbed into the back seat with the chest and Frank sped away.

"How the hell did you get away with that?" Joe asked.

"Local forces don't want the aggro so I fed him a story about a one night stand," Frank smiled.

"And he believed you?" Blake asked.

"There's still some mileage left in this ol' body yet," Frank laughed.

"I thought the local police forces had a filtering system to keep the idiots away from the front line," Joe replied.

"Unfortunately nothing is idiot proof anymore as whenever you think you've cracked it, someone finds a better idiot," Frank said as he drove through the country roads back towards Southward Cottage overlooking Lepe Beach.

"Idiots or not, we don't have much time. Sooner or later they're going to trace Blake's car back to us so we need to move fast," Joe replied.

When they arrived outside Southward Cottage, Blake and Joe carried the chest inside the cottage and placed it on the floor.

"Where's Frances?" Paula asked.

"She blew herself and the vicar up at the manor so we need to move fast to find the connection between her and what Vladimir Vasilievich have planned next," Blake replied as he began to pick the lock on the chest.

"What's that dirty old thing?" Michael asked.

"That is your father Michael, please have a bit more respect," Frank quipped.

Blake rolled his eyes. "It's something we've found buried underground."

"Wow, is this real pirate treasure Dad?" Michael asked.

"Don't touch it Michael, you never know what's inside it," Paula replied.

After a few minutes, Blake finally managed to release the lock. As he opened the chest, a plume of dust escaped into the air causing everyone to take a step back. He looked inside the chest and found a sheet of paper with a drawing showing a map of tunnels. In the top right corner of the paper, someone had written the code:

98 72 46 79 21

"I don't understand, she was convinced that the treasure was in Holbury Manor," Jenny said as she looked at the piece of paper.

"That map was the old extraction tunnels in the village from during the war," Blake said as he rushed into the study toward the old bookcase in the corner of the room.

The old mahogany door creaked open as Blake scanned his finger across the spines of the old books until he came to Ark Of Triumph, by Denis Bright. He opened the old book and found a map of tunnels on page fifty-five. He brought it back into the hall and compared it to the piece of paper that was inside the chest.

"How the hell did you remember that?" Jenny asked.

"Dad used to talk about what used to be down in the village before they turned it into the refinery in 1951. Those are the original tunnels. If we find them, we possibly find the gold," Blake replied.

"We have a bigger problem here," Joe said as he logged into the secure network of Special Branch on his phone.

Everyone looked at him.

"Alison and Samir are walking into a trap. That code isn't just any kind of reference number. If Vladimir Vasilievich is involved, that could well be the activation code for one of the old Soviet nuclear bombs that were used in the 1930's," Joe explained.

"Meaning?" Paula asked.

"If the gold is down there, it could also be guarded by an unstable nuclear bomb. If that goes off underneath the oil refinery with all of their pipes that run from here right across the country, you could end up wiping out the whole of the UK," Joe replied.

"We need an edge," Blake said as he scanned the map of the tunnels in the book. "Frogman's hatch, of course."

"You're not thinking what I think you're thinking," Jenny gasped.

"The old hatch at Ashlett Creek," Blake replied. "It's our only way past security."

"Blake, that hatch hasn't been used in over thirty years. It's only visible at low tide and it's about ten metres off-shore," Jenny said.

"Wait, what's the frogman's hatch?" Frank asked.

"When our parents used to visit Aunt Mary when we were kids, they used to take us to a local village pub in Ashlett Creek. People used to launch their fishing boats and kayaks from the little slipway at high tide but when the tide went out, in the distance, you could see a small metal drain cover that apparently led to a tunnel underneath the refinery," Jenny explained.

"Apparently?" Joe questioned.

"Nobody knew for sure but that was the story we were told," Blake replied. "If we want to sneak in and help Samir and Ali then it's our best chance. When is the next high tide?"

Paula rushed over towards a noticeboard in the kitchen and removed a small piece of cardboard with the tidal times written on it. "Quarter-to-eight in the morning," she said.

Blake looked at his watch. "We've got five hours."

"Blake, you don't even know if this will work. The water level is higher now so how do you even know if it hasn't rusted shut?" Jenny asked.

"I have to try Jen. It's the only way."

"Then I'm coming with you," Frank replied.

***

Angela Barnes arrived at the entrance to the oil refinery. Andre stepped out from the passenger seat and warmly embraced Pietro before handing over the briefcase full of money. The barrier was lifted and Andre rejoined Angela in the car as they headed inside the refinery. As they drove down the hill towards the heat exchange, Angela noticed the green Land Rover that belonged to Alison Pearce.

"Something wrong?" Andre asked.

She shook her head. "No, everything is as it should be," she replied as she parked her car and they both headed over towards a large building that overlooked a network of pipes that disappeared underground several metres further down the road.

Angela and Andre entered the large building, its interior dimly lit and filled with the hum of machinery. They were greeted by a man in a lab coat, his face obscured by shadows.

"Welcome," the man said in a low voice. "I trust all loose ends have been tidied up."

Angela nodded. Without a word, the man led them through a maze of corridors and staircases deep into the belly of the refinery. As they walked, Angela's mind raced with thoughts of Alison and Samir walking into danger. She knew she had to act fast to warn them, but she also couldn't risk blowing her cover.

Finally, they arrived at a heavily guarded door. The man typed in a series of codes and the door creaked open to reveal a vast chamber filled with rows of computer servers and monitors.

"This is where our transaction will take place," the man said as he led them inside.

"Angela Barnes," a man with a strong Russian accent called out.

Angela turned to see a tall overweight bald man wearing a military uniform with several medals attached to the lapel.

"It's been a long time since we met in Moscow," he continued.

"Vladimir Vasilievich, I should've known that you'd be pulling the strings," Angela replied.

"You too," he replied as he pressed a button to turn on a screen which showed Alison and Samir in a darkened room. "You seem to have led your team of agents into a trap with relative ease. Funny how one bad apple can rot the entire fruit bowl."

"What do you mean?"

"Samir Khalifa, so eager to save his own skin that he'd even lead the woman he loved astray for his own ends."

Angela's heart sank as she watched the live feed of Alison and Samir in captivity. She knew she had to think fast to come up with a plan to save them without blowing her cover.

"You don't need to concern yourself with them Vladimir, we can work something out," Angela pleaded, trying to keep her voice steady despite the rising panic within her. "Blake will bring you the gold."

Andre looked at her in disbelief. "You're a double agent?"

Vladimir Vasilievich chuckled, a cold and menacing sound that sent shivers down Angela's spine. "Oh, I have no doubt we can come to an agreement, Angela. But first, you must prove your loyalty to me."

"What do you want me to do?" Angela asked.

"I want you to retrieve an item for me from a secure vault within this facility. It's a small price to pay for the lives of your colleagues, wouldn't you agree?"

Angela nodded, her mind already racing with possible escape routes and plans. "I'll do it."

Vladimir nodded before leading her through the labyrinthine corridors of the refinery towards the secure vault. Her mind was a whirlwind of thoughts as she tried to formulate a plan to retrieve the item while also finding a way to warn Alison and Samir.

As they approached the heavily guarded vault door, Angela's heart pounded in her chest and her palms became sweaty. She knew that whatever lay inside was of utmost importance to maintain her cover and she had to retrieve it without raising suspicion.

The guards scanned her credentials and allowed her access into the vault. The room was filled with rows of lockers, each secured with intricate locking mechanisms. Angela's eyes scanned the room, searching for the item she needed to retrieve. Finally, she spotted it. A small metal box tucked away in the corner of the vault. With steady hands, she input the code Vladimir had given her and opened the box. Inside, nestled on a bed of velvet, was a shimmering diamond. As she reached up to take the diamond, a loud whirring sound echoed around her and suddenly the floor gave way underneath her, sending her down a large metal slide into a damp algae covered pit below. She could hear water sloshing against the walls of this newfound tomb that she had become encapsulated inside and soon realised that she was in an underwater bunker.

She looked around to find some kind of escape route but found nothing. She cursed herself for trusting Andre and Vladimir but she knew she had to find a way out and somehow work out where they were holding Alison and Samir.

Meanwhile at the heat treatment centre, one of the assistants, carrying a small laptop, was checking the radiation shields when he walked along the corridor and tapped a code into a keypad. The door lock clicked open before mechanically removing a large metal bolt and opening the door. As he walked through the door, Alison kicked the laptop from his grasp whilst Samir struck him on the back of his head, sending him to the floor.

The door quickly slammed shut behind him foiling their plan for escape. At that moment, a red light began flashing and a piercing alarm began to ring out. The assistant was groggy but managed to look up at them.

Alison slapped him around the face to bring him around again. "What is that alarm?" she asked.

"Why did you hit me?" he asked.

"We thought you were somebody else, now tell us what's going on!" Samir replied.

"Oh hell, no!" the man said as he staggered to his feet. "Quickly, we need to go!"

He stumbled and had to use the wall to maintain his balance.

"Go where?" Alison asked.

"That's the burner alarm!"

"What's the burner alarm?" Samir asked.

"They're going to burn off the excess fuel. If we don't get out of here, this is going to turn into your own private crematorium!" the man screamed as he hammered on the door but nobody answered.

"Can't you override it on your laptop or something?" Alison asked.

The man looked up. "There's only one way out," he said as the roof three hundred metres above them opened up showing the night sky. "Come on, this way!"

Alison and Samir followed him as they began climbing a series of ladders that led up to the top of the chimney. Each ladder had been drilled into the concrete structure of the chimney and was around twenty-five metres in length. There were thirteen small platforms between each ladder as the three of them climbed as fast as they could. The noise of the generators below them became louder and louder and they could feel the heat rising from deep within.

"Don't look down!" Samir shouted as he followed Alison up higher and higher.

"We're not going to make it!" Alison called out.

"We will just keep going!" the assistant replied as he led them higher and higher inside the chimney.

Their arms and legs ached from the constant climbing. Reaching and pulling themselves up ladder after ladder. The heat from below sapped their energy as they began to sweat. On the last ladder, condensation had begun to form on the rungs. Alison reached for the next rung and her hand slipped. She gripped as hard as she could with her right hand as she lost her footing and was hanging from the ladder by one arm.

"I'm slipping!" she shouted.

Samir reached out and tried to push her leg back towards the ladder. She swung her hand wildly trying to grip one of the rungs when she felt someone grab her wrist. She looked up and saw the assistant help her to take a firm hold onto the ladder. They finally managed to reach the top as smoke began to billow out of the chimney.

"Now what?" Alison asked breathlessly as she looked down on the vast drop below them.

The assistant held onto the metal rail as he walked around the edge of the chimney towards some ropes and metal clips. "What goes up must come down," he said.

"We're abseiling back down!" Samir gasped breathlessly.

"Unless you'd rather take the kamikaze route! Come on quick before the fire starts!"

Samir looked at Alison. "I'm getting too old for this shit," he sighed.

Chapter Thirty-Four

John Misses The Boat

Sunday 13th August 1977

At 1pm in Weymouth Bay, Frances, Timmy and Dmitri arrived in a removal van loaded with items from Thyme Cottage and some from the vicar's cottage. Timmy drove the van into a yard full of large metal storage containers. He parked it next to a container marked MC74921RU before stepping out and handing the keys and a roll of banknotes to a man wearing a beige t-shirt and matching shorts. The man inspected the banknotes before nodding in approval and signalling four other men to start unloading the van into the metal container.

Frances and Timmy then joined Dmitri as they climbed into a white Ford Cortina and drove down towards the marina where a small escort boat would take them out to the biggest yacht in the bay, SSJ St Petersburg VV. The sea was smooth in the summer sun and as they approached the yacht, a middle-aged man in a white suit looked down on them as they arrived.

Frances rushed up the steps at the side of the yacht to meet the man on the top deck.

"Any problems?" he asked.

"None that I can't handle," she replied as she handed him the envelope that Mavis Langford had given her the day before.

"One day you'll be a very rich lady," he smiled before placing it inside his suit jacket pocket.

***

Meanwhile, John and Emily Langford stepped out of a taxi outside Southward Cottage before rushing inside. Mary and James were already there waiting for them. Mary quickly told them everything that had happened whilst they had been gone.

"So Detective Hastings took all four of our parents in for questioning?" Emily asked.

"Dad's in hospital after being knocked out at the Vicar's house last night but Detective Hastings has got it into his head that they had something to do with it," Mary explained.

"No, it wasn't them. When we were in church yesterday, I saw mother having a very stern conversation with Frances King at the side before practically dragging her out of the church," John replied.

"You don't think she's tried to frame our parents to get back at you do you?" Emily asked.

"Anything's possible with her. Mary, where does Dad keep his briefcase?" John asked.

"Under the desk in the study, why?"

John rushed through into the study and picked up the briefcase. "If my guess is correct, this might give us a clue," he said as he furiously tried different combinations. "Damn it, do you know his combination?"

"Two, five, one, zero, one, two," Mary replied.

John turned the dials, moved the clasps and the case opened. "How did you..."

"Dad's date of birth, 25th October 1912. He uses that for everything that needs a combination lock."

Inside the case were two pens, two notebooks, a tie, a can of talcum powder and a bundle of at least fifty letters held together with elastic bands.

"Here it is," John said as he removed the letter with a postmark on it from August 4th 1977.

Emily looked into the briefcase. "What is all this?"

"Letters from Frances King to John. She kept sending them even after she got married to some Russian millionaire," Mary explained.

"Why would she do this?"

"She's been obsessed with him ever since they had a relationship when he was eighteen."

"That's twenty years ago."

Mary nodded. "That's why he had to move away and didn't want to come back here but your parents insisted and now the floodgates have opened again."

"Got it, read this," John said as he placed the letter on the table.

It read:

Dearest John,

It appears that the fight is over and I have lost. I will never forget the years we had together. The times we make believed our future would end in a beautiful white wedding and we'd sail off into the sunset. Now I guess that dream belongs to someone else.

I have sold Thyme Cottage and I am going to join my husband on his new venture far away from here. Too many familiar surroundings remind me too much of you. If you feel the need for closure, I will be in Weymouth Bay until 6pm on the 13th. If I don't see you there, I guess I'll have to let you go.

Yours always

Frances

"6pm, that gives you four hours," Mary said.

"You're not seriously thinking of going after her are you?" Emily asked.

"It makes sense. She has obviously tried to frame our parents and blackmailed mother for the gold. I need to go to Weymouth and bring her in for questioning!" John replied.

"If you're going then I'm coming with you," Emily said.

"It's too dangerous Emily," Mary replied.

"I'm not letting my husband go after that psychopath alone!"

"Then we all go," James replied.

John looked at Emily and then at Mary and James before closing the briefcase. "Come on, we don't have any time to waste!" he said as he led them out towards his car.

John knew he was clutching at straws but he needed answers and Frances was his obvious connection.

***

At Southampton Police Station, Detective Peter Hastings joined Sergeant Ted Newman and William Handanowicz in the interrogation room.

"You're wasting your time here, I had no reason to kill the reverend or injure Edward Langford!" William protested.

"Our sources have said that you and Mr Langford had some differences of opinion over the marriage of your children, Emily Handanowicz and John Langford. Would you care to clarify those?" Hastings asked.

"Our situation isn't normal. I knew what I was getting into when I met Dana. She had recently been widowed, had a young daughter and was pregnant with twins whilst she was at the convent in Portsmouth but somehow we connected in a way that I've never connected with anyone before."

"This convent, am I right in believing this was St Anne's?"

William nodded.

"And how did you gain access to this place?"

"I was doing some charity work to raise some money for them. Dana volunteered to make the teas and coffees at the event. We started talking and learnt that we had a lot in common."

"Such as?"

"Detective, sometimes in life, you need to hit the reset button. When life becomes unbearable, you need an outlet or you will just bottle things up over and over again and it will eventually consume you. As a middle-aged man who had focused solely on my business ventures throughout my twenties and thirties, I felt that the opportunity of love had passed me by."

"Until you met Dana."

William nodded. "She told me about her husband Gerald who had died fighting in the war leaving her a widow. Then she told me about the charming gent, Jack Smith, who visited her several times during the war. How she had fallen for him but both times he betrayed her. Left her pregnant, firstly with a son that she had to give up for adoption in 1940 and then she was pregnant again in 1948 with twins after they had had, I guess you could call it a one night stand before his death."

"The twins, Emily and Evelyn, you raised as your own," Hastings confirmed.

William nodded. "I loved Dana and thought we could make it work. And we did. We had James in '51 and finally had our own little family. Then, when Edith became ill, her dying wish was to return to Lepe. To be with her friends once again before she passed away. Little did I realise what a tangled web Jack Smith had left behind."

The interrogation room fell silent as William's words echoed in the air. Detective Hastings exchanged a knowing look with Sergeant Newman before turning back to William.

"You're suggesting that this man, Jack Smith, had quite the impact on your wife's life," Hastings observed.

William nodded slowly. "It's like a shadow from the past has caught up with us. Dana's past with Jack Smith seemed to resurface when we returned to Lepe. She was haunted by memories she had buried deep within her heart and Frances King knew what she had to do to cause maximum pain."

Detective Hastings leaned forward, intrigued. "And you believe this connection to Jack Smith somehow led to the events that unfolded recently?"

William's eyes darkened with sorrow. "I can't be certain, but it's as if the sins of the past have woven themselves into the present. Dana was a strong woman, but the weight of her history with Jack Smith... it was a burden she couldn't shake off."

Sergeant Newman cleared his throat, breaking the heavy atmosphere in the room. "Where does Frances King fit into all of this?"

"She knew about the pay-offs," William replied.

"What pay-offs?" Hastings asked.

"Jack Smith robbed a bank in 1938 in Portsmouth. The gold was never found and it had been written off. When he returned in 1948, he gave Dana and Mavis Langford two gold bars each. Dana cashed it in and used the money to pay for her stay in Portsmouth. It wasn't until after she left that she discovered that her home had been burnt down. The money that she had wanted to use to help with the children's education ended up paying to rebuild Sundial Cottage instead. That was why we returned to the village."

"Why did Mavis Langford receive the gold from Jack Smith?" Sergeant Newman asked.

"Because Jack Smith is the father of Mary and Frederick Langford," William replied.

Detective Peter Hastings sat back in his chair. Everything was beginning to make sense. The argument between the families, Fred leaving the wedding and having the accident that cost him his life. "I'm assuming Frederick Langford and Evelyn Handanowicz did not know about their paternity."

"Not until yesterday, no. We knew that Evelyn had been dating a young man at university but until recently, we didn't know who he was," William admitted.

"And Frances King used this information to her advantage?" Sergeant Newman asked.

"She was dating John Langford soon after he left school. When our family returned to the village, John left her to be with Edith."

Sergeant Newman looked at Hastings confused.

"Edith Wise passed away in 1956," Hastings confirmed. "Frances never let it go that John had picked Edith over her."

"Mavis Langford was so keen to save face that she gave her gold bars that Jack Smith had given her to Frances in an attempt to bribe her and keep her away from John now that he had moved on and married Emily," William replied. "My advice to you, if you're looking for someone with a motive to kill the reverend and injure Edward Langford, Frances King and her family would be a good place to start."

"We can't," Hastings sighed.

"Why?"

"Because she moved away last night. Packed everything up and headed off to Russia to be with her husband," Sergeant Edwards confirmed.

Detective Hastings felt a sinking feeling in his gut as he processed the latest revelation. Frances King, the woman at the centre of it all, had slipped away just when they were getting close to unravelling the truth. He exchanged a glance with Sergeant Newman, both silently acknowledging the setback.

"Well, that complicates things," Hastings muttered under his breath. But he was not one to give up easily. "We need to find a way to track her down. Newman, get in touch with our contacts at the border control. We need to know if any flights or shipments have left for Russia recently."

As Sergeant Newman hurried out of the room to make the necessary arrangements, Detective Hastings sat back in his chair, deep in thought. The pieces of the puzzle were scattered before him, waiting to be put together. Frances King's sudden departure only affirmed his suspicions that she held the key to unravelling the mystery behind the Jack Smith case that Hastings and his Detective at the time, Edward Langford, had stumbled upon in 1948.

"So what now?" William asked.

Hastings stood from his chair. "Now I need to speak with Dana Handanowicz and Mavis Langford but thank you for your cooperation Mr Handanowicz. You may well have answered the questions from a cold case that we've been working on for almost thirty years."

***

John Langford parked his car in the marina at Weymouth Bay. In the distance he saw a huge yacht far out at sea. He opened the boot of the car and found a pair of binoculars hidden under a windbreaker and a cool box. He looked out and could just make out the name on the side of the yacht, SSJ St Petersburg VV.

"That has to be it," John said as he rushed over towards the lock building.

Two men were standing high up on a platform as the lock gates that allowed boats in and out of the marina began creaking open and closed. John shouted out to the two men but they couldn't hear him over the creaking and whooshing of the water in the lock. He began climbing up the steel steps towards their platform.

"Hey! You can't come up here!" one of them shouted down to him.

John pulled out his ID. "Officer John Langford, Met Police, do you have any boats that could take me out to the SSJ St Petersburg?"

"That boat belongs to Vladimir Vasilievich," the man replied.

"I know who it belongs to, can you get me out there?"

"You're too late pal. They set sail half an hour ago. By the time you get out there, they'll be out on the open sea. Too dangerous."

John walked back down from the lock building towards his car as he watched the yacht disappear out of sight.

"You tried John," Emily said as she held him close.

"There has to be another way."

"How? She's married to a millionaire, she'll be protected come what may. All we can do is head back home and try to figure out how to get our parents out of custody," Mary replied.

"That's it, Mary you're a genius," John gasped as he quickly climbed into the driving seat.

"I am?" Mary asked, confused.

"They've moved house right?"

Everyone nodded.

"There's no way they would have got all of their belongings onto that yacht so it would have to go into the freight containers," John explained.

Emily sighed. "But John, there must be hundreds of freight containers in the port. How on Earth are we going to find out which one Frances has used?"

"Because every container has a reference number and the last two letters of the reference number are linked to the country they are heading to. All we need to do is find the containers with their reference number ending in RU."

"Needle in a haystack," James sighed.

"Maybe, but we have to try," John replied before starting up the engine and heading towards the freight shipping terminal.

Chapter Thirty-Five

Who Can You Trust?

Thursday 6th November 2008

As Blake and Frank arrived at Ashlett Creek, Blake's phone rang. He checked the caller ID before answering.

"Any news Sir?" Blake answered.

"Angela Barnes has been tracked to the oil refinery north of your position. The Prime Minister and the Ministry Of Defence have been in touch and have received demands from Vladimir Vasilievich for the release of funds from "The Crystal" totalling one hundred million pounds," Eric Gordon confirmed.

"Joe is working his magic to keep that door closed, however, we seem to have a bigger problem than just a potentially unexploded world war bomb under the refinery. When we uncovered what was buried at Holbury Manor, it gave us the code for a nuclear bomb as well as the location of the gold inside the tunnels that were there before the refinery was even built. Jack Smith was certainly clever."

"Our records show that when he stayed at Holbury Manor House during the war, he met an architect called Herbert Thomas. That would account for how he was able to know the layout of the tunnels and potentially stash away the gold whilst still having access to it."

"It was local history books that led us here but do we have any idea where the original maps were located?"

"Underneath the floorboards of the old manor house."

"Surely they would have been discovered by now?" Blake asked.

"You'd have thought so but the house burned down in 2006 and was then rebuilt. The old maps presumably went up in flames."

"Accident or deliberate?"

"Your guess is as good as mine."

"Have safety measures been put into place if things go south?" Blake asked.

"The oil companies won't want to shut off the supply completely however contingency plans are in place. If you come face to face with Vasilievich, say goodbye from us," Eric Gordon replied. "Good luck Blake."

As Blake cut off the call, a loud boom echoed around the area and a chimney in the distance shot a large flare of flames into the night sky.

"What are you thinking?" Frank asked.

"That the sea is going to be bloody cold tonight," Blake replied.

"Let's do this," Frank said as they waded out into the water and began to swim out towards the hatch.

The icy cold water attacked their muscles as they swam against the waves until they were around ten metres offshore. Treading water for a moment, Blake took a deep breath before going underwater. Mostly by touch rather than sight, he found the hatch. It was a concrete structure out of the seabed with a metal underwater hatch that had rusted over the years. Blake came back up for air before signalling for Frank to join him underwater. Together they pulled and pushed as hard as they could to open the hatch door. They both came up for air once more before going down again and finally managing to open the hatch.

Angela had begun to explore the tunnels of her underwater bunker when she heard a clanking and groaning of a metal hatch being opened. As she turned to look back from where she had come from, a huge wave of water suddenly flooded the pipes sweeping her up off of her feet and onwards through the tunnels.

The force of the water was overwhelming, pulling her with such ferocity that she lost control of her movements. Debris swirled around her, creating a disorientating whirlpool of chaos. Her heart raced with fear as she struggled to find something to hold onto in the dark, murky waters. A loud boom of a door or hatch slamming shut echoed around the tunnels. Desperately gasping for air, Angela's mind raced with thoughts of being swept away into the unknown depths of the tunnels. Just as panic threatened to consume her entirely, her hand brushed against a metal railing embedded in the wall. With renewed determination, she grasped onto it tightly, clinging for dear life as the relentless current tugged at her.

Finding strength she didn't realise that she had, Angela managed to anchor herself to the railing, her knuckles turning white from the intensity of her grip. The water continued to rage around her, but she held on. With each passing moment, she could feel a glimmer of hope beginning to stir within her. Summoning every ounce of strength she possessed, she slowly began to pull herself along the railing, inch by painstaking inch. The water surged against her, pressing hard against her body as if trying to tear her away from her lifeline. But she refused to yield, her muscles burning with exertion as she fought against the relentless current.

Time seemed to blur as she forged ahead through the flooded tunnels, her willpower propelling her forward in the darkness. The only sound was the rush of water and her own ragged breaths echoing off the walls. She couldn't see where she was going, but she clung to the hope that there would be an end to this watery labyrinth. Just as she felt her strength waning and doubt creeping into her mind, a faint glimmer of light appeared in the distance. It beckoned to her like a beacon of salvation, a promise of escape from the watery depths that threatened to consume her. With renewed determination, Angela quickened her pace. As she pulled herself up onto a metal platform above the water, she felt a hand reach out of the water and grab her.

She screamed for a moment before realising that it was Blake and Frank pulling themselves out of the water.

"What the hell are you two doing here?" she asked as she helped them out of the water.

"I could ask you the same question," Blake replied. "What were you doing running out of Gordon's office like that?"

"Andre has the codes. I needed to make sure that I was down here before he entered the refinery but Vladimir Vasilievich was one step ahead. He revealed that I was a double agent. He led me into a trap which then led me down here."

"We could have worked together and helped you."

"And then we'd all have been trapped. If Gordon had spoken to Andre about my involvement, my cover would have been blown long before we had gained any new intelligence. I had to go it alone. Vladimir already suspected Samir of being a double agent. I had to convince him of my loyalty but ultimately, I mis-stepped."

Blake pondered that for a moment before pulling out a small earpiece from his wetsuit and placing it in his ear. "Joe, can you hear me? Joe?"

"I've got you Blake but you're a long way from the source," Joe replied as he tracked them on his laptop from Southward Cottage.

"We got washed downstream," Blake replied. "We've found Angela."

"Did Andre get hold of the codes from the undertaker?" Joe asked.

Blake repeated the question.

"Yes and then he shot him," Angela replied.

"Did you see the codes?" Frank asked.

She shook her head.

"Joe, the whole place is flooded, I'm going to need a way out," Blake replied.

"From where you are there should be a tunnel that leads up to the surface near to the heat treatment unit. From there you can access the main well where it looks like the bomb has been buried."

"I can't see anywhere. We're running around blind down here."

"What about Alison and Samir?" Angela asked.

"They are safe. When the flares went off, they managed to abseil down a chimney with a radiation specialist," Joe confirmed before consulting the map on his laptop, plotting out the best route for Blake, Angela and Frank to take.

"Okay, listen up," Joe instructed through the earpiece. "Head straight down the tunnel you're in now for about fifty metres until you reach a junction. Take a right there and keep following that path until you see a ladder leading up. It will bring you to the surface near the heat treatment unit. Once there, you should be able to access the main well where the bomb is located."

Blake relayed the instructions to Angela and Frank as they prepared to navigate through the flooded tunnels towards their escape route. The water still raged around them, but with a renewed sense of purpose and direction, they pressed forward determinedly. Each step was a battle against the relentless current, but they refused to give up. As they followed Joe's guidance, their surroundings gradually shifted from the dark, claustrophobic tunnels to a slightly more open space. The rushing water began to recede, allowing them to move more freely as they pressed on towards the surface.

Every muscle in their bodies ached from the exertion, but the trio pushed onward, driven by the urgency of their mission. Angela could feel her heart pounding in her chest as they neared the ladder that would lead them to their destination. With a shared look of determination, they braced themselves for the final ascent.

One by one, they began to climb the ladder, water dripping from their sodden clothes as they ascended towards the light above. Finally, with aching limbs and breathless anticipation, Angela emerged from the tunnel onto the surface near the heat treatment unit.

The harsh light of a floodlight blinded her momentarily, but as her eyes adjusted, she could see the vast expanse of the refinery laid out before them. Smoke billowed from various structures, the air thick with the acrid scent of industry. In the distance, the looming shape of the main well stood ominously.

"We need to move quickly," Blake said. "The bomb could detonate at any moment."

Angela nodded, her heart racing as she followed Blake and Frank towards the main well. Each step felt like a countdown to disaster.

Inside the main well, the air was thick and suffocating, the sound of their footsteps echoing off the metal walls. They moved cautiously through the dimly lit space, their senses on high alert for any sign of danger. Angela's hands trembled slightly as she scanned their surroundings, her eyes darting nervously from one shadowed corner to the next. Suddenly, a faint beeping noise cut through the silence, sending a jolt of fear coursing through Angela's veins. She froze in place, her heart pounding in her chest as she tried to pinpoint the source of the sound. With mounting dread, she realised that the beeping was coming from a darkened alcove across the chamber.

"Over there," Frank pointed, his voice barely more than a whisper in the oppressive stillness of the well.

Without hesitation, Blake and Angela followed his gaze, their eyes locking onto a small, ominous-looking device nestled among a tangle of wires and circuitry.

"It's the bomb," Blake said.

"And look at what's behind it," Frank replied as he shone the light from his phone over around a hundred solid bars of gold.

"Son-of-a-bitch entangled it in the bomb. There are metal claws holding the gold bars in place. If you remove any of it or input the wrong code, the claws will destroy the gold. The only way to get to it is to either disarm the bomb or..."

"Blow it up," Angela gasped.

"It'll kill millions," Frank gasped as he looked behind it and noticed a huge drop that went as far down as the eye could see. "Jack Smith literally buried it in the centre of the earth. There's no telling how far down that goes."

At that moment, the whole area lit up and Vlaidimir Vasilievich, Andre Lewis and Colin Sanderson entered the main well. Angela, Blake and Frank rushed to the side of the well to hide in the shadows.

Andre handed a piece of paper to Colin. "The world's greatest cash card. It better not be rejected!"

"When this is released into Crypto, nothing can stop us," Vladimir replied.

"What do you mean Crypto?" Andre asked.

"Once this is invested in The Crystal, we will be unstoppable!"

"Crypto is dead. Special Branch closed it down. Wiped millions off of its value. Why would you risk everything we've gone through for online currency?"

"My wife, Frances, ran rings around them. They took her inheritance away from her and now I will reclaim what is rightfully ours. Do you honestly think you could launder ten million in gold bullion?" Vladimir snapped. "The kremlin can cover up a lot but that much merchandise hitting the market in one hit is a tall order for anyone."

Colin removed a sheet of paper from an envelope and read what was written on it out loud. "Death is a mirror, reflect on that. Everybody will die one day, just give them time."

"What is the code?" Vladimir asked.

"It's written in Roman Numerals. I need time to figure it out."

Andre sighed and snatched the paper away from him. "If you want something done right, do it yourself."

The note read: **XII XCVII LXIV XXVII LXXXIX**

"You get this wrong and we lose everything," Vladimir replied.

"Look XII is twelve. C is one hundred but a ten before it makes it ninety so the second number is ninety-seven. L is fifty plus fourteen is sixty-four. The fourth number is twenty-seven and the fifth number is eighty-nine," Andre said as he worked out the numerals.

"It's a riddle," Frank whispered. "Their numbers are a mirror image of the code. They'll set it off."

"If you enter those numbers, you will blow us all away," Blake called out.

Andre spun around as Angela, Blake and Frank stepped into the light.

"Well, well, Blake Langford. What an unpleasant surprise," Vladimir sighed.

"If you input that code, you will blow us all off of the face of the earth!"

"What would you know? Your family are part of the reason why we're all here! If your father hadn't left Frances King when she was a young and vulnerable single mother..."

"Then she wouldn't have ended up with you."

"Let's not split hairs here. Our paths would have crossed sooner or later. Blake Langford, the government's loyal terrier, a meagre wage for risking life and limb for what? A pat on the back, good job old boy, now onto the next. I could make you a very rich man instead of a poor dead one. Your grandfather learnt that before his untimely demise."

"The code was buried with Dana Handanowicz. Why would somebody go to such lengths to protect the code for it to be wrong?" Andre asked.

"Because the code we have uncovered is different from your code," Frank replied.

"And what if your code is wrong?" Colin asked.

"Do you really want to take that chance?" Blake asked.

Vladimir stared at him for a moment. "Frances always said you Langfords never know when to keep your nose out of things. I'm going to disarm the bomb and take the gold out of here. You've interfered with my plans for the last time."

Blake's jaw tightened as Vladimir reached for the bomb, his mind racing for a plan. Without hesitation, he lunged forward and tackled Vladimir to the ground. The bomb and the gold bars rolled backwards on what looked like some kind of wheeled trolley that it was situated on towards the huge hole behind it.

Angela and Frank sprang into action, restraining Andre and Colin before they could react.

"You're not getting away with this," Blake snapped, pinning Vladimir to the floor.

Vladimir struggled beneath Blake's firm grip, his face contorted with fury. "You fool! You have no idea what you're meddling in."

Blake kept the pressure on. "I know enough to stop you. Are a few gold bars worth the lives of millions of innocent people?"

As Vladimir's resistance faltered, a cold voice cut through the tension in the air. "There's no need for violence here!"

Blake looked up and saw Samir standing in the doorway.

Chapter Thirty-Six

Through The Years

On Sunday 13th August 1977, the flashing lights of police cars illuminated the night sky as officers swarmed around the shipping container MC74921RU heading towards St Petersburg just before midnight. Items from the Reverend Denis Black's cottage, Frances King's Thyme Cottage as well as a severed hand had been discovered inside the container. Three security guards and two supervisors from the shipping yard were taken into custody and there had been a worldwide APB put out for Frances King and her family. Whether it was through fear or money, no new information came forward and the local police had to close the case.

John, Emily, James and Mary all returned to Lepe where they were reunited with their parents, Mavis and Edward Langford and Dana and William Handanowicz. Evelyn Handanowicz never returned.

Edward and Mavis Langford lived out the rest of their lives at Southward Cottage until their deaths in 1984 Mary Langford then inherited Southward Cottage where she stayed until her death in 2002.

Dana and William Handanowicz moved back to Portsmouth after relations with the Langfords became fractured over the years. Dana Handanowicz died in 1984 with William following in 1987.

Emily and John Langford returned to London where John worked for the Met Police Force until his retirement in 1997. During this time, they welcomed the births of their three children, Blake William Langford, Jennifer Eleanor Langford and Steven Alexander Langford. John died after a short battle with lung cancer in 1999. Emily followed in 2008.

After disappearing before her sister's wedding in 1977, Evelyn Handanowicz battled anxiety and depression for seven years after emigrating to the Greek Island of Rhodes.

James Handanowicz approached John Langford in 1982 about creating a safe space for war veterans and people with mental health issues. James had studied psychology at University and had managed to raise over one hundred thousand pounds towards the new centre. A derelict hospital wing in Croydon became available and James began transforming it into a new mental health facility to help the local people.

As time rolled on, mental health specialists began asking for more money and the centre looked tired. The dream of helping people in need began to falter and the companies who had sponsored the project in the early days began to pull away. James became desperate and approached John Langford with the possibility of him becoming a partner in the business.

With his dealings in law enforcement, James convinced John that his knowledge and expertise would be invaluable in securing the future of the centre.

In January 1984, John invested fifty-thousand pounds into the Handanowicz Centre For Mental Health. A steady flow of patients continued to flow into the facility however the money was disappearing fast. Without John's knowledge, James placed the centre on the market, made the entire staff redundant and sold the business by May 1984. He fled the country with the money from the sale of the business and disappeared. For four years, John Langford used all of the options he had at his discretion as a Police Detective but there was no trace of James Handanowicz.

In September 1984, James Handanowicz joined his sister Evelyn on the Greek Island of Rhodes where they worked on an olive farm together. Evelyn never fully got over the death of Frederick Langford and was admitted and sectioned to a mental health facility in

Monolithos at the end of 1984 where she stayed until her death in 2008. After her death, James Handanowicz fled from the island and his location is currently unknown.

On the night of his death in 1984, Edward Langford sat on Lepe Beach with a flask of coffee and a fishing rod in his hand. He looked out as the sun began to set on the horizon and wondered where all of those years had gone. Years where he had been a young, energetic, enthusiastic police detective. All of the secrets that had crossed his desk. All of the lies and deceit that became the norm after the second world war. He thought about Frederick. How he had mourned his loss. How Mary had lived a life of solitude with her interests in birdwatching rather than any kind of relationship with the opposite sex. And then there was John. Determined and strong-willed enough that he would go far in whatever he did. He noticed his wife Mavis approaching him on the beach and she sat beside him in a fold-out chair. Together, they watched the sun go down and he placed his hand on top of hers.

"We did all right in the end, didn't we?" Edward asked.

Mavis smiled. "I think so," she said.

Edward wasn't sure if he heard the two pops. He wasn't sure if he felt himself slouch down in his chair. In a moment, it was over. Two lives so entwined through all of their ups and downs, had taken their last moments together under the setting sun. Mavis and Edward Langford had been shot dead before the engine of a Ford Escort roared away into the distance as it sped away from Lepe Beach.

Chapter Thirty-Seven

The Water Bomb

Thursday 6th November 2008

Inside the main well at the oil refinery, Samir stood in the doorway with Blake, Angela and Frank to his right and Vladimir, Colin and Andre to his left.

"Samir Khalifa, what an unpleasant surprise," Vladimir spat as he moved towards the bomb.

Samir aimed his gun. "I wouldn't do that if I were you."

"Looking to take it for yourself Khalifa? After all, you know all about treachery and deception don't you? Haven't you told Langford about your little adventure whilst your colleague supervised the rising of the dead?"

"What does he mean?" Blake asked.

"I've been your guardian angel Blake. Keeping a close eye on my investment whilst Tom Gibson attempted to get under your skin like some disease that needed to be destroyed," Vladimir replied.

"You killed Gibson?" Angela asked.

"No, chalk that one up to Frances. She knows all of the ways you can torture a human body for maximum pain before they die."

"Interesting role-model," Frank quipped.

"I've made mistakes in the past but I've paid for them. That gold doesn't belong to you Vladimir and you shouldn't be the one who decides who lives and who dies from a world war two secret," Samir replied.

"How touching, I almost shed a tear. Now let's get on with it," Vladimir snapped as he moved towards the bomb.

Samir fired at the top of the well. The bullet ricocheted off of the metal walls and flew in the air above them before coming to rest on the floor next to Andre.

"Neat trick but I don't have time for theatrics," Vladimir said.

"Neither do we," said Alison as she slid a gold key into the bomb and turned it, leading to the entire display to light up.

"What the..." Vladimir began.

"You see, if you had been following me, you would have known that I met with Christopher Anderson and he gave me the ashes of Jack Walter Smith. In those ashes was a gold key. I never knew what it was for until a radiation expert saved mine and Alison's ass from being barbecued in the heat treatment unit!" Samir replied.

At that moment, Andre pulled his gun but Frank reacted first, hitting it out of his hands. Angela charged at Colin who headed for the exit. Blake launched himself at Vladimir, knocking him into the bomb and the gold bars. The small trolley that it was on rolled closer to the hole. Alison tried to grab hold of it but the gold bars began to tilt on the edge of the huge crater. Blake wrestled Vladimir to the ground as they rolled ever closer towards the huge crater.

"At least I'll have the pleasure of putting you out of my misery!" Vladimir said as they rolled closer to the hole.

"Don't count on it," Blake replied as he aimed a sharp fist to Vladimir's chest.

"It was beautiful Blake. Your grandparents on that beach. I took them out in two shots. Pop. Pop. One after the other. And now it's your turn."

Blake remembered the story he had been told by his own father, John Langford, of how his grandparents had been sat on Lepe Beach and had died together. Now, it suddenly made sense.

"You!" Blake cussed.

Vladimir nodded.

A fit of rage consumed Blake as he began pounding away at Vladimir's chest. Vladimir gasped for air as Blake's fists pummelled his chest relentlessly. Blood trickled from the corner of his mouth as his body went limp under Blake's raw fury. The others stood frozen, watching the brutal scene unfold before them.

"Blake, that's enough!" Angela finally shouted, rushing forward to pull him away from Vladimir's lifeless body. "It's done!"

Blake stumbled back, panting heavily, his hands clenched into fists at his sides. His eyes burned with a mixture of grief and anger as he looked down at Vladimir's motionless form on the ground.

"We need to get out of here," Samir said urgently, his voice breaking through the stunned silence that had settled over the group. "The bomb is still active."

Alison quickly grabbed the trolley attached to the bomb with the gold bars, pushing it away from the edge of the crater as they all made their way towards the exit. The sound of alarms blaring filled the air as they raced against time to escape. As they got to the exit, they heard a beeping like a timer ticking down. As they turned to look back at the bomb, they saw Andre entering a code.

"I thought the key deactivated it!" Samir gasped.

"Only the nuclear reactor part. There's still enough explosive to blow this place sky high!" Alison replied.

"Now she tells us," Frank said as he wrestled Andre from the control panel.

"It's too late, we all go down together," Andre laughed before grabbing Frank's gun and shooting himself under his chin.

Angela turned away in disgust.

"Saved me a job, where's that code?" Frank asked.

Blake touched his ear-piece. "Joe, are you still there?"

"I'm with you Blake."

"We need the code to deactivate the bomb."

"We don't even know if that's going to work."

"I've got two minutes to find out or this place gets blown to shit!"

"Okay, okay, it's ninety-eight, seventy-two, forty-six, seventy-nine, twenty-one. Now get the hell out of there!" Joe shouted.

Blake entered the code but the countdown continued. Sixty seconds, fifty-nine, fifty-eight, fifty-seven...

"Get the hell out of here, run!" Blake shouted.

"What are you doing?" Alison asked.

"I need to disarm the bomb!"

"It's gonna blow!"

"If it does, we're all dead!"

They looked at the display. Forty-nine, forty-eight, forty-seven, forty-six, forty-five...

They both looked at the gold bars.

"Are you thinking what I'm thinking?" Alison asked.

Blake nodded and they both pushed the trolley of gold bars over the edge and into the huge crater behind the bomb. With a loud clanking boom, the gold bars and the bomb disappeared into the crater. Frank, Angela, Blake, Samir and Alison all ran out of the main well and rushed away towards the exit. A few seconds later and a loud boom echoed around the refinery. In the distance, a huge plume of water rose up into the air creating a huge wave that engulfed the lower part of the oil refinery before receding back down towards the sea.

"How the hell did you know that would work?" Frank asked.

"I didn't," Blake replied.

"That was one hell of a water bomb," Samir smiled as police and emergency services arrived at the oil refinery gates.

Frank, Angela, Samir, Alison and Blake watched as the officers and emergency personnel swarmed the area. Even though the gold was gone, they had the knowledge that the bomb had been destroyed too.

"Next time you decide to trace back your ancestry, warn me first," Alison said as she led them out towards the village.

Blake smiled. "I wouldn't be very good at my job if I did."

As they adjusted to the aftermath, a reality set in that there would always be someone or something hunting them for the mistakes of the past. They would all need to lay low and stick together, at least for a while until the bodies of those involved were recovered. As Joe Knight pulled up in his car to pick them up, they knew their wishes for a simple life seemed as far away as ever. It was the nature of the job and no matter how much Blake didn't want to admit it, being a family man and working for Special Branch would always keep himself, his team and his family in the firing line.

When they arrived back at Southward Cottage, Michael came rushing out and wrapped his arms around his father's waist. Paula walked over and they held each other close for what seemed like an age.

"Is it over?" she asked.

"It's over," Blake replied as dawn slowly began to appear over the sea that was the backdrop to their family home.

"You missed something really cool Dad. About an hour ago, a huge wave came up and it soaked the back garden at the top of the cliff. It was awesome. I've never seen anything like it!" Michael explained.

Blake gave Alison and Paula a knowing look. "I'm sure it was great Michael, now how about we get some breakfast."

"Yeah! I'm making waffles!" Michael said as he rushed indoors.

"How's he still got the energy after being awake all night?" Alison asked.

"Oh to be kids again," Blake laughed as they all headed inside Southward Cottage.

Chapter Thirty-Eight

Recover Your Soul
Monday 17th November 2008

Blake Langford entered the cemetery at All Saints Church near to Dibden Golf Club on the edge of The New Forest. He walked over near to the church where he found the grave of Mavis Irene Mary Langford and Edward George Ernest Langford. He placed a selection of artificial flowers into the rose bowl on the gravestone before standing in front of the grave and reading the inscription.

"We got him in the end, Grandad," Blake whispered to himself.

His mind cast back to kicking a football around in the back garden of Southward Cottage when he was seven years old. Using two metal bins as goal-posts, he would take shots at his grandad before enjoying homemade scones with fresh strawberry jam at the wooden picnic table.

As he was about to leave, he noticed a burgundy urn had been placed next to a white carnation on an unmarked grave in the shadow of the church alongside a wooden cross that had a remembrance day red and black poppy attached to it. Blake crouched down and looked at the urn. A gold inscription on the side read;

JACK WALTER SMITH
DIED: 21st AUGUST 1948
Aged 41 Years

Blake sighed. "Did they love you? I hope you made them happy even if it was only briefly," he said to himself.

As he stood up to leave, two robins hopped over the grass towards him. One of them flew up and sat on top of the gravestone next to the unmarked plot and looked at Blake for a moment before flying away. Blake smiled and looked up to the skies before continuing on his way back to his car. Alison was waiting for him in the passenger seat as he returned.

"You okay?" she asked.

"I think so. My father told me about how he felt cheated that his parents never had the opportunity to enjoy a retirement together. He'd searched for years to find out what really happened on that day at Lepe Beach."

"It must have been awful."

"When he came back here to identify them, the investigating officer at the time took him down to where it happened. He worked out that whoever had done it must have been standing near to the lighthouse at the top of the hill. If they'd just stayed on their own stretch of beach behind Southward Cottage, chances are they would have been all right."

"You don't know that for sure."

Blake nodded. "I guess. If Vladimir and Frances hadn't seen them on the beach they would have probably gone to the house."

"If you don't want to do this, I don't mind visiting the hospital alone."

"No, I need to have this closure. I need to know why," Blake replied as he started the car and drove into Southampton City Centre towards the hospital.

As they arrived at the hospital and walked along the glass corridors towards the Acute Medical Unit, Blake thought back to his father's last words before he died. He'd asked Blake to look after the family. To be the figurehead that for so long, John Langford had been. He'd sat at his father's bedside after rushing back from a Special Branch training course in Ireland to be at his bedside when he died. Now that the dust had settled following his mother's passing, Blake knew that he owed it to his father to keep the promise that he made to keep the family safe.

When they arrived at the Acute Medical Unit, Alison showed her ID to the nurse at the reception desk. She led them through the ward to a side room at the end of the corridor. Alison entered the room with Blake close behind. Machines beeped an endless monotone as they monitored the man laying motionless in the bed. The name plate above the bed read; Timothy John King.

"Timmy, can you hear me?" Alison asked as she sat on the chair at his bedside.

His eyes flickered momentarily before opening wide. He looked firstly at Blake before noticing Alison at his side. "Who are you?"

"I'm Alison Pearce, I work for Special Branch. We just wanted to ask you a few questions?"

"And who is he?"

"Blake Langford," Blake replied.

Timmy's eyes widened in recognition as Blake introduced himself. "Where is she? What have you done to my mother?"

"Your mother has sadly passed away, Timmy," Blake replied.

"You killed her!"

"No, she did it herself."

Timmy felt tears sting the backs of his eyes. "No, no, she'd never do that! You're lying!"

Alison placed her hand on Timmy's arm but he didn't respond to her. "Timmy, do you know Father Christoph Fischer from St David's Church in Lepe?"

Tears began streaming down Timmy's face. "I wanted to die," he cried. "My whole life has been one big lie. Mother would never let it go. My father had been alive the whole time and she lied to me. Her obsession with the Langfords consumed her." He looked directly at Blake. "And then you killed her!"

"She died with her first love. I hope you can find some comfort in that," Blake replied. "What do you know about Holbury Manor Timmy?"

He glared at Blake for a moment before answering. "It's a patch of woodland on the edge of The New Forest. During the war, the old Manor House was used to treat the wounded. They later turned the Manor House and the surrounding barns around it into a housing estate."

"Your mother believed that Jack Smith, the man who had robbed a bank in Portsmouth in 1938, had buried the gold within Holbury Manor."

"It was her inheritance and John Langford took it away from her. If I ever saw the bastard again, I'd kill him!" Timmy snapped.

"John Langford, my father, died of lung cancer in 1999," Blake replied.

Timmy didn't reply.

"He told me about his relationship with your mother when we used to fish off of Lepe Beach. How as soon as he left school, he helped her look after you and your Grandad. Your mother fell in love with him. They had a brief relationship but when it all broke down, she refused to accept it. She stalked him. She sent him letters. Thousands of them. Waited outside his house at Southward Cottage until he finished work and then hounded him constantly. Even when he moved to London she continued to send the letters."

"She loved him."

"It was through her letters that we discovered the truth about what had really happened all of those years ago. Mavis Langford, my grandmother and John's mother, signed over her share of the Smith gold to your mother, Frances King, on the understanding that she would leave John alone when he married my mother, Emily."

"And what a twisted family secret it turned out to be," Timmy snapped.

"Timmy," Alison spoke now. "You've spent your life hating and chasing a family that wasn't even related to you. All John Langford wanted to do was to help your mother after Christoph Fischer had left her alone with a young child and an ill father at a time where young single women had no support whatsoever."

"Christoph Fischer is dead to me. He was never there for us!"

"He is dead," Blake confirmed. "When he came face-to-face with your mother in Holbury Manor, he tried to help her. He wanted to help her to come to terms with the hurt and regret from almost sixty years ago. As he embraced her, she set off the suicide bomb vest that she was wearing and blew them both up. They died together. As it should have been. Christoph, who was a German soldier, should have been allowed to be with the mother of his child. If he had, maybe your mother would not have become involved with Vladimir Vaselievich. Maybe he would not have murdered my Grandparents, Mavis and Edward Langford, on the beach that day in 1984. Maybe, just maybe, if they had been allowed to be together, you wouldn't have jumped from that church balcony."

Timmy bowed his head. "They said I've broken my spine and I'm paralysed from the neck down. Oh my God, what have I done?"

"Your mind was poisoned by a manipulative and very mentally ill mother, Timmy," Alison replied. "The post-traumatic stress that must have put you and Dmitri through would have been immense."

"Where is Dmitri?" Timmy asked.

"He's been arrested and is going through the investigative procedure. We don't know for certain what the outcome will be," Blake replied.

"Thank you," Timmy said, looking straight at Blake.

"What for?"

"Being honest with me. It's been a long time since someone has been."

"You have a chance to recover your soul," Alison replied. "I know things may look bleak but you'll get through it."

Timmy smiled at Alison before closing his eyes once again. After a few minutes, Alison and Blake left the room and headed out of the hospital.

When they sat back into Blake's car, he let out a long exhale and ran his fingers through his hair.

"You okay?" Alison asked.

"I guess you never realise how much life can mess you up until much later when often it's too late," Blake replied.

"You seemed to have turned out alright though."

"Me? I'm a complete mess. I jump to conclusions. My anger management could do with some work."

"And you have a wonderful son and fiance who love you and if you didn't have those characteristics then you'd be a useless field agent. I know who I'd rather have watching my back."

Blake smiled as he started the car. "Thanks Ali. You're not too bad yourself."

"Believe me, you think your family has baggage, mine is a whole new level."

"Samir?"

"It's complicated."

"Meaning?"

"A sharp suit and a cute ass may be enough for some women but sometimes things need to go a lot deeper than that."

"Paula tells me that all the time."

"Does it cause friction considering your past with her sister?"

"If Rachael was still alive I think it would. As this case has shown, sometimes life doesn't always work out the way that we plan it. When Rachael disappeared in 1999, I thought I'd never see her again..."

"But you never gave up hope."

"Someone's been doing their homework."

"I like to know who I'm entrusting my life with."

"I followed that trail for eight years without so much as a glimmer and then Paula led me straight to her."

"So you can relate to the lost love that Frances experienced with your father."

"I guess. I never went out and killed people for Rachael though," Blake smirked.

"I know that but deep down, even after her disappearance and everything that happened, you still loved Rachael, right?"

"I did. I guess I still do. When she died, it felt like my whole life had been tipped up-side-down. Suddenly, I'd had a chance to be with the love of my life and then it was ripped away from me at the last minute. Then I found out I was a father to a son that I never knew for the first eight years of his life..."

"And now..."

"Now, I can't imagine a day without Michael or Paula. If you'd asked me three years ago where I'd be today, I'd never have predicted this."

Alison nodded.

"What are you thinking?" Blake asked.

"That, maybe, I guess, Samir deserves the benefit of the doubt."

"Only you can decide that."

Alison sighed deeply. "Why is love so hard?"

"That's what makes it worthwhile I guess. Where to now?"

"We need to catch up with Joe at Holbury Manor. Forensics would have hopefully finished piecing together whatever remains there were of the bomb that Frances had set off."

As the two friends travelled out of the city centre and back into The New Forest, Blake felt a renewed sense of purpose. The ghosts of the past had finally been laid to rest and he could focus on his family and his future.

When they arrived at Holbury Manor, blue and white police tape was surrounding the woodland whilst Joe Knight was directing police officers around the scene. He saw Alison and Blake approaching and walked over towards them.

"Glad you could make it," Joe smiled. "That bomb made quite a mess."

"That is what they're designed to do," Blake laughed.

"Have the police found anything interesting from where the trees were uprooted?" Alison asked.

"Nothing of note however, take a look at this," Joe said as he led them towards the third tree where the metal box that held the codes was found.

As he moved some of the mud and debris out of the way, he revealed a wooden handle. "Take a look at that," Joe smiled.

Blake reached down and pulled on the handle which released a knife with a six inch blade. "An old knife?" Blake asked. "Do I need to ask if it's Colonel Mustard in the Drawing Room?"

"Very funny. Look at the inscription," Joe replied.

"H. Boker and co." Blake read aloud.

"Boker was a rare knife maker around the time of the second world war. You're holding a museum piece there!"

Alison and Blake looked at each other. "Anything else?" she asked.

"Yes, down by the pond, this way," Joe replied as he headed down the mud path.

As Blake and Alison turned to follow him, they heard something growling behind them. Blake slowly turned around and saw two Staffordshire Bull Terriers growling and glaring at them.

"Don't move," Blake said as he slowly turned to face them.

"Amber! Mongo!" a man's voice called out.

Alison and Blake looked up towards the main path and saw a middle-aged man wearing grey shorts, a pale blue shirt and an orange hi-visibility jacket.

"Oh hi Blake, sorry about them, they're friendly really," the man called out.

"They look like it too," Alison quipped.

"Hi Steve, long time, no see. Are you still working at the local sorting office?" Blake asked.

"Not for much longer. I'm moving out to Boldre to enjoy some fishing and early retirement. The legs don't work as well as they used to," Steve replied.

"Excuse me Sir, you're trespassing inside a police corden!" One of the police officers called out.

"Sorry, just rescuing my dogs!" Steve replied as he attached Amber and Mongo to their leads and gave them a couple of biscuits each.

He handed some of the dog biscuits to Blake. "You'll probably need them if you're trawling through here. It's a dog walkers paradise."

"I'll keep that in mind, thanks," Blake replied as he watched Steve walk back up towards the main path.

"Old friend?" Alison asked.

"One of the local postmen I used to see around the area. Bristol City fan but nobody's perfect," Blake smiled as he followed Joe down towards the pond.

When they arrived, they found Samir crouched down on his knees with one of the forensic experts as they carefully dredged a fishing net through the murky water.

"What are they doing?" Alison asked.

"Removing traces of nickel and copper from the water. When that bomb went off, it sent shards of metal off in all directions," the forensic expert replied as he looked up at Blake. "You were lucky not to be torn to pieces."

"We found this too," Samir said as he handed Alison a small metal bucket.

Amongst the pieces of nickel and copper was a large gold and diamond wedding ring.

"It needs cleaning up but I'm sure somebody will want it back. It must have been worth a lot to whoever lost it," Samir continued.

Blake looked at the wedding ring and then checked his watch. It was just before quarter-to-three in the afternoon. He turned to Alison; "Are you okay to head back with Samir at the end of the day? There's somewhere I need to be."

Alison nodded. "Sure, is everything okay?"

"It will be, thanks," Blake replied before rushing off and heading back to his car.

Fifteen minutes later, he was parked outside Forest Way School. He walked through the side gate and up the slight incline of the path that snaked its way through the trees and hedges before walking past the school playground. He spotted Paula on the far side nearest to the entrance talking to another parent. As he walked over towards her, a teacher opened the door and allowed the children to run out of the doors towards their parents. Michael rushed over and wrapped his arms around Blake's waist.

Blake held him close as Paula joined them.

"Well this is an unexpected surprise," Paula smiled. "What brings you here?"

"A promise that I made to my father nine years ago that I intend to keep. Looking after my family first," Blake smiled.

"Dad, can we go over and buy some cakes from Mrs Prince's cake stall on the playground?" Michael asked.

Blake nodded and as Michael led them over towards the playground, he noticed three stalls had been set up selling homemade cakes, books that had been written by the children in the school and freshly baked bread.

As they looked at the stalls, Michael pointed out the book which had the poem inside that he had written a few months ago and explained how his class had used yeast and flour to bake twenty loaves of bread. Paula took hold of Blake's hand as Michael ran off to play briefly with one of his friends.

"This means a lot to him," she smiled as Blake held her close.

"I've spent too long rushing from one mission to the next. If mum's death has proven anything, it's that life is too short and I need to make the most of the life we have now."

"Michael needs you in his life right now. The transition to secondary school is going to be tough for him."

"Then we'll face it together as a family," Blake replied.

"You mean that?"

"When I proposed in London, you said yes. I hope that still stands."

Paula laughed. "Of course it does."

"Then let's do it. Let's book the church and make it official."

Paula looked into his eyes. "You're serious?"

"Never been more serious about anything," Blake smiled.

Paula held him close for a moment before Michael came running over towards them.

"Dad, can we get some chocolate cake?" he asked.

As they approached the cake stand, Blake recognised the lady standing behind the stall. "Hello Gloria, what brings you to the school?"

"Blake Langford, I haven't seen you in over twenty years!" Gloria smiled. "You haven't changed a bit!"

"Mrs Prince, can we have one of your amazing chocolate and marshmallow cakes please?" Michael asked.

"Of course you can. After all, everything's better with cake," Gloria replied.

As Paula and Blake continued to chat with Gloria and the other parents in the school playground, a navy blue BMW with a Greek number plate slowly drove along the road just outside the school gates. The driver waited for one of the parents to drive away before parking in their space next to the school gate. He picked up his binoculars and managed to peer through a gap in the trees towards the cake stall. He saw Paula and Blake laughing and chatting with a group of people.

"That's right Blake, play happy families for now. It's only a matter of time," a man said as he watched them for a moment.

"Excuse me Sir, is everything okay?" a lady carrying a large black and yellow lollipop asked as she approached the car.

The man placed his binoculars onto the passenger seat. "Everything's fine, thank you," he smiled.

"Does your child attend this school?"

"No, but my nephew does."

"And who is he, may I ask?"

"You seem very suspicious..."

"It pays to be when strange men are looking into a school playground with binoculars during school pick-up time. Do I need to speak to the headmaster about this?" the lady asked.

"That won't be necessary, I'm just going."

"Then may I ask who your nephew is?"

"His name's Michael. Michael Langford," the man replied before driving away.

BLAKE LANGFORD WILL RETURN...

Catch Up With The Previous Blake Langford Adventures:
WHERE NO ONE STANDS ALONE

Blake Langford works for the Special Intelligence Branch of the British Government. In 1999, he was assigned to a case in Italy regarding some smuggling of blood diamonds into the country from Africa.

Rachael Evans, Blake's fiancee for two years, said goodbye to him at Heathrow Airport and then vanished with no explanation.

Eight years later, whilst Blake is taking some long overdue leave from the service, Rachael's sister Paula, pays him a visit at his holiday home in southern England with a message that Rachael is in trouble and needs his help.

Blake had never let go of the love he had for Rachael but had learned to live with the reality that she had gone. Now reopening long forgotten deep wounds, Blake travels across America and into Mexico to crack a diamond smuggling ring that he had stumbled upon in Italy all those years ago but this time, for Blake, the stakes are much higher.

Catch Up With The Previous Blake Langford Adventures:

UNDERNEATH THE COVERS

As the countdown to new year echoes around the streets of Edinburgh, Blake Langford is seeking comfort in a bottle of whiskey. His life torn apart by his previous assignment, Blake has shut himself off from the world.

When a police spotlight shines on a body hanging from the top of Edinburgh Castle however, Blake discovers that the past still has many unanswered questions.

As he travels up to the Scottish Capital, nothing is as it seems and Blake has to fight against his own demons to unravel a murder that happened ten years ago. The only connection being a message telling the victim that they will die.

Can one woman's need for closure help catch a killer or has Blake been fooled again?

Catch Up With The Previous Blake Langford Adventures:
IN THE SHADOW OF MY LIFE

When a London Underground Train makes an unscheduled stop at a disused station, Blake Langford realises that something is not quite right.

As he follows the abandoned staircase up into a rundown building above the station, he discovers the body of a young girl.

As Blake pursues the case, London's cruel streets provide little explanation of who the girl was or how she was killed until a surprise confession from his sister changes the case completely.

When blood runs thicker than water, Blake is left with two women wanting answers and a brother in need of an alibi, but who can he trust?

Coming Soon:
EVERYTHING

How can you protect your child from themselves?
When Michael Langford posted a live video on social media, he
never knew who was watching. After agreeing to meet the new girl
in class, Michael disappears.

Blake Langford is arrested during a routine training exercise and
accused of compromising Her Majesty's Government by using a
new spyware known as The Crystal.

When secrets from the past bring new developments into the
investigation, Blake and Paula have to risk everything to discover
what happened to Michael.

When everything you thought was true turns out to be a lie, where
do you turn next?

Coming Soon:
QUESTIONS FOR THE DEAD

Blake Langford, wrongly implicated in a cyber attack on the British Government, returns to Special Branch.

Whilst attending a friend's 40th birthday with his colleague, Alison Pearce, Blake becomes a suspect in a murder investigation at Farnborough House.

The inquiry into Colonel Francis Stanislav's life exposes connections to a mysterious Egyptian organisation, adding layers of complexity to their quest for the truth.

As more witnesses die, Blake must act fast to apprehend the killer before another wealthy businessman is murdered.

The race against time leads him to the heart of an Egyptian pyramid in The Valley Of The Kings and an archeologist with a deadly secret but who can answer the questions for the dead?

Coming Soon:
HOME FOR SEPTEMBER

James Turner, freed after five years, reunites with his sister Gabby outside Florida State Prison, only for her to be kidnapped moments after his release.

Alone and under suspicion, James, accompanied by CIA agent Simon Buxton, faces a web of intrigue.

Meanwhile in the UK, Blake Langford, investigating a prison riot on the Isle Of Wight, receives a mysterious diamond with the initials RF lasered inside it from an inmate with information on a past case.

As Blake returns to Miami to assist the CIA in their search for Gabby, haunting memories and local connections take an unexpected perilous turn leaving Blake to wonder who he can trust when the price of one woman's freedom is death.

Coming Soon:
PIECES OF MY LIFE

When Graham Evans is discovered dead aboard a millionaire's yacht in Monte Carlo, Blake Langford senses there's more to the story.
With a sudden inheritance from Paula Langford's aunt, previously unknown relatives suddenly emerge seeking their share, prompting Blake and Paula's journey to uncover the truth.
In Monte Carlo, they encounter Joseph Perks, a wealthy financier backing a new racing team for the classic Monaco Grand Prix.
As investigations continue, Blake discovers Graham's involvement with counterfeit casino chips leading into a dangerous investigation unveiling a network of intrigue and money laundering that stretches far beyond the French Riviera, revealing a clandestine organisation operating on a global scale.
When money talks, how much are you willing to lose?

John's First Non-Fiction Book:
AN ASPIRING AUTHOR'S ARTICULATION OF AN AUTHOR'S JOURNEY TO PUBLICATION

With so much information flooding the internet these days, it's often difficult for aspiring writers to know where to start and what advice they should take.

Falling victim to this madness, I began writing a blog on Substack where I shared my own experiences of becoming an author and gave my own take on issues that I encountered along the way.

None of the blogs featured here are meant to be 100% accurate. This is just my own interpretation of subjects that cropped up in my author journey across 2023 and 2024.

To find out more about the blogs and the various writing projects I have going on, please visit www.CorneliusCone.co.uk[1]

---

1. http://www.corneliuscone.co.uk

Children's Books By John Roberts & Steve Boyce

John Roberts is also the author of the new Bennie Barrier's Big City Adventures series and a co-author of the Amazon children's book series; The New Adventures Of Cornelius Cone And Friends with his friend, Steve Boyce. Over 80 ebooks are currently available as well as 23 paperback and hardback compilations.

Bennie Barrier's Big City Adventures - Volume 1

Bennie Barrier's Big City Adventures - Volume 2

The New Adventures Of Cornelius Cone And Friends - Part One

The New Adventures Of Cornelius Cone And Friends - Part Two

The New Adventures Of Cornelius Cone And Friends - Part Three

The New Adventures Of Cornelius Cone And Friends - Part Four

The New Adventures Of Cornelius Cone And Friends - Part Five

The New Adventures Of Cornelius Cone And Friends - Part Six

The New Adventures Of Cornelius Cone And Friends - Part Seven

The New Adventures Of Cornelius Cone And Friends - Part Eight

The New Adventures Of Cornelius Cone And Friends - Part Nine

The New Adventures Of Cornelius Cone And Friends - Part Ten

The Whole Cone

The Whole Cone 2 - Above The High Visibility Belt

Cornelius Cone And Friends - The Story So Far - Volume One

Cornelius Cone And Friends - The Story So Far - Volume Two

Cornelius Cone And Friends - The Story So Far - Volume Three

Cornelius Cone And Friends - The Story So Far - Volume Four

The New Adventures Of Cornelius Cone And Friends Novel - The Return Of Susie Suitcase

Bennie Barrier's Best Bits: My Adventures With A Cone Named Cornelius

Susie Suitcase's Selected Stories: My Encounters With A Cone Named Cornelius

Postman Pete's Predicaments: A Catalogue Of Errors With A Cone Named Cornelius

Tricia Trolley's Tea Time Treats: Bitesize Tales With A Cone Named Cornelius

For all the latest John Roberts news, please visit the website:
www. CorneliusCone.co.uk

Milton Keynes UK
Ingram Content Group UK Ltd.
UKHW030345240824
447344UK00001BA/71